Betrayed
SECOND EDITION
a novel

by

R.P. McCabe

Pen & Ink Publishing, Ltd

To: Patt
Love
Warm Thanks!
R.P. McCabe
Ronnie
7/4/2014

Cover Designed by Yevin Graphics

Cover Art: Shutterstock
Copyright © R.P. MCCabe

Published by Pen & Ink Publishing, Ltd.
1468 James Rd.
Gardnerville, NV 89460

Visit the author website:
www.novelistrpmccabe.com

Follow the author on Facebook and Twitter:
http://facebook.com/novelistrpmccabe
http://twitter.com/#!/R_P_McCabe

Version 2014.07.15

Also by R.P. McCabe
Thick Fog In Pacheco Pass

Coming Soon
Slaughtered

For: Birdie ~ Phoebe ~ Fiona ~ Rudy
And
Bobby Dale Clark

My life can never again be as full as it once was—

"This, then, is the test of your manhood: How much is there left in you—after you have lost everything outside of yourself?" ...<u>Orison Swett-Marden</u>

TABLE OF CONTENTS

ACKNOWLEDGEMENTS

When a writer sits down to write a novel, there is this sense of committing a solitary act; something akin to seppuku. And to be sure, as one word becomes two and more, and those words develop into sentences, and those sentences turn into paragraphs that create pages, which ultimately grow to be a manuscript, there is but one set of fingers that will tap across the keyboard.

But along the path of the arduous journey to a finished novel are the voices of family, friends, colleagues and scores of accidental influences from people you don't even know that fortifies the psyche of the solitary mind staring at a blank computer screen; infuses you with the audacity, if not outright arrogance, to believe you actually can do the deed and in the end someone might reward you with their most valuable of possession—the *time* to read the damn thing!

I can't thank every single individual who had some influence on me in the writing of Betrayed, but I would like to remember some of those without whose belief in me this novel would have never become a reality.

My closest friend and greatest fan was Robert D. Clark. Bobby Dale was one of the most extraordinary human beings I have ever known—that I will likely ever know. Though he was never *my* shrink, he was a shrink (Okay…psychopathologist for those of you who require the deference.) to the stars … literally. And because you still see many of them in movies we'll just leave it there. One day, nearly 30 years ago—time ultimately becomes our enemy, doesn't it?— Bobby Dale asked me to read one of his manuscripts. (He was a writer, too.) When I mentioned to him I'd secretly harbored thoughts of being a writer, he wanted to know why I hadn't acted on the idea. Until Bobby Dale died, three years ago now, the first words out of his mouth every time we were able to get together were, "What have you written lately, and when do I get to read it?" Bobby Dale finds his way into Betrayed in the persona of FBI Special Agent, Clark Reynolds. He'd have gotten a kick out of that. I'd have never written this or any other work if I hadn't gotten a kick out of him!

When I finally did become serious about wanting to test my skills for becoming a writer, I enrolled in a two-year creative writing program with Long Ridge Writer's Group. That was more years in the past than I want to recall. I had a number of writing coaches over the duration of the program, but it was Author Lou Fisher who mentored me through the final stages of the program who wrote a letter to me upon graduation that to this day hangs above my writing desk and I reread every time I think about giving in to my demons and casting this all aside for another bottle of good red wine. The Steve Jobs commencement speech at Stanford University a few years ago was another watershed moment for me. We never know who we are going to influence in a meaningful way, do we?

My closest friends: Alisa Proctor-Mullins, Devan Mullins, Ted Keyes and Hope Busto-Keyes, besides listening to me harp about how horrible certain chapters were or sequences I couldn't seem to get right and the thousand other calamities going on in my life during the writing of the novel were rewarded with the dark task of being beta readers. They were all warned lying was not only acceptable, but required in some instances. Their suggestions, corrections, technical input (Dare I mention love?)—Alisa is a well known Southern California artist, Devan an attorney I can actually feel affection for, Ted a hematology oncologist and one of the finest human beings I have ever known, Hope a Nurse Practitioner and political *mamacita* making sure our president gets reelected—all contributed critically valuable expertise that not only validates but enriches scenes throughout the work. You can't write like this without people like these behind you.

And then there is Ann Clark. If I could make a wish for every person I have ever known, or will ever know, it would be that you have the good fortune to have an Ann Clark in your life. Her's is not a friendship that can easily be articulated? Our friendship spans thirty years and more shared experiences than can or should be enumerated here. Most afternoons over the last two years, after I have finished my writing day, I've enjoyed sitting with her on the terraza of her lovely home overlooking the Sea of Cortez. We leisurely consume a bottle—sometimes two—of the best red wine the two of us can afford while Ann listens to me carp over and over about every maniacal misgiving I have about my writing—and life in general. When I don't have anything legitimate to be worried about, I make something up—insecurity being my most familiar state.

I often look out across the open sea contemplating the bleakness of the empty horizon. Sometimes I can feel its forlorn pull dragging me toward the ends of the earth. Ann looks out across the same expanse and sees unlimited possibilities. I'm finally beginning to see a bit more than an empty horizon, too. That's a pretty powerful friendship.

And finally, I remind all of you that ten thousand Americans are reaching retirement age every day. But there is one group of Americans who will never be able to retire at any age through no failure of planning or lack of work ethic nor four in the morning wake up calls nor any other failing of their own doing. Criminals, most of who walk free, have stolen their lives from them.

It was through their heartbreaking stories I saw the foundation for writing Betrayed. This novel is their story.

PROLOGUE

At some point over the course of our lives—most of us anyway—are forced to glimpse the penalty of misfortune in someone else's life. I am not speaking here of those hapless disparate factions of mentally ill who fall through the cracks in our system, populating empty doorways and back alleys of every major city across the country. No—I speak here of that singular downtrodden human being stumbling along a busy street, wearing clothes that had once been fastidious but have now been slept in for so many nights they seem vacuum-sealed against the flesh. You know, the one that sticks in your head for days after the encounter, leaving you dwelling on what might have happened to him or her to end up like that? Because on the face of it, he or she didn't look all that different from you. What you can't see, of course, is the event that turned life upside down. Was it a thing beyond his or her control with consequences irrevocable, an event so devastating if you could know the details it would cause you to pause, consider for a moment how something like that could be? Maybe you'd feel a shiver run up your spine and hear yourself whisper, *"There but for the grace of God—"*

Cliché? Sure. But, as George Orwell noted, the thing about clichés is—they are mostly true.

~~~~

One-thirty a.m., August 20, 2009—1602 West Osborn Road, Phoenix, Arizona—Offices of Perfect Property Investments, LLC—Arizona Department of Public Safety Homicide Detective Bill Garcia and FBI Special Agent Clark Reynolds pushed out the front doors of the building into the gyrating aura of red and blue halogen lights flickering urgently across the parking lot. The backcloth was full of radio chatter and hot air blow-by whooshing out from under the front wheel-wells of the running diesel engines of fire trucks still on the scene.

"So what do you think?" Garcia asked without ceremony. The two officers had known each other a long time.

Reynolds shoved his hands into his pockets and looked off toward the street. Even without the added heat blowing out from the fire engines, it was still above one hundred degrees outside at that hour. He looked back toward the front of the office building. "Pure hatred," he said. "Odds on … one attacker. Hated those two so bad he didn't want them to die. Act of pure vengeance." Reynolds went on. "Your vics did something to this guy. Or somebody he knows ... family member ... friend, maybe." The FBI man shifted his weight, cocked his head and thrust his hands deeper into his pockets. "... Notice there was no sign of an altercation ... no struggle?"

"I did, Clark," Garcia said. "Only things out of place in that entire office are the things on top of those two desks, because the perp needed the shit on them out of his way."

"I agree," Reynolds cut back in.

"Excuse me Detective." The captain commanding the firefighters approached Garcia. "We're gonna pull outta here. Your people have it now."

"Thanks for the cover, Cap," Garcia said.

The captain raised his hand, spun on his heel and headed to his command vehicle. The driver revved the engine and the behemoth eased around in a large arc heading back toward the street. There was nothing to do but watch the three giant engines pull away; the sound was the near equivalent of a space shuttle launch. The moment the ladder trucks pulled away, the absence of sound from clanging diesel engines was prominent.

Clark Reynolds turned back from the street. "... Exactly! Like I was saying ... no sign of a struggle. One individual overpowers two relatively young, healthy men ... seemingly without much of a struggle ... ties them up and unleashes the fury of hell. Money says he drugged 'em somehow. The hospital will confirm that. Ask them to do a tox-screen ... see if we can determine what he used on them.

"But look, that's the *how* of it. Let's talk about the *who* of it," Reynolds said, shifting gears. "This guy knew these two and I'm betting they knew him. Like I said, this was personal. The vics might be able to tell you who your perp is.

"I can tell you he's above average intelligence. Middle age or older, most likely. Probably has military training. Doesn't place much value on his own life. Obviously quite cunning. Found a way to surprise 'em, gain control over them."

"Doesn't leave me a lot to go on," Garcia complained.

Reynolds went in another direction. "What about the vics?"

"Uniforms that answered the call had the EMTs recover their wallets," Garcia said. "Guy by the name of Bud Pace ... the second one's name is Carl Taylor. They run some kind of real estate investment company."

"Not doing too bad for themselves," Reynolds observed casually, pointing to the Maybach in the lot.

"Registered to Taylor."

"What about the other guy's vehicle?"

"Maybach was the only vehicle here. Ran a DMV on Pace. He's got three vehicles registered. No way of knowing which one he was driving until I can talk to his wife."

"Well I'd get to that the minute you can," Reynolds suggested. "Good chance your perp's getting away in it right now."

"Got APBs on all three plate numbers until I can confirm with the wife which one he was driving."

"Good call," Reynolds agreed. "We need to interview these guys the minute we can. They're gonna know who this guy is."

"We're fucked there," Garcia groused looking down at his feet. "My lieutenant called from the hospital. Doctors say these two are in such bad shape, had no choice but to place them into medically induced comas for several days … said the trauma of learning what happened to them tonight would likely kill them. Gotta stabilize 'em first—let 'em find out the situation slowly."

"Meanwhile, our perp has all the time he needs to cover what few clues he might have left us. You gotta squeeze the wives, Bill."

"Being interviewed right now. I'll keep you informed on anything we turn up. Don't see any reason to turn this over to the Bureau … you?"

Reynolds shook his head no. "Not for now, anyway. Get as much as you can. I'll alert my team. We'll support you the best we can."

"You'll work with me?"

"We don't nail this guy in the next thirty-six hours … he's gonna be tough to find and you might well have another night like this one on your hands."

With that prediction, FBI Special Agent Clark Reynolds headed out to the street where his vehicle was parked, glanced at his watch; 1:43 a.m. He whispered under his breath. "Better pray this madman isn't pissed off at anybody else.

CHAPTER 1

October 2008

Retirement Day—not that abstract goal most of us strive to get to, but the actual day itself. The ultimate moment in our lives when it's acceptable to disengage—give ourselves permission to go and do and be all of those things we never could find time to pursue over the course of lives too busy. *That day* had come to Wally and Poppy Stroud ten months before this story begins.

November crept in almost imperceptibly except for the incessant political ads that made it impossible to watch anything on television. Wally and Poppy accepted a dinner invitation to watch election returns with their neighbors, Dan and Fortunada Dolan who lived a mere hundred yards down the lane.

Early exit polls from the east coast began to roll in. Tom Brokaw was on air with Brian Williams and David Gregory was at a desk somewhere in the bowels of the NBC News organism scribbling rapidly on a white oil-board doing his best to imitate the deeply missed Tim Russert.

Wally stood in front of the TV in the den of the Dolan home holding a glass of red wine. "Please don't let us get stuck with another four years of Bush," he pleaded to no one in particular.

"I second that," Poppy mumbled.

By seven o'clock PST it was clear a third term of Bush's failed politics would not occur in the incarnation of John McCain and Sarah Palin. West coast polls remained open ensuring every American the opportunity to participate in the revolt against the ultra-right-wing-neo-con-pricks who'd done everything they could over the past eight years to turn American society into the Christian extremist equivalent of the Islamic terrorists from whom they claimed to be protecting the nation. Equally significant was the election of the first African-American president.

"Now, if we could just charter a ship and load Cheney, Rove, Rummy, Wolfowitz … the whole friggin' lot of 'em—" Wally was saying.

1

Betrayed

"*Pul ... eeze!*" Fortunada Dolan shouted from the kitchen, cutting him off mid-sentence, "don't leave out the *Limbpublicans*; Rush, Hannity ... God, that sick fuck, Glenn Beck!" she shouted, grunting those last few syllables as she conveyed a large casserole dish from the oven to the island countertop.

Fortunada Dolan was a shortish, robust, cherub-faced woman with red hair, fiery blue eyes and a grandmotherly gentleness that belied her political activism during the late sixties. She believed in God, loved her family and was not loath to express her deep disapproval over the right-wing extremist movement in America.

"We'll save a spot in the hold for 'em, Fo," Wally shouted, then added laughing, "where they can sling shit, which is what they do best anyway!"

"That would be funny if they weren't inciting so much intolerance," Poppy added.

"You gotta be a dumbass to listen to those jerks," Dan Dolan claimed, then sipped some red wine. He turned his trim frame away from the TV and wandered toward the kitchen. "Smells good," he said.

"Lot of dumbasses out there," Fortunada argued. "Prop 8 was defeated in California."

"Where you gonna send 'em?" Dan argued.

"Good point," Wally agreed. "The hell of it for a guy like me," he went on, "I'm a former Republican myself. Hate to admit it now, but a Nixon Republican ... still a fiscal conservative. Party just went too far with this Puritan based bullshit philosophy they try to beat us over the head with. Every time we turn around we're hearing God is on our side and the rest of the world doesn't exist." Wally paused, stared into his wineglass as though it were a reflecting pool. "Just can't abide that kind of parochial isolationist horseshit any more. It's as if there isn't anyone left in the party who made it out of middle school."

Wally admitted to being a social moderate but he didn't believe in a free handout for anyone. And he was for providing a solid education to poor kids as well as rich ones and supporting scientific endeavor. What gay people called their relationships was unimportant to him. It seemed to Wally the 'Limbbags' suffered under the asinine notion if gays were allowed to say they were married, being gay might somehow become contagious. He humorously described himself a heathen-moderate-apolitical-non-homophobe fiscal conservative neither party would want to claim.

Dan Dolan seconded that assessment and took a long pull from a bottle of Pacifico.

That November fourth evening in 2008 had come and gone with lighthearted banter among new friends—some deeper philosophical exchanges celebrating the victory of hope over fear, intellect over religious dogma, social conscientiousness over political ideology—maybe? They're all politicians in the end, they'd all agreed.

CHAPTER 2

Wally Stroud, just shy of six feet, thinning gray hair he wore cropped neatly but full over his ears; it touched his collar at the nape of his neck. He made no effort to cover the creeping inevitability of the bald spot that was evident on the crown of his skull. Wally was frequently judged younger than his actual age, which was sixty-five.

Wally had a geometric symmetry to his face that matched, on most days, his convivial personality. You might have called him good looking but not overly striking. He had dark brown eyes with moderately full eyebrows hooding a Greek nose that had been broken twice, complemented by full lips that parted mischievously when he smiled, revealing straight white teeth; the entirety set affably between a pair of *Selleckesque* dimples.

To compensate for what he felt was a personal failing in not having finished his college education, he drove himself to work harder than his peers. *"Show me a job somebody won't do and I'll show you an opportunity,"* was his credo. He read extensively and travelled when he could. The residue of his efforts yielded what he thought of as a happy, productive life. But when Poppy Zinsser came into his world, a kind of contentment settled over him. Privately he felt at peace: newfound confidence. Poppy offered balance in a life that up to then had been dedicated primarily to work. Wally was a grinder. What he lacked in credentials, he made up for in obdurate determination. With Poppy at his side, Wally was a happier, more complete human being.

Wally and Poppy Stroud traversed the landscape of thirty-three years of life together, and when scored by the universal measurement of achievement in American Society—*money*—they were about middle of the pack. They'd worked hard, saved, and planned well.

Poppy Zinsser-Stroud was five feet, six inches tall with a ballerina body beginning to soften around her middle. She wore her saddle brown hair cut in a short bob. It was flecked with accents of golden honey hues the shades of majestic canyon walls bathed in an Indian summer sunset. She was a woman of patrician elegance as she drew near sixty years of age. It took Wally's breath away to watch how gracefully she moved after all their years together.

Poppy's peridot eyes twinkled like fireworks on a fourth of July night. Her skin was soft and smooth, but not artificially so, and when she laughed, which she didn't do often enough these days, it made Wally feel all was right with his world. For in Wally's mind, Poppy Stroud was the world—or at least the part of it that mattered to him.

Until those last three years, Poppy Stroud met each new morning of her life awakening with a smile on her face, resilience of spirit that sent Wally forward into his day with lightness in his heart. It made facing the rigors the day-to-day grind a lifetime of hard work can morph into palatable. Poppy Stroud was an exceptional woman who had begun to fight demons Wally did not see, nor would he have understood had he the insight to have detected the depth of Poppy's troubles. In his eyes, she existed in an exalted state: erudite, kind, compassionate—loyal—one-of-her-kind. Not another woman was the equal of Poppy if you were asking Wally. Watching the two of them strolling arm-in-arm, one felt a sense of a beautifully matched pair of special human beings, the kind of people who inspire love stories.

To her credit, Poppy Stroud did not define herself by the measurement of things possessed, but the fact she and Wally could possess nearly anything they wanted—within reason, of course, elevated Poppy's sense of self image—and, perhaps, self-worth to a dubious pinnacle. She was certainly not inflicted by the despair of wanting for things. Poppy worked side-by-side with Wally all of their married life. She was entitled to anything she wanted they could afford. That's how Wally rationalized it.

The accumulation of money can become a game; one to which Poppy found herself a certified convert—to an extent Wally did not understand. For while it was true Poppy did not despair of wanting, it was also true her ego was fed, to a great extent, by the fiction of having. That is to say, Poppy Stroud had come to suffer unease, restlessness, boredom, anxiety and dissatisfaction as a result of unfulfilled wanting; a thing of which even she was unaware. Add the associated hormonal anomalies resulting from menopause, with which she was struggling, and one begins to glimpse how Poppy Stroud was a conflicted woman.

Had Wally understood the implications of seventy-five pairs of shoes sitting in his wife's closet, many having only been worn once, and her telling him about the *cutest pair of Manolos she just saw at Nordstrom's she was dying to have*, things might have turned out differently. But he did not understand the deeper implications of what Poppy's incessant need for more told him. All he believed was if she wanted it, it was his responsibility to get it for her—whatever *it* was.

CHAPTER 3

Four days before Thanksgiving, Wally and Poppy waved goodbye to Dan and Fortunada. Wally pointed his pickup north where he'd connect with I-8 to Phoenix. It was damp and foggy as they drove away that day.

They arrived home around 6:30 Monday evening. The house looked fine except for the runaway growth of Cat's Claw hanging over the front edge of the garage and the climbing fig covering the front of the house, which was, quite literally, growing between, under, over and through the joints around the doors and windows.

"Couple hard days of gardening," Wally grumbled pointing to the overgrowth.

"I'll help," Poppy offered. "It won't take long."

They unloaded the truck and made the rounds opening the house.

Wally uncorked a bottle of Chardonnay for Poppy and a Pinot Noir for himself before calling out for pizza. Spinato's Pizzeria said it would take about thirty minutes.

The next two days were a blur of activity. A mountain of mail waited on Wally's desk. The thought of going through it was even less appealing than getting the patio in shape, but it had to be tended.

The morning before Thanksgiving Wally decided he couldn't put the mail off any longer. Grudgingly, he grabbed a cup of tea and retired to his office where he spent most of the morning reading offers from banks and the premium renewal notice for car insurance. Just before lunch he noticed an envelope from Perfect Property Investments, LLC; the company that now managed their retirement savings.

Two years earlier Wally'd contacted Todd Davidson, his longtime Wealth Management Consultant and told him he wanted out of the stock market. Davidson didn't like the move. He was about to lose a lot of commission. Davidson's task was to find Wally and Poppy a solid, steady income-producing investment that would generate regular monthly cash flow they could plan and budget against. Between the savings in their stock portfolio and the cash they received from the sale of their business, they had a sizable nest egg to invest.

Some weeks went by before he received the call that led to the presentation by PPI. Their business model seemed sound enough. The company had a twenty-year track record. Davidson-Timmons Wealth Managers claimed they were solid as a rock. They were, themselves, invested with PPI. They didn't, however, disclose the hefty commission they'd get for the referral.

It seemed to Wally and Poppy PPI was what they'd been hoping for. And what was proposed was a business model with a social conscience. A suitable property in the inner-city would be found that would lend itself to being rehabilitated and subdivided so it could be resold as a co-op or condo-style housing to first-time home buyers.

A year passed and payments from PPI were deposited to the Stroud's checking account on the fourth day of every month like clockwork. Wally guessed the envelope now in front of him contained another performance review since they were coming to the end of the year. But when he opened it and read the first sentence, a rush of chemicals went to his brain that obscured his vision, made it difficult to breath.

The letter read:

Dear Perfect Property Investor,

Because of the catastrophic deterioration of real estate values in Arizona, and the recent withdrawal of mortgage financing from the market place, PPI is herewith forced to temporarily suspend interest payments to all investors—*(The letter went on in broad, vague terms to explain the problems as identified by PPI.)*

Sincerely,
Bud Pace
Carl Taylor

No discussion of a reduction of interest payments as contractually promised. Simply the appalling assertion that yesterday you had a solid income, today you have zero.

His last conversation with PPI (Bienvenidos, the portfolio manager.) took place just before they drove to Baja in October. The meeting left them feeling fortunate Davidson-Timmons came up with this investment opportunity.

When his vision cleared, Wally read the letter again. It did say, "temporarily suspend" payments. Maybe I'm overreacting, he thought. He took several deep breaths, but the dizziness didn't go away. The sickening feeling of impending doom was powerful. He finally gave up and just sat there staring at the letter, rereading it periodically.

That's where Poppy found him when she returned from shopping.

"You still at that mail?" she puzzled, coming in carrying an armful of groceries.

Wally didn't jump up to give her a hand as he normally did.

Poppy set the groceries on the counter and walked back into his office. "You okay, sweetie?" she asked more softly, sensing the aura of anguish surrounding him.

Wally felt incapable of speaking. He dropped his head forward onto his chest and held the letter up in his left hand.

Poppy stepped to his side and took it from him. She read in silence. After a few moments she placed her right hand on the base of his neck. "What are we going to do?"

He leaned back in his chair.

"I already tried to get someone on the phone," he whispered hoarsely. "Got a recording … says they'll be closed until Monday."

Poppy didn't say anything. She set the letter down and walked back to the kitchen.

Wally sat several moments longer before following her. "Let's not panic, Popp. I'll go have a look at the property Friday. You can come along." He pulled her to him and held her. "Let's start there."

"That's our entire life savings, Wally. We could lose everything we've worked for." Poppy's voice broke, and then her body trembled.

"Don't jump to judgment, Popp." But that was exactly what he'd done himself.

"I have a bad feeling about this, Wally."

Wally didn't reply. He had his own bad feelings but he would never put them on Poppy's back. She was too fragile to handle both her fears and his.

"It'll be okay, Popp," he reassured her in a stronger voice. "Let's wait until we can properly evaluate this thing before we get upset … anymore upset than we already are."

It was hard for Wally to lie convincingly to her. She could read him like a book, and he knew she knew he was just as frightened as she was.

They managed to get through Thanksgiving Day without revealing to their family what they were facing. It would do no good for anyone, they'd agreed, to bring it up now before they could explain exactly what they were facing.

Neither of them got much sleep Wednesday or Thursday night. Around 2:00 a.m. Friday morning Poppy asked softly out of the darkness, "You asleep?"

Wally's voice was absent the edge drowsiness would have produced. "No," he replied simply.

He reached out, took her hand and they lay, wide awake, side-by-side until around five thirty when, gratefully, the first gray strands of dawn began to claw their way across the darkness of their bedroom prison.

Wally could lie there no longer. He climbed out to start the coffee and tea.

Poppy wallowed in the warmth of the sheets with a headache, feeling hung-over from sleep deprivation. She required several hours more sleep than Wally. Now she remained in bed feeling like her limbs were weighed down with lead.

Wally brought her two Advil and a cup of hot coffee. He was the tea drinker.

Betrayed

He shaved and performed his morning toilet, flipped on the *Today Show* and listened mindlessly to the good-natured banter between Meredith and Matt. By the time he'd finished another cup of tea, Poppy was up and nearly dressed. "Let's go," he groused.

"Take it easy, Wally," she fought back. "Sun's just up."

He grumbled a bit, but settled in with one more cup of tea. Poppy generally had a better sense of tempo about things, he conceded.

A while later she up-ended her second cup of coffee and drained it. "Let's go find out what we're up against."

CHAPTER 4

At the time Wally and Poppy's business was sold, PPI was just launching a new development project. Sonoran Plaza, located on South 34th Lane in downtown Phoenix was a sixty-five-unit co-op conversion project. The proposal presented an attractive pro forma anticipating twelve percent equity growth over the four-year life of the project. When added to the interest payments they were offering investors, it was an appealing consideration.

The fact a New York trust fund was the single largest investor in the property went a long way toward providing the sense of confidence they needed to get involved. The bulk of their retirement savings went to fund their buy-in.

As Wally pulled his pickup to a stop in the parking lot of Sonoran Plaza, he and Poppy exchanged a puzzled glance. They hadn't visited the project since their due diligence tour the previous year. Timely interest payments and glowing quarterly reports lulled them into believing it unnecessary.

"What the hell?" Wally said, more to himself than Poppy. "I don't think they've even painted the place, have they?"

Poppy went numb. "Maybe they completed the insides and left the outside for last?"

"Not a very smart idea, you ask me. Let's go see." He stepped out of the truck slowly. On the passenger side of the vehicle, he opened the door for Poppy and pointed. "Office is over there."

Wally pushed the door open and walked in. An attractive young Hispanic woman who identified herself as, Olivia, the manager, greeted them. Wally pulled his first question short and glanced to Poppy.

"Snowbirds," he told Olivia. "Looking for a place for the winter." Olivia explained she had only one small unit currently vacant, but one of the larger three bedrooms would be available beginning the first of the month.

They masked another perplexed glance before Wally pursued the question. "Are you generally this full?"

"Oh, *jes*," Olivia answered, her accent thick, "we no *hab* many *bacancy* here."

"Are the condos refurbished?"

"Oh, *jes*, we cleaning *dem ebery* time somebody moving out."

"No," Wally clarified. "I mean, are the condos rebuilt inside? Are they like new?"

"They nice," Olivia admitted, "but is no like is new. Come on, I *cho* you *de* one I *hab righ* now."

Olivia, in her early twenties, Wally guessed, couldn't have been more pleasant. She walked them across a quadrangle with a huge gated swimming pool in the center they observed was clean, and looked to be in excellent condition. But the landscaping and exterior of the buildings offered no curb appeal.

When Olivia swung the door open, their hearts sank.

"*Done* look *de mess*," Olivia encouraged them. "We gonna clean that."

There was dry cereal, corn flakes of some kind, scattered over the shabby, chocolate-colored carpet. The walls were dingy and marked by a child's hapless scribbling in a rainbow of Crayola. A cupboard door hung by one hinge in the kitchen and neither Wally nor Poppy could fathom storing food in the refrigerator. On top of the way the place was trashed, it exuded a nasty combination of odors ranging between stale urine and rotting food.

"Are all the units like this?" Poppy wanted to know.

"Only when *dey* moving out," Olivia confessed. "But we gonna fix all you see. *Dey* clean *de* carpets good 'n fix *de* door. We gonna paint *dis* one, too," she promised, walking over, pointing to the wall with the crayon all over it. "*En* we got really good cleaning staff. *Dey* gonna make that *refreehador* 'n *estufa* good like new," she announced proudly. "No more it gonna smelling bad."

Wally'd seen all he could stomach. Now he wanted an explanation. That would not likely happen before Monday morning.

They thanked Olivia for her time. They'd make a decision soon. Walking back to the pickup, they observed more deferred maintenance around the grounds and exterior of the four buildings that comprised the complex. They didn't speak to each other again until they were nearly home.

"What do you think's going on?"

"Don't have a clue, Popp," Wally admitted honestly. He turned to look over his right shoulder checking traffic. "But I can tell you it isn't the economy prevented PPI from renovating those units. Hell, they haven't painted the place."

"What do you think it means?"

"Means they still have three million dollars from investors they haven't expended."

There was a long pause.

10

"I should have been checking up on these bastards," he mumbled, clenching his teeth so tightly Poppy could see the muscles in his jaw straining.

She didn't say anything. She didn't have to.

Wally pulled the truck into their driveway and killed the engine. They sat in contemplative silence staring straight ahead, stunned and confused by what they'd just seen.

"The place is fully rented," Poppy finally said, reciting an obvious truth. "But PPI hasn't spent a dime to upgrade the property. They're holding three million dollars in reserves. They have to have good cash flow from rents … why'd we get that letter, Wally? What's going on here we can't see?"

"I'll try to get someone on the phone," he said on his way out the driver's door. As with his attempt to reach someone on Wednesday, there was no answer. He hadn't expected one. It was merely an exercise that had to be performed in view of the gravity of it all.

The balance of Friday and the entire weekend were lost. They couldn't focus on anything but the looming crisis. They attempted to start projects around the house, but neither could concentrate on anything except when they'd climbed out of bed last Wednesday morning they'd had a substantial monthly income to be retired on. And today, thirty hours later, they were trying to figure out how they could live on the paltry amount of Wally's Social Security check. But that wouldn't cover the cost of utilities, let alone allow them to survive. The implications were abysmal.

Wally'd had chest pains twice on Saturday, but said nothing to Poppy.

CHAPTER 5

At nine-fifteen Monday morning they were in the parking lot of PPI's offices at 1602 West Osborn Road in downtown Phoenix waiting for someone to unlock the front door. It looked like the whole company, employers and employees had barricaded themselves inside. At nine-thirty a youngish female employee walked out of the building and got into a parked car. At that moment, four couples rolled out of their vehicles and marched solemn-faced into the lobby. Each understood why the others were there.

Wally didn't ask to see Sonja Bienvenidos, the portfolio manager on Sonoran Plaza. Instead, he demanded to see Bud Pace, one of the two principals of the company. To his surprise, Pace stepped out within a few moments and invited them to join him in his office.

Pace looked to be in his late fifties and stood around five-ten with smartly clipped sandy colored hair that might have actually been some shade of blond in his youth but was now turning whitish-gray at the temples. He was all smiles and overly pleasant, offering them coffee or bottled water. Pace crossed the spacious suite and sat down at a round glass-top table in the corner of his office, folded his hands together and adopted a cocksure, condescending demeanor. He wore an expensive blue suit with a smart yellow tie and looked the picture of success. They declined his attempted diversion with the bottle of water.

"I wish you were here under different circumstances," Pace began.

"What circumstances would that be?" Wally countered.

Pace hesitated. His cherub-cheeks reddened slightly, exaggerating the pasty pallor of his complexion. The man was not accustomed to being challenged. "I presumed you were here about the letters we mailed out." His voice was high-pitched, afflicted with too much treble.

"We are," Wally affirmed, not an affable nuance in his manner. "So what are the circumstances?"

"Well, as the letter explained," Pace went on, the swagger beginning to leach out of him, "the dreadful decline in property values has caused financing to dry up and we just cannot meet obligations to our inves—"

Poppy cut him off. "What do declining property values or credit and financing have to do with anything?" she demanded in a tone that said, *don't bullshit me.* "We … we and a lot of other investors," she went on, "gave you people three million dollars in reserves to perform renovations to Sonoran Plaza that you haven't done, and we," she continued, indicating she and Wally, "know for a fact the property is fully rented, so cash flows can't be bad."

Wally let her go. There were few events more deflating than receiving a full-out rebuke from his wife. She was a smart, competent businesswoman with the ability to affect a certain air, *noblesse oblige* that all but dared one to lie to her. Pace was no exception. "You bragged you didn't need banks for your business model to work," she reminded him. "You haven't touched that property. Where's our money?" She demanded coldly, coming to the edge of her seat.

She engaged Pace's vapid, watery gaze and held it. His confident stare slowly shriveled, his gaze falling to focus somewhere near his shoes. His face began to redden, but before he could manufacture a response, Wally pounced on him.

"My wife and I visited that property. You people haven't touched those buildings." Wally watched Pace's hands as he fidgeted with a pen. "You've had control of this property for more than a year. So what's going on?"

Pace's reaction time and body language were too tentative. Every word the prick uttered was a lie; of that Wally was certain. He knew before Pace opened his mouth to speak again they, he and Poppy, along with a lot of other people, were in serious trouble. The Madoff Ponzi scheme flashed into his head, followed by a hopeless internal plea that it not be so.

"I'm sure we made mistakes along the way," Pace argued, "but this situation is not our fault … we're victims just like all of you," he whined.

"Where's our money?" Poppy demanded once more, her voice rising.

"There is no money, Mr. and Mrs. Stroud."

"What the hell do you mean … *there is no money*?" Wally hissed. "Where are the reserves and the rents you've been collecting?" That was the moment the sledgehammer hit Wally in the solar plexus.

Pace, perspiration beading on his forehead and upper lip, began to spin the story he and his business partner, Taylor decided on. "Look, we thought we were doing the right thing for all of you," he said in a near whisper. "We used the reserves to prop up other projects that were in trouble. And we had to use some of the money to cover our overhead … keep our office doors open and manage your investments properly. Things would have fallen into chaos long ago if we hadn't done the right thing and used the money to maintain a stable environment on all of the projects."

Before he could take a breath Wally went at him, "You're sitting there telling us you took the money invested by all of us on Sonoran Plaza, more than seven million dollars total, with three million of that as advance reserves, and used it to pay other investors on other projects … and what, pay your own salaries and your operational overhead with our money?" Wally's voice had become hoarse and visceral. The darkness in his eyes served warning to the man in front of him he'd better choose his words carefully.

Pace slid back in his chair, spread his hands in a gesture of capitulation … as if to say, what else was there to do? "We did what we thought was in the best interest of the majority of our investors, Mr. Stroud."

Wally Stroud's face was white with rage. He stood and looked down at Pace, who flinched as Wally rose from his chair. Pace slid backward, getting out of Wally's reach. "You fucking fraud!" Wally growled. "How the hell is it in anybody's best interest but your own to use our money to pay obligations you have to other investors, all the while paying yourself a salary?"

"Listen, I understand you're upset," Pace said, wincing at Wally's attack. "I can appreciate you're angry. But if you will just not panic … we're going to do everything we can to fix this." Bud Pace looked up into Wally Stroud's threatening face. "We can't make this go away overnight, Mr. Stroud, but if you can just stick this out with us for a year or two—"

Poppy cut him off. "You've taken our life savings. We sold our business and entrusted our retirement savings with your firm. We have no place to turn. We can't go get jobs …" Poppy stopped and stared hard at the man. "When our emergency savings are gone in the next few months we won't have any way of making our mortgage payments or paying the cost to maintain our existence. How in hell do you think we are going to be able to 'just hang in there for a year or two?'" Each word coming now was spat into Pace's grimacing face. "How do we eat? How do we pay for our medications? How do we keep the electricity on in our homes? Are you thinking about that while you casually tell us you misused our life savings and now you see yourselves as victims like us … all we have to do is, hang in there with you another couple of years and you're going to be our salvation from all of this?"

Poppy was in a near frenzy. Pace leaned forward in his chair, elbows on the table, bowed his head and stared down at his clasped hands.

There was silence for several seconds.

Wally forced himself to pursue the truth. "This situation didn't just happen. How long have you been pilfering money from the reserves?" he demanded in a level tone.

"I know you're angry, Mr. Stroud, but—"

"I'm not angry," Wally mocked, jutting his contorted face toward Pace. "I'm pissed off!" The crusted spittle in the corners of his mouth and the gray pallor of his skin was enough to cause Pace to squirm in his chair.

"What do you want me to say?" Pace pleaded.

"I want you to tell me you're going to return our money."

"I can't tell you that, Mr. Stroud. The money is gone."

The room went coldly silent once more.

"Then you'd better start by providing us with a detailed account of where it went and when it went there," Wally said, a threatening edge in his voice.

"Let me see what I can do for you," Pace lied. "That's all I can do. I've got your address. Let me see what our accounting department can put together for you," he said, standing. "It could take a week or two."

"We'll be waiting," Wally threatened, continuing to stare Pace down. He knew there was never going to be any accounting. Someone … or several some ones looted the investor reserves that included his and Poppy's life savings. Wally felt certain of that. But who, besides Pace, was in on it? What were the chances of getting it back? How much time did he have to recover his money before these thieves buried it so deep he'd never be able to find it? Those were the issues on which he knew he needed to concentrate now.

Poppy stood and Pace slid out from behind the table. He made a puny demonstration of trying to thank them for coming in to let him explain and promised to get back to them soon. In the doorway of his office he proffered his hand. Wally glared at him. It was all he could do to control the urge to bust the weasel in the nose right then and there. Pace looked down at his shoes nervously, sensing the danger in the moment and said, "I'm sorry."

There was, by then, a lobby full of older faces all wearing the same mask of despair and fear. They looked from one to the other, weary, frightened eyes searching for some one of them to have an answer or a solution that would undo the devastation they all now learned had been delivered unto them. But there was no such person or revelation, and one by one they trudged, in a hopeless fog, out to their cars, not one among them having the slightest idea of what to do next.

Wally and Poppy sat quietly together in the cab of their pickup truck in the parking lot. People were now coming and going in and out the front door of PPI. The silence was oppressive. Poppy broke down and wept. It was not necessary to give voice to the terror gripping her.

Wally was still gray-faced with a sense of impending doom—and rage. "I won't let them get away with this, Popp," he swore gently, patting her knee. "They won't get away with this!"

CHAPTER 6

Two weeks came and went. Wally'd gone first to the Arizona State Attorney General's office where the first bucket of ice water was poured over him. Little effort was made to hide their lack of interest in his complaint. They passed if off to the Securities and Exchange Commission. That agency was even more aloof. They offered little hope of any investigation. It was becoming clear; none of the oversight agencies had any intention of pursuing the matter. The FBI said they'd look into it and get back to him. The State Board of Realtors said they'd review ethics or license violations … a nice way of saying, "Get lost, fella."

Wally tried every agency he thought might help. He did everything asked of him and more; spent hours documenting what took place; where and when and who was present. He provided hundreds of pages of documentation substantiating his claims. Copies of documents for each separate agency ran into the hundreds of dollars. But there was little hope if he didn't try. When the FBI deposed him, he believed someone was finally listening. There were three agents present during questioning. Alternately each jumped in with questions that seemed to promise action. But weeks passed without further word.

Poppy's state of mind continued to deteriorate. Wally could see in her eyes and hear in her words her sense of hopelessness was deepening. He did what he could to reassure her he would find a solution. He'd get their savings back somehow. But Poppy could see he was getting nowhere. It was as if they were in a horrible car crash and the people who could help were standing by, doing nothing, while they slowly bled to death.

Wally was gradually putting the pieces together. He spent hundreds of hours tracing Pace and Taylor's business activities through public records. They'd been failing all along. One convolution in uncovering their scams was the illusory way in which they used limited liability companies sequentially owning other limited liability companies, diverting the trail far away from PPI and themselves. The technique had further served to isolate investors from each other.

Through the utilization of a privacy policy cleverly fashioned after legitimate laws, Pace and Taylor were able to prevent investors on the same development project from knowing each other. The two carefully controlled the details investors were allowed access to: divide and conquer.

They were brainy, Pace and Taylor. But once Wally detected the pattern it became a simple matter of assiduous pursuit. He found more than two hundred shell companies he could tie to the two. A trail emerged. If he followed it far enough he'd eventually find their names.

The people they claimed were lined up waiting to buy homes were a fabrication. There was no demand for their inventory of properties. They'd created a shell game. They moved the same money into or out of projects, as required, to make it appear the project was tracking successfully.

When Wally went to Davidson-Timmons for an explanation of why *they* had not discovered these irregularities, he was stonewalled. "Goddamnit, Todd," Wally railed at Davidson. "You've managed our investments for years. How the hell could you let something like this happen?" Davidson sidestepped the accusation pointing out they were victims as well with millions of dollars invested. He produced the hold harmless document all Davidson-Timmons clients were forced to sign and reminded Wally he could not now look to them claiming this was in any way their responsibility. It was clear; the company he'd relied on to guide his investment decisions failed miserably to protect his interests.

He took the matter before the law firm he'd used for years. "Pretty standard stuff, Wally," Allen Cohen deadpanned, reading the copy of the hold harmless document. "Trouble with these damn things," Cohen flipped a page, "the burden for proof of malfeasance falls to you if we're going to overcome its protection to Davidson-Timmons." Cohen looked up at Wally, dropped the document onto his desk.

"So I rely on these guys to keep me safe from scams like this, they screw up and the only one who loses is me ... right?"

Cohen leaned back in his chair, rested his elbows on the armrests, arched his bushy eyebrows; a gesture of capitulation. His body language answered Wally's question.

"We can overcome it, Wally. That isn't the point. Point is they have deep pockets. They'll keep us in court for years until you're broke—"

"You mean more broke than I am now."

"Sorry. Didn't mean to be insensitive." Cohen took a deep breath and then went on to further explain. "That's why they make investors sign these things; whether they drop the ball or not, you have to prove it. Most people haven't the resources or the will. It's all upstream against the system. They're off the hook."

"Is there *anything* you can do, Allen?"

"We can write a letter. Threaten a suit. See if it moves them to offer a settlement. Wouldn't count on it."

Wally folded his hands and sat silently for several moments. "Thanks for your time, Allen."

"This one's on the house, Wally," Cohen said, referring to his fee.

Betrayed

"Appreciate it."

"You'll get through this," the lawyer attempted to reassure him.

"Yeah," Wally said, sardonically, "I'll get through it."

~~~~

The unfolding picture looked like this: Bud Pace and Carl Taylor sold investments in projects under their original business model—for sixteen years it'd been honest—which called for raising twice the capital needed to purchase an investment property. That eliminated the need for institutional financing for marketing and managing. Instead of paying banks interest on loans, they paid interest to their investors over the cycle of a project, then shared a small portion of the capital gain as additional incentive.

When things turned bad in 2004, rather than go to investors with the truth, Pace and Taylor made the decision to *borrow* from the reserve funds of more than forty projects. They needed to meet operational expenses and gain time to find new investors to infuse more cash. Perhaps the original plan was to catch up and replace the borrowed money. That was unclear and intent is a major component in proving fraud.

Established reserves from investors that would have insulated them from the vagaries of the crash in the housing market had been systematically diverted. The money was used to pay Pace and Taylor seven figure salaries. Key managers received six-figures with expensive country club perks keeping them motivated to continue harvesting capital from new investors (a la Enron). Capital is the lifeblood of the Ponzi scheme PPI had become. They used the residue to cover obligations on the next project due to be sold out so investors would believe the plan was working as advertised. Shareholders were duped into reinvesting their capital in new projects making it unnecessary for Pace and Taylor to have to do more than show the funds on paper, though the money no longer existed inside the company. And why wouldn't investors continue? They believed they were receiving solid returns against a proven business model that was performing in an economic climate beginning to resemble the Great Depression. Pace and Taylor utilized a page right out of the Madoff playbook by reporting steady returns.

But out-of-state businesses and state governments began a systematic disengagement with Arizona in protest over the draconian SB 1070 law being viciously enforced by America's toughest Sheriff, Joe Arpaio. Right-wing xenophobes may have been placated, but when thousands of Hispanics moved out of the state in protest, Arizona's economy collapsed. Pace and Taylor's scheme abruptly ran aground; the house of cards was falling.

Knowing exactly what they were doing, the two systematically *diverted* enough money to become disgustingly wealthy. Once they'd stepped across the line, it became easier to continue than go back. A plan to guarantee their financial security ultimately morphed into an orgy of pure greed. Pace and Taylor lost all sense of morality where money was concerned. They acquired fabulous homes; ownership embedded safely in trusts that were virtually impossible to pierce. The idea was to remove any possibility investors could later sue and expose their assets. When the two were satisfied their own needs were secure, they turned to stealing the cash reserves from projects like Sonoran Plaza Condominiums, simply because they could. What Pace and Taylor did was the equivalent of abandoning a sinking ship in a life raft filled with food and water, then pushing their fellow passengers overboard to ensure their own survival.

Wally managed to locate several ex-employees by networking from one to the next. Two believed it likely there existed an offshore bank account in the Cayman Islands since Pace and Taylor made regular trips there, ostensibly to go scuba diving and fishing.

A former comptroller of the company resigned suddenly twenty-four months earlier. Wally found the man working for a large restaurant chain in Southern California. Leon Herrera claimed to be under the burden of a nondisclosure agreement he'd signed with Pace and Taylor. He reluctantly confessed to Wally about the shenanigans he'd uncovered ... how he'd personally confronted Pace and Taylor. They were running an illegal scam by then and it was very close to collapse. He said he couldn't stomach what the two were doing to people. Some had been loyal investors with PPI over many years. Herrera warned Wally unless he was subpoenaed and compelled to testify, he had no choice but to keep his mouth shut.

Wally documented each new revelation, what *he* considered evidence. He amended the complaints he'd filed, sharing information between agencies. In every instance the response was the same. "That may be the case, Mr. Stroud, but we have to develop evidence according to our rules and as part of our own investigative process."

And there had begun a new, more subtle theme from those oversight agencies, the ones consumers believe they will be able to turn to when they've been taken advantage of: Investors who accepted the advice of management companies like Davidson-Timmons, one smug bureaucrat said, who were being compensated by companies like PPI to recommend them to investors, were guilty of not performing proper due diligence. Ms. Shontel, in her heavily accented drawl, inferred to Wally that what happened was his own fault. Investors were somehow deserving of what happened.

Wally's resentment was deepening with each failed effort to find help. And to hear a bureaucrat who was supposed to be there to protect him actually suggest this was somehow his fault—he and Poppy deserved what was happening—chiseled into his psyche the first of many harsh resentments that would ultimately lead him to a decision he would have never dreamed himself capable.

CHAPTER 7

Four months dragged by. Just as Wally feared, not one investigation was launched. When he called the Attorney General's office they told him they were burdened with caseloads and budget cutbacks. They'd look into the matter when they had the resources. Wally now believed that was a euphemism for 'if we let the thing sit long enough—the complaint, or he—would simply go away.' The criminals had the advantage, pure and simple. The FBI at least accepted the evidence he'd given them with a suggestion they would try to look into his claims. But he'd heard nothing. The SEC sent him a letter advising he was not allowed to make further inquiry regarding the matter.

Wally and Poppy were growing more despondent. He tried to keep a positive outlook. He continued to assure her everything was going to be all right. He'd find some way to get them through this nightmare. But every door he tried remained closed.

By then Poppy had withdrawn deep inside herself. The level of communication between them was becoming perfunctory. Wally's continuing reassurances sounded hollow. They were words without substance. She had little to say because she had no ideas of her own that might help. She watched his efforts fall short again and again, and admired the fact at least he was still fighting. That was something she could no longer muster the strength to do.

While Wally was busy looking for ways to recover their investment, Poppy spent a good part of her time analyzing what options were left if he failed. Her assessment was harsh. She'd concluded life as they knew it was over. The planning, the saving—a lifetime of work—gone. She knew for a certainty the real estate they owned had been rendered worthless by the collapse of the economy. The deflation of values in Arizona was so precipitous even if they'd been able to find a buyer, they owed more than it could now be sold for. Their equity had evaporated like the Mexican's who'd fled the state. Poppy saw no possible way they were going to escape this.

Their bank account finally ran down. They couldn't make the April mortgage payment. Their personal collapse was beginning. They simply couldn't survive on Wally's Social Security check and there was no place left to turn.

On the tenth of April Wally gathered the courage to go talk to Commercibank, his mortgage holder, about what had happened to them.

One aspect of being the victim of a crime like the one Wally and Poppy found themselves victimized by is the humiliation the victim feels. The despair over not having seen the thing coming is exacerbated by the sentiment of those who watch the train wreck, baffled by how the victim could have *let* this happen. It was difficult for Wally to discuss what occurred, even with close friends. The prospect of telling the story to his mortgage banker was about as agreeable as contemplating a root canal.

Poppy was uncharacteristically animated that day. She wished him good luck and told him how much she loved him—believed in him. It was more than he'd heard from her in a month.

"Sorry I haven't been able to find a solution yet, Popp," he told her, holding her gently.

"You've done everything anyone could, Wally. What else can you do?"

"Well, I can convince the bank to give me more time," he answered unconvincingly.

"It's going to be okay, sweetie," Poppy assured him.

It was a relief for him to hear a sense of optimism coming from her. Could it be she was beginning to recover from the deep stupor she'd fallen into over the last two months? There were days Poppy would sit inside their courtyard, never uttering a single word. She wouldn't eat or drink the entire day. She'd sit quietly in a deep meditative state and listen to the birds or stare at the flowers, a total absence of emotion in her demeanor.

"Thanks, Popp," Wally said, squeezing her to him. "I need you to keep believing in me."

"We deserve better than this, Wally," she said. "We put in our years, saved our money. Remember the year we decided not to go to Greece so we could save an extra ten thousand dollars?"

He didn't reply. He turned his head slightly and kissed her on the cheek.

"We did everything right," she went on. "We took care of ourselves and made sure we could live out our lives carrying our own weight. No burden to anyone." She struggled to find the words. "Those—*people*—stole it from us—simple as that, Wally. They stole our lives and we aren't going to get them back."

Wally didn't deny the possibility.

"Come on, Wally," Poppy said. "You need to get going." She gently pushed him away from her and wiped the tears from the corners of his eyes with her thumb. "You don't want to be late to your appointment with the bank." She looked up into his eyes. "It'll be all right, Wally. You've done everything anyone could." She smiled at him lovingly. "No matter how things go, you keep in mind how much I love you, okay?"

"I love you, too, Popp," he whispered. "I'll figure something out."

"I know you will," she said. "You always do. Now … go wash your face and get going. You're going to be late."

She walked with him out to the driveway and smoothed his shirt before he climbed in behind the steering wheel of his truck. "Want anything special for dinner?"

Wally shook his head. "Surprise me," he said.

Poppy touched his shoulder, then leaned in and kissed him on the lips. "Good luck," she said, and waived. She waited while he backed out of the driveway and pulled away.

CHAPTER 8

One complicating reality accompanying the occurrence of any shattering event, is while the thing that happens may be common to any number of victims, it is a guarantee the rippling effects will be processed in vastly different ways by each individual. Poppy Stroud had given up. No longer could she find the will to believe a solution to their troubles was possible. Life had conspired against her and there seemed no hope any measure of joy or wonderment would ever return. Malignancy existed everywhere she turned. It broke her heart to watch Wally's every effort be mired by inaction from the agencies he'd turned to for help. She finally lost all hope he would ever recover their savings—even a small part of it.

Wally, for his part, lived in a state of constant grief that permeated every waking hour. Sleep came artificially, supplied by a small bottle of green and white pills he'd managed to con an urgent care physician into prescribing. Even then, four consecutive hours was the best he was getting. Once the mild chemical euphoria wore off, he'd lay, wide-awake, paralyzed and at the mercy of the darkness gripping his life. He maintained one focus; find their money. His greatest frustration was becoming a resentment that would have shocking consequences. The indifference to what happened to him and Poppy by those agencies he believed would protect them constituted nothing short of abandonment. Wally felt betrayed and isolated. He needed help to locate his money—now! Pace and Taylor were being given too much time to hide their assets.

~~~~

Roger Watkins was a portly, white-bread man of about fifty years. The nameplate sitting on his desk announced 'Mortgage Officer.' The man was cordial. He'd listened with feigned empathy to Wally's story. When Wally finished explaining what he was faced with, Watkins assured him the bank would not initiate foreclosure proceedings until he and Poppy were a full ninety days delinquent.

This is his idea of help? Wally thought.

"From that point, the process would take another ninety days to complete," Watkins went on to explain. "So if you can get something worked out by then," he said, "you can pay your mortgage current and start the clock all over again." He concluded this critique with such energy it suggested he believed he had just handed Wally the definitive solution to his predicament.

Simple! Just work something out. The fucker's a genius, Wally thought, getting into his pickup. But what should he have expected from Roger Watkins? The man was an employee. And what was realistic to ask of his bank? Shit—he had no answers himself, only frustration after frustration while the criminals played golf and hid their assets—his life savings.

That was it then—six months—maximum.

He drove from the bank to the nearest Border's bookstore. He couldn't bring himself to drive straight home and reveal yet another dead-end to Poppy. What would it accomplish anyway? For the first time in weeks she seemed—what, he thought? Not up, but—better? What purpose would it serve to go over the details of the ridiculous suggestion *mortgage-man* Watson made? She was smart. She knew without him having to explain the gory details anyway. Except keeping something like that from her was a thing Wally had never before done in all the years they'd been together.

One thing was certain. For the first time since he was a child, Wally Stroud found himself at a complete loss to know just what it was he would do next. His thoughts meandered through a litany of banal absurdities that cluttered clear thinking. There were a thousand voices screaming inside his head all at the same time. Noise—so much noise, yet no solutions.

But the only possible answer to the dilemma was obvious right from the moment he began to realize he was never going to recover their savings. There never was any other option. Wally understood the *absolute* of what would be required of him. If he could not recover their life's savings, he'd have to start a new company, begin again—just as he had after he'd been discharged from the military forty years in his past.

His responsibility was to provide for Poppy and he had no intention of letting her down. But the journey this time around could only end at his death. It was a bleak contemplation as opposed to the optimism he'd felt in viewing the challenges in front of him as a young man. This journey would not end with leisure years to travel and savor the joys of a productive life and marriage; celebrate the final act that was the story of his and Poppy's life together. Well, he thought, maybe they would discover something positive, if not good, in all of it. What else can a person think when there are finally no more options?

Still, they both had a good work ethic. And hadn't Poppy been grousing about how she was not taking up the *rocking chair on the front porch of retired life,* anyway? He folded his arms across his chest, leaned back against a bookcase and closed his eyes. He knew that wasn't it. It wasn't that he or Poppy felt sorry for themselves because they would have to continue working. Millions of people have only that option.

No—it was the grief over the loss of what amounted to the representation of thirty-five years of hard work and sacrifice he and Poppy'd expended over a lifetime to provide themselves with security and a measure of grace as the end of their lives began to close in. It was that all of their choices were gone, replaced by the mundane necessities for survival. And in the near term, it would be subsistence survival until they could reestablish themselves. Who knew how long that might take? And then there was one final demon that, somehow, Wally realized was going to have to be exorcised: The knowledge this penalty was being imposed on them by two criminals who had literally stolen their savings, negated in an instant all of their life's efforts to ensure dignity in their final years, yet would be allowed to go on in the lap of luxury while he and Poppy, along with hundreds of other families, suffered.

He opened his eyes and turned to face the books on the shelves. Bile rose into his mouth as the image of Bud Pace's imperious face snapped momentarily into his brain recalling that Monday morning back in November when the arrogant prick lied to him and Poppy about the stolen reserve funds.

He browsed the fiction section trying to remember which John Irving novel he hadn't yet read. He realized he'd read them all—some twice. He would have picked up the newest Grisham novel but hardbacks were expensive. It struck him his life was changing in ways he'd not even considered. He loved books—but he could no longer afford to buy one.

He moseyed over to the magazine section and thumbed through several claiming to identify the hottest new trends or businesses if you intended starting your own. They were 99.9 percent bullshit, but people—desperate people like him—bought them. He turned away without one.

CHAPTER 9

Wally finally trudged out to his pickup, climbed in and sat behind the wheel steeling himself for the gloomy drive home. Poppy should be finished with her grocery shopping. They'd sit, drink a bottle of wine while he explained what he planned next.

He pulled to a stop along the curb at the front of his house, slid out and gathered the two folders of documents from the front seat. Had circumstances been different, they might already be sitting in the courtyard together watching the Cactus Wrens flying in and out of their hiding places in the Fichus, busily building nests or reinforcing old ones from last season in preparation for the new families of chicks they'd soon hatch.

It was a warm spring day. Shadows had begun to grow long. The ornamental pear tree in the corner of the courtyard was sprouting a healthy profusion of tender young leaves that would mature, turn a deep forest green, and ultimately provide shade to the entire northwest corner of the yard once the scorching hot Arizona summer was under way. He inhaled deeply, breathing in the sweet perfume of orange blossoms.

He was home ahead of her. Some shopping trip. He glanced at his wristwatch. It was four-thirty. He'd use the extra time to find a bottle of Chardonnay. Maybe surprise her with it opened and chilled—chunk of cheese and a few crackers. Just the kind of celebration they used to end every day with before this nightmare began.

Wally could just detect an unusual soft humming sound coming from somewhere deep inside his house when he pushed the front door open. When he walked into the kitchen he realized the source of the sound was coming from the garage. He crossed the kitchen and flung open the service door expecting to find an off balance load of laundry in the washer. They'll do that sometimes. A pair of Levis or a bed sheet gets balled up and throws the spin cycle off. The machine wants to try to launch itself across the floor, then sits buzzing for attention. Instead, he found Poppy's Volkswagen parked inside, idling. The convertible top was up. She was sitting behind the wheel. Above the din of the car's engine he heard the muffled sounds of a soft jazz track coming from the speakers.

"Poppy? What the hell—" He lurched toward the car. It was dark. Suddenly the full impact of what he was seeing exploded in his brain.

"Oh, God ... No! Poppy, what ... have ... you ... done? No!" Wally did not scream the words. They were soft ... simply regurgitated from the core of his being: a rhetorical, desperate plea from a man who already knew the unbearable answer to his question. Hysterically he fought with the door handle. She'd locked herself in.

He smashed his fist into the driver's window. The pain didn't register. Nothing happened. He turned sideways and hit the glass again with his elbow. Again, nothing. Insane with dread and a sense of helplessness he searched in the grim darkness of the garage. There ... five-pound dumbbell.

Wally grabbed the weight, used it like a ramming bar and bashed the window in its center. The safety glass exploded sending pea-sized shards everywhere. He used the dumbbell to score off the sharp edges at the door and groped to get the latch up. "Sonofabitch," he yelled. Couldn't get a grip with his fingers. It dawned on him to reach in along the armrest and press the electric door release.

At the click he fumbled urgently with the handle. He pulled the door open and dragged Poppy's clammy body out onto the glass-riddled floor of the garage. She was covered with tiny bits of safety glass.

The garage began to fill with toxic fumes, which poured out of the car like water over a breached dam. Wally stumbled across her, falling toward the car. Fumbled to turn off the key. Then he wove his way back to the kitchen entrance and slammed his hand against the electric garage door opener.

For a split second he was addled. Chaos and dread confronted him brutally. What to do next? Think! He grabbed the phone and ran back to where Poppy's limp body lay. He punched the 911 autodial then the speaker button and dropped the handset next to him on the floor. He was performing CPR in the few moments it took for the ring to be answered.

"911 operators," a metallic, robot-like voice answered. "What is your emergency?"

Wally pulled his mouth away from Poppy's and pumped on her chest. "It's my wife! I need help," he gasped. "I'm ... per ... forming CPR right now."

Wally went back to Poppy's mouth, gently squeezed her nostrils closed and forced air down her windpipe.

"What is your name, sir and your loca—?"

"Wally Stroud, 307 E. Glendale. There's been an accident. My wife isn't breathing."

Wally placed his mouth once more over Poppy's and forced air into her lungs. Her chest expanded a little and he returned to massaging her heart.

"Goddamnit, send somebody to help me! Now!"

"Try to remain calm, sir." The voice was evenly modulated. "Help is already on the way. Can you tell me what happened?"

"Just get the paramedics here, fast," Wally said, breathing hard, crying openly.

"Mr. Stroud," the operator said, "if you can tell me what happened, it will help the paramedics when they get to you."

"Carbon monoxide," Wally shouted, and then forced another gulp of air into Poppy's lungs. "Oh, Poppy ... come on! Wake up, Popp!" He sobbed.

Two minutes later the fire department paramedics pulled their large red ambulance to a screeching stop directly behind Wally's pickup.

Two athletic EMTs jumped out and jogged up the driveway with a large black bag that broke down the middle and exposed the tools of their trade.

"Please stand back, sir," the one with the stethoscope around his neck said, placing the listening tubes into his ears with blue latex-gloved hands. He ignored the broken glass on the floor as he knelt down beside her, but brushed the pieces around Poppy's neck away.

The EMT in charge of the black bag questioned Wally while setting up to insert an IV line. What happened? How long? Taking any drugs? Been ill?

The barrage of questions made Wally's head hurt.

The EMT with the stethoscope opened the front of Poppy's blouse and was listening. Abruptly he commenced to massage her heart. Then he stopped and listened again.

His partner was ready to insert the IV. He was having trouble finding a vein. While he struggled to get the needle in, a ladder truck pulled to a stop alongside the ambulance. Three firefighters launched themselves toward the frantic scene underway next to the open driver's door of the black car parked in the garage.

"Talk to us, Brad," one fireman said.

"Clear out some of this glass," one of the EMTs said.

The three firemen went to work. One of the heavily jacketed men knelt alongside the EMTs and brushed glass off of Poppy's inert body.

The EMT with the stethoscope was preparing the paddles of a defibrillator. "Clear," he shouted, and Poppy's body jerked.

The guy with the IV worked frantically. "Clear," the other EMT yelled. Again, Poppy's body jumped.

Two of the firemen worked silently sweeping away glass shards from around the working paramedics and Poppy's body.

While the two EMTs worked to try to save Poppy Stroud's life a police car pulled up and blocked the street in front of the Stroud's house. By then heads were popping out of doors and front yards to see what the commotion was.

"Oh, my goodness," shouted one neighbor. "Is it Poppy or Wally?"

"Please stand back," the uniformed officer ordered.

Finally the EMT with the IV needle found a vein. They were preparing her to be transported. John C. Lincoln Hospital was only a few blocks away with one of the best trauma centers in the southwestern U.S.

"I have no heartbeat and she isn't breathing," the lead EMT said to his partner. "We need to transport her right now." Their eyes met momentarily. The lead EMT wobbled his head faintly, his partner understood.

Within seconds they had her stuffed into the back of the ambulance. Wally managed to shove his way in with them. The siren burped and the driver pulled away. Wally watched from his pinched corner seat, dazed and in shock at what he was witnessing. His emotions were cascading through his psyche like an avalanche, the strongest being denial. This could not be happening. The lifeless blue-gray form the paramedic was trying desperately to aspirate was the love of his life.

Back at the Stroud home a uniformed officer ran a strip of yellow crime scene tape across the front of the driveway and asked the gathering crowd of neighbors to please stay back.

The ride to the hospital took less than five minutes. The resident on duty pronounced Poppy DOA.

All motion stopped abruptly. Silence sucked into the void as if a vacuum had been broken. The stillness was palpable. The desperation etched on Wally's face caused the two EMTs, the resident, an intern and the two nurses assisting to bow their heads. The very spirit of Wally Stroud's *inspiration-to-be* was ebbing out of him like a shooting star entering the atmosphere, expending the final reserves of its cosmic energy before collapsing into oblivion. These were professionals, accustomed to witnessing the pain anyone experiences when a loved one is lost; but somehow they each understood something beyond the loss of a loved one had lodged itself inside this man.

The two nurses broke the silence. "Follow us, sir," the heavy-set nurse instructed quietly, taking charge. The EMTs took over once more and wheeled the gurney slowly, somberly down the hall toward a small, private room. No one spoke. The wheels on the gurney squeaked from need of oil and echoed eerily in the empty hallway. Wally followed behind them and the two nurses, his shoulders slumped, eyes cast downward. It was an effort to get one foot in front of the other without stumbling forward. He was utterly unaware of the swelling beginning to show in his right hand. He followed the nurses into a tiny room and took Poppy's hand, weeping openly. They told him he could stay as long as he needed.

Before they closed the door, the taller nurse said to Wally, "Your hand looks broken, sir. We'll take a look at it when you're ready."

~~~~

Betrayed

That was where CSI Dan Jenkins from the Phoenix Crime Lab found him an hour later. "Mr. Stroud," Jenkins said. "Could I have a word with you?" He pointed toward the partially open door.

Wally looked up reluctantly, eyes swollen and red. He placed Poppy's hand on her stomach. His right hand was swollen so large by then he could no longer move his fingers. He followed the detective out into the hallway without speaking.

"You need to have that looked at," CSI Jenkins began, observing the size of Wally's swollen fingers. "Mr. Stroud," he nearly whispered, "I've been at your home while you've been here with your wife." Jenkins stopped and looked at Wally before holding out his hand. "It's a suicide note, Mr. Stroud. I'm sorry. Your wife been under a lot of stress lately?"

Wally held the letter in his left hand but could not see it through the blur of tears in his eyes. It was several seconds before he could compose himself enough to answer. "Yeah," he said simply. "... But I didn't see this coming." With that admission he broke down again.

Dan Jenkins put his hand on Wally's shoulder. "I'd like to drive you back to your home, Mr. Stroud. I'll tell the nurse's station you'll be back. I'll ask them to have a look at your hand then."

Wally shook his head in agreement but didn't speak.

Jenkins took the suicide note out of Wally's hand and walked toward the nurse's station a few yards down the hallway.

Wally went back into the room where his dead wife lay. "I gotta go for a while, Popp ... but I'll be back," he whispered, his choked voice barely audible. "You rest now, baby. Everything is all right ... these folks will take care of you until I get back." He leaned down and kissed her on the lips. "Just rest, Poppy."

CHAPTER 10

The detective backed an unmarked, white Crown Victoria out of a covered parking stall and Wally got in. Jenkins turned onto Hatcher Road and headed west to Seventh Avenue.

"You wanna try reading this?" Jenkins held Poppy's letter out to Wally.

Wally didn't answer: reached over and took the letter. He continued to ignore the condition of his right hand, which exhibited dark purple and greenish-yellow hues across its back from his four knuckles. He dropped the piece of paper into his lap. The stock was the copy paper they kept loaded in their printer ... 12 pt., Times New Roman. The default setting in the word processor.

My Sweet, Sweet Wally,

I know this is going to be difficult for you, but I know what is coming and I cannot bear thinking about it or living through it.

I know you've done everything humanly possible to fix what happened. It wasn't your fault, Wally. Criminals always seem to win. Whoever said, "bad guys finish last" clearly did not have much life experience under her belt. In all our nearly forty years together, the criminals have gotten away over and over again and I just cannot bear to see you struggling to fix things one more time.

This time you've been dealt such a blow I know in my heart you are not going to be able to fix it and I know what that is going to do to you.

Please don't be angry with me, Wally. I figured out a way to fix things this time: I verified the life insurance company could not get out of paying you the full death benefit on my policy. The policy is old enough to be beyond their rescission period. They'll no doubt try to get out of paying, but they have no choice. I took the policy to an attorney just to make sure.

Betrayed

You've always been excellent with money and $250,000 will make it possible for you to get through this mess.

And Wally, just take the money and go spend the rest of your life in Mexico. Let all of this pain and agony go. Go live your life. This is the gift I want you to have. You can buy a lot of golf with that much "dinero" and look ... you won't have to worry about being late for dinner. (Please laugh. I want you to remember my smart-ass wit.)

By now it's over and you're reading this. You know what I've done, but I'm just fine, Wally. You'll be fine, too. Give it some time. In a while you'll see the wisdom in my decision.

Trust me this time, Wally. I love you so very much. Not because you've been the perfect man all these years, but because you've always admitted your shortcomings and made a sincere, if not always successful, effort to fix your screw ups.

You made my life as rich as I could have ever asked. This is as good a place as any to get off the bus.

Love,

Popp

Wally let his head fall back against the headrest and closed his eyes. A steady stream of tears flowed into the crow's feet at the corner of each eye, and then down the sides of his face. He sniffed snot down his throat, ran the back of his left hand under his nose.

"What's she's talking about, Mr. Stroud?"

Wally didn't respond. Instead, he looked down at the letter and took the time to read it again. "Goddamnit, Popp," he croaked, "I would have found a way."

Jenkins didn't say anything.

When he was ready, Wally began to recite what he and Poppy had been going through. He went back to the beginning: The letter at Thanksgiving—the meeting with PPI. The ensuing revelations about Pace and Taylor.

Then the frustration of taking the complaint to all the different agencies, all the while watching helplessly as the last of their emergency savings was consumed trying to keep their heads above water while he tried to find some way out of the nightmare that consumed them.

Long before Wally finished the woeful tale, Jenkins pulled to a stop in front of the Stroud home and parked across the driveway, as the ambulance driver had done, behind Wally's pickup truck.

"Christ!" Jenkins said as Wally finished the story.

"And today I met with our bank," Wally went on. "I don't know what I thought would come of that."

He looked over at Jenkins; Wally had no idea how carefully he was being observed.

"I suppose I keep hoping every time I tell that story to someone, they might come up with the magic solution for me to make it all go away."

"I wish I could, Mr. Stroud. But I don't have the answer either," Jenkins said. "Come on, looks like my people are finished processing the scene." He rolled out of the car.

Wally stepped out of the unmarked car and stood looking straight into the garage where he'd found Poppy in her car. Everything was just as he remembered when the ambulance sped away.

His feet felt cemented to the pavement. It was nearly impossible to make the march up the driveway.

He'd been so consumed when Poppy was positioned into the back of the ambulance he hadn't noticed how she ran the large black hose from the shop-vac over the end of the exhaust pipe of her Volkswagen EOS, under the partially closed trunk lid then into the access port from the trunk into the backseat. She'd been efficient setting things up. That was Poppy. She never did anything halfway.

Dan Jenkins said, "You can remove that and return things to normal around here, Mr. Stroud. We have everything we need."

"What the fuck could you think is ever going to be *normal* here again?" Wally replied angrily.

"I won't pretend to understand how you feel, Mr. Stroud," Jenkins admitted. "I don't know how you pick up the pieces from something like this."

Wally didn't respond. He walked around the back of the EOS, through the garage and entered the kitchen. Dan Jenkins followed a few paces behind.

"I'm sorry we had to invade your privacy, Mr. Strou—"

"Wally," Wally said. "It's all right to use my name."

"Thanks, Wally," Jenkins went on. "We have to do it ... the investigation. It's policy."

"That's fine," Wally said, "do what you have to."

"We're finished, Wally. It's just routine procedure, I wanted you to understand."

"I understand, officer."

"Has your wife ever attempted anything like this before," Jenkins probed almost as an afterthought.

"Never," Wally replied rejecting any discussion along those lines. "Before those fuckers stole our lives from us, we were set to immerse ourselves in everything we loved to do together for however much time we had."

"Sounds like the two of you were very happy together." Jenkins said. He eyed Wally's body language closely. His statement came out as a probe—or gouge depending on your point of view.

Wally looked up and engaged Jenkins' gaze. "What kind of shot was that?"

"I apologize, Wally. I have to explore every angle in these situations."

"Well, you explore all you want," Wally countered vituperatively. "What Poppy did, she did out of—," he agonized for the words, "confusion ... misguided confusion. She didn't mea—," he couldn't continue his thought. Wally caved to the cascading grief once more.

"It's all right, Wally," Jenkins said, placing his hand on Wally's shoulder. This time Wally shrugged it off. "We have everything we need for now," Jenkins repeated. "I'll have to hold on to this note until we've completed our report. We have no choice but to have an autopsy performed. We have to do it."

Wally looked at him with bitterness. "You're going to cut my Poppy open?"

"We don't have any choice, Wally. It's the law," Jenkins explained. "The Medical Examiner's office will pick her up from the hospital. They'll need a couple of days."

"Jesus-fucking-Christ!" Wally yelled.

He didn't wait for Jenkins to continue. He stomped over to his liquor cabinet, pulled out the bottle of Johnny Walker Red Poppy gave him at Christmas and poured himself a full tumbler. He ignored the pain and clumsiness in his right hand.

Without hesitation he lifted the glass with his purple, swollen fingers that had begun to resemble a baseball glove and downed half the glass. "That all, officer?" he growled.

"You want to take it easy with that, Wally," Dan Jenkins cautioned. "Would you like me to ask the ME to give you a couple of hours with your wife at the hospital before they pick her up?"

Wally set the glass down on the counter and stared straight into the wall in front of him. A full half-minute of tense silence elapsed before he answered. "I'd appreciate that," he said pushing the glass aside. "You finished?"

"Yeah," Jenkins responded softly. "I need to fill in any blanks, I can give you a call."

"Whatever you need," Wally said, and walked off leaving CSI Dan Jenkins standing alone in the kitchen.

Wally staggered into the master bathroom and splashed cold water onto his face. Leaning against the front edge of the countertop, he studied his broken hand, and then slowly raised his eyes to meet his reflection in the mirror. Wally studied his face as though it belonged to someone else. "How can I go on without you, Poppy?" he whispered. "Did you consider that? How am I going to be able to go through another day without you?" He searched the vacant eyes of his reflection and understood the man he'd always thought he was—was no more.

Dan Jenkins was halfway out the open garage when he heard a primal scream so painfully guttural, from so deep within the creature that unleashed it, it made the hair on the back of his neck stand up. They were agonized screams—hopeless. Jenkins did understand the desperate sorrow he heard emerging from a place deep within Wally. He spun and ran to him.

Wally was curled in a corner on the floor of the bathroom, his knees pulled up tight to his chest, his forearms crossed over them, his face buried. He rocked back and forth, screaming from the depths of his being. Jenkins was used to seeing the painful reactions of victims and family members to such events—yet tears crept into his eyes as he knelt down and put his hand on Wally Stroud's back.

If we can learn anything from this, it is that you can never understand another person's illusions—even if that person happens to be a wife or husband. No matter what you try to say, they cling to their version of the truth with a fervor that mystifies and infuriates you. But you will not realize until later that it is the only defense against a truth that would undermine

34

everything of which they have become convinced. Once they embrace the lie, nothing you can say or do is going to shift them away from the truth they have created. The lie becomes the truth.

"You'll get around this, Wally," Jenkins promised. He slid down into a sitting position on the floor next to Wally Stroud, stretched his legs out in front of him, crossed his ankles, and let his head fall back against the wall.

CHAPTER 11

Whether Wally believed the words of Dan Jenkins or, for that matter, even wanted to believe them, they proved irrelevant. For life will not give you a time out. Time won't stand still no matter how much you need it to—life continues relentlessly coming at you. You *will* move forward because there is simply no other choice.

Arranging to have Poppy cremated had proven a tedious affair. Wally found the pomp and circumspection disingenuous. It amounted to little more than money grubbing behind the guise of respectful consideration for the dearly departed and the bereaved survivors. Nevertheless, he'd agreed to a beautiful marble urn to hold her ashes. A peculiarly cantankerous regard for mainstream convention was beginning to manifest itself in Wally's behavior as he dealt with the transition he felt forced upon him—unbearably unjust.

~~~~

March 25th was a quiet, warm Sunday. The Barbara Karst Bougainvillea clinging to the front wall of the courtyard at the Stroud home had exploded into a cornucopia of brilliant new color. The ornamental pear tree in the corner was beginning to gain its new white blossoms and somehow the carroty/scarlet hibiscus in the blue ceramic pot next to the pond had burst open to display three brilliant saucer-sized blossoms. It felt to Wally as though there was a consciousness in the plants, like they were competing to be a part of the moment, perhaps to somehow reward Poppy's nurturing care of them over time. He didn't share that idea with anyone, too loony; but he'd pondered the notion.

While the few neighbors, friends, and family he'd invited to celebrate Poppy's life straggled in, he greeted each of them, shook hands left-handed and hugged those who seemed to expect that intimacy. He accepted sympathetic wishes and inquiries as to the condition of his heavily bandaged hand. To a person, they artfully ignored the fact that Poppy had taken her own life. The gathering evolved with people filtering in and out of the house, filling small paper plates with hors d'oeuvres he'd had prepared for the occasion. He noticed how once each individual issued the appropriate sentiment to him, they'd slip uncomfortably away to congregate quietly in small clusters of two or three or four people huddled together at a safe distance speaking softly, as if the sound of their voices might wake the lady in the jug. Maybe that's the way people acted when someone committed suicide.

In the southeast corner of the courtyard, under the dwarf date palms Poppy affectionately named "Desdemona & Little Jimmy," Wally had leaned a cork bulletin board with pictures of her pinned to it, pictures taken at various times throughout her life. To one side he'd nestled the marble urn containing her ashes in amongst some clusters of Purple Katie in a large decorative cement planter.

Dolores Zinsser, Poppy's mother, was a look-alike for Acquanetta, the Venezuelan Volcano of 1950s B-movie fame, without the trademark black braids. She and Liz Zinsser, Poppy's youngest sister, along with Ellen Craig, Poppy's middle sister, stood near the urn accepting condolences for their loss. Dolores wept openly and said little, a nonstop flood of tears streaming down her face. Ellen didn't say much either, accepted thoughts of encouragement, and absurd assurances from a few that if she put her pain in God's hands it would somehow all go away. Ellen graciously deferred to her younger sister, Liz, who was holding court, having adopted the role of official family spokesperson.

Wally watched Liz work her audience. She was ten years younger than Poppy. Liz had always been jealous of her older sister. Wally was not the least bit surprised to see even that day—a special day to remember her dead sister—Liz felt the need to compete with Poppy to be the center of attention. Poppy was a natural beauty, the girl-next-door kind of innocent beauty that caused people to gravitate to her effortlessly. Everything about Liz, on the other hand, was manufactured: the phony come-on of her personality, her nervously over-exuberant gestures, the strikingly platinum hair she coiffed to hide the fact that she was prematurely gray, and you couldn't miss the thirty-eight double D cleavage she kept on prominent display. Liz proudly referred to her enhanced breasts as, "the girls." She wore her stock-in-trade stretchy black "T" a full size too tight, but outlined her nipples perfectly. Liz was a popular Hooters girl at the restaurant where she waited tables. She might just as well have been attending a cocktail party. Wally looked on and could not deny that physically she was an attractive woman, one might even have argued—pretty—until she opened her mouth, which she was overdoing at that moment.

As she lectured on the probable mindset of her poor depressed sister during these last difficult months, in volume loud enough to be heard across the courtyard, she continually glanced toward Wally, sending him the unmistakable message about her assessment of who was to blame for what happened.

Betrayed

Wally'd listened to her myopic lecture on how they all needed today to give closure to what happened. *Closure?* What bullshit, he thought. As if a simple ceremony was going to somehow allow him or anyone else to put what happened behind them and move forward. Wally knew if he was ever able to sleep completely through another night he'd be doing well. If he could find a way to live with the pain he might be able to survive, and that would be a great enough accomplishment. He wondered who the genius was that came up with the concept of closure to begin with. It had to have been someone similarly afflicted with the profound wisdom his sister-in-law, the expert, currently was putting on display. The only closure for which Wally was grateful was the closure of Liz's mouth when her father, Jake Zinsser, fell in beside her and whispered in her ear to shut up.

Wally endured the next two hours sipping a glass of Scotch and recalling those first queasy baby steps he'd taken twelve days earlier, which propelled him into this bizarre, awkward existence that now controlled his life like a canker. Once he'd pulled himself together enough to go back to the hospital that night to hold and touch and say his final goodbye to Poppy, her spirit, really, an intern checked his hand. The nurses on duty arranged it and insisted. They gave both Wally and the young doctor-in-training orders neither man cared to challenge. The x-rays showed several small hairline fractures, but nothing that could be set in the conventional way of most broken bones. The intern placed Wally's hand in a slightly curled position on a rigid, pre-shaped rubber form and then bandaged it securely so his fingers could not move and the damaged knuckles were protected. The fabrication produced the manifestation that was the current object of curiosity. After a brief discussion with Wally about not blaming himself for what Poppy had done, the same intern arranged for a half dozen Valium pills. He was instructed to take one the moment he returned home. The others he could use as required. He'd needed that first pill to make his eyes close that night. The remaining five were still in the bottle.

When the nurses deemed Wally's immediate physical needs adequately tended to, the tall one, her badge identified her as, Alice, RN, lead him silently down the hall to the holding room where Poppy's body awaited the next step in its journey into eternity. He recalled being curiously entranced by the up and down jiggly rhythms of the cheeks of the kind nurse's rotund ass, dancing competitively against the insides of her scrubs as she shuffled forward down the hallway. "You take all the time you want, Mr. Stroud," Alice had said, and closed the door quietly.

The room was cold, the silence harsh but welcome. Just being close to her was a balm to his mangled psyche. Wally walked to her and looked down at her lovely face. This could not be happening. Her eyes were closed, her mouth was closed, but she did not seem at peace to him. Deep crevices turned downward at the corners of her mouth and ran to merge with the loose skin that was just now beginning to form the first signs of jowls along the bottom of her jaw line. Her mother had them. Poppy would have had them, too. She looked sad, he thought—very sad.

"What have you done, Popp?" He spoke softly and tears filled his eyes. Wally was conflicted by the feelings of profound love he held for his wife, because now he also harbored raw anger toward her as well. He wanted to hold her gently, and yet he wanted to yell, "You left me for … *money*? You thought *money* was that important?" He used his good hand to pull her blouse closed. A portion of her breasts had been exposed during the efforts to shock her heart back to pumping.

He brushed her hair so that it fell tidy away from her face, and then gently touched her cheeks and lips. They were cold now—completely cold. His tears fell onto her shoulder and left a darkened spot on her blouse. "This is so final, Popp. I didn't see your pain. This is my fault. If I had understood what was happening to you … maybe … I don't know. I feel so confused." He shook his head, stared up into the ceiling, but found no inspiration there. "I obsessed about getting that fucking money back, didn't I? I was so focused on that I didn't see what was going on in your head. I let you down Popp. And you were drowning in things I didn't see or understand."

Wally pulled the sheet back so he could look at her entire body. She'd worn her Calvin Klein jeans, a baby blue Liz Claiborne blouse and black Ferragamo ankle boots. He recalled the Christmas he'd given them to her. He smiled. "You dress for every occasion, don't you Popp?" Without looking he knew the lingerie she was wearing would be lacey and matched. Knowing these simple truths tore at his heart. Why could he not have known with equal clarity the profound psychosis lurking inside her?

He bent down and kissed her cold lips. His mouth lingered on hers. Then he slowly, gently brushed the cold skin of her face with his nose and lips. His sobs were silent and bitter, erupting from the core of everything he was as a man.

He finally straightened up, coughed the phlegm out of his throat, leaned against the gurney and laced the fingers of his good hand into hers. He'd remained there, head bowed, playing a movie in his mind's eye that was a fast-forward of every precious memory they'd created in thirty-three years together. There was that: The very first home they'd bought; that Christmas they'd stumbled into the pet shop where they found Phoebe their Cocker Spaniel. (She'd lived eighteen years and was as much their child as any human child could have been.) The traveling—Central America, South America, London, Paris … China. They'd traveled around the world together. There was all of that and more coming at him then in fast forward.

Then there was the bargain he was willing to make with a deity he had no faith even existed if he could just have her back. There was the promise the motherfuckers who drove her to this would not walk cleanly away. His brain was in overload. For several cloudy, tortuous moments he believed he understood *why* what Poppy had done made perfect sense, because right then—he wanted to be dead, too. Though he did not believe in an afterlife, he focused every ounce of his brain's energy into attempting to breach the barrier of death and tell her one last time just how much their lives together meant to him and how much he loved her—would always love her. Death—so painfully final, he lamented.

He'd lost all sense of time, fallen into a transcendental state. He could not recall how long he'd been there when the door opened slowly. It was Nurse Alice. "Mr. Stroud," she'd said, "the attendants from the Medical Examiner's office are going to have to take your wife now. Is that all right with you?"

They'd all been more than generous in allowing him this time. He would not repay their generosity with petulance. "Sure," he'd said. "I appreciate your kindness."

With Nurse Alice standing in the doorway and the two attendants from the Medical Examiner's office looking on, Wally bent down and kissed Poppy one final time. "Goodbye, Popp," he'd said softly, turned and walked out the room. It was nearly 1:00 a.m. He remembered realizing then he would never again see his beautiful wife: the love-of-his-life—his best friend—the only human being in his life that made anything worth enduring—gone—forever.

It had been worse calling family and friends. What the hell do you say to people? Poppy's father, Jake Zinsser, was seventy-eight years old and suffering from emphysema after a lifetime of smoking cheap Crook cigars. He also sported a scar that ran from just below his sternum up to his Adam's apple and attested to the double bypass surgery, which had narrowly saved his life. He wouldn't have been anyone's first choice for notifying Poppy's family about what happened. That will attest to the regard Wally held for Poppy's younger sister, Liz or her mother, Dolores. Ellen Craig, Poppy's middle sister, was the exception to whom he might have turned, but she lived in California; urgency, befuddlement—his addled mental condition dictated practicality.

"Jake?" Wally said into the phone.

"Hey, Wally. Whatcha up to?"

"You alone?"

"Shit! You know, Dolores. Lives at the mall. I'm considering turning her in to the county for abandoning her invalid husband." He laughed but detected something profoundly wrong in Wally's tone. "Everything all right?"

"I'm less than a block up the street. Can we talk?"

"Come on over," Jake said suspiciously.

Jake was waiting for him, sitting in his favorite lawn chair just inside the open door of the two-car garage that faced onto the street at the front of the Zinsser home. It was an observation post from which Jake regularly sat silently for hours, a hunter of sorts, up a tree waiting for the game to arrive, accomplishing nothing more than taking in the comings and goings, lives in motion, of the small community in which he resided. It was a substitute activity for the life in which he no longer participated.

It was nine-thirty the morning after Poppy died. The wheels of life were unrelentingly grinding forward. He was the only one in the family—maybe the entire universe—who knew the horrible message he had to deliver. Wally had not spoken to anyone since—well, since. He felt drugged. Maybe the Valium hadn't completely worn off? He felt responsible. He felt ashamed. He felt fear. He suffered the notion he might burst into flames, combust from the inside out and evaporate. The pain he bore was unspeakable—and he was about to have to share it with people who loved Poppy, too.

R.P. McCabe

He pulled his GMC pickup into the driveway and slid out. Jake Zinsser saw Wally's eyes and fear echoed on the old man's face. The two men said not a word, just held each other's gaze.

Wally said, "We better go inside."

Poppy's father lowered his eyes, stood paralyzed staring at his feet several seconds before turning and walking toward the door. He shoved it open and went through leaving Wally to navigate his own entry.

Jake went straight to his liquor cabinet and retrieved a half gallon bottle of Jim Beam. He pulled out a cocktail glass and filled it, looked down into the amber liquid anticipating dreadful news he could not begin to guess, but instinctively feared.

He had not waited to receive the blow. Jake lifted the glass to his mouth, tilted his head back and drained it slowly. "How bad is it?" he asked without looking into Wally's face.

"Bad, Jake."

"Somebody t-bone her in an intersection?" Jake asked, wiping his mouth with the back of his hand.

Wally didn't answer.

"If I've told that woman once," Jake went on, "I've told her a thousand times not to jump off a green light. Some asshole runs the red light and she's gonna get hit."

Wally was fear-frozen. He could not coax words out of his mouth.

"Why'd they call you? Poppy with her?" Jake glanced inquisitively at Wally. "Where'd they take her?" he continued, not waiting for a reply. "Let me change shoes. I want to see her. How bad is it?"

When a message of doom is imminent, as Jake Zinsser sensed it was, people often react with an odd, disjointed staccato of babble, attempting to force the message to be what they want to hear rather than what their deepest fear tells them they are about to learn.

"Sit down, Jake," Wally ordered gently.

"Ah, shit," Jake replied, and poured himself another glass of Beam. He downed the full glass as he had the first, looked furtively to Wally and said, "She's dead ... ain't she?"

Wally's eyes brimmed with tears. Jake Zinsser was a watery blur when he replied, "It isn't Dolores, Jake ... it's Poppy."

Jake wobbled. Wally grabbed him and forced him into a chair. "Is she—?" Jake cut himself off and looked up into Wally's eyes, his countenance pleading that his fear not be given voice and thereby become reality.

It was all Wally could do to say the words.

Jake demanded another tumbler of Jim Beam and Wally did not deny the man. He poured the glass full and delivered it to him. Wally took a seat adjacent to his father-in-law and recounted the story. At the revelation his eldest daughter committed suicide, Jake fought to breathe, his eyes bulged out of their sockets. In all the years Wally'd known the man he'd never seen a tear fall from in his eyes. They filled now and the very essence of the man's life flowed over his face in a steady stream.

41

Betrayed

Wally had more than once observed the stoic fortitude his father-in-law exhibited in crisis situations. He was a stronger man than he ever received credit for. The moment he was managing to get through then was testament to that strength. Jake calmed himself, and then began questioning Wally on every incredulous detail he could imagine. He wanted to be able to steer his wife and daughters to understand this tragedy as best he could. Jake understood nothing he could say or do was going to be enough, yet he instinctively knew how critical those first moments were going to be when his girls received the agonizing news—a daughter—a sister—was dead.

Jake Zinsser was a good husband and father, though he was not respected by his wife or his daughters. The women of the Zinsser family routinely belittled the man, but in every moment of crisis Wally witnessed through the years, it was always Jake to whom they turned. He knew this time was going to be no different. They'd berate him later. They'd berate and discount him until the day they would find *him* dead. But in the meantime, it was his shoulders they would lean on through this nightmare.

Wally'd stayed until Jake asked if he didn't need to be somewhere. Wally acknowledged the cue. Jake simply wanted to be alone. He appeared unaffected by the alcohol, though that was patently impossible.

~~~~

Wally came back into the moment. The afternoon was winding down. Friends and neighbors managed to camouflage their retreat. The Zinsser's remained. They lingered around the patio table as though they could not decide how best to withdraw. Jake was beginning to press his wife and daughters into action when Ellen's son, Colin, arrived.

The hinges on the heavy Mesquite gate creaked as Colin pushed it open and let himself in. For a few seconds everyone looked on in somber silence.

"'Sup ya'll?" he said quietly.

The kid seemed a foot taller when standing next to Wally, but at six-two, Colin had only four inches on his uncle. He was lean, but not skinny. When he turned and saw his uncle standing under the pear tree, Colin's ice-blue eyes went shiny.

Wally set his glass down and paced over to him. They stood motionless facing each other for several moments before Wally embraced the young man. They clung to each other for several moments.

The silence was broken when, at the opposite end of the courtyard, Jake announced, "Dolores, you girls gather up your stuff … time to go."

"We're not going to just leave Colin here with—"

"Dolores." Jake raised his voice slightly, cutting her off before she could shoot her mouth off. "You and the girls get your stuff together right now. We're gonna give Wally and Colin a little privacy."

"No—we're—not," Dolores argued, enunciating the words as though they were syllables in a single word.

"Mom," Ellen interrupted, dragging the word out in a fatigued tone while rising from her chair, "Daddy's right. Colin needs some time alone with his Uncle Wally."

Dolores and Liz made no effort to conceal their disgust over the idea of leaving Colin alone with Wally but they could not overcome Jake's determination to leave once Ellen backed him. The two women huffed their way around inside the house gathering handbags and sweaters.

Jake and Ellen waited at the gate. "I'm sorry, Wally," Jake said. "This is a real strain on all of us."

"You gonna stay with me at Gramma and Grampa's tonight?" Ellen asked Colin.

"Not sure, Mom, I'll call."

Dolores and Liz joined the cluster as they began to inch their way out the courtyard gate. "I can't believe you're just gonna go off and leave Colin with *him*." Liz sulked at Ellen as she scooted around Wally.

"Stuff it, Aunt Liz," Colin reacted, defending his uncle.

"Okay … okay," Ellen cut in. "Let's go Daddy. This is hard on all of us Wally. We're doing the best we can."

"I understand, Ellen." Wally hugged his sister-in-law.

Jake didn't bother trying to shake hands. He herded his wife and youngest daughter out the gate, then turned and raised his right hand. "Good luck, Wally," he said. He turned back and coaxed his peeved wife and daughter on toward the parked car out front. Ellen followed close behind.

Wally's instincts told him he'd never see any of Poppy's family again. The conflicts inside his head were growing. The voices were always there tearing at him, one frosty, bitter, ugly revelation after another. Bottom line—Poppy's family was dysfunctional. They'd been dysfunctional all the years he'd known them. Hell, he and Poppy were probably dysfunctional as well, but they were his family, too—at least he'd always considered it so. He cared deeply about each of them. That there were imperfections in each of them was balanced in his mind by his admission that he was afflicted with his own imperfections. Dolores and Liz could never be nasty enough that his affection for them could not overcome petty differences because in between all of that—there was a lot of love going around as well. It never occurred to him they would turn away from him. It was another crushing epiphany to add on top of the crumbling legacy that had been his life.

Two criminals started an avalanche that was stripping away everything that had ever meant anything to him, and they were going to walk away free, no accountability for any of it. Right before his eyes, the family he'd considered his for thirty-three years was blaming him for Poppy's death, drifting away just as his entire life's efforts had.

One internal voice screamed that in spite of her intention, Poppy had betrayed and abandoned him in a foul and cruel way. The voice that countered that argued she had been driven mad—pushed beyond all limits of reason into a state of despair that was so hopelessly toxic she simply could not see a way out any longer. It wasn't her fault, and it wasn't his fault either. Behind it all—at the very root of this nightmare—were two pricks that were not considered responsible for anything that happened to her—or him.

CHAPTER 12

"Want a beer?" Wally offered, closing the gate.

Wally had a special place in his heart for Colin. As a child Colin fought juvenile leukemia. He was only a baby, two and a half, when he and Poppy received the news. They'd taken a couple of months off work when the call came. Could it have been twenty-four years ago, he thought now? He and Poppy had gone to stay with Ellen and her husband Ross to help however they could. A special bond that went beyond family grew between them.

Wally thought, here is this young man today, twenty-six years old, healthy and Hollywood-handsome with a personality to match. He had that Ashton Kutcher innocence in his baby face that made him an instant heartthrob with the girls and a sweet boy-next-door look that left every mature woman wanting to mother him. He was also endowed with a quick, bawdy wit that belied the underpinning fact Colin Craig was of near genius intelligence.

Colin was just three years past graduation from UC San Diego with a degree in computer science. Wally didn't know what you did with a degree in computer science. What he did know was his nephew was considered a genius of some measure. Every big tech firm in the country was constantly trying to recruit him. As a consequence, Colin accepted consulting projects for compensation amounts that astounded Wally. Thus far, Colin hadn't expressed any interest in working for one company over another. Why would he? The kid makes more money at twenty-six than I earned during my best years.

"You drinkin', Uncle Wally?" Colin wanted to know before committing. His tone and demeanor were subdued. The pain he was feeling was palpable.

"I could do with a refresh," Wally admitted, taking the direct route to the bar. Wally's feelings were as evident to Colin as Colin's to him. He grabbed a cold Amber Bock and held it out to Colin, then filled a tumbler with ice cubes and poured it full with straight Johnny Walker Red.

Betrayed

"Shit, you're gonna get hammered," Colin predicted, watching his uncle's glass fill. "I thought you were exclusively red wine?"

"Recent development," Wally deadpanned, "and with any luck, I *will* get hammered … *salud*." He clinked his glass against Colin's beer bottle.

"I get it." Colin acknowledged.

They meandered in silence back out to the courtyard.

The French doors remained wide open. The warmth of the day had begun to dissolve. The accent lights came on. A soft cyan glow spread across the courtyard. At least the silence offered aloneness, Wally thought.

They walked to where Poppy's remains sat nestled under Desdemona & Little Jimmy. Wally said nothing, stared several moments at his favorite picture of his dead wife.

Colin stood quietly by his side.

"Here's to you, Popp!" Wally whispered, and held up his tumbler.

"I miss you Aunt Poppy," Colin managed, and broke down.

Wally slipped his hand up onto his nephew's shoulder. The gesture said what he felt. The two men stood in silence several minutes.

"I don't know what to do, Uncle Wally … I want things to go back to the way they were."

"Yeah," Wally replied.

Silence.

"This is my fault, Colin."

"It isn't your, fault, Uncle Wally. I know that."

"I try to make sense of what she was thinking. I don't know how I couldn't have seen it coming. If I hadn't been so caught up in this fucking financial fiasco—" Wally's voice trailed away. He slid his hand down from Colin's shoulder and stared into the glass of Scotch before taking a long slug.

"Can't keep beating yourself up, Uncle Wally."

"Why not?" Wally objected. "I'm her husband, Colin. It was my responsibility to take care of her … watch over her. I let her down.

"The fucking criminals who stole our lives turned our world upside down. I didn't know which way to turn … still don't. I was doing what I thought I had to do. Your Aunt Poppy was severely depressed. I could see that, but I had no idea.

"She left me a letter, Colin—" Wally looked again into his glass fighting the guilt of what he felt over Poppy's words. "Colin," he began again, "she did this because of what she thought the loss of our life savings was doing to me … because she thought I wouldn't survive this ordeal. She thought she was saving me by figuring a way for me to get the money from her life insurance. Can you fucking believe that?" Wally's voice rose and broke. "She thought the fucking money meant that much to me," he repeated, putting the guilt he felt on display. "I want her back, too, Colin. I want to tell her everything we have can go away and it won't mean a thing to me as long as I have her. We would have figured something out. But—" Wally stopped himself. "I'm sorry, Colin. I know you're struggling with this, too."

"Not like you, Uncle Wally," Colin said softly, "not like you."

"I want to be strong for you, Colin, but I feel so broken. Instead of accomplishing what I guess she thought she was doing for me, she's made me feel responsible for her death. The two motherfuckers who stole our lives made her think this way, but I didn't see how far she'd gone. I should have stopped it. I want to get a gun and go shoot the fuckers, but I want to take that gun and shoot myself, too."

"And where do you think that would leave me, Uncle Wally." Colin recoiled, shocked at the depth of emotion coming out of his ordinarily mild-mannered uncle.

"Don't worry, kid. I'm not about to go postal on these guys. And in spite of how I feel about how your Aunt Poppy left me, I know I have to find a way to deal with this. I have to keep going … somehow. I just don't know how to do that right now."

They drank in silence several moments.

"You gonna keep this place, Uncle Wally?"

"No," Wally replied matter of fact, lifting his glass to his lips once more.

"Know what you might do?"

"Working on it."

"Anything I can do?"

Wally contemplated his nephew's offer. "Not that far along yet," he confessed.

"Any chance you'll move to your place in Mexico?" This was more a suggestion than a question.

"That's exactly what I'm going to do for now, not sure longer term. How you fixed for furniture?" Wally walked across the courtyard. Colin followed him. They settled into the two rattan club chairs next to the pond.

"I have the necessities," Colin replied.

"You want anything Aunt Poppy and I have here in this house?" Wally pointed with his glass around the courtyard and toward the open French doors.

"What do you mean?"

"Our place in Mexico—" Wally's voice caught, "is furnished. Thought I'd give you first choice at this stuff," he said lifting his glass. "I'm going to keep all of the art … pieces with sentimental value anyway," his face was damp with tears again. "Thought I'd give the rest away … you interested?"

Colin seemed to ponder the question a few moments. "Sure, I'll take some stuff if you're really gonna get rid of it." His heart wasn't much into dispersing his Aunt Poppy's things.

"I need to empty the house in the next month, so think on it before you head back to California." Wally had a thought. "Hell, if you want, you can use my pickup to take a load. I've got Aunt Poppy's EOS."

Colin drained his beer.

47

Betrayed

"You hungry?" Wally pushed himself up out of the chair.

"I could eat." Colin looked up from his iPhone as he dialed his mother.

"Okay with your mom?"

"She's cool … Gramma's having a cow. She wants me to stay with them."

"Don't feel you have to stay—"

"I'm doing what I want," Colin said, cutting Wally off.

"Just don't wanna create any more trouble than I already have in that quarter, if you know what I mean."

"She'll get over it. What do we have to eat?"

"I'm really not interested in these hors d'oeuvres," Wally confessed pointing to the bits and pieces left on the kitchen counter. "What do you say to a pot of spaghetti?"

"I say, yeah. Want me to open some red wine?"

Wally looked up and smiled. "Colin … you can't know what you mean to me." Tears came into his eyes once more. "I'd really like that a lot."

While the impromptu dinner heated on the stove, they strolled through the house deciding which pieces Colin would be removing to his condo in Escondido, California. It wasn't a happy occupation for either man, but they understood life was going to happen while they continued to try to make sense out of what a beloved wife and aunt had done to herself and how her decision had changed both of their lives forever.

Suicide—it's an ugly word with ugly implications. For four months Wally Stroud grieved the loss of the savings he and Poppy worked an entire lifetime to create and preserve. In the face of constant fear and despair over the abysmal implications of their situation, he'd fought every way he knew to extricate them from their nightmare. But that grief and fear paled now in comparison to the devastation he felt. This new state of agony was so profound he now willingly forfeited the possessions he'd fought so hard to preserve. It was not difficult to walk away from all of the *things* that had before seemed so important, but he could not walk away from the loss of the love-of-his-life. There was no pharmaceutical that could bring him momentary relief from the pain that was lodged forever in his psyche. He found himself possessed of a despondency that had taken over his very being and begun to rule his way forward.

And to believe the individuals who precipitated those falling-domino events that brought him to this dark place would spend the rest of their lives in a secure life of luxury was— unconscionable.

CHAPTER 13

The gray haze of dawn was giving way to a pale orange halo around Piestewa Peak. Three red-breasted finches warbled to their mates. Wally wondered if there could be any more elegant way to be ushered into a new day. Yet he felt not an ounce of joy over the melodious songs of the innocent little birds. They flitted back and forth between their nests hidden deep inside the climbing fig on the front of his house, and those secret gardens from whence they judiciously selected only the most perfect of twigs, string and linty fibers from some wayward dryer exhaust. But no magical piece of colored yarn was likely to help Wally pull his life back together.

Spring Equinox just occurred and the sun's warming orb was clawing its way above the horizon by six-thirty each morning. That was an astronomical fact for which Wally was grateful, for the dark desolation of night had become his persistent enemy. He lifted his mug of tea to his lips, fully aware of how much his hand was shaking: sleep deprivation. He recognized the signs, but the urgent care physician who'd accommodated him with two refill prescriptions refused a third for the tiny green and white pills that for the past three months he'd relied upon for three or four hours of nothingness each night.

The effects of the two bottles of red wine he and Colin polished off last night had worn off by one o'clock in the morning, replaced by a pounding headache, the reward of having consumed so much wine on top of so much Scotch. For one confusing moment when he'd first opened his eyes, he'd felt—uncertain. Then he'd reached out to touch Poppy. The cold contact of the sheets in the empty spot where she should have been plunged him backward toward his hideous reality. Voices in his head began to churn. Seemingly, hundreds of angry spirits assaulting his sanity. He lay in agonized reflection through the rest of the night, as he did every other night, staring into the cruel abyss of his tortured mind searching for any piece of an answer as to how he could have let something like this happen.

Betrayed

It was nearly nine o'clock when Colin came bounding into the courtyard, barefoot, shirtless, spiked hair smashed down on one side, which made his head appear lopsided. He held his iPhone against his ear. "Let you know in a while," he said into the phone, and dropped it from the side of his head.

Wally was slumped in a chair next to the pond working on the dregs of his third cup of black pekoe tea. Colin shuffled over to stand in front of him, his face contorting while he yawned; he stretched his arms up and out, then behind his head letting his ribcage bulge. "Jesus, you look like shit, Uncle Wally," he said, noting the dark drawn lines in Wally's face, purplish green bags underscoring dull, blood-red eyes.

Wally scoffed. "I wouldn't be entering any beauty contest if I was *you*, Ace—coffee?"

"I'll get it," Colin said, turning toward the open front door.

"Already made ..." Wally said, speaking to the back of Colin's head, "milk's in the fridge."

Wally listened to the spoon chinking against the side of the kid's cup. "How 'bout you?" Colin shouted.

"Good," Wally replied

Colin trudged back out to the courtyard. He dropped heavily into the chair next to his uncle and sipped loudly from the steaming cup of hot coffee. The cup quivered precariously to his mouth several times before giving it a rest. "That was mom on the phone. Wants to know what I have planned today."

Wally was lethargic, unfocused. No response.

"I was thinking about what you talked about last night ..." Colin went on, "I mean, emptying the house in the next few weeks." Quick sip. "The project I'm working on right now's pretty casual." Colin waited for a response but none came. "I could take a week off without much interruption ... give you a hand getting things under control." He hoisted his cup once more. "Whattaya think?"

"You really have time for that?" It was like Wally had drifted off someplace confusing.

"Even if I didn't ... I'd make time." Colin sipped again. "But, yeah ... it wouldn't be any hassle."

Wally considered the offer. "When's your mom going back?"

"I was just trying to talk her into cancelling her flight and driving back with me. Don't think it would take much to convince her."

The significance of having Ellen and Colin give him a hand slowly penetrated the fog in Wally's head. Ellen was the perfect person to divvy up Poppy's jewelry, clothing—all of her personal things. He really had no alternative but to turn it all over to her mother and sisters.

Those things probably should have mattered to him, he figured—but they didn't. Without Poppy—it was just stuff. He found it curious he no longer felt any connection to things that, in some cases, he'd spent large sums of money acquiring. Now—in his new reality—it amounted to little more than debris he had no practical alternative but to get rid of. He'd found it all but impossible to contemplate, and yet—it had to get done. And the obscene fact of the matter was,

the sooner he could accomplish the nasty business the better it would be. If Ellen would agree—
"You and your mom *could* give me a hand …" Wally said, interrupting his thought. "Well …
you guys talk it over...but if this works a hardship for either of you—"

"Let me call her," Colin offered, setting his coffee cup on the table. He pulled his phone
from his pocket and touched the screen once before moving it to his ear. In seconds he said, "Sup
my ho?" Wally could hear Ellen erupt from as far away as he was sitting. Colin grinned easily
while he listened to his mother's tirade.

Wally watched and listened while the kid lit her up over and over again for several minutes,
inching her ever closer to doing just what he wanted her to do. Each time he jacked her up and
received the response he was looking for; he'd sit quietly, an innocent smile on his face, pure joy
apparent over how he could manipulate her with his playful wickedness. Wally believed that
Ellen Craig must have been taking as much pleasure in her role as her son was in his. What else
would prevent her from doing bodily harm to the kid?

Presently Colin pulled the phone away from his ear. "Bitch is down widit," he announced,
looking over to Wally.

"Goddamnit, Colin," Wally objected, "that's your mother you're talking about."

Colin broke up. "Shit, Uncle Wally … you're as easy as she is." Colin levitated himself out
of his chair, stuck out his hand for Wally to grab and pulled his uncle to his feet. "Must be an old
fart thing," he chortled. "Come on … let's get this *bidness* started," he said, dragging Wally
toward the house.

Colin was in a roguish mood that morning. The kid was going to lighten the mood. He made
an open challenge. "What … you don't think I respect my mom?" he growled playfully at Wally,
locking his arm around his uncle's neck, pulling him into his chest. "You don't think I respect
my mom?" Colin repeated, his voice feigning incredulity. "Shit, Uncle Wally … didn't think
you'd ever turn into a tight-ass. You goin' all neocon on me?" Colin laughed and released his
uncle from his affectionate grip.

~~~~

Having Ellen share his burden was a circumstance Wally had not considered, but which softened
one of the most painful obligations facing him. Poppy's middle sister spent the rest of the week
paring out jewelry and clothing; the shoes, the handbags, the belts and scarves—just thinking
about it sent pangs of misery through Wally's brain. "We'll get through this, Wally," Ellen
promised each morning as she beat forward into the chill, brutal wind of acceptance—of
reality—not a scrap of confidence detectable in her face. And yet she bent forward, leaned into
what was equally as bad for her, if in a different, yet linked, doing what had to be done.

"Would it be okay with you if I kept this for me?" she'd asked sheepishly one morning,
holding out an elegant emerald ring. Wally remembered buying it for Poppy when they'd spent a
month in Cartagena, Colombia twenty years earlier. Ellen's long black hair was pulled back in a

Betrayed

ponytail that draped over her shoulder against the white sleeveless blouse she wore tucked into her jeans. Ellen was blessed with an alabaster complexion and shimmering blue eyes, like the one's she'd given her son. Her hips had grown womanly with age but she never lost the girlish quality Wally always appreciated about her. She was the sister Wally wished Poppy had gravitated to, but she hadn't; they were not close. She held her hand out at arm's length and admired Poppy's ring on her finger. He couldn't remember the last time he'd seen Poppy wear the ring. The fact was—he'd forgotten it even existed. Sadly, he had to concede; Poppy had most likely forgotten it, too. The illusion of the significance of things, Wally thought—they'd always seemed so important to Poppy. Then he'd stop himself, ashamed of the anger he couldn't stop feeling over her having abandoned him.

"Poppy would want you to have anything you'd like, Ellen." But she wanted only that one keepsake for herself and suggested they pass the bulk of Poppy's things to Liz.

There were certain key items, of course; a four-karat round-cut yellow diamond being one such piece. It was circled by two-karats of tiny round chocolate diamonds set in an elegant eighteen-karat white-gold setting. Dolores coveted it. Ellen set it aside for her.

Wally witnessed countless instances during the week when Ellen held a particular item up in front of her, examined it lovingly, then hugged it to her breast or buried her face in it and wept long moments. When he caught sight of his sister-in-law in collapse, he'd disappear—for her sake, and because he was himself about to disintegrate. By the time they tumbled forward into late afternoon each day, Ellen, Colin, and Wally were drained to the point of exhaustion.

~~~~

The grueling week was finally finished, and with it, one of the obligations Wally'd considered most offensive. It was a herculean undertaking he realized he'd never have gotten through without his sister-in-law.

Colin helped Wally move the bits and pieces he intended taking to Mexico into the living room; ready for Wally to load into his truck when the time came. It didn't amount to much. In the closing days before he was ready to move south, Wally planned to let the Salvation Army come for any remaining—*things*—he might be unable to dispose of. The thought pissed him off. A lifetime of loving acquisition—tramp through shops, find the perfect little what-not that fit one specific corner of their world and none other—find some ridiculous way to get the damn thing back home—and the best fucking word he could come up with to describe it now was—*things*— before the Salvation Army came to haul it away.

Thursday afternoon around three-thirty when Wally drove away in Poppy's EOS to keep the same appointment he'd kept at that hour each day for more than two weeks, Colin followed his mother to the rental-car-return at the airport to drop off her car. Wally's GMC pickup was parked inside the garage of the Stroud home loaded with the few items Colin wanted for his Escondido condo and the miscellaneous pieces Ellen acquiesced she could take to her home in Glendale.

52

Colin dutifully delivered everything his mother boxed up that week to his Aunt Liz or his grandmother, Dolores. That left only the few miscellaneous pieces going to California. There was no more practical way for getting the stuff there than for Colin to haul it over by truck and drive back for his car.

At four o'clock, while Colin and Ellen fought the Sky Harbor airport traffic, Wally pulled into the parking lot of Encanto Elementary School on the northeast corner of 16th Ave. and Osborne Road, across the street from the offices of PPI. While he sat patiently noting the comings and goings of employees, matching specific faces to specific cars, and watching people he speculated must have been other devastated investors, he reflected on what he'd been able to accomplish during the week because of the help from Ellen and Colin.

Come morning, Wally thought, checking off the departure from the PPI office building of another employee he recognized, Colin and Ellen would head for California in his pickup. It was a six-hour drive. The kid considered a drive like that a short break. "I'll have your truck back in a few days," he'd insisted. "Day after tomorrow if you want." Wally'd told him to take his time. There was nothing pressing for which he needed the truck. He didn't bother to explain why to Colin, but he figured to be busy in Phoenix another full month—at least he hoped he could wrap things up in that time.

The ghostly silence of his empty house was all Wally could bear. Colin probably would never completely understand what it meant to Wally when he offered to stay on with him. Wally needed to be gone from all of this as soon as he possibly could.

As each familiar face came out of the office building, he checked it off on the chart he'd made matching faces to cars. Except for two people, names were irrelevant. He'd created a simple numbering system to identify all of them. He used #1 to signify Bud Pace, #2 was Carl Taylor, and so on. He used the actual make and model of car with which to place a number, for example: Bud Pace (#1)—Range Rover. It wasn't clever. But it *was* efficient. And what, exactly, was the purpose, or even the usefulness, of such an exercise? Well, he hadn't figured that out yet, but the abiding frustration he felt over what he knew this company, its owners anyway, was getting away with was enough impetus for now. What he felt deep in the emptiness that once must have been his essence was he had to do something. For the moment, this apparent waste of time was the something he'd chosen.

The men he now surveilled were criminals who'd remorselessly destroyed hundreds of lives. Pace and Taylor's scheme was cold, calculated and ruthless. How the hell, then, could it be they were still playing golf at their country club twice a week? How could it be Poppy had been driven over the edge by what they'd done, and they would never have to give her so much as a thought? One thing was certain; watching them carry on their carefree lifestyles while he endured his nightmare was an injustice he was struggling mightily to appreciate. Turning the other cheek would have to be reserved for the bible-thumpers; it wouldn't work for Wally—not this time.

Betrayed

Working hours extending beyond four-thirty every afternoon at PPI were dictated by what time Bud Pace and Carl Taylor decided to call it a day. It was easy for Wally to know whether the two were leaving for the afternoon or whether they'd be returning. If they planned to be out the rest of the day, within fifteen minutes of their leave-taking the next highest ranking employees, (#3, #4, #5) identified by the status symbol of the vehicles they drove, would slip away also. There was no definitive way to know if the status symbol of a person's car was by any means an exact method of measuring their position with this company, but the obscene reality of *thingness* in American society, Wally figured, offered sufficient argument to make the unsophisticated numerical assignments for his purposes. And besides—it didn't matter.

Twenty minutes behind #3, #4 and #5, the next ranking class of employees would evacuate until finally the grunt-workers, those driving the '98 Dodge Neon or the '01 Honda Civic with the occasional hubcap missing would feel safe enough to slink away early. And every last one of them was receiving a full paycheck, money stolen from unsuspecting investors. Wally could feel his brain contract, squeezing a chemical poison out of the neurotransmitters into his arteries that temporarily blurred his vision at the very notion.

The monotony of his routine, together with the doubtful usefulness of the frivolous information he was amassing, had finally convinced him to modify his surveillance. After all, what difference did it make to anyone what time employee #7, in her Lexus ES-300, left work on Wednesday afternoon? Of even less value: employee #16 in her beat-up green Honda Civic?

Fridays, however, had proven another matter. That, Wally allowed, in the absence of any clear objective, was why sometimes he simply went with the first idea that popped into his head. In this instance, his lack of any better idea led him to discover that Pace and Taylor left early every Friday—at least they had on the last two Friday afternoons, and drove together to the Adams Hotel in downtown Phoenix where they spent a couple of hours together over drinks.

Two Fridays in a row Wally followed them there, parked only a few stalls away in the underground garage. He'd taken the next elevator behind the two men up to the lounge. Inside, at the bar, he found a corner seat at the opposite end of the room where he could keep an eye on them. The young woman behind the bar knew by his second visit he would order Dewar's on the rocks, and smiled pleasantly when he confirmed what she thought she remembered. The lounge was crowded with over enthusiastic business types: older men, mostly, competing to buy drinks for younger women. The place was filled with clusters of youngish women doing their best to attract the men with the most money—marital status not a requisite, apparently. Pace and Taylor appeared to be well known but generally kept to themselves.

The previous two Friday afternoons Wally tailed the two to the Adams. They'd had two drinks each and didn't hang around longer than an hour and a half. By five-thirty they were looking to pay their tab and be on their way. He watched the elevator doors close behind them then stepped forward to follow them down in the next car. They'd gotten back into Pace's Range Rover and driven back to the empty office building. On that first Friday he followed them they'd gone back inside for a short while. Last Friday, Taylor stepped out of Pace's Range Rover, slipped into the driver's seat of his black and gray Maybach, and drove away.

Wally followed at a distance while Taylor drove from his office to his country club. The gym bag he carried in with him was a clear enough clue he went to work out before heading home. It was going to require more time to know if this was his regular routine.

What about Pace? Where did Bud Pace go on Fridays after the stop off at the Adams Hotel? The coming Friday, tomorrow, Wally intended to know the answer to that question.

He still had no idea what, if any, the practical application of knowing these men's habits might be. For now, this ridiculous undertaking was providing some partial focus on something other than the pain that was irrevocably lodged inside him, pain so unspeakable he instinctively knew it would never go away. He'd decide another time whether what he knew about Pace and Taylor was of any value to him, the FBI—maybe the AG's office if they ever got around to pursuing his complaint.

He glanced at his wristwatch, after five o'clock. Colin and Ellen would be back soon. Wally set the yellow legal pad on the passenger seat and clipped his seatbelt on. There were only two cars left in the parking lot of the PPI office building; older model, low-end cars.

It was six-ten when he pulled into the driveway of his home. Colin's roadster wasn't parked out front, so Wally was surprised to find his sister-in-law sitting at the kitchen counter with a warm pizza still in the box, and a cold bottle of Chardonnay opened. She was already into the wine but bravely controlling her urge to attack the pizza.

"If you'd been much longer I'd be putting a hurt to that pizza," Ellen confessed warmly. "You ready?" She tipped the bottle of wine toward the edge of a glass.

"Sounds great," he said, side-stepping into his office to deposit the notepad. "Don't wait, Ellen," he shouted, "you been back long?"

"Not long," she said. "Hungry?"

"Didn't know I was until I smelled that." Wally pointed to the box that was the source of the inviting aroma.

"Pepperoni, sausage, Cremini mushrooms … 'bout everything except the anchovies."

"Coward," Wally accused, moving around the counter. He mounted the stool opposite her.

Ellen slid off her seat, grabbed a quick sip of wine on the fly and pulled down two plates. "Doesn't feel right … seeing these cupboards empty," she said. "You and Poppy have so many dishes … platters."

"Yeah …" Ellen could hear in his voice the pain dispersing his and Poppy's things added on top of the devastation of her sister being—gone. "Colin joining us?" Wally asked.

"He'll be back after dinner at Mom's," Ellen explained. "She's been gritchy she hasn't seen much of him this week. Since we're leaving in the morning I thought he should go have dinner with her and Daddy and Liz."

"You're right … he should."

Betrayed

Ellen put two pieces of pizza on each plate and pushed one over in front of Wally. "Chilies?" she said, sliding a small plastic cup of crushed red peppers into his reach. She sprinkled her two slices with Parmesan cheese. "Rough week for both of us ... thought it might be nice to have a quiet moment together. That okay with you?" Ellen scooted back up onto her barstool.

An awkward silence followed while they chewed and sipped wine.

"I can't tell you how much I appreciate what you—"

"I know how you feel, Wally." Her tone was kind.

Oppressive silence followed once more.

Ellen mercifully took the lead. "I spoke with Poppy by phone several times during these last months," she said softly, pouring a little more wine into his glass. "I didn't see it coming either."

Wally lifted his wine glass, peered reflectively into the lemony colored liquid and then took a short sip. He didn't reply. He was content for now to live in a sort of self-imposed internal exile. If he could have known Poppy's mind in those final weeks, he would have recognized in himself now a familiar bitterness. Life had conspired against him, too. Ellen's kindness was but a tiny counterpoint to the malignancy he constantly felt surrounding him.

"The thing is," Ellen went on, "*I'm* worried about *you*."

"That's not—"

"Listen to me, Wally." Ellen cut him off, deflecting any attempt on his part to escape what was coming. "It *is* necessary for me to be concerned about you. Poppy was my sister ... but you were married to her for thirty-three years. You have no living family left except us, God help you, and the person you've spent your entire adult life with just killed herself." Ellen paused, having said the words so matter-of-factly. Her watery-blue eyes began to moisten. Reading the ache in her heart was not difficult. "Wally ... I'm seriously worried about you. You're carrying on ... but it's like watching a zombie; you're here, but you're not."

He stared at the half eaten piece of pizza on his plate as if magically it would tell him how he should respond to his sister-in-law, but said nothing. Poppy had done just that—killed herself. She hadn't come to him and cried out for help, or had she, and he just hadn't recognized it? Well, clearly, he berated himself, he hadn't seen it. And that's why he knew the misery he felt then was never going away. It didn't matter what wizard or shrink he turned to for help. No one was going to be able to exorcise from his psyche, the truth of what he knew; he'd failed Poppy. If he could somehow get to the point of being able to close his eyes for a few moments and still find life bearable, he might survive. He considered from where he was at that instant—that was a mighty big *if*.

Ellen swallowed her food and chased it with another sip of wine. "Have you thought about talking to a professional?" she asked tenderly. She waited, but Wally didn't answer. "Wally, you can't keep this bottled up. It isn't healthy. Poppy was confused and depressed. She made a really bad decision we are all going to have to find a way to live with—you more than the rest of us. I've got Ross to go home to ... Colin," she shook her head and rolled her eyes, "to keep tabs on.

Mom and Liz have Daddy. I know … not the most functional trio, but at least they have some semblance of a support system.

"You need to find somebody you can discuss your feelings with, Wally. I can only imagine after what you and Poppy had been going through," she paused momentarily, "and now this … I can see it in your face, Wally … hear it in your voice. You're not the same man I once knew. You look desperate. You look angry. You look scared." Ellen paused briefly. "You've got to find some balance, some sense of normalcy you can hold on to."

There was that word again, *normal*. Did anyone seriously believe there could ever be anything normal for him again? It was a relatively simple matter for Wally to acknowledge the truth in Ellen's assessment. The trouble was in bringing himself to do something about it. That is to say, to look to therapy as a means of doing something about it.

It occurred to him pretense would ultimately be the only place he could hide. For a sense of normalcy was what everyone wanted, what they all needed to see or sense in him for their own sake. Because if he could not get back to normal—how could they get there?

"I've thought about it," he lied.

"You need to act, Wally," Ellen persisted. "You need to find someone … now … tomorrow. You need to be able to process what has happened without blaming yourself."

He considered Ellen's words. Similar words came out of everyone who was forced to speak to him; he shouldn't blame himself. At least in Ellen's case the words represented a heartfelt, honest sentiment.

Well, he did blame himself—and Bud Pace and Carl Taylor, too—even Poppy could not escape responsibility for what she'd done. They were responsible for stomping her down into the dark void she'd descended into. But it was ultimately his fault, he considered, for not seeing the desperation that obviously consumed her. For if he had, maybe she'd be here with him now, instead of her sister Ellen. Wally doubted there was any influence on this earth that would ever convince him he was not to blame.

"I'll make some calls in the morning after you and Colin leave," he lied again.

"Promise?" Ellen looked over the top of her glasses.

"Promise," Wally agreed, and clinked his glass against hers.

When Colin came in around nine o'clock there were two pieces of room-temp pizza the consistency of cardboard sitting in the open box. The smell had grown stale: congealed grease. Wally and Ellen sat across from each other, an empty bottle of Chardonnay to one side and a near empty bottle of Malbec positioned conveniently between them on the counter.

"Dessert!" Colin announced, and bit off a healthy-sized piece of the dried crust.

"Were you nice to Gramma?" Ellen seriously wanted to know. Colin chewed the hard, crunchy pizza noisily, picked up his mother's glass and drank half its contents. "We have a long drive tomorrow," She warned.

"Yeah, Gramma wouldn't let me have any either," he said, going for another bite. "I'm cool. We all set for morning?"

Betrayed

"Just have my overnight bag in the bathroom," Ellen said. "Everything else is in the truck."

"Tank's full," Wally added.

"You gonna be cool, Uncle Wally?" Chewing noisily, Colin glanced sideways at his uncle.

"Gonna be ... cool," Wally said, dragging out the pronunciation of the word, smiling at his nephew. "Gonna miss you, though. Drive careful and be nice to your mother. Remember, she'll be trapped in that truck with you."

"Her good fortune," Colin bragged.

And Ellen Craig allowed privately that it *was* her good fortune to have her son all to herself for a few hours.

To use Ellen's words, it had been a rough week. She'd wanted to help. She'd wanted to show a personal kindness to Wally, and she had. But when the flurry of dreaded deeds is finally put behind you, the thread of that focused energy dissipates quickly. No one knows quite what to say. What is there to be said? The acknowledgment that, where there had been entropy and miserable duties to be performed, order had now been restored—and still, the awfulness of it all persisted.

They small-talked their way to a mercifully early turn-in, the emotional vaults of the three of them, finally bankrupt.

CHAPTER 14

Wally turned into the underground parking garage behind Pace and Taylor. Pace was driving, Taylor riding shotgun. Four fifty-two on the dash clock. Wally followed a few car lengths back and when Pace pulled into a space near the elevators, he continued down the line a few stalls before choosing a spot on the opposite side of the aisle. He watched Pace talking animatedly with his hands while Taylor listened. They strolled casually to the elevators and pressed the up button.

He settled back to wait out happy hour. Wally knew the routine up in the lounge. Not in the mood. The position button on the side of the seat buzzed softly while it slid back. He slouched down, made himself comfortable. Pace and Taylor wouldn't be back for at least an hour.

Colin should be arriving at Ellen's home in Glendale any time, though it was a reasonable guess with Colin at the wheel, they might already be there. They'd driven away by ten-thirty that morning. Neither Colin nor his mother had shown any interest in an early leave-time. Ellen cooked a light breakfast. They'd taken their time, eaten slowly, cleaned the kitchen and drove away as if they might be running out to errands. No fanfare. No prolonged, overburdened silences—just a pair of hugs, a quick buss on the cheek from Ellen. "See ya in a couple days, Uncle Wally," Colin promised and then they were gone.

Wally flipped to a clean page on his note pad and began a new list. Periodically the elevator doors opened, regurgitating a hotel guest or a lounge victim. Wally watched couples walk to vehicles holding hands or stumble arm-in-arm toward his or her car. His list grew:

Follow up complaints: AG, SEC, FBI.
Commercibank: late credit card payments.
Insurance company: death claim.
List house with realtor.

Betrayed

Cancel credit cards.

Delinquent mortgage payments.

With one foul obligation behind him, a dozen more were thrust into his face before he could take a breath. He'd had a nasty voicemail from somebody named Johnny about the late payments on his Commercibank credit card. The list represented the obstacle course of details still before him as he prepared to leave Phoenix for good.

It seemed longer than an hour and forty-five minutes when the elevator doors opened and Pace and Taylor stepped out. The conversation they were having on the way in was obviously concluded as the two men walked in silence back to Pace's Rover.

Wally allowed the Rover to clear the space and make the turn at the end of the aisle before starting the Eos and turning on the headlights. There was no reason to crowd Pace.

At the PPI offices Taylor did a repeat performance of the previous Friday; slid into his Maybach and drove away. He'd be headed to his country club.

Pace pulled out and drove east on Osborne. Wally gave him room to stop at the light at Seventh Avenue before pulling out of the school parking lot and falling in behind him. Tailing someone with one surveillance vehicle was proving tricky. He couldn't get too close; yet, falling far behind and getting caught at red lights could easily cause him to lose sight of the Rover— force him to have to start all over again a week later. He had no intention of getting himself behind that eight ball. He edged close enough behind Pace to ensure he could floor his accelerator and speed through any lights Pace went through threatening to trap him.

Rush-hour traffic had begun to thin. It was getting easier to maintain visual contact with the Range Rover from several car lengths back. Wally was confident Pace had no idea he was being shadowed. Downtown traffic continued to lighten as Pace drove into residential sections. The Rover continued on Osborne all the way to 32nd Street. There Pace gave a left turn signal, slowed for the light but continued north on 32nd. Wally gave no signal and followed. He was forced to race against the yellow light to keep from getting caught on red.

Pace followed 32nd Street all the way to Lincoln Drive. They were getting into the high rent district, Paradise Valley. Wally knew Pace lived somewhere in PV, but never actually drove to the address he'd discovered on one of the LLC filing documents he'd uncovered. Perhaps he'd get around to a visit, soon.

When Pace came to the light at Tatum, instead of continuing straight ahead into the heart of PV, he turned north, toward Scottsdale. At Shea Boulevard he turned east and drove a couple of miles before turning into another upscale residential area. There, elegant single-family dwellings lined golf course fairways along sweeping curved lanes. A wide equestrian path ran between the cozy streets and fairways of the golf course. Wally followed several car lengths back while Pace rounded the streets before pulling in to a small cluster of condominiums. The units were two-story. But based on the parking, there were only eight large units. The upstairs had to be bedrooms. He drove on eyeing Pace pull into an empty space.

R.P. McCabe

Wally made a quick left at the next corner, spun a U-turn and pulled to the curb. He sat quietly several minutes glancing here and there, learning the lay-of-the-land. It was a quiet, high-end community, crime literally non-existent. The residents were relaxed; they didn't anticipate the need for vigilance. *Nosey* would be the Block Watch policy in this neighborhood.

Wally got out and sauntered to the corner. It was less than two hundred yards back to the condos. He glanced both ways once more to satisfy himself some neighborhood busybody wasn't observing him. It was six o'clock, turning dark. The streetlights came on illuminating front lawns. Still, there was enough cover if he was resourceful.

He edged slowly up to Pace's vehicle and looked around. There were lights on in all eight of the condos. Directly across from Pace's Range Rover was another vehicle Wally recognized. It was easy because it was #3 on his surveillance list. He knew the owner of the late model Cadillac. He read the white number painted on the pavement just below the rear bumper of the car: Unit 1. Large brass numbers were easily visible under well-lit entries at the front of each unit. Number one was at his far left as he faced the building.

Wally squinted over his shoulder. He still felt safe. He crept to the east edge of the building and saw the back of the condo faced onto the golf course fairway, no dividing barriers. The edge of the tree lined fairway rough spread all the way to the backs of each condo. He slunk out onto the grass under the trees and was well concealed in the shadows. Lights were dim on the lower level, the upper was totally dark. The patio was no more than twenty yards in front of him. If anyone wandered out he'd be vulnerable. In the shadow of the stubby, fat-trunked Ponderosa Pine he'd cozied up to, he was invisible for the moment.

Abruptly, the lights on the upper level came on. In another instant the drapes were being drawn back. A moment later, the French doors opened and Sonja Bienvenidos stepped out onto the balcony. She'd changed out of her work clothes and wore a simple sleeveless blouse and a pair of loose-fitting cranberry-colored shorts. In one hand she held a glass of white wine.

She tossed her head. Her mane of thick black hair flung to one side as she lifted the glass to her mouth. Pace glided up behind her, slipped one arm around and his hand down the front of her shorts. Her head fell backwards and he cupped one large breast in his hand as he kissed her down the side of her neck.

"Why'd you take so long getting here?" she gushed. Wally was so close to them he could hear their softly spoken words.

Pace didn't bother to answer. His left hand explored her femininity; his right gently worked its way into her blouse and over the top of her low-cut bra to get at her bare breast.

Sonja's breathing increased while Pace worked his fingers inside her panties. She set the wine glass clumsily onto one of the balcony supports and slid both her hands behind.

"God … I love it when you touch me like that," he whimpered in that high-pitched treble-infected tone of his.

Within a few minutes the two were tearing at each other's clothes. The scene degenerated rapidly into a shitty version of an amateur porn video. Wally slipped away without waiting for the ending. It was all he could do to control the rage growing up in his throat. A human being as gentle and … good as his Poppy was dead because of what the two pieces of dung who were at that moment cavorting like a couple of monkeys in a tree had done to them. They would never know how lucky they were to have escaped those moments with their lives.

Gliding quietly along the edge of the golf course, working his way westward toward his parked car, Wally thought about the scene he'd just left behind. There was nothing prurient in it for him. It had only served to reignite the ache deep within him that felt increasingly limitless. Poppy's memory loomed large over everything coming before him. How to reconcile himself with the appalling knowledge of what had happened? One thing was certain, the two people he'd just observed flaunting life bore an irrevocable responsibility for the fact he would never touch Poppy again as Pace had just touched Sonja Bienvenidos.

CHAPTER 15

The voice on the other end of the line was indifferent, detached from any sense of empathy or possibility of consideration—annoyed would describe the attitude. Wally seethed over how government agencies, it seemed to him—he'd throw public utilities and large corporations into the tirade if you'd like—trained Homo sapiens to perform like this. He allowed these jerks were the result of stem-cell-research-gone-bad. But they were, in the genetic sense at least, human, and couldn't be tossed out at the end of the experiment. Instead, they were recycled, given jobs such as the one occupied by the *light bulb* on the other end of his phone, with whom he was currently attempting to communicate.

"Ah'm sorry, suh. Ah don't have no reference in mah file for no company name o' PPP."

"PPI, miss ... Perfect Property Investments, not PPP." Wally corrected the woman. "I filed the complaint. My name is Wally Stroud."

"Do you have a complaint numba, Mr. Stroud?"

"Just a moment," hen grumbled. He rifled through the thick folder on his desk and found the filing number for the complaint he'd laboriously filed four months earlier with the Attorney General's Office.

"Here it is," he said, and read the twelve-digit number to the woman.

He waited impatiently against stone silence for several minutes.

"Ah found it, suh. Less see ... oh yeah, well, they ain't had time yet to investigate on tha—"

Wally hit the red button on his cell phone. He rested his elbows on his desk and buried his face in his hands. At least the AG's office had taken the call. The SEC refused to pass his call into their system with a curt message that if there was any progress in the matter he would learn about it like everyone else: through the public news media. He'd simply left a message for agent Clemmons at the FBI with whom he'd spoken on several occasions. The guy'd been courteous enough to return his call, and let him know the investigation was moving … slowly. Wally understood that to be a euphemism for—we haven't done shit.

The silence inside his office was oppressive. The silence everywhere in his house was only marginally bearable. He slid back from his desk, leaned backward in his chair and stared at the trio of framed photos of 1920s nude dancing girls hanging on his office wall. He usually smiled when he gazed to those photos; now it had been a long time since he'd noticed them. He couldn't manage a smile for the girls that day.

There was a flashing light on his voice mailbox. It wouldn't be good news, that was a given. Only ten days had passed since his meeting with the life insurance agent. He'd hated that encounter. There were forms to complete, a copy of the police report to be provided, death certificate. The whole ordeal turned his stomach; felt as if he was attempting to collect on a lottery ticket based on the suicide of his wife. But Poppy'd killed herself. She hadn't given him the courtesy of a vote in the matter. It was a reality he continuously did his best to confront. He was having little success. Anyway, wasn't likely to be the insurance agent, way too soon. He pressed the play button.

"Yes, sir, Meester Wally Stroud!" The high-pitched, rapid-fire voice was thickly infused with East Indian accent making it hard to follow. "This is Johnny with Commercibank. I am calling again about your late credit card payment. I regret to inform you that you are two months past due with our payments and we are obliged to increase your interest rate to twenty-three percent. Of course," Johnny went on, "you are also responsible for two late fees totaling an additional sixty-four dollars. If you are to avoid further action by Commercibank you must send me two hundred fifty-three dollars and seventy-one cents, immediately. If you have any questions you may call me at: 888-bad-credit."

Wally went purple in the face. His fingers trembled as he attempted to punch the numbers into his cell phone. A metallic voice answered and began the usual litany of options from which a caller could choose. "Press option four on your digital phone," the voice instructed, "for delinquent payments."

The voice of the young woman or man who answered the extension, Wally couldn't be sure, was so densely accented communication was uncertain. He asked for, Johnny. "One moment, please," he thought he or she said.

The familiar high-pitched, rapid-fire voice he'd heard on his voicemail came on the line. "This is, Johnny. How may I help you?"

"This is, Wally Stroud."

"Thank you for calling, Meester Stroud," Johnny said. "Can you please take just a moment and punch the number of your credit card into your phone … please?"

"You left *me* a message to call *you*."

"I leave hundreds of messages each day, Meester Stroud," Johnny said, just a little too imperiously for the circumstance. "If you will be kind enough to input your account number, I will be able to locate your file."

"Sonofabitch." Wally complained while he dug out his Commercibank credit card and punched the numbers into his cell phone.

"Ah, yes...there you ar—"

Wally was fuming. "I've had this card with Commercibank for fifteen years," he jeered. "I have my house mortgage with Commercibank and I kept my business accounts with you people all those years, as well." He hardly took a breath. In any case, he allowed no opening for Johnny to get a word in. "Your fucking bank knows my wife recently died and I've had serious financial problems—"

Johnny attempted to apologize. "I am so sor—"

"I'm not finished!" Wally shouted cutting Johnny off. "So I miss a couple of payments," he continued, "and you're going to knock my interest rate up to twenty-three percent and charge me a bunch of late charges ...? That's what Commercibank is going to do ... Johnny?" Wally's words dripped with contempt. "Tell me something ... Johnny!" He pronounced the man's name disdainfully. "Where are you?"

"I'm here, of course," Johnny said, clearly rattled.

"Well ... where the fuck is, here?"

"Please, Meester Stroud. There is no reason for crudity."

"Where ... Johnny, are you calling me from?"

"I am located in Mumbai—"

"India?" Wally shouted the word.

"Yes, India."

"So, let me get this straight ... Johnny from Mumbai, India ..." Wally's inflexion had the clicking-quality of the hammer of a gun being cocked. "Commercibank hires some goddamn foreigner half way around the world who doesn't know *shit* about *my* life or what's happening to me, to let me know that since I missed a couple of payments to those parasites, they're going to increase my interest rates to," he pulled the trigger, "twenty-three-fucking-percent-plus-late-charges! Is that about right ... Johnny from Mumbai?"

"Meester Stroud, you are obviously very upset and—"

"You can bet your Hindu ass, Johnny—you got that part right!"

"All right, Meester Stroud, that is quite enough," Johnny said indignantly. "I do not have to listen to those kinds of disrespectful words." There was a distinct harrumph in his manner; "I am going to terminate this call if you do not calm down immediately."

Several silent moments went by.

"You're right, Johnny," Wally admitted implacably. "You're just some poor schmuck trying to make a living. This isn't your fault. I apologize," Wally mumbled into the phone.

"Thank you, Meester Stroud. Now then ..." Johnny went on, "Commercibank's policy is quite clear on this mat—"

Wally terminated the call, stood up from his desk and kicked his chair. "Motherfuckers!" he yelled. For several seconds he stared at the credit card lying on his desk. His eyes clouded with tears, pure rage. He glanced at the wall clock above his desk: 1:35. "Close enough," he said, and went to the liquor cabinet. He pulled out the half empty bottle of Johnny Walker Red, laughed at the irony, and poured himself two fingers. "Here's to you, Johnny … in Mumbai."

The first sip of the astringent room-temperature liquor burned all the way down his esophagus. He could feel it hit his stomach. He leaned back against the bar, raised the glass and drained it. The sense of his life spiraling out of control gripped Wally as it had only threatened to up to this point. He stood there playing the movie of his life since last Thanksgiving in his mind. It was clear the system had turned its back on everything that happened. Worse, if he didn't use the blood-money from Poppy's death to appease the bank parasite, they'd take his house and cancel his credit cards. Wally imagined there were going to be other revelations he'd not considered that would begin to drop on him soon enough, because that's how it works, he thought. That's how life works; as long as you don't need any help, everything you don't need comes to you whether or not you ask for it, like the unsolicited credit cards sitting in his wall safe, never applied for, never used, but pushed onto him for no better reason than he didn't need them. But if you do use one and you stumble—look out for Johnny from Mumbai.

Wally halted his internal monologue a moment, pulled the back of his forearm across his face wiping away most of his tears. He marched back into his office and picked up the Commercibank credit card. He stared at the thing several moments before he turned to the credenza and retrieved his last statement. Almost miraculously his frustration was supplanted by laughter—pitiless, maniacal laughter. On the front page he found what he was searching for; available credit: $15,000; cash advance: $10,000. He smiled, turned the card over and dialed the 800 number for customer service. An answering system picked up and began to go through the categories of options from which customers could choose. He selected the 'increase credit limit' option.

"This is Allison," the pleasant sounding young woman began, "may I verify the last four digits of your social security number please?"

"6342," Wally said.

"And your date of birth, sir?"

"Five, ten, forty-seven," he replied.

"Thank you Mr. Stroud. How may I help you today?"

"Yes, hello Allison," Wally began, calm and friendly, "I've had this card with you folks for fifteen years and I do my checking with you as well as the mortgage on my home …"

"Yes, I see those accounts, Mr. Stroud. You've been an excellent customer of the bank for many years and we appreciate your business. What can I do to help you?"

"Allison, I've got a few things I want to take care of, and a trip I'd like to take. Would there be any problem increasing my credit limit by ten thousand dollars?"

"You'd like to raise the limit to $25,000?"

"If you would, please," he said.

"Ordinarily, Mr. Stroud, I'd be able to say yes immediately," Allison said. "But I see here you are two payments behin—"

"Allison," Wally interrupted, adopting an avuncular quality in his demeanor, "My wife recently passed away and I simply forgot to make the payments. I just spoke with your credit department and made arrangements to bring the account current."

"Oh my goodness Mr. Stroud—" The shock in the girl's voice was genuine. "There was no way I could have known that. I'm sorry … I … I … I don't—"

"Thank you," Wally said, saving the young woman the grope to find the right words. "So what do you think can be done?"

"May I put you on hold a moment? Briefly...only a moment or two." Allison reiterated. "Give me just a few moments? I'm going to put you on hold." Wally could hear Allison was flustered.

He waited patiently imagining the probable conversation taking place on the other end of the line. Presently, Allison returned. "Thank you for holding, Mr. Stroud. My supervisor has approved your increase. I have that noted, but she says we'll have to keep a hold on the increase until your payments are received."

"Not a problem, Allison," Wally replied amiably. "I'll make an electronic payment right now."

"That would be perfect Mr. Stroud. If you make it before two o'clock it will post tonight and your credit increase will be effective tomorrow. Will that work for you?"

"Yes, Allison," he said, "I can make that work. I can't tell you how much I appreciate your help with this."

"My pleasure Mr. Stroud," the customer service representative (Allison) said. "Will there be anything else I can do for you today?"

Wally could hear in Allison's voice she wanted off the line as quickly as possible. "No thanks," he said, and concluded the call.

He flipped his cell phone closed and went immediately to his computer, logged into his Commercibank account and initiated an electronic payment in the amount of two hundred fifty-three dollars and seventy-one cents. "There you go—Johnny in Mumbai."

Wally shoved his office chair back and trotted off to his bedroom. He moved the framed watercolor on the wall to reveal the safe. He fumbled with the dial missing the combination twice before getting it correct. On the third try he could hear the pins drop in place inside the lock and the door opened. He took down two envelopes each holding six unsolicited credit cards and carried them back to his office.

Over the course of the next two hours he confirmed credit and cash withdrawal limits on a dozen different cards, ensured they had all been properly activated. He called each customer service department giving them advance notice of anticipated abnormal activity in connection with a vacation he was planning. If the bank employee offered credit increases, Wally readily accepted the maximum increase that could be granted there on the phone without any formal application required. More than seventy-five thousand dollars of increased buying power had been added during the process. It was there for: not asking. All he seemed to need was a credit score above 780; his was still 820. It never would be again.

When Wally added up the total available credit on his cards, he grimaced. Two hundred ninety thousand dollars was available for credit purchases; two hundred three thousand was available for cash advance.

There is order in our universe. There are complex laws of physics and mathematical formulae to predict the movement of cosmic bodies. We understand the minutest influences of gravity or the speed of sound and light: the likely path of random particles. Quantum physics explains the behavior of subatomic particles, which we know exist but have never seen; but there is apparently no such formula to predict what causes a human being to snap. Even when we know the *why* of it, there seems to be no clear message to tell us *when,* at what point a man or a woman comes to the end of their ability to endure one more shred of adversity; the moment when a woman sees connecting a hose to the exhaust pipe of her car, starting the engine and locking herself inside as her only option, the instant of insanity when a man says, "Fuck the system, I'm going to make a new set of rules to play by."

Wally wheeled his chair in front of the credenza once more and fumbled for the folder that held his car titles. He pulled the entire folder out of its hanger and examined its contents. He found the title to his GMC pickup as well as the title for the VW EOS. Both vehicles were owned outright. He paper clipped a copy of the current registration to the title of each vehicle. Finally he folded the two titles and organized the stack of credit cards so they all fit into a blue bank-deposit bag, which he zipped closed.

CHAPTER 16

Wally's silver GMC Sierra was parked in the driveway. Colin suggested he have the front alignment checked soon because he thought the vehicle pulled to the left on the drive over and back from California. Until a few hours ago, it had been on Wally's mind to have the problem investigated one day during the coming week.

Instead, he pulled onto Seventh Street and headed north. Five miles ahead he made a left on Bell Road and drove west. Traffic was heavy with rush hour beginning to gain purchase. It made better sense to stay on the surface streets as opposed to getting onto the freeway, which would soon enough be reduced to a snail's pace with bumper-to-bumper frustrated commuters. He drove all the way to 86th Avenue, to Liberty GMC, where he'd originally bought his truck. He took his time, thoughts wandering.

His Sierra 1500 was in excellent condition with the only criticism possible: it was a little heavy with mileage, otherwise, the truck was spotless, looked like new, never had a mechanical problem. He accounted if he'd been inclined just one day earlier to negotiate for a new truck, this might have mattered. He smiled as he pulled onto the lot of the auto dealer and spotted the next salesman in line rub his hands together while he watched Wally park in front of the new truck showroom. "Today's your lucky day, *Snake Oil*," Wally said under his breath, ascribing the name that popped into his head.

A sweaty-faced tawny headed youth of twenty-something with the sleeves of his white shirt rolled part way up his arms swaggered out toward him like he was sneaking up on a coiled rattler. The rolled up sleeves apparently were intended to give the impression of a hard-working stiff. It looked to Wally like the kid figured if he sneaked up he'd have a better chance of making the sale or, at worst, Wally wouldn't figure out what he was up to until it was too late.

"Howdy Pard," the salesman began.

Jesus, Wally thought.

Betrayed

"Looks like one of ours," *Snake Oil* went on, pointing at Wally's truck. "I'm Dale," he continued, before Wally could get a word in. "Ready to let me put ya in a new'un?"

"Yes," Wally said without elaborating.

Dale became tongue-tied, failed with the follow up. "Well ... yeah, well—" That wasn't the way the script he'd learned went.

Wally took control. "I want a white 2500 Sierra Crew Cab with air, power doors, and power windows. Doesn't need a towing package, but I want the heavy-duty coolant system and I want the upgrade on tire size and rims. Oh, and I want a burgundy velour interior with an opening center console between the front seats."

Dale stood flatfooted, couldn't speak for a few seconds.

"You have a truck like that in stock?" Wally coaxed him.

Snake Oil arrived to the party. "Uh ... yeah, I think ... I mean, yeah ... we do. But the interior is a dark cranberry more than burgundy."

"Not that picky ... Pard," Wally said sardonically. A piece of Wally's gentle nature had spalled away. "Show me," he said.

Suddenly Dale was recovering his wings. "Name's Dale Crockett, no relation to Davy ..." he laughed at his own joke, "what'd you say yours was?" he asked, attempting conviviality.

"I didn't," Wally said, and continued walking behind Dale (no relation to Davy) Crockett to a far corner of the lot. "Wally Stroud," Wally reluctantly divulged finally feeling the slightest twinge of guilt over his restive treatment of the kid.

"Nice to meet ya Wally. You gonna be tradin' your 1500 for this one?"

"And a second car, too," Wally confirmed. "Too many cars," he added without elaboration.

Dale didn't like the revelation of a two-car trade. His boss might not go for it. Wally registered the negative reaction. "There she is," *Snake Oil* announced, pointing to a shiny white three-quarter ton Sierra Crew Cab pickup.

Wally noted the truck sported large tires and chrome rims. It was a handsome vehicle with four fully opening doors that made it as much a car as it was a truck, but with all the utility value he'd grown accustomed to over the years. Dale pulled the driver's door open and the cozy interior illumination spilled out along with distinct new-car smell. The short-knapped velour was too dark to be called cranberry. It would have been more accurately described as currant. Wally was certain *Snake Oil* didn't have that analogy in his repertoire, not part of the script.

The truck was fine just as it sat with the exception of a sprayed in bed liner, which Wally knew Dale was going to throw in at no charge. When he climbed behind the wheel he was taken with how much bigger the truck felt under him than his 1500. He reached down to start it.

"I'll have to go get the key," Dale apologized.

"Wait!" Wally ordered, and then climbed back out. *Snake Oil* didn't like the move. Wally closed the door and read the window sticker. As it sat, the truck was priced at $45,995. Not $46,000 ... $45,995. "I'll take it," Wally said.

Snake Oil became unsteady. "Well ... uh, you wa—"

"I'll take it," Wally repeated. He turned and began the walk back toward the showroom. "Just bring it up front when you get the key."

"Yes, sir, Wally!" Dale exclaimed, suddenly feeling very familiar. Wally cracked a smile, his first in weeks, the kid couldn't see because Dale was now following him like a puppy to its feeding.

The process of buying a vehicle was a thing Wally detested all of his life. Today day was going to be different. There wasn't going to be any haggling, no up-sale negotiation, no discussion about financing, and no bargaining over trade in values. They'd fuck him. He had no plan to fight them.

By the time Dale's sales manager was finished, Liberty GMC had sold Wally the 2500 Sierra Crew Cab for the full sticker price of $45,995 less $18,000 for his EOS which was actually worth $26,000 and $8,000 for his 1500 GMC which was actually worth $14,000, the entire process having been completed without a single objection from Wally. Periodically Wally noted the look of puzzlement on the sales manager's face expecting at any moment this moron, Wally, would surely come out from under the ether. By the time the auto dealership calculated taxes, licensing and dealer's preparation fees, another of their bullshit tactics for stealing from customers, Wally owed them $22,495. Not $22,500 … $22,495. And yes, the dealership would be happy to throw in the sprayed-in bed liner, which they would deduct from *Snake Oil's* commission check. Dale was happy with the terms.

By his calculation, Wally figured he'd paid roughly $62,500 for the truck considering the real value of his two trade-ins against the value he was allowed.

Wally pulled two credit cards from his blue bank bag and handed them to the sales manager. The luck of the draw went to Desert Hills Bank and New York Bank. One was a Visa card, the other a MasterCard. Wally instructed the sales manager to split the amount owed between the two cards. The charges represented about 24 percent of the available credit on each card. Within minutes the sales manager was back with a wide grin on his face and two credit card slips for Wally to sign.

"You want to drive it home tonight?"

Dale stood to one side having been pushed out of the process by the professional in the house. No way was this guy allowing some dumb kid to fuck up a sweetheart deal like this one.

"No," Wally said, "how long to do the liner?"

"We'll have everything ready for you tomorrow afternoon," Mr. Professional guaranteed. "You could pick it up any time after three."

"Let Dale come with me now and I'll send him back with this truck," Wally suggested, indicating his gray Sierra. "I'll bring the EOS in tomorrow when I come for my new truck."

"Done," the sales manager agreed, sticking out his hand.

Salesman Crockett scrambled around making sure he had his cell phone. He was doing the best he could to conceal the glee he felt over what he calculated his commission check was going to look like. It would ultimately be declared the largest single commission ever paid to a salesman in Liberty GMC's history; Dale (no relation to Davy) Crockett would become a legend in truck sales.

The following morning, Wednesday, Wally was up early with purpose. He felt infused with energy he'd forgotten himself capable of. His gray pickup was gone and he needed to go through the EOS, make certain he removed anything personal of Poppy's. Once more he was reminded of his wife's thoroughness; there was nothing left aboard the vehicle but the owner's manual and a few wayward shards of broken glass.

It was the twenty-seventh of April. Spring was in full bloom. He backed the car out of the garage and activated the convertible feature. The driver's window, which the VW dealer replaced for free, made a clunking sound when its electric motor engaged but otherwise functioned just fine. Buzzers buzzed, windows clicked, and the hardtop of the vehicle moved up and backward while components chirped robotically like a Transformers movie until the hardtop had screwed itself inside the tiny trunk of the sports car. Wally marveled at the event. For this he'd paid $42,000. But Poppy had wanted it and that was all he'd needed to know at the time— Poppy wanted it.

He backed out of his driveway, pressed the button to close the garage door and headed south on Seventh Street. At Bethany Home Road, he cut west to Central Avenue and continued south to Camelback Road. It was nine-thirty when he parked in front of the Good Egg restaurant. The early business crowd was filtering out. A few high-level management types, or professional people who could afford to take their time, lingered. Wally was seated immediately and didn't wait for a menu to order. The waitress dropped off a pot of hot coffee and scurried away to get his orange juice. While he waited for his omelet he unzipped his blue bank bag and rummaged around for the Bank of America Visa card. When he located it, he set the card on the table and dove back into the bag until he found the Discover card. He collected the two cards together and slipped them into his shirt pocket. On his napkin he began a list of the cards he carried in his bank bag with amounts noted next to each.

The young waitress smiled at him standing next to his table with his order on a tray. Wally scrambled to move his notes to make room. The waitress situated everything in front of him and asked could she bring anything else?

"Not right now thanks," he said. He ate slowly and scribbled amounts next to credit card names. Next to the cards with $20,000 limits he jotted $14,000; $25,000 limits were indicated with $17,500. His two $50,000 cards were indicated with $26,600 shown next to each because Wally had already used the two cards to purchase his new pickup. Those purchases reduced the amount available for cash advance against those cards.

He leaned back in his chair, brushed a clean napkin across his lips and sipped from his coffee cup. When he set the cup down, he picked up his pen and began a quick calculation. Wally openly worried about people who could not seem to add simple sums without the aid of a calculator. He rested the point of the pen next to the rows of numbers on the napkin as he moved down through his scribbled notes. Finally he drew a line at the bottom of the column and wrote down, $200,200. He hooked the pen in his shirt pocket, picked up his fork, and lifted a bite of omelet into his mouth.

"Can I bring you anything else?" his waitress asked, noting Wally was nearing the end of his food.

"Just the bill please." He smiled at the pretty young girl.

She nodded, collected his empty plate and juice glass. "Back in a flash," she promised.

Wally paid his tab and dropped a five-dollar tip on the table. The young waitress saw the bill, grinned broadly and waved. He raised his hand toward her as he went out the door.

Outside the sun was bright and already elevating the temperature above warm. He left the EOS parked where it was and walked to the crosswalk at the corner. He crossed at the light and strolled seventy-five yards east to the heavy-glassed double front doors of the Bank of America branch on the corner of Third and Camelback. When he pushed through the weighty doors a young girl greeted him. To Wally she looked to be just out of high school. The nametag on her blouse said 'Kelly—Assistant Manager.' The state of the banking system had long since perplexed and annoyed him. There was no longer an individual in any branch office of any bank with the authority to do anything more than authorize the opening or closing of accounts, approve deposits and withdrawals and—sign off on credit card transactions.

He showed Kelly, the Assistant Manager, his card and explained that he was doing some—fix up—no elaboration, just—fix up—and needed some cash. Kelly walked him to a teller window, then went around inside. When he swiped his card the teller asked how much he wanted. "$17,500," Wally said evenly.

Kelly peered momentarily at Wally's account history, looked up, smiled and scribbled her initials on a slip of paper the teller put in front of her. "I'd be glad to have our loan officer begin processing a home improvement loan for you Mr. Stroud. The interest rate would be considerably less than this credit card."

"No thanks Kelly," Wally said smiling. "I'll be taking care of this within the month."

"Okay," she acquiesced, still smiling sweetly at him, "just let us know if you'd rather convert this ... then you won't need to worry about paying it all off at once." They had no authority to do any banking, Wally was thinking, but the bloodsuckers in the tower had them all trained like robots to keep sucking people into the trap. (Yes. Always say yes to the customer. Bury them as deep as you can in debt.) The state of 'personal banking' in today's America.

"I'll keep that in mind," he promised.

The teller asked how he wanted the cash. He opted for large denominations, which the girl placed in an envelope after carefully counting it back to him.

Kelly, the Assistant Manager, walked him to the door and invited him back any time they could be of service. Outside under the latticed porte-cochere, Wally smiled, shook his head, and walked casually back to the corner. He pressed the pedestrian crossing button and waited patiently to retrace his path back to his car.

Betrayed

By two o'clock he'd visited four of the dozen banks through which he'd been issued credit cards. His blue bank bag bulged with four envelopes of large bills totaling $66,500.00. He drove from downtown Phoenix back to his home and pulled the EOS into the garage, closing the door while he sat in the vehicle.

Back inside the house he went to his bedroom, pulled aside the painting on the wall once more and opened the safe. He'd placed the appropriate credit card inside each envelope with the cash advance he'd obtained on the card. Wally then transferred each envelope into the safe from the bank bag and began a stack on the middle shelf.

He was still satiated from breakfast but a Diet Pepsi from the refrigerator would wash away the metallic taste of bile before heading into his office. Shuffling through the documents on his desk, he pulled the sales receipt for the new truck from the bundle, found the phone number, and punched it into his cell phone. It seemed only right "*Snake Oil*" should be allowed to wallow in his moment of triumph. He asked for Dale Crockett.

"This is Dale."

"Wally Stroud here Dale. My truck ready?"

"Yes, sir, Mr. Stroud!" *Snake Oil* announced loud enough for everyone in the showroom to hear. "Got 'er sittin' right out front."

"Be there in a half hour," Wally predicted, and collapsed his phone. He stood still for a few moments staring at the three framed photos of the nude dancing girls on the wall. Then he picked up the entire folder of documents pertaining to the new truck and slid them under his arm as he headed back out into the garage. He squatted and folded himself into the EOS, laid the folder on the passenger seat, and tried to figure out where the cup holder was in the car. He finally pressed a button on the dash and a flimsy holder folded out. He settled his Diet Pepsi into it before he hit the garage door opener on the sun visor.

The heated air felt good as he backed the car out of the driveway and accelerated to the corner. This was the one pleasure he could relate to in driving the car; warm, windless days with the top down did feel luxurious. Its usefulness, however, ended there as far as Wally was concerned, and he was not going to be sad to have the car gone. Its other associated memories didn't help.

It was still early enough to make getting onto the freeway practical, but once again he found himself in no particular hurry. He'd had enough for one day. Finishing up the business of picking up the new truck would be all he'd want for the rest of the day. He couldn't generate any enthusiasm at all for the new vehicle. The truck was a chunk of metal, nothing more. He connected only the contempt he felt for being betrayed by the system to it. None of what was in his mind would have ever occurred to Wally had he not finally been completely convinced by Johnny from Mumbai that nobody in the entire world, least of all Commercibank, gave a shit about his troubles or the helplessness he felt over the state of his existence.

Sometimes the hardest thing in life is to know which bridges to cross and which to burn. Wally'd made that decision. Now that he'd crossed over, he had no clear idea of what path he was set upon, except to say he no longer felt constrained by any established rules of society. On an existential level, it was quite liberating. Where this new restive philosophy was likely to plunge him was patently unclear for the moment but, surprisingly, he no longer felt burdened by the state of uncertainty with which, heretofore, the chaos in his life had been punishing him.

That next day was Thursday. He had no commitments. By the end of the day he planned to have completed collecting the cash advances from the remaining credit cards. More than two hundred thousand dollars in cash would be tucked away in his safe. He felt certain that to pull off what he was doing he must complete the cash advances rapidly, because when $200,000 in cash withdrawals began to appear in the system, he was pretty sure alarms were going to sound. As it was, he'd been forced by each bank to sign a form they would ultimately send to the IRS because he'd withdrawn more than $10,000 in cash. The government was tracking every cash dollar withdrawn by every American citizen these days. All-in-all, Wally felt more serene than he had since last November. If you'd only held on a little longer Popp, he thought.

~~~~

That Friday he planned another surveillance trip to the offices of PPI. The previous Friday found him following Carl Taylor again, who was by then establishing, pretty convincingly, Fridays after drinks with Pace at the Adams he went to his country club for a workout before heading home.

This particular Friday was Pace's turn to be tailed once more. Though Wally had been unable to develop any prurient interest in the performances, he thought the guy should have invested in a porn studio the way he and Sonja Bienvenidos regularly tore up the sheets on those Friday evenings. Clearly the two thought they were engaged in something righteous or romantic. It seemed to Wally a lot of wasted moaning and groaning. He suspected the pair spent many more evenings together, but he had no interest in pursuing that. For now, all he was interested in was what Pace and Taylor did every Friday after work. He still had no clear idea of how he might ultimately use that intelligence, but a crazy idea with no clear resolution had begun to buzz around in his brain like an unseen planet in the outer reaches of the solar system; a body unseen, yet its effects on life around it clear to the trained observer.

CHAPTER 17

The middle of May was rolling up. Spring had given itself over to the first waves of summer. Wally'd lost thirty pounds; didn't eat much—drank his lunch and dinner as often as not. Some days he'd shave; others he couldn't seem to generate the energy to lift his hands to his face to hold his electric razor. He'd remained in contact with Colin. They emailed. But Wally masked the truth of things, and without any outside input, Colin was buying his uncle was doing all right.

Wally'd finally mustered the courage to phone Dan and Fortunada Dolan. Fortunada had taken Poppy's death particularly hard. At some point Wally felt he'd have no alternative but to sit down with her, provide what insight he could. He had no idea how to discuss suicide. It seemed such a personal act. How do you discuss that with a friend—anyone—when you have no idea yourself how someone makes such a desperate decision—then carries it out as flawlessly as Poppy had? Fortunada and Dan called him every Sunday evening without fail. "Get your ass on down here," Dan kept insisting. "You need to get away from things Wally. Just drop everything and get down here!" But Wally resisted. There were issues to clear up, details to be attended to. He wouldn't share that with Dan Dolan, or anyone else for that matter, but doors were slowly closing; doors that would never open again and therefore the closing of those doors required focus and attention to detail. When he did make the transition to Mexico, it would be a one-way trip.

The depth of night remained his constant foe. He was suffering severe sleep deprivation. His *demons* habitually visited between one and two in the morning. First Poppy's face in the seat of her EOS, then came listening to the confused, at times vicious, voices babbling inside his brain, ripping him first one way then another. He'd toss and turn until mercifully the gray steaks of dawn would begin to filter through his bedroom window turning the room into a scene from an old black and white movie. And recently, yet another layer crept in, a fantasy. One in which Pace and Taylor would pay for having driven Poppy to take her own life. For as far as Wally was concerned, both of them may as well have held her down in the car, started the engine and led the hose back inside the vehicle. As sure as they drew breath, they'd killed her with their own hands. Both men were culpable in Wally's eyes, but a distinct and abiding contempt for Bud Pace developed in his mind. The creep was a scumbag of unparalleled nature, cheating on his wife and young son right along with the rest of the world. He was a fraud, absent any moral fiber. It was only a minor redemptive quality elevating Taylor to a fractionally higher regard in Wally's mind, for he was a cruel fraud as well. At least he appeared true to his family, a commitment that mattered in Wally's estimation. Unlike Pace who'd clearly committed his sins for the sake of his own greed and lust, Taylor had, at least in part, perhaps, done it for his family.

Wally'd now been surveilling Pace and Taylor a full two months. He'd focused his attention on their Friday afternoon activities for the most part, but he'd recently extended the reconnaissance to discover how late it was before the men finally went home on those evenings. Surprisingly, both routinely arrived at their homes not much later than eight-thirty and on one occasion they'd met their wives at the Camelback Inn Restaurant for dinner.

Friday evenings looked something like this: four/four-thirty p.m.—leave PPI offices drive to Adams Hotel for happy hour—five/five-thirty p.m.—Pace heads out for a bit of sport-fucking with Bienvenidos—Taylor goes to his country club to work out—eight-thirty p.m., plus or minus, they arrive home.

A window of approximately three and a half hours, when neither man would be missed, seemed to open every Friday evening. That might have been significant had Wally any idea how to use this knowledge. For the moment it was just intelligence; but his brain was working. A fantasy was coalescing like the fierce gathering wind before a tornado into an identifiable form that if it ever came to fruition might be equally as devastating—maybe as deadly as any monster storm.

~~~

Thursday morning the eighteenth of May around nine-thirty Wally's cell phone rang. He saw on the caller ID it was potentially the call for which he'd now been waiting impatiently for more than a week.

"This is Wally," he answered.

"Mr. Stroud," Mass Mutual agent Peter Broch replied gently, "I was hoping I'd catch you this morning." Broch was a kind, portly man of about Wally's age with whom Wally'd been acquainted for years, but was not friends. His tone was detectably uncomfortable. "The benefits check for—" Broch let the specifics of his thought fade. "The benefits check arrived in yesterday's mail," he concluded rapidly.

"What now?" Wally wanted to know, offering no relief for the difficulty Broch was finding in addressing the subject.

"Wally," Broch began again, "this is always a difficult conversation to have."

"Why?" Wally's manner was unyielding.

Betrayed

"Well ... the circumstances. The loss of someone so close to you ... what to do with such a large sum of money."

"Let me make that simple for you, Pete," Wally said. There was a crass chirpiness in his voice. "Is the check made out to me?"

"Yes, of course it is," Broch confirmed.

"Is it a cashier's check for the full two-fifty?"

"Yes, Wally," Broch said, "and that's why I'd like to sit down with you and discuss ho—"

"No need for you to worry Pete. Nothing to discuss. When can I pick it up?"

"Well, Wally ... I was hoping we might talk about converting this to an annuity or something that would allow you to manage the money mo—"

"No thanks, Pete. When can I come by?"

"Bu—"

"I said, *no thanks*, Pete." Broch heard clearly the pain-filled, edgy dissonance in Wally's voice. There was no point to continuing the conversation.

"Okay Wally," Broch acquiesced. "I'll be in all morning. Drop by anytime you'd like."

Wally'd been sitting quietly next to the pond in his courtyard, a glass of iced tea in one hand, the nightmare of his new existence looping through his brain like an HBO movie when Broch's call arrived. He snapped his cell phone closed, took a sip of tea, and then let his head fall back against the rattan chair. He stared up into the pear tree. A tiny redheaded finch sat on a branch above him, a piece of blue twine hanging from its boney nub of beak. Somewhere hidden in the bushy fig on the front of the house his mate warbled to him. "Time to move on my friend," Wally said softly to the little bird. "I'm going to miss you." His voice broke and he wept quietly.

After a few minutes he collected himself, tossed what was left of the now warm tea onto the cobbles of the courtyard and worked his way to his feet. He walked into the kitchen and surveyed the near empty house.

"It's done, Popp," he said aloud, leaning against the counter in the kitchen. "Our lives have been completely dismantled. Everything we worked for is gone. Our things ... your things ... they're all gone. You're gone. I feel so confused Popp. I love you, but I'm angry with you. I'm alive and yet ... I feel just as dead as you."

Wally moved slowly through the house stopping here and there as if remembering certain instances or recalling significant moments across the years he'd shared this space with Poppy. In his bedroom he changed slowly into the same Levis he'd worn nearly two weeks. He sniffed the armpits of the shirt lying on the foot of his bed. He tossed it into a heap of other clothing next to the closet door and took down a clean shirt.

Shaving and brushing his teeth left Wally feeling only marginally renewed. He made another slow stroll through every room in the house. No one knew better than him how badly he needed to get out of the place. It felt as dead as Poppy. This house had once been so alive with color and laughter and music and happiness, sounds of life. All that was left was the void of space and silence that was created when Poppy was sucked into the vacuum of eternity. He had to get out. He knew he must. But then what? Would he fall off the edge of the earth? Would he encounter the tribulations of Odysseus on his quest to return to Penelope? Would he finally face his own demons and giants and sorcerers he would have to slay to survive? Or would he simply cease to exist? The fact of the matter was he didn't much care one-way or the other. He was getting by mindlessly putting one foot in front of the other letting his steps fall where they may. If he was actually moving in a direction it would have to reveal itself, for Wally was incapable of making conscious decisions. He had no alternative for now but to trust the currents on which his life was being tossed and turned and carried forward each day.

It was late morning when he walked into the office of Peter Broch. As promised, the agent was in to receive him.

"Can I have Miriam bring you a coffee?" he offered.

Wally declined.

Broch went to his desk and picked up the check. He didn't hesitate handing it over to Wally who held it in his lap examining it as if he was looking for something specific.

"Everything all right?" Broch asked.

"Yeah," Wally said, but his voice was barely audible.

Broch did not follow up. It was awkwardly quiet for several moments. Finally he said, "Wally, I hoped to discuss with you some options for preserving your money. I know you've been through some rou—"

"Pete," Wally cut in, "I know your heart's in the right place. It's just … not right now. Okay? I'm just going to deposit this in my bank for now. Maybe we can talk another time."

"Understood Wally." Broch honored his client's wishes seeing the pain screwed across Wally's face. "Is there *anything* at all I could do for you?"

Wally sat motionless. He made no reply. After a few agonizingly silent moments he stood, shook Broch's hand and said, "No thanks."

He drove back to his house. The pickup turned over its first one thousand miles as he pulled to a stop in the driveway. While he was still sitting behind the wheel the mailman walked up with his delivery. Instead of inserting the stack of envelopes into the mail slot he offered them to Wally. Wally accepted the stack and pressed the button to open the garage door. He hit the closer as he walked into the kitchen and dropped the mail on the counter.

Inside his office he leaned the Mass Mutual check against the computer screen on his desk. He stared aimlessly at it for several seconds before turning his back and returning to the kitchen. He was hungry but didn't feel up to making himself anything. "If you were here Popp, I'd take you up to El Bravo for lunch. You'd like that, wouldn't you?" The reply was sullen silence.

Instead, he poured himself a tumbler of Johnny Walker Red and began going through his mail. The envelope on top was from Desert Hills Bank. He tore it open and read the brief letter inside. The bank temporarily suspended his credit card until he reduced the amount owed. The letter went on to say they were concerned about his recent credit activity and could he please call the woman's name at the bottom of the page to discuss the matter. He smiled, tossed the letter aside and snatched up the next envelope in the stack.

Not surprisingly, it was from New York Bank. Wally ripped the edge of the envelope and pulled out another letter nearly an exact duplicate of the one he'd just read. He wasted no time, ignored its message and tossed it aside with the Desert Hills letter. He didn't bother opening the envelopes from Discover, Chase and Wells Fargo; tossed them carelessly, but significantly, into the heap of ignored letters.

The next envelope was from Commercibank, but it was clearly not a letter about his credit card balance, although he fully expected if such a letter was not lower down in the stack it would surely be arriving soon. He opened the Commercibank envelope and read slowly. He knew this letter was due to arrive, but reading it now was the equivalent of replacing the blood in his veins with ice water. His house, the one he'd shared some of the best years of his life with Poppy and his family, was now officially in foreclosure.

The letter drifted to the counter in slow motion. Wally staggered to the liquor cabinet and refilled his glass. He didn't sip the Scotch. He up-ended the tumbler and drained the burning alcohol down his throat. He closed his eyes, held the empty glass in one hand and leaned against the liquor cabinet. Returning the empty vessel gently to the counter, Wally drifted back across the room. He read the letter once more before setting it aside. By the time he'd worked his way to the bottom of the stack of envelopes, he'd been notified by seven of his twelve credit cards they had, for all intents and purposes, been cancelled, his house was in foreclosure, and he'd received the month's electric and water bills.

It struck him how utterly perfect the moment really was. As if he were living the moment of crescendo in *Eskimo* as Damien Rice's voice fades with the haunting lyrics … *down … down … down …* and the song gives way to its emotional operatic culmination. It was a moment of intense pain in which sublime clarity leeched into his consciousness offering the perfect climax to his tortured psyche. He knew in that instant what he was going to do next.

Instead of El Bravo for Mexican food, Wally drove up Seventh Street to Burger King and bought a Whopper Junior. He pulled around into the lot and began to eat the burger sitting behind the wheel of his new truck. Before he could finish, his breathing became rapid and shallow. It was impossible to gasp enough air into his lungs. He was forced to open his door and regurgitate the last bite of the burger right there in the lot. Tears streamed down his cheeks, but he didn't think he was weeping. Wally began shaking uncontrollably, like a machine was vibrating him. His chest felt heavy, as though someone was on top of him with a knee buried in his solar plexus. The thought went through his head—heart attack! "Not now Wally!" he screamed at no one—at himself.

He tossed the remains of the burger out the window, started the truck and squealed out of the parking lot. Light headed and psychologically out of control he screamed, *"Hold on, Wally! Hold on!"* While the truck was still moving he hit the garage door opener and jammed the brakes just short of crashing through the lifting door. He tumbled sideways out of the driver's door and slid along the side of the truck but managed to make it inside the house. As he stumbled into the kitchen, he hammered the garage door closer, barely breaking his fall, grabbing the side of the counter. While he still had the strength, Wally crawled the short distance into his bedroom and made it up onto the bed. If I'm going to die, he thought, let it be right here, right now, as his convulsions reached the climax of their intensity. Wally considered he was about as ready as any man could be to make the journey into oblivion. But his breathing began to return to normal, and the tears he was not weeping began to abate. He had to concede whatever this episode was—it scared the hell out of him. An anxiety attack was a foreign concept to him, but in the weeks and months ahead, Wally would learn to become better at controlling himself whenever the unanticipated assailant visited.

He fell asleep in a puddle of sweat and sheer exhaustion. He didn't awaken until the *hour of demons*. By then he'd slept nearly a full twelve hours. He awoke in a confused daze. Gradually the memory of what had happened returned. Wally sat up knowing there was no point pursuing sleep any further, and unwilling to endure the torture of lying there until dawn.

He shuffled in a fog out to the kitchen and sat in semi-darkness, the room lit only by the backlights of the glass front cabinets. A fresh cup of hot tea steeped while he scribbled a short to-do list. It was a very short list. He stared at it feeling he must be forgetting something. In the end, he had not.

The first item on his list was to call his father-in-law and let him know that Monday morning would find him headed to his home in Mexico. Jake was an early riser. The minute light began to appear outside, Wally made the call.

"Hello," Jake said cautiously. Late night or early morning phone calls usually boded ill news.

"It's Wally, Jake. Good morning."

"Thought I was the only one up at this hour," Jake said.

"How are you getting on?"

"Surviving," Jake replied. "You?"

"Yeah," Wally answered.

"We haven't heard from you since Ellen and Colin left."

Wally didn't say anything for several seconds. "How's Dolores?"

"Constantly on the go," Jake said. "I guess that means she's doing okay. She doesn't talk to me."

Wally knew Dolores's routine. It wasn't just Jake she didn't talk to. Wally suspected the woman was tormented, so damaged and dysfunctional from something in her life never revealed she'd been rendered nearly useless as a mother, wife—friend. One could almost feel sympathy for her were it not for the fact she seemed to enjoy inflicting cruelty.

"And, Liz?"

Jake hesitated. "I'm worried about her Wally. This hit her hard. I know she was jealous of Poppy, but she loved her, too."

"We all have something," Wally conceded.

"She's drinking way too much."

"Well … I can't say much about that," Wally admitted. "I'm guilty of it myself."

"Anyway," Wally went on, changing gears, "I wanted to let you know I have things cleared up … finally. I'm leaving Monday for Mexico. Not sure when I'll get back this way Jake."

"Whatta ya gonna do down there?"

Wally knew it was useless to get too deep into the subject of living in Mexico with his father-in-law. Jake was never going to appreciate the attraction Wally felt for the country. "Play a little golf … drink too much wine," Wally explained, letting the subject drop.

"I'd like you to say goodbye to Dolores and Liz for me," Wally went on. "I think nerves are still too raw for me to come around, but I want them … and you … to know I've considered all of you my family, for better or worse, over these thirty-odd years. I'm going to miss all of you."

"Jesus. Sounds like you're moving to outer space instead of Mexico. We'll be seeing you from time to time."

Wally didn't argue. "You're right, Jake. Just feels like the end of everything to me right now. I guess that sentiment finds its way into what I have to say."

"Why don't you come and have dinner with us tomorrow night?" Jake suggested. "I'll have Dolores barbecue a couple of slabs of baby-backs."

"Too normal, Jake," Wally countered. "I wouldn't get through it and neither would all of you."

Jake didn't respond. Neither man could seem to find a way to continue the conversation. "Take care of yourself, Wally," Jake finally said.

"You, too, Jake. I … I gotta go."

Both men listened to the silence for several moments before Wally hung up.

Wally stared at the cell phone in his hand. His instincts told him he'd never hear from or speak to Jake, Dolores or Liz Zinsser again. For the remainder of his life his only connection to Poppy's—his family would be through his nephew, Colin, and his sister-in-law Ellen or her husband Ross. He decided then and there that was an acceptable condition to him.

~~~~

At nine o'clock Monday morning Wally was parked in the lot of Commercibank's administrative offices where its mortgage department was housed waiting for the doors to be unlocked.

At nine sharp he saw the shadow of a female form on the inside of the frosted glass doors fumbling with a set of keys. He didn't wait. He stepped out of his truck wearing a pair of navy-blue Dockers shorts, a yellow and blue striped golf shirt and a baseball cap that said Taylor Made across its crown. He could have just as easily been headed to a tee-time as to the task he'd chosen that morning.

He pulled the heavy doors open and went inside. The receptionist was fussing with a Starbucks coffee cup and a bran muffin. "Good morning," she greeted him. Her tone was pleasant.

Wally nearly sang the words back to her. "Goood mooorning!" he replied melodiously, and then walked passed her.

"Wait!" she shouted after him, clumsily detaching herself from the coffee cup. She came chasing him down the short hallway, the urgent click, click, clicking sound of her high heels against the tile floor echoing the sharp distress their occupant was feeling. "Who are you looking for? What do you want?"

"It's okay." Wally reassured her, ignoring her breathless pleas. He carelessly raised his right hand, made a motion so as to indicate she should calm herself, "Roger Watkins is expecting me."

Just as the frantic receptionist caught up to him, he arrived at the door he was looking for and let himself in.

The receptionist rushed in behind him peeking around his shoulder. "I'm sorry, Mr. Wat—"

"Roger!" Wally greeted the man, merrily dismissing the receptionist. He continued into the office he'd sat in several months earlier—the same day Poppy died—explaining to its occupant the predicament he was faced with. Wally crossed the room deliberately. "I just wanted to drop these off to you," he said, dangling a set of keys from his hand. He approached Watkins' desk, held the keys at shoulder height and dropped them noisily onto the desk in front of the bewildered man.

"What's this?" The blood drained from Watkins' face. Wally read fear.

"Take it easy Roger," Wally ordered petulantly. "Those are the keys to your new house," he continued, a menacing, fake grin grinding its way across his face. "I know you folks are going to enjoy it!" The words he uttered did not begin to convey the resentment or wretchedness Wally felt at that moment.

Watkins may have thought he understood what was taking place. "Mr. Stroud," he began, "Things have been tough for you, but this is not what you want to do."

"Nonsense Roger," Wally shot back. "This is precisely what I want to do. I'm moved out as of right now. She's all yours. Oh … and when you explain to your bosses what went wrong here," Wally drawled on, ragged dissension in his voice, "make sure you let them know your compassion in the face of what my wife and I were dealing with when I came to you for help played no small part in my final resolution of the matter."

"But the insurance money," Watkins pleaded.

The moment he'd learned of Poppy's death, Watkins pulled their file. Sifting through the loan documents he'd observed the life insurance policy. He'd concluded all the bank would have to do was wait until Wally collected, and he would bring the mortgage current, if not pay it off outright. "You can bring everything current." The banker's voice was little more than a whimper.

Betrayed

"Sorry, Rog ... made other plans." With those words, Wally turned his back not just on Roger Watkins and Commercibank, but the entire system he felt had betrayed him. He retraced his steps up the hallway, left the building, and never looked back.

He climbed into the cab of his pickup. It was eight minutes past nine when he pulled out of the parking lot of Commercibank. Thirty miles west on I-10 he turned south onto State Highway 85 and drove toward Gila Bend where he would pick up I-8 to San Diego. At the stoplight where Buckeye Rd. intersects Arizona 85, he looked east to the distant skyline of Phoenix. It appeared as a fading mirage on the horizon, just as the entirety of his life had vanished in what seemed a blinding flash. In that moment he envied Poppy's wisdom and courage; again he wanted to join her.

CHAPTER 18

Miles and time slipped by. Wally lost himself to the subtle drone of muffled road noise inside the cab of the moving pickup. The rhythmic white sounds were hypnotic. He was grateful that what he was listening to was not the usual chorus of mean voices that continued to punish him each night at the *hour of demons*. There in the cocoon of the plush cab of the truck he sensed metamorphosis in his life; the end of one incarnation, the genesis of another existence in which the previous Wally Stroud was not recognizable.

He'd never enjoyed driving for the simple pleasure of it. That no doubt accounted for one reason he'd never been able to enjoy Poppy's EOS the way she could. He glanced over to the passenger seat where he'd secured the granite urn that held her ashes. "So what do you think of the way this machine rides, Popp?" he said, aloud. He knew if she was there to respond she'd have said, "I hate it." Poppy wasn't the truck type.

The response was as silent and barren as the bleak open stretches of desert across that part of southern Arizona; greasewood, jojoba, fishhook barrel cactus, ocotillo—the odd cholla against a dry, volcanic cinder-strewn plain dotted by jutting volcanic hogbacks and mesas in the distance. Even the wind made little sound here.

Wally turned his focus to his recent fantasy: making sure Pace and Taylor didn't get to just walk away from what they'd done. His thoughts began to sharpen. At first he saw only broad, blurry strokes in an out-of-focus image. Before long he began to fill in the spaces with—"*what if?*" The process continued while the miles and his former life continued to fall away behind him.

Not until he noticed the first warning sign for the U.S. Border Patrol inspection stop halfway to Yuma did he realize how far he'd driven. A mile before the inspection point, orange traffic cones were placed on the roadway forcing traffic down to one lane. Speed zones dropped; 75 to 65 to 55 to 45 to 35 to 25. It wasn't until he was the second vehicle back, reading the prominently placed *brag placard* of achievements in uncovering illegal aliens, drug busts, catching DUI drivers, or identifying wanted criminals the significance of getting caught with

Betrayed

$200,000 in cash stashed inside his golf bag occurred to him. He knew he could forget any attempt to explain the money was not stolen or about to be used for a drug purchase or any number of other accusations that could be made. In the new order of things in America, Wally accused "W" and Cheney—especially Cheney—for this one; he knew he'd be fucked until he could prove otherwise—*if* he could prove otherwise. Hell—who knew? They might even have him waterboarded!

From about the age of fifty-five, Wally resented the avuncular treatment that seemed to be bestowed upon him all too often. That day, when the pretty young border patrol agent smiled at him and asked, "U.S. citizen, Sir?" He smiled back, content to be regarded as an elderly uncle figure and said, "Yes."

"Have a nice day," she said waving him through.

He drove on and accelerated back to highway speed. He gave consideration to the fact that inside his briefcase he carried the life insurance check for a quarter of a million dollars, in his golf bag, two hundred thousand more in cash. For as many years as he could recall there had been a sign at U.S. ports of entry when exiting or entering the U.S. which notified travelers it was a federal crime, punishable by imprisonment and confiscation, for not declaring funds of more than $10,000 in one's possession, regardless of its form. With the stepped up cooperation between Mexico and the U.S. over the drug war in Mexico, there was now the same notification hanging above the border crossing entering Mexico. Wally had no intention of voluntarily putting himself on every radar screen from Homeland Security to the FBI. And there was the dubious matter of the Mexican Federal Police. But he knew the odds were dramatically in his favor. The ace-in-the-hole was his profile didn't set off any alarms and he intended to use that to his advantage.

Long before he saw Yuma off in the distance he'd returned to the trance-like state in which he painstakingly peeled away the layers of complications plaguing the insanity of the horror movie being played in his mind. Each time he rolled the clip he'd address a new flaw, acknowledged that it could realistically be overcome, or decided he'd have to take another turn in the maze if he was to find his way through.

It was closing in on one in the afternoon, but he figured to gain an hour when crossing into California. The woman with the reflective vest at the port of entry asked where he was travelling from. He wanted to say, "Fucking outer space," to the ridiculous question. Instead he smiled and said, "Phoenix."

California's maximum speed limit was seventy miles per hour. He pushed his truck up to seventy-six and set the cruise control. Before ten miles passed, the movie in his brain was rolling once more. There was a plot now. The story had a beginning and middle, but its ending was problematic. Each time he went back to the beginning he found something suspect—logic that didn't hold up; but he persisted. Again and again he went back, worked his way through the parts he could see. It was the ending he couldn't peg. If he could concoct and carry out something as insane as he was considering, what then? Where would it leave him? Could he get away with it?

What if he didn't get away with it? He went back to the beginning and began anew. He decided to concentrate on execution; making it doable. He'd worry about getting away with it if he ever got that far. In the end he acknowledged it probably amounted to nothing more than virtual catharsis, mental masturbation. It was a palliative pursuit at best. He figured nobody in his right mind would seriously consider what was on his mind. But that was precisely the point; he was no longer in his right mind and that made the whole idea not just conceivable, but maybe—just maybe—doable—if he really had become insane.

He looked down at the urn. "So what do you think, Popp?" he asked his dead wife. "Am I insane?" He worked off of what he knew her reply would have been. He wasn't sure he wanted to admit that to himself.

He glided down the Tecate Summit dropping into the coastal suburbs of San Diego around three-thirty that afternoon. Rush hour was getting underway. At least, he thought, he'd be driving against the worst of the traffic until he arrived at the southbound approach to the International Border at San Ysidro. He was funneled into another border patrol checkpoint at El Campo. Traffic was heavy and backed up for nearly a mile. It was another slow crawl up to the inspection point but the patrolman, this time a middle-aged Hispanic man dressed in green camouflage fatigues and a Smokey-the-Bear-hat, waved him through without any question. Wally knew he was being profiled each time. If he actually worked up the courage—or stupidity—to attempt what was now percolating in his brain, that fact would be a welcome one, not so good if you were a dark-skinned person with all the kids crammed into the front seat of the family pickup.

It was approaching five o'clock when he found himself weaving his way into the traffic headed into Tijuana. Impatient commuters blew horns, flipped each other off, cut in and out; made themselves and the people around them generally miserable in an effort to jump two car lengths ahead. Wally relaxed and left room in front of his truck for another vehicle to work in or out. The confusion and tempers worked to his advantage when it came his turn to cross. The customs officers simply wanted the crazies out of their hair and pushed cars through in order to keep traffic moving. He received a green light with the word "PASE" and wove his way through the scramble of vehicles jockeying to make lane changes and turnoffs on the Mexican side.

He skirted downtown Tijuana taking the road that went along the *Zona Rio,* which ran next to the border fence with the U.S. until it merged with Mexico Highway 1 South. Wally worked his way into the southbound lanes of the toll road to Ensenada. His home was only about twenty miles north of that seaport, an hour's drive south from the border.

As he'd dropped from the Tecate Summit earlier, the sun had slowly become obscured by heavy, dark marine layer, only occasionally showing itself as a subdued orb that looked more like the moon leeching through a cloudy night sky than the sun, until it was totally obliterated by the "May Gray." As dusk settled, darkness advanced rapidly, assisted by thick patches of fog descending to the ground. He didn't like the driving conditions, but he had little choice. When he was south of Rosarito Beach, the marine layer lifted enough for decent visibility and remained at

Betrayed

a ceiling of a few hundred feet until he reached La Misión, where the cloud layer came right down to the road once more and made driving treacherous. He never saw the sign that said Bajamar, but he recognized the turnoff when it came up. At the security gate the guard had to walk up to his truck to identify him.

Inside the entrance, Wally pulled onto the cobbled lane, unhooked his seatbelt and said, "We're home, Popp … finally home. And the sonsabitches can't touch us here." He fought back tears. Wally felt he'd wept enough for a lifetime, but being there with Poppy reduced to ashes in a jar was simply more than his fragile psyche could absorb. The tears leaked and kept leaking while he wound around the curving cobbled lane to the street that turned down to his beach house.

The beautiful Moorish style tri-level home sat no more than a hundred fifty yards off the main road, on the edge of a cliff not more than two hundred yards from the crashing breakers of the Pacific Ocean. The narrow lane arched northward and downward as it dropped from the main road before curving back south to the front of the house and terminated in a large cul-de-sac at the end of the lane. As he turned, his headlights cut into the fog and revealed the silhouette of the house as a brooding dark angular edifice devoid of life—and, Wally knew—joy. Although in fairness, it was not the house that was devoid of joy.

He pulled up in front of his home and backed his truck into the carport on the north side of the house. There was no chance a truck of that size would fit in the single-car garage attached to the house. When he pressed the garage door opener on his visor, the heavy copper door began to retract and the light inside came on. It was enough to bathe the passenger side of his truck in a soft sepia glow that made it possible to see well enough to unload a few of his things. He left the truck doors open and entered the house through the garage. In a few moments lights were on and he'd turned on the heat. It was cold and damp inside.

While the house unfolded itself from hibernation, Wally made several trips with armloads of clothing, framed paintings and suitcases. Everything in the bed of the truck could remain except his golf clubs, which he carried upstairs to the master bedroom along with his brief case. There was a library located just off the master bedroom where he deposited those two items.

He'd accomplished all he intended to tackle in four loads. The rest could wait until morning. He locked the truck, went inside and let the garage door seal him in like a tomb, which was the feel the place had inside with the storm shutters in place. Before he began the process of waking the house up any further, he looked around its capacious main level. The greatroom was 1400 square feet, with a ten-foot ceiling spanned entirely to its outer principal walls but for one column near the kitchen counter whose structural significance was disguised by its artful employment.

Wally cradled Poppy's urn in one arm with her photo clasped under the other, and looked first to each of the four lamp tables around the room. None of them suited his purpose. The fireplace mantle, maybe? No—no good either. But the fireplace begged to be lit. He took the time to get it going and was instantly rewarded, for the golden ochre glow of its light across the room and the lively flickering shadows cast about, transformed his tomb into a kinder place where Wally hoped he might find a little peace.

When he stepped toward the liquor cabinet he discovered just the spot he'd been searching for and retrieved Poppy's urn from the kitchen counter. He moved a fluted blown-glass vase to the opposite end of the buffet and replaced it with the funeral urn. Next he retrieved his favorite ten by twelve photo of her; one a friend had snapped a few years back that caught Poppy standing in front of him with his arms wrapped around her from behind, her head tossed backward looking over her shoulder at him adoringly, her bobbed hair glimmering golden with the first strands of silver beginning to show in the sun, and both of them laughing as though it would not be possible for a care of any kind to ever displace the love and joy they found in each other. It broke his heart every time he looked at that photo, and yet it captured the essence of both of them and a time in life he needed desperately to be able to cling to.

The room was becoming warm and dry. He poured himself a double Scotch straight up and went in search of the remote controller for the storm shutters. Wally found the controller on the lamp table nearest the French doors, pointed it at the shutters and pressed the button. The aluminum battens began to retract. Instantly the aluminum shield was replaced by dark, heavy fog that closed right up against the glass doors and began to condense in droplets. Wally felt oddly attracted to the gloominess of it all. He was lately of the opinion that, with time, a person acclimates to his condition in life; sadness felt more normal, more comfortable than being engaged in a constant struggle to change that which he now believed could not be changed.

But there was the world outside of his head with which he had to contend. People were watching. There was Colin and Ellen. He was going to have to add his neighbors, Dan and Fortunada. They were all touched by what he was going through; what happened to Poppy. They would all be watching and waiting for his return to some form of normalcy; a signal he was going to be okay, that life could begin again—permission for them to be okay again, too. He sensed this dynamic rather than possessed any true understanding of it. And he was ready now to give those around him what they needed. *Pretense*, he'd learned from Poppy, could be as good as the real thing if he was convincing enough.

The utility door at the back of the kitchen opened, scaring the hell out of him. No less startling was the vision of Dan Dolan stepping inside with a Louisville Slugger resting on his shoulder ready to brain the intruder.

"Jesus-fucking-Christ, Danny Boy! You scared the shit out of me," Wally yelped, setting his Scotch on the liquor cabinet.

"I scared the shit out of you? What about what you did to me?" Dolan walked into the room and lowered the bat. "The fog lifted a little and I could see a light on over here. Didn't recognize the rig in the carport—looked like somebody was cleaning you out."

"Goddamn, Dan," Wally said, "I'm sorry. I wasn't thinking." Wally turned and pulled the door to the liquor cabinet open and found a glass. He poured a stiff slug of Scotch into it and passed it over to Dolan. "Here," he said, "let's start over."

Betrayed

Dan Dolan smiled, shook his head and accepted the glass from Wally's outstretched hand. "Could've called, asshole," he complained.

"It was that kind of day, Dan," Wally said, attempting an apology. "I intended to. Then once I was on this side my cell dropped its signal and—cheers!" he said suddenly, and they both swallowed a healthy slug of Scotch.

Dolan set his glass on the buffet, spread his arms. "Get your ass over here," he ordered, and hugged Wally heartily. "Good to see you, Wally. Need a hand with your things?"

"Thanks. I'm gonna let the rest go 'til morning."

"Good," Dolan said in agreement, and then he drained the glass of Scotch. "Fortunada just pulled one of her casseroles out the oven."

"Jeeze, Danny ... no warn—"

"She's gonna be a little shocked, but there's no problem with dinner. You know how she is—cooks enough for six people no matter it's just the two of us. Come on ... better grab a coat ... wet'n cold out there," Dolan said, pointing toward the French doors.

There was no use to argue. Wally didn't try.

A few minutes later Dan Dolan pushed the front door of his house open and waved Wally in behind him. His two dogs, Jena and Charlie were there to greet them. Charlie barked at Wally, then worked his way in for a pet. Jena was already slobbering for her share.

Dan yelled up the staircase. "You won't believe what I found, Fo."

"Everything all right over there?" she shouted back.

"Go ahead," Dan indicated, pointing to the stairs. "She could use a nice surprise."

The dogs scrambled up ahead of them. Wally followed with Dan on his heels. Wally came onto the upper landing, standing at the edge of the kitchen. "Could you stand an unannounced guest?" he asked Fortunada Dolan.

Fo Dolan looked up from the salad she was tossing and froze. No words came out of her mouth. She looked like a statue when Dan came around Wally and said, "Pick up your jaw, Fo, before it falls in the salad."

"Oh ... my ... God!" And a gusher of tears sprung from her eyes. Before she could get to Wally her face was soaked. She clutched him close to her. "I can't tell you how wonderful this is, Wally."

"I know, Fo ... for me, too."

Charlie barked again.

Fortunada let Wally go and affectionately shushed her dog. "Why didn't you call?" she admonished, returning her attention to Wally.

"I was trying to explain that to Dan. It just turned into one of those days. I wasn't even sure I would get here today. Just started driving this morning and the next thing you know—" He shrugged his head to one side. "Damn near got a baseball bat between the eyes for my trouble."

"Would'a served you right," Dan chimed in. "Okay, okay, let's cut to the important stuff. Fortunada's got a bottle of wine open. You want some of that or you stickin' to the booze?"

"What are we drinking, Fo?" Wally wanted to know.

"Cheap red," she replied giggling.

"I'm a cheap date … long as you intend to feed me some of what I smell."

Dan already had a glass of Scotch poured when Fortunada finished filling a wine glass for Wally. "Well …" Fortunada began. She suffered a momentary loss for words. "Here's to some sunshine," she finally said.

"I'll drink to that," Dan agreed.

Wally sipped the wine. Fortunada ushered him to the dinner table where she was adding another place setting. "Had a lot of this?" Wally asked, pointing to the fog at the door.

"Damn near the whole month," Dan complained.

Fortunada set the casserole dish in the center of the table. When she came back she scooted the salad bowl next to Wally and a basket of toasted French bread next to Dan. "That's it, boys," she announced. "Nothing fancy tonight."

"Fo," Wally said, more honestly than Dan and Fo could possibly know, "this is the fanciest meal I've looked at in a couple of months."

"Well, stop gawking and start eating then," she ordered. Fortunada and Dan stole a furtive glance while Wally piled his plate high. His emaciated condition was shocking to them.

CHAPTER 19

The week that followed was busy. Fortunada called her housekeeper and asked her to bring her sister. The two of them took charge of cleaning Wally's home. Dan and Wally transferred the few items from the truck into the house, mostly paintings and clothing.

There'd come an interesting moment when the cleaning girls realized the urn on the liquor cabinet contained Poppy's ashes. In a culture where the dead are remembered each year in a national holiday, you wouldn't expect much of a reaction to a dead person in any form. Apparently that did not extend to strangers, because the two girls crossed themselves and slunk back when it was revealed they were dusting around Poppy's ashes. During the remainder of the week neither girl would come into the room alone. When they did find the necessity to be in the greatroom, they skirted the liquor cabinet, nervous as a couple of alcoholics battling the temptation.

The heavy marine layer persisted all week, the first in June. Clouds continued heavily laden with moisture in a chill, misty fog leaving everything soggy. On Thursday Wally'd let the fireplace burn the entire day. He'd initially resisted Fortunada's insistence they all jump in and get his house in order. What he really wanted to do was slump down into his cushy-stuffed chair-and-a-half in front of the fire and slip silently back into the depressed stupor that was the reality of his existence, the state that had come to feel to him where he belonged. But when Friday afternoon arrived, he looked around and could not deny the wisdom and genuine service his friend had done him. He thought of Ellen.

He popped a bottle of wine for Fortunada and himself while Dan drove the cleaning girls home.

"Leftovers tonight," Fortunada said absent-mindedly.

"Your stuff starts out fabulous and gets better every time it's reheated!"

"That petroleum by-product junk they put in processed foods." Fortunada chuckled, lifting her glass.

Wally took a long lug from his glass—then, "Dinner's on me tomorrow."

"Where we goin'?"

"Right here. Found a package of filet mignons in the freezer ... couple of potatoes left from Phoenix that need to get baked."

"I'll throw something together for dessert," Fortunada offered, emptying her glass. Wally leaned across and poured her a refill.

"You're on."

"You doing okay, Wally?" Her directness caught him by surprise.

He paused, stared deep into the rich garnet liquid at the bottom of his glass as if it was a crystal ball. He lifted the globe to his lips and let a deliberate flow come into his mouth. "I have my moments." Wally fell into a contemplative silence before he went on. "When you consider what's happened since the last time I saw you two—" His voice trailed away.

"Gonna take a lot of time, Wally," Fo sympathized. "Don't be too hard on yourself."

"Yeah," he acquiesced before reminding himself—*pretense, Wally—pretense.* He smiled, looked directly at her. "Just being here with you guys is turning the whole thing around for me," he lied.

"Dan knew it would be good for you to come down here and relax. That's why I wanted to get you organized so you can just kick back ... do what you want." Wally noted the muscles in her face relax.

"Well, you've gone way beyond the call, Fo," he said, according Fortunada the appreciation she deserved. "And your girls did a fine job on the house. You've fattened me up some already. I'm feeling better." He raised his glass to her. "Thanks," he said.

Fortunada grinned, blushed a little and patted Wally's knee. "Just come on over when you see Dan's car." Fo stood, finished her wine and rinsed the glass on her way out.

Saturday morning arrived like the calm after a great storm. The sky was a crisp, clean cerulean color, the closest visible clouds—half way to Hawaii. A gentle, warm breeze blew from off the land and began to dry the air. Quivering vapors of steam rose up off of plants and the wrought iron railings along the side of the house. Wally shuffled, still tired, to the south end of the upper terrace and let the warm sun bathe his nude body. He figured if there was anyone around to see him—they wouldn't want to look long. Even the sea was glassy calm. The breakers that normally crashed on the rocks below had quieted to mere soughing ripples lapping against the black lava crags like water being gently sloshed back and forth in a bucket.

Air in the house was still cool and damp. He wandered downstairs and lit the fireplace. It was a bacon and eggs morning if he ever saw one. Two eggs sizzled while the teapot built up a head of steam. The toaster popped up while he flipped the eggs and slid them onto a plate.

Wally was doing the best he could with this idea of normalcy. The day setting up outside was a balm to his state of mind. But the *demons* that plagued him nightly in Phoenix had arrived at the appointed hour here, obviously having hitched a ride to remain with him. He'd lain awake from a little after two on, tossing and turning in the warm flannel sheets, listening to one voice after another, mostly all at once.

One clear benefit endured from the long, silent drive from Phoenix the week before; his developing fantasy. More accurately, the clarity and detail he'd brought to that insane idea had grown to become the plot in a story Wally thought about constantly. Instead of casting the thoughts aside as absurd as he once had, he now gave careful consideration to the details he realized would have to be overcome if he actually wanted to carry out such a scheme.

That old cliché: Keep it simple, he reminded himself. That's when the light came on in his head. Wally'd been a staff sergeant in the army during the Vietnam War. He'd served as an operations specialist. He recalled how they'd laid out field-ops; all components given their assignments: insertion, support, extraction. That was it. Lay out an operations plan, just as he had forty-five years earlier.

A second cup of tea steeped. The house was dry enough to shut down the fireplace. Outside the air warmed enough, he thought, to throw the doors open. He conquered the spiral staircase two steps at a time without spilling the tea. The cup sat on his desk in the library while he flung the doors wide open.

"Oh … you'd have loved today, Popp," he said, noticing the profusion of California Poppies, spangled with misty dew, bursting out to the warm sunshine: Poppy and her poppies. It had been a stupid little thing between them. But it didn't feel stupid that morning. "I miss you so much, Poppy," he whispered.

It was cool in the library. Wally sipped the warm tea appreciating how it slowly drained down his esophagus warming the core of his body. On a piece of copy paper he began to sketch out the plan: injection, target, objective and extraction. He created a heading using each criterion, made notes and lists as he considered what had to be accomplished in each phase. He was immersed in concentration when he noticed it was two in the afternoon. He skimmed over his work. Lots of details to be considered, but it seemed clear enough; this was no longer just some hare-brained fantasy. This was a mission if he decided to pursue, could be carried out; at least he could have twenty years earlier. For now it was enough he had something engaging his focus and made him feel as though he had a purpose to continue into tomorrow. He couldn't recall the last time he'd sat concentrating on something other than Poppy's suicide since—well, he couldn't recall.

When he stepped out onto the terrace a smile crossed his lips. The strip of poppies he'd noticed that morning had erupted into a broad meadow of brilliant cadmium orange. Had there been any reason, he'd have found his camera and shot several photographs.

Dan showed up at four. Wally was slumped back in a club chair on the terraza with a glass of Scotch. A plate of white cheddar, a few remaining garlic-stuffed olives and a few crackers Wally'd mangled sat on a small table.

"Party of one?" Dan inquired coming up the short staircase.

"Hey, Danny Boy—" Wally started to wiggle up from his arrangement, but Dan placed a hand on his shoulder.

"Stay put," he said. "I know where things are."

"Help yourself," Wally said, settling back. "Grab that box of crackers on the counter."

The tinkling sounds of ice against glass certified Dolan didn't need his help.

"Been a month since we've seen sun," Dolan mused. "Sure as hell wasn't like this!"

"Just letting the UVs cook my face and head," Wally said. "Feels good."

"Should've played golf today," Dan babbled mindlessly, looking up and down the links below.

"Why spoil a beautiful day?"

"Bullshit," he argued. "Just need to get you cranked up again, that's all."

"We'll see," Wally said, eyes closed, masking his indifference to the idea.

"Let's play nine Tuesday, if this weather holds."

Wally didn't respond, lifted his glass and sipped a slug of Scotch. Dolan reached over and took a slice of cheddar, placed it on a cracker and shoved the whole thing in his mouth. He followed it with two olives.

"We'll see," Wally said.

Normalcy, Wally, he reminded himself—*pretense*.

Fortunada showed up around five-thirty carrying something chocolaty with walnuts on top, still warm. Wally thought they should eat it first and cook dinner later. Fortunada shot him down. Dinner was simple but perfect.

Once the sun was down, it turned chilly quickly. He lit the fireplace and they moved over around the gentle flickering flame. Dan sipped his Scotch slowly while Fortunada and Wally uncorked a second bottle of wine. Fortunada served up a healthy sized portion of the crusty chocolate treat for Wally. The middle was filled with dark bittersweet cocoa pudding. As large as his serving was, he was interested in a second. A gleam of approval twinkled in Fortunada's drowsy eyes.

"You gettin' shit-faced, ole girl?" Dan exclaimed. It was an accusation, not a question.

"Maybe a little," Fo admitted. "Dinner was wonderful, Wally."

"This *dessert* is wonderful," Wally countered, filling his mouth, closing his eyes.

"Got plans for tomorrow?" Dan asked Wally.

"Couple of projects," Wally said. "And I need to call my nephew, Colin."

"Where does he live?" Fortunada was curios.

"Up the road," Wally said. "Escondido."

"Close!" Dan noted. "We gonna meet him?"

"Guaranteed," Wally said. "Poppy's sister, Ellen's boy."

"Makes me feel better knowing you have family nearby," Fortunada confessed.

"You and Dan are my family, too, Fo." It was obvious to Wally both Dolans appreciated the sentiment.

Betrayed

"Well," Fortunada said, "family or not, we need to drag ourselves home while we can still walk."

"Speak for yourself," Dan objected.

"I just did," she countered, "and you can haul your carcass up outta that chair and march home with me."

Dan didn't argue.

Wally returned to sit in front of the fire in the vacuum of sound created by the departure of his friends. He stared hard into the flames, looked up to where the picture of he and Poppy sat on the liquor cabinet and said, "I miss you so much, Popp. How am I going to survive without you?"

Wally was awake again at the *hour of demons*. He would sleep no more the rest of that night or many more to come just like it.

The sunrise Sunday morning was spectacular, but Wally could find only pain in the beauty around him. He almost couldn't bear to look at his surroundings. There's this bullshit notion that if you talk about things like this, get it out, it somehow magically makes things better. He didn't even need to try; instinct told him after all was said, talking about it would amount to just that— it will have been said. But not a fucking thing was likely to be changed.

He brewed a mug of tea and went back to work on the operations plan he'd started the day before. He worked through most of the day again. At four in the afternoon Dan showed up once more for what was to become a quotidian observance either on Wally's terraza or Dan and Fortunada's. Wally decided not to fight it. Simpler just to quibble over who was hosting sundowners next.

Monday morning promised another day of sunshine. By eight-thirty Wally was pulling through the exit gate at Bajamar and turning south toward Ensenada. He'd offered to pick up anything Fortunada needed while he was in town but he'd made no offer for either Fortunada or Dan to ride along. His first stop was Bancomer.

It was close to ten o'clock when he pulled up in front of the bank. Several cars filled the lot and lines had formed inside. When he presented himself at the information desk the beautiful Mexican girl, who spoke some English, dropped what she was doing and made a quick interoffice call. When she hung up, she looked up at Wally and said, "Follow me, please, Señor Stroud." He was presented without any wait to Amado José Romero Garza, the branch *Director*.

CHAPTER 20

The pretty receptionist doted over Wally's needs while Director Garza completed his phone call. Garza was a fortyish, handsome man with thick black hair manicured like fine topiary, every hair in its place. He maintained elegant, patrician manners. Jet-black eyes were set wide apart in a friendly face of light olive complexion. Wally could see the Castilian, Conquistador blood in the man, but the *sangre* was not pure, and Mexico is a caste society. Therefore, *Bank Director* Garza—would never be—*Bank President* Garza.

Wally handed the insurance check to Señor Garza, who stared at it several seconds. Wally had to admire the way the man concealed his glee. He felt certain the director had never been handed a check that large directly from a client. Wally offered no explanation about the check except to say his wife had passed away and now he intended to live permanently in Mexico.

Señor Garza set the check down between them and expressed his deep sorrow for the loss of one as beautiful and young as Señora Stroud. He remembered her well, as he said. Wally could feel the man's sentiments had nothing to do with the fact he was about to deposit a quarter million dollars into his bank.

Director Garza suggested it could be a mistake to deposit the check into the existing account with Poppy's name still on it. The account, of course, allowed either Wally or Poppy to withdraw funds. "But under the circumstances." Amado José spread his hands; gestured toward the check. "Why risk any complication?" He recommended they close the existing account and open a new one into which the insurance check could be deposited.

Wally thought for a moment, "I did plan to add my nephew as a co-owner on the account," he added thoughtfully. "Can we do that at the same time?"

"That will be no problem, Señor Stroud," Garza assured him. "I will have the papers prepared for your nephew to sign." He fidgeted a moment. "I'm sorry our system is so … cumbersome," he apologized. "The government has become very strict because of our drug war," he went on to explain. "If your nephew will not be able to come here to my office, he will be required to appear before a Mexican *Notario* to sign the documents … it is merely a precaution, but I have no control."

"I understand, Director," Wally said. "It's not a problem. I'll bring him here."

"Of course," Director Garza assured him. "You should go ahead with the deposit of the check anyway, *porque* with such a large sum of money, there is going to be very close scrutiny by my government as to where these funds are coming. And Bancomer is going to require the funds be fully transferred to our bank before you will be permitted to withdraw any amount. I apologize for all of this, but it could easily take thirty days, Señor Stroud. The sooner we begin the process the better for you," he concluded authoritatively. "Do you wish to hold the money in U.S. dollars or Mexican pesos?"

Wally hadn't thought he'd have an option. He considered how utterly contemptuous he felt toward a government claiming to protect its citizens but turned its back on him when the time came; U.S. dollars didn't seem so significant to him any longer. "Are there other choices?" he asked.

Amado José pondered the question a moment. "Actually, you do have a few other alternatives, Señor Stroud," he said. "You could hold your money on deposit in Bancomer in: Swiss Francs, Deutsche Marks, British Pounds Sterling, Canadian Dollars or Japanese Yen … I can set up such accounts for you … Ah … *permiso*, I nearly forget," Garza added quickly, "you may also maintain your account in Euros."

"And once I make a decision … what if I change my mind?"

"Then we must do what we are doing now," Garza explained. "You must close this account and open a new one to your new preference. The money must be converted."

"British Pounds," Wally decided serendipitously. "Convert it all to Pounds Sterling … can't be any more risky than holding it in U.S. dollars," he mused.

It required more than an hour for the documents to be drawn. Wally sat patiently to one side while the director attended other matters. Another elegant Mexican woman brought the stack of papers to his desk when they were ready. It looked as if the signing of a major international treaty was about to take place, right down to the designated pens for the signing. "Mexican officials," Garza explained, "require a specific blue ink be used in the signing of all signatures, and the color must be consistent throughout the document."

After Wally'd signed all the documents, Director Garza rose and shook his hand. "Thank you for opening such a prominent account with my bank, Señor Stroud," he said. "I'm sure you must understand this will cast a great deal of prestige upon me with my superiors."

"Then I have a friend in Mexico," Wally replied. "No doubt I'll be back for your advice on other matters."

"*Para servirle*, Señor Stroud," Director Garza offered crisply.

With those salutations, Wally collected his documents and excused himself.

"It would be helpful, Señor Stroud," Garza added while walking Wally to the door, "if you could bring your *sobrino* here within the next thirty days."

"Shouldn't be a problem," Wally promised, and shook the director's hand again at the door.

~~~~

From the bank he drove the short distance to the supermarket, *Comercial Mexicana*. He checked the items off his own shopping list before making sure he'd picked up the few things Fortunada asked him to get.

CHAPTER 21

It was after one o'clock when he backed his truck into the carport at his beach house. He hauled the three bags of groceries inside. When he opened the refrigerator to store the bacon and eggs, he pulled out a cold beer. It was warm outside but beginning to cloud over. Nothing in Fortunada's bag was perishable. He left it sitting on the counter and headed upstairs.

He went straight to the library and pressed the power button on his laptop. While it booted he opened the French doors. The breeze was too chilly. He closed them and went back inside. His wireless Internet was slow connecting. While he waited he opened the folder from Bancomer. His debit card was in the slotted holder in front; Colin's wouldn't get issued until he personally appeared at the bank.

When the browser page opened, Wally signed into his Yahoo account and pulled up the contact list. He started to send Colin an email, then stopped abruptly and decided to activate the international service on his Verizon account instead. He stood up and pulled his cell phone out of its holster. The service didn't take long to set in motion. He terminated the customer support call and thumbed down his auto-dial numbers.

Colin was #3 in the speed-dial list. He pressed it and waited. On the forth ring he heard his nephew's voice on the other end. "Hey, Uncle Wally. 'Sup?"

"Never a surprise with that caller ID, is there?"

"You don't want to listen to who's calling—snuff the call. Couldn't live without it," Colin said.

"Can't argue that," Wally agreed. "Got a minute?"

"All the time in the world ... for you!"

"I'm trying to get my affairs back in shape ... you know, getting set up here in Mexico."

"Yeah ... so how's that going?"

"Progress, you know? Making progress. Actually, that's why I called." Wally hadn't discussed his plans with Colin. Primarily because he had no idea what his plans were from one day to the next. "I want to put you on my bank account," he told Colin.

"Why?"

"I'm alone now kid," Wally explained, stating the obvious. "Anything goes wrong … I need somebody I can count on to help me out. Withdraw some cash, pay the bills. You up to that?"

"You already know the answer to that, Uncle Wally," Colin dropped the street slang sensing his uncle was trying to discuss a serious matter with him.

"Yeah, I knew … but—"

"What do I need to do?" Colin interrupted. He was a cut-to-the-chase kind of guy.

"I need to get you down here," Wally said. "Gotta take you to the bank in person for a few signatures—not much, really—inconvenient."

"When?"

"Sooner the better," Wally said. "Next thirty days."

"Why screw around?" Colin said. "I can be at your place for dinner. We do the bank first thing in the morning—I can be back here by two o'clock tomorrow afternoon. What do you think?"

"I think that would be pretty great. But you don't need to drop what you're doing for this."

"I'm not. That's why I'm offering. Do it now, I have no conflicts. We wait—"

"Can't deny it would be great to see you, Colin."

"Dinner in—you do the cooking," Colin ordered. "I want to know what you've been up to. You got enough wine or should I bring a couple of bottles?"

"I don't keep much around here, but there's no shortage of wine!"

"Cool," Colin shot back. "See you in a few hours," then he added, "anything you need from up here?"

"Not this time," Wally said. "But I have a list of things we can talk about when you get here."

When the call was finished Wally sipped from the beer; it wasn't what he wanted. He pushed it aside and pulled out his operations plan. He studied each list separately before starting a consolidated list on a new sheet of paper.

While he worked, he thought carefully about how he was going to enlist the help he was going to need from his nephew without making the kid suspicious. There'd have to be some legitimate purpose for the supplies he would ask Colin to procure. The explanation would have to be—an idea came to him through the back door of his brain: raccoons and coyotes. Lame, he conceded. But it might work. They were a goddamn plague around the entire neighborhood. He needed to get rid of the marauding bastards, but he was an animal lover. Colin knew that to be true because it was a sentiment the two of them shared. It would be only reasonable he'd want to get rid of them without hurting or killing them. But Colin was smart, too smart for any flimsy shenanigans.

101

Betrayed

He pulled out his cell phone and dialed the Dolans.

"Hi, Wally," Fortunada answered (caller ID again). "How was your trip?"

"Hi, Fo," Wally replied. "Successful. And I didn't forget your things."

"They were just convenience items anyway," she said. "Whatcha up to?"

"My nephew, Colin, is driving down for dinner. Gonna spend the night. You and Danny Boy be offended if I invited you for drinks but didn't offer dinner?"

"You really think you needed to ask?"

"I wouldn't hurt your feelings for anything, Fo," Wally said. "Just that I haven't seen the boy since Poppy's memorial service. Wanted a little private time with him."

"What time for drinks?" Fortunada asked laughing into his ear.

"Call you when he gets here."

"See you then."

Wally frowned and went over his list again. There'd be a lot to add, but Colin didn't need to know any of that. He highlighted the few items he'd need Colin's help with and ran his story through his head a few times while he finished up.

Downstairs he dug a package of chicken thighs out of the freezer and set them to defrost in the microwave. Over the next hour Wally organized a simple dinner.

For the past two hours Wally'd been brooding out on the terraza with a half empty bottle of wine when the doorbell rang a little passed five; normalcy he reminded himself—*pretense*; none needed it more than Colin, he figured. He scrambled to his feet and jogged to the front door.

"Hey, Uncle Wally," Colin said when Wally swung the door open. He didn't wait for an invitation to come in. "You look … okay … sort of," Colin lied. The way his uncle looked scared the hell out of him. He sidestepped the four steps down from the foyer with the heavy bag he carried.

"The paradise effect," Wally lied, ignoring how he knew his appearance must seem to his nephew. "What's in the bag?"

"Figured we'd punish a couple of bottles of your wine tonight," Colin said. "Picked up some replacements." He set the bag on the counter and pulled out two bottles of Brunello di Montalcino and two Far Niente Cabernets.

"Goddamn, Colin," Wally said. "Those aren't replacements. That's the start of a cellar!"

"They won't survive long enough to be cellared," Colin assured his uncle laughing. Then he turned and engulfed Wally in a bear hug. "Seriously, you look pimpin' … comparatively speaking, of course." Colin laughed. It was forced.

Wally wasn't a hundred percent sure just what that meant but went with it. "Neighbor friends've been force-feeding me." He managed a grin and realized just how much he'd needed to touch flesh that was part of the life he'd shared with Poppy.

"Don't fight 'em," Colin said, pushing Wally back by the shoulders, scrutinizing him more closely.

"I'm doing better," Wally went on lying. Perhaps it was only a partial lie. He was doing better. He was gradually regaining focus, even if it was in the form of some absurd obsession. But what he now contemplated required he not just regain some strength—he needed to get stronger, and he was going to have to conscientiously work on his endurance. He'd soon need a lot more stamina than he could muster for now.

"You'll meet them," Wally said. "I invited them for drinks. Hope you don't mind."

"I'll behave," Colin promised, chuckling.

"You don't need to be anything but yourself kid," Wally said too seriously.

"Joke, Uncle Wally … just a joke. Lighten your ass up!" Colin ordered with a toothy grin. "Or I'll be forced to put you in one of my hammer-locks!"

"Oh God … not your smelly pits!" Wally feigned a painful grimace. "You gotta forgive me kid," Wally said, throwing his hands in the air. "Everything feels serious to me these days. I gotta lighten up, I know." He shook his head and went around to the kitchen side of the counter, "Ready for some wine?"

"Now you're talkin'," Colin said.

The sun was still above the horizon but obscured by distant clouds. It was warm enough to sit outside but cooling fast. Wally set out the cheese and crackers. "Here," he said, stepping out onto the terraza to recover the half empty bottle of wine he'd been teasing. "Let's finish this before we get into … wait. Forget that," he said, walking back into the kitchen. "Fortunada loves this L.A. Cetto Zinfandel. You and me … we're going straight for the gold." Wally retrieved the corkscrew and proceeded to liberate the cork from a bottle of the Far Niente.

"Now that's what I call good resource management," Colin approved, following Wally's instructions.

Wally took down two clean glasses and poured the Cabernet. He held his glass up to the window and let the light glow through the deep blackberry flush of the wine. "Even a depressed psycho like me has to appreciate the pleasure in this," he said, as honestly as he'd spoken to anyone for a long time. He stuck his nose all the way into the wide globe of the glass, closed his eyes and inhaled the bouquet of the dark, rich wine.

When he looked up, Colin was having a whiff himself, watching him over the rim of his glass. "It's great to see you really enjoy this, Uncle Wally."

They savored the wine in silence several moments. Wally set his glass down, opened his cell phone and dialed the Dolans.

"Just got here, Fo," he said into the phone. "You and Dan come on over." He looked up at his nephew. "If I get them over here now," he explained before sipping again from his glass, "we can have the whole of the evening to ourselves."

~~~~

103

Betrayed

Dan slowly nursed a Scotch and bragged about the golf course. Fo was a bit more aggressive with what was left of the bottle of Zinfandel and hoped out loud Colin might come for a longer visit sometime when she could make dinner for everyone.

Wally'd struggled to find an opening to bring up the subject of the pack of raccoons and coyotes plaguing the neighborhood trash cans. When he did, Dan Dolan dismissed the problem out of hand suggesting poison or a twenty-two rifle could solve the problem. Colin raised his eyebrows and stared at Wally over the lip of his glass listening to Dan's solution to the problem.

It was a fleeting moment but Wally couldn't have scripted it better if he'd tried.

"You don't have to leave already," Wally said when Fo announced it was time for them to go.

"You guys need to have your evening. There'll be other opportunities," Fo predicted.

"It's not that big a deal for me to get down here," Colin affirmed.

"Well then, don't make it too long 'til we see you again," Dan said jovially. "You swing a club?" he continued.

"Been known to hack it around," Colin admitted.

"Drag your clubs down sometime," Dan said, jostling Wally's shoulder. "I haven't been able to get the big hitter here back on the course yet."

"You got it," Colin said, intending to do as promised.

Wally hugged Fortunada and she immediately turned to Colin for the same. Dan settled for a slap on Wally and Colin's shoulders before he and Fortunada slipped down the staircase at the side of the terraza.

"Give us a call for drinks and dinner tomorrow," Fortunada called to Wally over her shoulder.

"I'll let you know, Fo," he promised.

CHAPTER 22

Wally had the chicken ready to go onto the grill. He set the flame low. "Get you anything?"

"I'm good."

Wally went back inside, dumped a can of refried beans into a pan and lit the oven. "You'll love my Mexican-style garlic bread."

"I'm gonna pop one of those Brunellos," Colin announced. "Whadda ya say?"

"Here … couple of clean glasses." Wally pulled open a cupboard door, retrieved two large-globed goblets.

"Chicken smells pretty good," Colin noted, stripping the foil cover from the wine bottle. "You wouldn't actually let your friend do that to those coons and 'yotes, would you?" he asked absentmindedly, worrying the cork from the bottle.

"They're trouble, but you know me," he went on. "Bad as you and your mom. I don't want to kill them." Wally stirred the beans, and then headed out to the grill. Colin handed off a glass of the elegant red wine as his uncle came around the counter. "What gave you the idea to buy this?" Wally pointed to the bottle with his glass.

"Remembered how much you and Aunt Poppy liked it. Just thought it sounded nice."

"Expensive as hell!" Wally said over his shoulder.

"Caught a nice gig with Siemens," Colin replied without elaboration.

"You mean, Siemens … as in the global technology giant?" Wally asked looking up from the chicken.

"Yeah," Colin confirmed. He made little of the detail. "They want me to interface a software system between them and NASA on an emergency vehicle response control system." Wally simply stared at his nephew who sipped casually from his glass. "You know …" Colin went on explaining, not noticing the look of admiration and wonderment on his uncle's face, "make all the lights turn green exactly when the cops or firemen or ambulances need them."

"Jesus Christ, Colin … you know how to do that shit?" Wally marveled.

"Nope," he admitted matter-of-factly, then grinned mischievously, "but I know how to make their computers talk to each other and interface with NASA's satellites."

Wally started pulling the chicken from the grill. "Slide that garlic bread in the oven, would you? And give the beans a quick stir if you don't mind.

"You know, Colin," Wally said, shutting the grill down, "your Aunt Poppy would be proud of you. That sounds like one helluva job you're working on."

"Consulting fees are nice," he said closing the oven door. "They like my work ... I could potentially pick up contracts all over the world to convert municipalities onto the program as they adopt the system from Siemens."

"Wow!" That was all Wally could think to say.

"So what's your plan for the coons?" Colin asked, moving the conversation.

Wally put two pieces of chicken on Colin's plate and took one. He shifted around the counter and finished serving the food.

Colin poured more wine.

"Like I said ... bigger problem for me ... I'm not into killing them." Wally only half lied. "I have this idea to tranquilize and relocate them."

"Sounds complicated," Colin was saying, cutting into the chicken.

"It'll give me a project," Wally countered, biting into a thigh. "Good!" he mumbled, chewing the hot fowl.

"Yeah," Colin agreed. "How you gonna do it? Tranquilize them, I mean?"

"Did a little research on the Internet," Wally said without looking up from his food. "Thinking I might ask if you could find a way to get me what I'd need."

"Been waiting for you to let me give you a hand," Colin said, noisily crunching a piece of garlic bread—completely oblivious of the trap he'd just stepped into. "You were right," he went on, indicating the piece of bread, "this is great."

"You're about to get your wish, kid," Wally said looking sideways as he lifted a fork full of beans to his mouth. "Enjoy your food. We got a lotta ground to cover tonight."

While they ate Wally let Colin catch him up on the state of affairs with Poppy's family. His mom, Ellen, was busy. His dad was constantly on the go. He said he didn't hear from his grandmother or grandfather but Liz called his mom fairly regular. Jake seemed to be failing slowly but steadily. The weight of Poppy's death was so heavy on him the sisters doubted he'd ever recover. They worried knowing Dolores hid her feelings from everyone. No one could ever be quite sure about the hurt that dwelled inside the woman. From what Colin gathered from his mother, Liz was on the juice all the time, smoking marijuana and popping meds for her depression—hallucinogens when she could score some.

"And you?" Wally wanted to hear.

Colin swiped his napkin across his mouth, wiped chicken grease from his hands, pushed his cleaned plate away, refilled his and Wally's glasses and leaned back in his chair. "You want it sugar-coated Uncle Wally or straight up?"

It was the first time Wally ever noticed that demeanor from his nephew. Truth was, it was hard for Wally to see the young man as grown up, an accomplished professional, respected and sought after in his field—an independent thinker. Colin was Poppy's little boy. "Straight up, Colin …" Wally replied, "you doing okay?"

"I guess you could say I'm doing all right. I miss her in ways I had no idea I would." He paused a moment. "You know, she emailed me every week. I took her being there for granted. Now …" he paused again, lifted his wine glass, "I mean how the hell was I supposed to know what was going on in her head?"

Wally didn't say anything.

"I feel guilty a lot. I didn't know how she was feeling," Colin admitted.

"I was sleeping next to her every night and I had no idea," Wally confessed. "How in the world could you imagine you should have any insight about anything? Don't let it do that to you, Colin."

"Yeah … I talk to mom about it sometimes. Think I'm getting okay with myself. But I'm pissed off all the time about it. Know what I mean? Just feels like … I … somebody … should do something, but I don't know who or what. Guess I'll get passed that, too," he concluded unconvincingly.

Wally made no attempt to address Colin's issues. He fought so hard against his own he literally felt incapable of offering any advice a young man as intelligent as Colin could use. "Help me clean up," Wally said, getting up with his plate, "we have a lot to go over before we call it a night."

~~~~

"The bank's just a formality," Wally explained as they finished up in the kitchen. "The papers've already been prepared. It won't take long for your signatures. Here's what I want you to understand, Colin. I want you on my account so if anything ever happens to me, that money is yours."

"Like what could happen to you?" Colin demanded to know.

"I'm an old geezer, Colin. People my age … the stress I've been under … still under, have heart attacks and strokes … that kind of, *'if something happens to me.'* "

"You having problems?" Colin was eyeing Wally now, alert for any signs of deception.

"No," Wally assured him. "Simply precautionary. So here's the thing: I deposited all of the life insurance check from—" he couldn't finish the statement. "Two hundred-fifty grand," he finally spit out, "into an account in my name and yours at Bancomer in Ensenada."

"Holy shit, Uncle Wally! I'm not so—"

"Hold on, Colin. Don't get your feelings hurt, kid, but this isn't a debate. The money's been deposited. I've had it all converted to Pounds Sterling. I just want you to know it's there and you will have full access to it. And most importantly, should something—and it will sooner or later,

107

none of us are getting off this space ship alive, Colin—happen to me, I want you to have what's there."

"That's a lot of money, Uncle Wally."

"Okay," Wally continued, ignoring the observation. "So the bank thing is straight forward. You'll get a debit card tomorrow. Use it whenever and for whatever you need. Understood?" Wally engaged Colin eye-to-eye, forcefully. "Understood?" he repeated.

"Uncle Wally, I appreciate what you're doing, and I don't want to hurt your feelings, but I don't need your money."

"No offense taken kid. It isn't about you needing my money. Young man like you ..." Wally went on, wistfully, "brilliant mind, a lifetime in front of you—when you're ready. Find something worthwhile to do with it, Colin."

Colin could see arguing was pointless. "If that's how you want it, Uncle Wally."

Wally'd had no plan to do it, but the wine—the momentum of the moment—he found himself saying, "There's more. Follow me." He led Colin to the wine cellar, which had been fashioned in the cavernous area beneath the wide circular staircase leading to the upper level of the house. At the far end of the cellar, where the staircase descended into the foundation of the main level there was a dark and seemingly useless confined space nearly impossible to access. "See those cases of wine?" Wally pointed to the cramped corner.

Colin squinted into the darkness. "I see 'em," he said.

"Here," Wally said, and turned on the soft backlighting in the cellar. The illumination was a burnt sienna glow, not light, actually, but it did the job. "Better?"

"Yeah."

"Work your way in there and slide those cases of wine over here." Wally pointed to the opposite corner.

Colin did as asked.

"Whatta ya see?"

"Nothing." Colin squinted into the dark space.

"Good ... good," Wally declared. "Slide your hand around behind that right edge there," he said pointing with a long skinny finger. "Doesn't look like there's room, but there is. You'll feel a metal object. It's a release. Press it."

Colin followed instructions. In the shadows it looked like the wine cases had been stacked against the back corner wall of the cellar where the stairs pinched down to the point there could be nothing there but solid wall. But when he found the latch and pressed it, a small door the moment before appeared as the back wall of that part of the cellar, maybe three feet high and the full forty-eight inch width of the staircase at its base, swung inward and opened into a space, dark as the inside of a cow. The small cavern could be accessed only while crouching very low or sitting on the floor.

"There's a light switch close to the latch," Wally coached.

Colin found the toggle switch and instantly the small space was lit. "Holy shit!" Colin half shouted. Colin estimated the space to measure about forty eight inches wide by forty-eight inches deep; since the door pushed all the way open against the wall to the left. Its height must have been about thirty-six inches because Colin figured sitting cross-legged he could actually slide inside the space, which he rearranged himself to do. The right wall was a warren of cubbyholes, half of them filled with orderly stacks of money. "What the hell is this?"

"My safe," Wally confessed.

"I mean these stacks of bills," Colin went on incredulously.

"Yes, well … I told you there was more," Wally said. "Familiarize yourself with the whole space in there. You'll see some of those shelves have documents stored on them. There's more than just the money. Bring one of those stacks when you come out, would you please?" Wally instructed, meaning a stack of money.

Colin spent a few minutes admiring the space and the way it had been designed. From the outside there would be no way to guess a space like that could be housed where it was. The area had been hollowed and reinforced from the inside during construction of the house. His only complaint was the awkward inconvenience of access. But that was, in itself, part of the camouflage keeping the safe undetectable.

He slid himself backward and plucked a stack of money from the cubbyhole closest to the opening before turning off the light and pulling the door closed. When the latch engaged, it clicked a solid sound of connection; it was a high quality device.

Wally stood at the entrance to the wine cellar. "Slide those cases back in place, if you would."

Colin grunted as he spoke. "Okay … we gotta talk." He exhaled heavily, backing out of the space.

"Exactly what I have planned," Wally said. "Brush the dust off," he suggested when Colin was recovering from the back of the cellar.

"Pour us a refill of that Brunello while I get some things from the library."

Wally bounded up the staircase intoxicated by the excitement of having revealed the first layer of the convolutions taking place in his damaged psyche to his nephew.

Colin brushed the front of his black Levis and the tails of his peachy-salmon colored dress shirt, and worked his way back to the great room. He dropped the stack of money on the kitchen counter. Only then could he see the entire stack of bills was hundreds. He spoke to himself under his breath while he poured the wine.

CHAPTER 23

Wally scrambled down the stairs, notes in hand. "Why don't we sit in front of the fire?" The flames made a soft whoosh when the gas ignited. "Come, sit," he encouraged, indicating a chair in front of the hearth.

"Tell me you didn't rob a bank or something." Colin was only half joking. There was no humor attached to his usual casual affectation.

"Well." Wally fidgeted uneasily. "In a manner of speaking ... I did, actually."

"Ah ... Uncl—"

Wally cut short the moaned utterances. "Hold your milk, Colin," he said. "The FBI isn't after me. At least I don't think they are! It wasn't that kind of theft." He went on to confess what he'd done with his credit cards. He admitted Johnny from Mumbai simply represented the final straw from a system, in Wally's sincerest condemnation, contrived to plot specifically against him. "It wasn't my finest moment ... I know ... but—" He seemed to run out of rationale for what he'd done.

Clearly, Colin saw, his uncle felt little remorse over what he'd done.

"I'm afraid there's more." Wally confessed his decision with Commercibank—how he'd barged into Roger Watkins's office, dropped the keys in the middle of the guy's desk and walked away from the house, hadn't looked back—didn't intend ever looking back.

Colin couldn't seem to find his voice. It was the only time Wally could recall the kid having nothing to say.

"I'm sorry if you feel let down, Colin."

"You know you'll never be able to get credit again?" Colin sipped some wine. "And you're gonna be lucky if they don't come after you for credit fraud."

"And what would I need credit for?" Wally scoffed. "I'm sitting, quite literally, on half a million dollars ... guy my age ... what the hell do I need that much money for anyway? And as far as the credit fraud ... those bloodsuckers won't even flinch: too much trouble to come down

110

here and get me. Screw 'em!" Wally concluded, bitterness and contempt dripping from every word. Then he enjoyed a slow, deliberate swig of the expensive red wine.

Colin had no rebuttal.

"You okay?" Wally asked after a prolonged silence.

"Sure," Colin said. He appeared to shake off the revelations. "So what will you do with the money?"

"Well," Wally brightened, "for starters, I'd like you to help me spend some of it to get rid of these pests."

In a pitch that betrayed his disbelief, Colin said, "You mean those raccoons and coyotes?"

"The very same!" Wally affirmed gleefully. He handed Colin the list of items he'd need to get the job done.

Colin studied the list, looked away into the fire, and sipped a little more wine, "Where'd you learn about this drug?" Colin wanted to know, referring to the Ketamine on the list.

"The Internet," Wally answered innocently.

"You even know what this shit is?"

Wally heard the edge in Colin's voice. He held his ground. "Just a tranquilizer—found it on a veterinarian website."

"They call it 'Special-K' on the streets, Uncle Wally. Kids get high with this crap. It's an illegal drug." Colin's mood had begun to turn dark.

Wally didn't back down. "Internet says it's a tranquilizer used to incapacitate animals when zoos or vets need to examine them or treat them." Wally looked right at Colin when he lied. "I had no idea, Colin, there was any other purpose for the stuff."

Colin ignored the exchange and went back to the list. He read aloud, ".50 caliber dart pistol, six darts, and six hypodermic needles for manual injection … a dozen vials of Ketamine—" Colin pronounced the words with total incredulity. "Do you have a clue about how to use any of this?"

Wally was anxious as a loon to let Colin see how he'd been preparing for what he'd started calling his little project. "The articles I've been reading say you get the dosage right—vets get the stuff in ten milliliter vials—you can bring down a pretty large animal. The critter will lose muscle control before the injection is even complete."

Jack Nicholson—the 'Here's Johnny' scene—*One Flew Over the Cuckoo's Nest*—flashed briefly in Colin's mind. "And how would you know the correct dosage?"

"Weight," Wally announced authoritatively, "the animal's weight. I see them all the time. Raccoons go twenty-five, maybe thirty pounds, coyotes probably forty. I know I'm not off by much."

Colin eyed his uncle suspiciously.

"What?" Wally said. "You think I plan to shoot myself with this stuff and get high?"

Colin wanted to tell his uncle he didn't need drugs to get any wackier than he was sounding right then, but he didn't.

Betrayed

It was the first time they'd had words of discord. Neither man wanted this to escalate and end in a way that damaged their relationship.

Colin broke with a softer response. "Of course not, Uncle Wally … but Jesus … I mean all this shit with the credit cards, all this money laying around, you walked away from your house—

"Look, I know what kind of stress you've been under. I don't want to see you dig yourself into a hole so deep you can't get out."

Wally fell back into his chair and stared long into the fireplace. He denied any delusion of being in control as a way of accepting his depression; he held to the underlying fury and rage he felt toward Pace and Taylor. "Well, Colin," he spoke in a subdued, pensive voice, "there is no way out of where I am kid. All I can do is try to survive one day and live into the next and do the best I can. I know I come off a little nutty these days. That's why I came up with this idea of collecting these animals, getting them out of here. It's just a diversion to keep me occupied a while."

Colin set his empty wine glass on the lamp table. He'd had enough alcohol for the evening. "You know I'll help you, Uncle Wally. I told you I would. I just don't want you to get yourself into any trouble—or hurt yourself."

Wally brightened and sat forward in his chair. "Listen, the pistol and darts are not controlled. Cabella's carries both. I could drive up and buy those if you aren't comfortable with the idea." Wally hesitated; he knew the critical element here was the tranquilizer. "I really need your help with the Ketamine."

"I'll have no way to get that stuff except on the street."

Wally shifted uneasily in his seat. "I really don't want you to do that," he admitted. "I was hoping you might have a friend or two … somebody out there on the edge a bit … maybe get one of them to help us out."

"I don't hang out with drug addicts, Uncle Wally."

"No … Colin, of course you don't. I know that." Wally's manner was contrite. "I just meant you're young, on the go a lot … I guess I imagined you probably knew someone who is … not as polished as you … you know … a friend of a friend of a friend kind of thing."

Silence.

"There's this girl I know," Colin began slowly. "Has a brother works at the San Diego Zoo. She told me he's been in rehab a couple of times … I don't know … I can talk to her."

"You need to be careful kid," Wally cautioned needlessly, feeling ashamed for what he was doing—but not ashamed enough to stand down from where he was headed. It occurred to him at that moment to simply confess the plan to Colin—let him decide to be in or out—right from the beginning. Then he instantly considered the insanity of it all and knew he could never cause his nephew to consider what he thought *himself* incapable.

"You think I don't see that, Uncle Wally?" Colin shook his head in disbelief over the conversation he was having with his uncle. "This is scary business we're talking about … to get rid of a few raccoons and coyotes?"

"Colin," Wally gambled, "if you think this is too far out there, just say so … I can find another way." The statement was nothing more than a gambit, for he understood just how difficult it was going to be for him if his nephew did make such a decision.

"I'll talk to my friend, Victoria … that's her name," Colin said. "I'll let you know." He paused, looked to Wally, "Until I get back to you, don't buy anything on this list and don't do anything. Let me think about this … do some research of my own."

"That stack of bills," Wally said, pointing to the money Colin retrieved from the safe, "is $5000. I figure that ought to cover costs … whatta you think?"

"I have no idea, Uncle Wally," Colin said honestly. His voice carried an aura of annoyance in it. "All I can do for now is check it out."

"Okay," Wally agreed nervously, "that's the right approach. But take the money with you just in case you decide there's a way."

"I'll let you know," Colin said.

"We good kid?"

There was a horrible contemplative pause. "We're good, Uncle Wally. Like I said, I just don't want to see you get into trouble … or worse." Colin's body language made it clear he was in think mode. "Just seems like a lot of bullshit to get rid of a few animals."

Wally decided to turn up the heat one final time. "Well," he connived, "guess I could forget relocating the animals … smuggle a gun down here and kill 'em all."

"Shit! Don't do something like that," Colin went off. "DEA or the Mexicans catch you smuggling a gun across the border, we'll never hear from you again." Colin rubbed his hands on his thighs. "Just give me some time to work this through."

"Right," Wally said, satisfied he'd planted the correct seed.

Wally managed to rationalize by lying to his nephew he was protecting him. It is not clear whether he accepted the fact if Colin went through with helping him, he would be defenseless if he did get caught. What would he be able to say? "I was just helping my poor demented uncle get rid of some raccoons and coyotes." Good luck with that!

"Okay, kid," Wally agreed, "just a couple more things to go over."

"Jesus, you mean there's more!" Colin groused.

Wally was truly ashamed he'd generated such a mood in this normally gregarious young man. But the further he went with this scheme the more obdurate his determination. It was a character trait Wally'd relied upon his entire life, tenacity—persistence. *"Show me a job nobody wants to do,"* he'd say, *"and I'll show you an opportunity."*

In the case of Colin, there was, Wally knew, an underlying contempt for anyone who fucked with him or those he cared about. Colin was not above going after his enemies with the intent of exacting his own assessment of justice. Would he go as far as Wally was willing to go? Wally suspected given the right motivating event, the perfect storm of grievance—Colin could easily become a dangerous adversary—and if he chose to be, a considerably more cunning opponent than Wally could ever be. He would never know how accurate his assessment of Colin Craig was.

"You saw the documents in the safe?"

"I did," Colin said.

"All you need to know is that is where I keep every important document I have. As I've told you, my concern is over any complication that might arise if I should become ill or … hell what about a car accident?" he exclaimed reaching over and patting Colin's knee. "The point is … something happens, everything you need, you're going to find in there."

Colin lightened a little. "Anybody besides me know about that safe?"

"Your Aunt Poppy, me and now you."

"We should keep it that way, Uncle Wally."

"I won't tell if you won't," Wally promised, a demented grin spreading across his lips. "One important document in there," he went on, "Popp and I executed a couple years back; the trust on this house. We told you about it because you're already the named beneficiary. Anyway, you'll find it there and a lot of other stuff I'm sure you would need if something came up."

"I really don't like the way you keep saying that," Colin said. "Stay healthy and I won't need anything."

"That's my plan."

"What else?" Colin asked.

Wally climbed out of his chair and looked at his watch. It was eleven-thirteen. He sensed Colin had had enough of more than just the alcohol. He needed to back off. "Whatta ya say we call it a day?"

"Yeah," Colin readily agreed. "It's been a full one." He broke the hold his chair had on him and came to his feet. "What time in the morning?"

"Bank opens at nine," Wally said doing a quick calculation. "It's a half hour drive … figure we'll need about thirty minutes if we can get right in."

"Make the call," Colin said.

"Leave here by eight-thirty … be there when they open … you can be on your way between ten-thirty and eleven." Wally put his arm around Colin's shoulder. "How's that sound?"

"See you in the morning," Colin said, grabbing his tote.

"I really appreciate what you're doing for me, Colin."

"Don't thank me yet, Uncle Wally," he stood holding the handrail a few seconds and stared down to the bottom landing, "but you know I'll do what I can."

"Good night kid."

"Night …" Colin said, and disappeared down the stairs.

CHAPTER 24

Colin was blessed with one of those resilient personalities that allowed him not to dwell, overlong on other people's lunacies. By morning, the previous night's adversities had been evaluated and decided upon. It was Colin's approach to life; evaluate, commit. Do, or don't do, the deed, and be done with it. Too much agonizing complicates life to an extent for which he had neither the time nor the disposition. Had the considerations before him been for the benefit of anyone other than his uncle, Colin would have turned his back, walked away. But the bond with Wally was too strong for that. Besides, what could it hurt if his uncle wanted to chase around in the night trying to catch a few raccoons and coyotes. The truth was, Colin estimated, Wally'd probably never get close enough to the creatures to actually tranquilize anything. The whole idea would fade away due to Wally's inability to hit anything with a dart. Then the tranquilizer would dry up and lose its potency because in the end, his uncle wouldn't use it quickly enough or store it properly.

Colin and Wally'd been close since he was a baby. It went all the way back to when he was still a little boy fighting for his life against the leukemia. What made up his mind about his Uncle Wally happened one day when he was thirteen years old, in remission from his cancer, but still under the cloud of fear that death was just too fucking close for comfort; a comprehension that had come to him all too vividly each time he was sent to the hospital for chemotherapy and he learned another of his friends had died.

His Uncle Wally and Aunt Poppy had come to visit. His dad, Ross, had to work that day and his mom and Aunt Poppy went off for a morning of shopping.

Wally'd asked him what he wanted to do for the day. He remembered vacillating, then asking his uncle if he wanted to watch some porn. Wally'd stared at him several seconds; that deer-in-the-headlights kind of look. "I don't mean go rent some," he'd clarified. "Watch this." He could still visualize the look on Wally's face when he picked up the TV remote, turned on the set and in less than sixty seconds hacked the parental controls his mom and dad had set and went straight to the porn channels. "Jesus, Colin," Wally'd said. "You're gonna get us both in serious trouble." Colin remembered saying back to him, "I won't tell if you won't." And his uncle never ratted him out. What Wally did do was sit with him through a half hour of what Colin later understood to be some pretty raunchy hard-core porn and explain to him this was not about love, and this was not how girls you respected or cared about should be treated. (Sometimes now Colin wasn't so sure about that.) Later when he'd pressed him, his Uncle Wally bought him a *titty* magazine he'd masturbated to for nearly the full year between the ages of thirteen and fourteen.

This was the same man who, the night before, asked him for help with something pretty off-the-wall, but it wasn't any more off-the-wall than what he'd asked of Wally when he was thirteen. So if chasing raccoons and coyotes around in the night with tranquilizer darts was going to help his Uncle Wally deal with the suicide of his Aunt Poppy—how could he say no?

~~~~

The trip to Ensenada was pleasant. The drive along the craggy cliffs of coastline was as spectacular as any stretch of the Pacific Coast Highway. Parts of it were reminiscent of the Oregon coast, absent the hateful winds and arctic cold.

Wally's assurances about the bank proved accurate, and the eye-candy sitting at the reception desk was a bonus, Colin allowed. In less than a half hour he'd signed next to all of the Xs and received his debit card. Director Garza walked them to the ATM where they activated both cards. "I will notify you, Señor Stroud, when the funds are released for your use," Garza promised, and the task was behind them.

"Whatta ya say to an early taco?"

"Sorry, Uncle Wally," Colin said. "I really need to get back before two."

"No need to apologize," Wally said. "I'll make you a cold chicken sandwich at the house while you collect your things."

"Deal," Colin said.

The drive back seemed quicker than the drive in to Ensenada. The atmosphere was relaxed and good-natured once again. Both Wally and Colin felt the tension of the previous night dissipate. Colin spoke with ease of how he planned to talk to his friend Victoria about making a contact through her brother. When Colin drove away that morning, Wally knew the cam in the lock had been turned and it would only be a matter of time before the first pin fell into place that would ultimately open the door to—what? He still wasn't sure.

"I'll give you a call when I figure out how to get this stuff," Colin promised before he goosed the accelerator and sped north.

~~~~

Located south of Rosarito Beach, twenty minutes north of Wally's beach house, perched on a point jutting out into the warm blue waters of the Pacific Ocean, Fox Studios has three sound stages, a huge back-lot and scores of movie sets and memorabilia. Major segments of notable films—*Titanic, Pearl Harbor, Captain and Commander*—even Will Smith in *Independence Day* shot several scenes at the facility. Wally'd taken friends and family to tour the studio many times over the years.

The standout performance of every visit was watching the re-enactment of the rats *(the four legged ones)* abandoning ship as the Titanic was sinking. A Mexican man on site at Fox trained the rats, and they lived there, fulltime, reliving the terror of the horrific event over and over again. They scurried to safety, abandoning ship, each time a tour came through and the lights began to flash and the horns began to blare, signaling the eminent catastrophe. Meanwhile the water would advance—rising cruelly up through the bowels of the dying ship, once more.

Equally fascinating to Wally had been watching what could be achieved with makeup, the way the human form could convincingly be transformed. Wally scrolled the website for a contact number. The best he could do was a number for booking tour reservations. He called it. "I'm looking to contact someone in your makeup department," he told the person at the opposite end of the connection.

The young woman explained those resources were housed in L.A. and those crews and equipment only came down when a movie was shooting. But this young woman, unlike the zombies Wally'd dealt with when contacting the oversight agencies in Arizona, was actually able to make alternative suggestions. She gave him phone numbers for three different makeup artists, but highly recommended a small, oft-used studio in San Diego.

~~~~

At three-thirty in the afternoon Wally knew within the half hour Dan Dolan's right hand would be aquiver in anticipation of his first Scotch of the afternoon. "Never before four o'clock," Dan preached, "but once the bell has tolled—"

It had been one of those strange weather days. It began clear, warm, and sunny during the morning drive into Ensenada. By midday the ocean breeze turned abruptly cool and damp; gossamer clouds slung low and streamed ashore. The warm offshore breeze reversed. The threat of the heavy, dark marine layer hovering out over the water like a beast of prey was about to return—only to be thwarted once more by a shifting warm breeze that blew it all back off the land. The waning sun shone through, brilliant and hot once more.

Wally punched the #5 in the speed-dial list of his cell phone. "Sun's melting the ice," he said to Dan Dolan when he picked up. "We on?"

"Bet your ass," Dolan sang. "Saw the boy leave this morning. Didn't hang around long," Dolan wheedled.

"Bought him breakfast in Ensenada. He had to be back by two."

Betrayed

"Wasn't much of a visit?"

"He'll be back," Wally said. "Get Fortunada. Come on while this sun lasts."

Wally heard muffled conversation through the phone. When the voice cleared again Dan said, "Fo says she's in the middle of something. Wants to know if you wanna come for dinner in a while?"

"Sure," he said, "seems a waste not to throw down a couple while the sunshine's so nice though."

"Didn't say I was too busy," Dan said. "On my way."

"Like I said … ice is melting."

While he waited, Wally dragged two rattan club chairs close together and put out a bag of pretzels.

Dan climbed slowly up the stairs at the side of the terraza. "Man, this feels great."

"Gets my vote, too," Wally said holding out a glass of Scotch to his friend.

Dolan took a long hit from the glass before he collapsed into the chair next to Wally and reached for a handful of pretzels. "Let's play golf tomorrow," he offered.

"Can't tomorrow," Wally said, "but I think I'd be willing to go out later in the week. Whatta ya say?"

"Let me know when you're ready to donate a few bucks."

"Forget the betting bullshit, Danny Boy," Wally admonished. "Been almost a year since I played. Not a chance I'm gonna let you into my pocket just yet."

"Practice!" Dolan warned, "you're gonna need it." Then he laughed.

They sat quietly several minutes, the only sounds, the crunching noise of pretzels being chewed over the top of the ceaseless soughing of surf against craggy lava cliffs, and the distant sharp whistle of a Ferruginous Hawk.

"Bullshit aside … you doin' okay, Wally?" Dan asked, breaking their silence.

"Bullshit aside," Wally replied honestly, "I have my days."

Often in life the spread between success and failure comes down to knowing which bridges to cross and when. Wally saw an opening he hadn't anticipated, but which he recognized as one of those opportunities.

"I need to ask a favor, Dan," he began sincerely.

"Shit! Anything you need you got it," Dan answered too quickly.

"Not that kind of favor, Danny Boy," Wally explained. "This could test our friendship."

Dolan grew wary, "What the hell you askin' me to do?"

Wally held back a moment considering how best to explain something he hadn't completely worked out in his head yet. "In the near future," he went on finally, "not really sure just how far out yet … I'm going to need to cross back into the States without having my passport or Sentri Pass scanned." He let the statement lay there.

Dan didn't say anything. What he'd heard was a dangerous proclamation, but he didn't think he'd understood anything being asked of him in it. "What the hell you up to?"

118

Wally ignored the question. "You know ... if I borrowed your old Honda and didn't look directly into the camera, I'll bet I could slide straight through, flash your Sentri card ... matches the windshield sensor ... nobody'd be the wiser ... guys like you and me ... we're all but invisible to the world."

Dolan drained the rest of the Scotch in his glass and set it on the table. Neither man spoke. Wally felt the press of straining two close relationships in as many days. He slid out of his chair, picked up Dan's glass and treaded off toward the liquor cabinet.

"Won't do you any good ... tryin' to get me shit-faced," Dolan shouted after him.

New ice cubes made clinking sounds as they dropped into the glass. "And ..." Wally continued, "anybody comes asking ... I'd need you to swear I was here at the house the entire time I'd be gone ... anybody comes asking ... I was right here, watching golf, playing golf ... whatever." Wally stood in front of Dan Dolan, held out the refilled glass of Scotch.

Dolan's face was bright red. "You listen to me, you old fart," his voice hoarse with menace, "you're too old to be running around like James-fucking-Bond ... you hear me?" He grabbed the tumbler out of Wally's hand sloshing some onto his pants. "See what you made me do?" he groused, and sucked the top inch out of the glass. "What the fuck are you up to, Stroud?"

Wally ignored his question, made no explanation about anything. "I'd never implicate you in anything, Danny Boy. Something goes wrong ... they nab me at the border ... I stole the car and the card ... give you my word." Wally stood before his friend and looked him directly in the eyes. "When I'm ready, Dan ... I'll need your help."

Dolan dropped his gaze, sat back in the chair, grabbed another handful of pretzels and tossed one in his mouth. He chewed nosily while Wally walked around and settled back into the chair beside him. Dolan sipped long once more from the Scotch, popped another pretzel into his mouth.

Wally knew it was time to keep his mouth shut. His friend would have to come to the decision on his own from here.

After what seemed an eternity, Dolan asked, "How we gonna do this?"

Wally responded thoughtfully, showed no exuberance or satisfaction at his friend's question. "I'll let you know a day in advance. Just leave the car parked in the driveway with the keys under the driver's seat with your Sentri Pass the night I ask. It'll be gone next morning."

There was another long pause.

"How long?"

Wally didn't waver this time. "Seventy-two hours ... more or less," he said. "Need some flexibility. You'll find it back in your driveway ... gas tank full."

"Like I could give a shit about that!" Dolan said, mordantly. "You're crazy as a loon you old coot," he went on. "Just make goddamn sure you don't get your ass caught!"

"Hey!" the familiar voice shouted from below. Fortunada was halfway up the stairs when the two of them clambered to their feet to greet her. "You guys got a monopoly on this heavenly sunshine or can anybody get in on this?" She glided over and deposited a small plate of sliced cheese next to the pretzels.

"One red wine … coming up!" Wally announced. "Take this chair," he insisted, pointing to the seat he'd just vacated.

"Dinner's almost ready," she said to no one in particular. "You two tuned up?"

CHAPTER 25

During the night the thermal engine supporting the warm offshore breeze, holding the lurking marine layer at bay, finally spent the last of its energy. Heavy, wet clouds descended right down to the ground, clawed their way back onto the land making visibility dangerous. It was hard to believe it was the twenty-third of June with summer just getting into full swing. June Gloom was living up to its full potential.

Wally turned on the fireplace. He stood with his back to the hearth drinking a second cup of tea while the air warmed. It was only seven-thirty. The fog was likely to lift as the sun's warming rays penetrated its misty veil. Besides, he thought, he sure as hell didn't want to get hung up in rush hour traffic in Tijuana.

At eight forty-five when he climbed into his truck and headed north, the fog was still truculent. But, with the light of day it had become wispy enough to forfeit tolerable visibility. He'd decided to test his theory about the Border Patrol's indifference that day at the Otay Mesa crossing. San Ysidro was strictly for non-commercial automobile traffic returning to the U.S. from Tijuana, a million cars a day. Otay Mesa handled the commercial truck traffic out of Mexico into the U.S., and was three miles to the east, nearer the airport. He figured to find less traffic and a more relaxed atmosphere in the few lanes devoted to automobiles alongside all the semi trucks and trailers being combed through with drug dogs and random searches.

He cut through Tijuana's narrow streets and drifted the circles around its Gloriettas like a mouse trying to finds its way out of a maze. He was able to Q in the Sentri lane no more than twenty yards from the border gate. There was so little traffic that day the U.S. Border Patrol shut down two of the three lanes they kept open for non-commercial traffic.

Wally pulled his golf cap down low over his eyes and slipped his Sentri Pass card out of his passport holder. When it was his turn to pull forward, he held the card out the window for the scanner—looked down and away for a split second, as though he was grabbing something from the console in the truck. A bright flash from the camera signaled for him to pull the rest of the way forward. At the booth the officer glanced at him and said, "Have a nice day, Mr. Stroud."

"If the card-scan and the windshield chip match," he'd told Dan Dolan, "*guys like you and me are invisible.*" He was convinced that if he remained calm his idea to cross into the U.S. using Dan's car and Sentri Pass would go undetected.

At nine fifty-four Wally was back in the U.S., negotiating his way onto the 905. Less than four hundred yards after he'd entered the freeway a sign read, "Toll Road—El Cajon—Tecate Pass." He'd forgotten the bypass was there.

A few miles north he glided onto the ramp that exited to the 905 Expressway. Just before the 905 rejoined the 805, he turned onto the frontage road and drove another two miles north. The place he was looking for was easy to spot. There was a large orange sign on a very tall steel pole he'd seen many times from the freeway, Allied Storage.

It was an easy left turn off the access road when he came upon it. Wally pulled into the lot and parked. There were no cars around. It seemed so hushed he wondered if the place was even open. When he tugged on the right side of the double doors it pulled open. There were two people behind the counter. One was a thirtyish Hispanic man who looked up but didn't acknowledge him. The other was a young Latina woman with long black hair falling onto petite shoulders that were covered by a tight black stretchy t-top accentuating her large breasts.

"May I helped chu?" she offered. Her nametag read, Xochille.

"I need a garage to store an extra car," he told her. Wally wanted one that was easily accessible; preferably a corner unit.

"Chu like me chow de one I think?" she offered. Xochille didn't wait for him to answer. She grabbed a large ring of keys from a peg on the back wall and came around the end of the counter. "Come," she ordered him, moving in the direction of the front doors. She couldn't have been taller than five-four and probably tipped the scales around ninety-five pounds, but wearing five inch black patent stilettos she stood eye to eye with him.

Wally walked slightly behind her; letting her lead the way. The bottom of the black t-top hugged her petite, curvy hips snugly. The tight jeans she wore defied his imagination as to how she had managed to squirm her way into them.

On the east corner of the farthest row of storage buildings from the office, she announced, "Here ees de one." She fumbled with the keys and finally inserted one into the heavy-duty lock. When she squatted down to grab the handle at the bottom of the door, Wally feared she was about to topple off the stilettos and hurt herself.

The door rolled up to reveal a twelve by twenty-five space. "Just what I was looking for," he pronounced.

The amount of documentation involved in renting the space felt to Wally like he was completing an escrow for the purchase of real estate. Had he been forced to endure the process with someone other than Xochille, it would have been an unbearably tedious event. Listening to the musical lilt of her accent, watching the insouciant way she embraced her job, almost mitigated the boorish procedure.

It was eleven-thirty when he finally eased into the northbound lanes of Interstate 5. When he came off I-5 at the 6A Exit toward downtown San Diego, he saw a Taco Bell and peeled off into the parking lot. He and Poppy liked the ninety-nine cent Taco Supreme. Who the hell could get drippy over a Taco Bell, he thought? And yet, there he was. They always ordered two. "I'm doing the best I can, Popp," he said to himself. "I miss you so much."

~~~~

Colin Craig was just taking the ramp onto State Highway 163 West. He punched the accelerator of his Crossfire Roadster and zipped seamlessly into the fast moving traffic. He'd been driving south on Interstate 805 coming from a late-morning business meeting in Escondido with a Siemens VP. Now he was racing not to be late to a lunch date with Victoria Elliott and her brother Kyle.

He whipped off the 163 at Park Boulevard exit and took the next left onto Presidents Way. The winding, short streets gave him a brief opportunity to put his sports car through its paces. One block ahead, he made a right onto Pan American Road East and took the first space near Plaza de Panama at the west "Employees" entrance to the Balboa Park Zoo.

Unbeknownst to Colin, his Uncle Wally was sitting at a Taco Bell, less than two miles away.

Colin slid out of his pearl-white Roadster wearing a pair of snug-fitting designer jeans accented by Alessandro Dell'Acqua suede sneakers. The espresso-colored t-shirt he wore with the red silhouette of a stripper bending over was topped out by an unstructured tweed, single-button blazer with the sleeves pushed part way up his arms.

Victoria and Kyle were seated at an outdoor table of a quaint French bistro next to the museum entrance. Victoria saw Colin walking across the plaza and ran to him.

Victoria was a stunning twenty-two year old who worked for one of the makeup companies at Nordstrom's department store. She had delusions of creating her own makeup line someday. Victoria was a leggy brunette with jet-black eyes, always in costume. As you might expect, her makeup was impeccable, highlighting every elegant feature of her photogenic face, and she had the body to match. That day she wore a slinky crimson sleeveless dress that stopped about three inches below the knee. The black peep-toe platforms she wore turned her into a Victoria's Secret model.

He gave her a peck on the cheek. "'Sup, my ho?" he asked, a wide grin spreading across his handsome face.

"You're pimped out!" Victoria shot back. "You do that just for me?"

"You know I did!" Colin lied. Victoria liked to club. Plus the sex was without risk. So far—no strings attached. He treated her well, spent freely on her, although they were not yet exclusive.

Betrayed

Victoria's older brother Kyle worked at the San Diego Zoo. She said he was a coke-head but he'd never been arrested; had no record. She confessed her family'd done two interventions and her parents paid for two trips to rehab. She wasn't sure but suspected he still snorted from time to time. But, according to her, he loved what he did at the zoo. He shoveled shit out of cages, but he did a lot of other things, too. She had no idea whether he'd be willing or able to help, she'd told Colin honestly enough.

"Kyle," Victoria said when they strolled up to the table, "this is my friend, Colin."

The brother was not at all what Colin expected; tall, thin, average looking with light brown hair. He seemed shy, almost intimidated. Colin extended his hand to find a solid grip but indirect eye contact. Kyle wore a khaki shirt with the sleeves rolled up and ordinary Levis. If he was still snorting, any evidence of it was undetectable.

"How's it goin'?" Kyle asked, showing no actual interest in an answer.

"Things are good," Colin replied.

"I need to eat and run," Victoria announced. "Sorry."

The waitress fetched another iced tea like the two she'd brought earlier and collected their orders.

"So," Colin began, "Victoria says you've been at the zoo a while."

"Little over two years," Kyle answered before taking a sip of tea.

"Like animals a lot, I guess," Colin said.

"Better than people," Kyle replied evenly, and glanced up at Colin. Then he looked at his sister as if to ask what she was getting him into.

What Victoria had not disclosed to Colin was the genuine affection between brother and sister. Kyle cared about his sister. It was instantly apparent to Colin, and Victoria's eyes told him what she had not about her fondness for her brother.

"When we were kids," Victoria disclosed, "all he harped about was how he was gonna be this big important veterinarian when he grew up." Kyle fidgeted uncomfortably in his seat. Victoria made the pronouncement with a degree of detectable admiration.

"So what derailed you?" Colin asked sipping his tea.

"Just shit," Kyle replied, his demeanor and tone letting Colin know he wasn't interested in a probe of his private life. "Vic says," Kyle went on, "you want to get rid of some coyotes or something. What's that all about?"

Colin glanced at Victoria momentarily before he turned back to Kyle, "Something like that," he said. "It's a little more complicated. My uncle has a place out in the country, coyote and raccoon problems. But he's not down with just shooting 'em. He has this crazy idea about relocating 'em."

"I like your uncle," Kyle said deadpan. "So why doesn't he just hire a company to take care of the problem for him. There are people who do that kind of thing you know."

"Yeah, well, he wants me to help him figure out how to play Wild Kingdom or something so he can open up a can of—knock-'em-on-their-asses-long-enough-to-cart-'em-away-before-they-wake-up-and-have-him-for-lunch." He lifted his glass of tea. "He lives in Mexico. They want to shoot them."

"Assholes," Kyle said under his breath. "Full grown male raccoon's a bad-ass animal," he admitted. "Go forty … fifty pounds. Better be damn sure he's knocked him down before he tangles with one. Piss one off without controlling it and you're gonna be in serious shit!"

"So you know quite a bit about how to do that?" Colin asked.

"I help out once in a while when we need to examine some of the animals."

The waitress appeared with their orders. Colin turned his attention to Victoria.

Kyle ignored them and ate quietly. Colin caught the occasional hooded glance from him.

"Haven't seen enough of you lately," Victoria said to Colin after she'd taken a sparrow-sized bite out of her sandwich.

"New gig," he said. "Big deal … you know how it can be."

They ate without speaking.

Colin dropped his left hand to Victoria's knee, discreetly slid it under the edge of her dress and grazed the outside of her thigh. She gave him a lascivious grin and spread her legs slightly. "Anything goin' down Friday night?" he asked, withdrawing his hand slowly.

"Me on you … if you're taking me out," she said.

Colin looked over at Kyle. Kyle's disgust was apparent. "She does have a way with words," Colin said, shaking his head.

"He's heard worse out of my mouth," Victoria said, defending herself. "Remember … we grew up in the same house."

Kyle glared at her.

Victoria rushed through the rest of her food in a flourish. "I really do have to get back to work," she explained. "Regular coming in for a makeover."

Colin stood to walk her to her car but she declined the offer. "I'm just over there," she said, pointing a few yards away to her VW Beetle.

"Call me if Friday night is for real," she shouted back to Colin from several yards away. She spun in a full circle that caused her hair to flair out around her head like a shampoo commercial but continued toward her car, smiling prettily over her shoulder.

"We're on," Colin shouted, watching the swing of her butt as she walked away. She either had no panties on or the thong she wore was very, very tiny. With Victoria, Colin knew, it was an even bet as to which it might be. He enjoyed her naughtiness and was reluctant to apply his Uncle Wally's standards for treatment of women to this one.

"You love her?" Kyle wanted to know. "Or's she just a good lay?"

"I like her a lot," Colin answered without holding back. "Love … that's a big question for now … know what I mean?" Kyle looked down at his empty plate.

Colin stacked his half-full plate onto Victoria's two-thirds full plate just as the waitress appeared to see if they wanted anything else. "Everything all right?" she asked, noticing the uneaten food on the two plates.

Betrayed

"Everything was fine," Colin replied. "Got time for a beer?" he added quickly, looking to Kyle.

Kyle looked at his watch, "What the fuck," he said. He reclined into his chair and stole several furtive glances at Colin.

"So, how does your uncle figure to get the tranq he's going to need for this project?" The waitress set two twenty-ounce drafts down in front of them. "Guns and darts are easy enough," he pointed out.

Colin studied Kyle for several seconds. "You're not what I expected, Kyle," he began. He stopped for a swig of beer then returned the glass casually to the table. He decided to let the guy reveal himself rather than make any unilateral judgment. "Use a quick couple grand?"

Any previous attempt at bravado fizzled instantly. Kyle's fingers played at the base of his beer glass. "Who couldn't?" he said less assertively.

Colin continued to measure him several seconds. There was a considerable pause before he said, "Let's talk about taking down that full grown male raccoon." He leaned forward in his chair, placed his elbows on the table. "What am I going to need? What equipment? What tranquilizer? The works ... everything I'd need to do the job professionally ... safely ... no risk of injury to me or the animal?"

Kyle leaned in with him to the table and glanced around the space. There was one other table left that was safely out of earshot. "Equipment's no problem," he said softly. "I can get the gun and darts from a lot of places."

"Untraceable?" Colin asked.

"Why?" Kyle wanted to know, instantly suspicious.

"Because the tranquilizer that's going to be used in it will be illegal," Colin said. "Because it would just be smart business for both of us ... all of us. I want to keep it invisible. Know what I mean?"

Kyle simply shook his head in agreement.

"The tranquilizer?" Colin followed up rapidly.

"Depends," Kyle explained. "*Special-K's* all over the streets. Just gotta be careful making a buy."

"Got any contacts?" Colin asked eyeing Kyle carefully.

"Vic tell you I'm using again?" That possibility clearly pissed Kyle off. He leaned back in his chair, pulled his glass of beer with him and took a long pull.

"Are you?" Colin asked. His tone was compassionate, not accusatory.

"None of your fucking business," Kyle shot back loud enough for the waitress to look up. They were silent several seconds after the vituperative outburst.

"Didn't mean to pry," Colin offered.

Kyle settled down. "Look," he said, "Ketamine by itself won't do what you want, anyway. I mean ... it'll do it, but it takes several minutes to work. If the animal is in open ground, it's gonna run a long way before it drops. Your uncle handle that?" Kyle asked, back under control.

"No," Colin answered emphatically.

"Okay," Kyle began quietly again, leaning back into the table with Colin. "If you want to knock the animal down fast … almost instantly … you'll need a cocktail."

"Cocktail?"

"A cocktail," Kyle repeated. "When we want to knock down say … a baboon, for example … and those fuckers are serious bad-asses … we use a cocktail; Rompun, Sucostrin, Ketamine combo. Our vets use it to immobilize the animal within seconds. They want 'em back up, they use an injectable antidote; brings 'em out of it in minutes." Kyle's eyes were bright; he was animated as he spoke and Colin didn't doubt anything the guy said.

Now Colin glanced around at the tables. The other couple was gone. The waitress was across the courtyard. She looked at him as if to ask if they wanted something else; he shook his head no.

"Okay, Kyle," Colin said. "Clear enough to me you know what you're talking about. So what I need for you to get me is the dart pistol … untraceable … six darts with that cocktail you described and enough of the antidote … just in case. Oh … and clear instructions for determining the required dose."

"Just like that?" Kyle jeered at Colin. "Like you're ordering another beer?"

"Can you do it?" Colin asked.

Kyle sat back and studied his hands like some magic solution to the proposition before him might pop out of them. "No way in hell I do this for two grand," he finally said.

"What's it gonna take?"

"Four," Kyle announced defiantly. Colin sat back and looked away. He gave the impression he had other options but Kyle knew there were no other options like the one he was offering his sister's friend. "I'm taking a big risk doing something like this for you," Kyle added.

Colin appraised him carefully. "How long?"

"How long, what?"

"How long will it take to get this together?" Colin asked.

"Can't say," Kyle said. "I have to have the right opportunity. Can't just go marching in and lift those drugs."

"How you gonna do it?"

"How the fuck would I know?" Kyle said agitated. "You think I do this kind of shit all the time?"

Colin didn't respond to Kyle's abusive outburst.

"You gotta be patient," Kyle went on. "I need the right set up … when we're working with the animals. Not gonna put myself at risk by stealing that shit outta the drug locker. Gotta come from stuff we're using on a project. Lots of times they send me to retrieve the drugs and clean up after. I'll get it first chance … best I can do … if you want me to help you."

Betrayed

It wasn't what Colin wanted to hear, but what Kyle was telling him was perfectly reasonable. And the last thing he wanted was to be responsible for Victoria's brother getting nailed because of something as incredibly stupid as this project his Uncle Wally set him on.

"Okay," Colin agreed, "in your own time."

Kyle watched Colin pull out his money clip and begin peeling off hundred dollar bills. He counted twenty before he stopped and returned the bulk of the wad to his pocket. Colin cupped the bills in the palm of his right hand, palm down, and slid his hand across toward Kyle.

Kyle looked up again. The waitress was inside. He raised his left hand slowly to the table and eased the bills out from under Colin's palm.

"Balance on delivery," Colin said.

Kyle knew it was not negotiable.

Colin scribbled his cell number on a napkin and slid it over in front of Kyle. "Call me when you have everything," he told him.

Kyle stood up and shoved the napkin in his shirt pocket. "Gotta go. Thanks for lunch," he said, and walked away leaving Colin to pick up the tab.

~~~~

At the Taco Bell off Exit 6A Wally was just finishing his two Taco Supremes. The lunch-rush was easing, but the place was still jammed full. He ceded his table to a couple of young Hispanic guys wearing shirts that advertised a local landscape company.

128

CHAPTER 26

Wally pulled his pickup onto Sixth Avenue. At West Date he made a right turn and doubled back a block onto Columbia, driving south. He was in the heart of Little Italy. It seemed like there was a restaurant in every storefront.

Odd area for a makeup artist to be located. Maybe they were somehow connected with the community theatre he'd noticed near the corner of Beech and Ash. He'd driven passed where the address should have been twice and still couldn't locate the place. Frustrated, Wally pulled into a public parking lot paid five dollars and walked.

The environs had a lot going for them, more than just the abundance of great Italian restaurants and offbeat coffee houses. The streets making up Little Italy were also crammed with small jewelry shops and art galleries, tattoo parlors and eclectic furniture stores. If you substituted the exotic furniture stores with head shops and tie-dye boutiques, there was a distinct feel of Telegraph Avenue, Berkeley in the late sixties, (They tie-dyed everything in the sixties.) though Wally imagined not a single pedestrian he'd bumped into would've had the slightest notion of what he was talking about had he made that analogy.

Walking back north along the west side of Columbia, he found a funky, narrow stairway leading off the street to small rooms above a storefront advertising a Notary Public and Currency Exchange.

At the top of the staircase he found three doors opening off the cramped landing. The splintered wood flooring creaked as he turned slowly in the tight space. Two of the doors were solid wood, vintage—caked with years of bubbled, flaking russet paint revealing more than a few coats of light green and cobalt—specks of white over-coated through the years. Their only identification were dense collections of cobwebs and pulverized dirt at the corners of the jams informing a visitor they hadn't been opened in an extraordinarily long time.

The third door had a pane of glass in the upper half that brought to Wally's mind the image of Raymond Chandler's classic P.I. character, Phillip Marlowe from his 50s novels. The glass was opaque, discolored—yellowed with age—octagonal shaped wire embedded. The lettering read: Shoe Repair instead of Private Detective. The address above the door was the correct number. He figured the makeup artist was gone, or maybe the girl at Fox Studios made a mistake.

Cracking the door slightly, Wally peeked in. A skinny Asian person, Wally wasn't immediately certain about gender, with false eyelashes, dark red lipstick and both cheeks rouged bright pink peered back at him from behind the counter as though he/she might have been hiding there; eyes enlarged with—who the hell could know—just enlarged. The Joel Grey character of the movie *Cabaret* came into Wally's head.

"Can I help you?" the person ventured cautiously, with a strong lisp. There was the heavy scent of ginger in the foyer.

Wally stuttered.

The vision recovered. "Come on in, honey," he said. "I'm Carl. I won't bite ... unless ... oh dear, I'm just teasing. How can I help you?" Carl smiled. Wally wasn't sure which feature, the bright gold front tooth or the blond-tipped cascade of hair atop his head, being restrained by the neon-periwinkle scrunchy, he found most remarkable.

Wally collected himself and asked about the makeup artist.

"You're in the right place, honey," Carl answered. "Everybody knows us around here. Just never got to changing the door. Who needs the expense? Right?" Carl giggled easily at everything coming out of his mouth. Maybe it was his reaction to the look on Wally's face. "So what can we do for you?" Carl batted his eyes. Wally wasn't sure the guy, and by now he was pretty sure it was a guy, wasn't pulling his leg. In the background, Crosby, Stills & Nash had, "*eighty feet of waterline—lightly making way.*" The loft was capacious and disparate.

Wally stepped toward the counter, no doubt a holdover from the place's former incarnation as a shoe repair shop. He explained what he wanted. Carl listened thoughtfully, asking questions here and there.

"You came to the right place, sugar," Carl declared suddenly.

"Maurice!" Carl screeched in a lungy burst of reverberation. "Maurice! Where-are-you?" Carl sang the last words escaping his glossy crimson lips like a skier schussing off a giant ski jump.

Presently, a bulky young man bearing a remarkable resemblance to Gerard Depardieu appeared from some distant warren, moving with no sense of urgency in spite of Carl's bleating. "*Bonjour,*" he said to Wally in a thick French accent before turning on Carl. "*Qu'est-ce tant important pour que tu m'appelles de cette facon, mon amour?*—And what is so important you 'ave to cry out for me in this way, my love?" ·

"Calm down, Maurice," Carl ordered the Frenchman. "This is Wally," he announced in a febrile frenzy, smiling and giggling. "Wally wants to know if we can show him how to ... look like someone else?" Carl continued to giggle as if he were an insider to a well-kept secret.

"Ees no treek," Maurice said, looking Wally up and down, "No treek at all."

"There, you see, handsome boy," Carl said, busting a toothy grin. "I told you so."

"Follow, please," Maurice ordered, taking control. He led off down an aisle between two rows of double-hanging racks of costumes. There was a distinct odor of stale perspiration or maybe it was cigar smoke—interesting more than offensive.

Maurice was about five-nine, built like an NFL linebacker with thick, powerful shoulders and no neck. His waist was narrow and the gray polyester slacks he wore were stretched too tight over his muscular thighs. His head was topped by a mop of disheveled, sunburned curls and he sported a gold ring in one ear; altogether conservative by his partner's standards.

At the back of the loft were two dressing mirrors, each equipped with all manner of makeup brushes, creams, liners; paraphernalia of the trade. Wally was overwhelmed and suddenly uncomfortable. The two shop owners seemed harmless enough, but he felt ill equipped to control where the situation might lead.

"Sit," Maurice ordered, pointing to a chair looking a lot like an old-fashioned barber's chair to Wally. "Now," Maurice began, his accent punctuation to the exotic setting, "what it ees you 'ave in mind, *mon ami*?" It felt to Wally more of a demand for the information than a request.

What if they wanted to know the why behind what he wanted? It hadn't occurred to Wally what he was asking from them was what they did—make up actors—usually for studios or larger productions—but once in a while for small neighborhood productions from surrounding communities. *Every* client walking through their doors wanted to look like someone else. That's what a makeup artist was about—turning actors into characters. And as Wally was about to discover, Maurice and Carl were very good at their trade.

After Wally explained what he wanted, Maurice stalked around one side of the chair framing his features from a variety of angles. Carl crept like a cat in the opposite direction making his own appraisal.

Maurice was clearly the man in charge. "*Quel visage souhaitez-vous voir où vôtre était une fois, monsieur?*—who shall I transform you into, monsieur Wally?"

During all of Wally's maniacal imagining he'd never actually considered who he might want to look like performing the hellish acts he was edging ever closer to committing.

Sometimes, deep in the abyss of darkness—beyond the *hour of demons,* when he would lay tossing and turning, agonizingly awaiting the first glimmer of day, desperate for any relief from his torment, Wally would turn on the TV. Lately *The Bourne Identity* was the HBO loop running through the *demon's hours.* Wally wasn't sure exactly how many times he'd seen bits and pieces of the movie, but Matt Damon's face jumped into his mind's eye when Maurice pressed him for a face to create. "Matt Damon," he answered. "You know ... like *The Bourne Identity*?"

"Ah, monsieur, Wally," Maurice declared. "You wish to challenge my skills!" Maurice crossed one arm over his chest, placed an elbow in a palm and rested his chin in his hand. Again he pussyfooted about, studying his subject. In a flurry he ordered, "Carl, you will bring for me, please, a composite chest plate."

Betrayed

Unquestioning, Carl spun on his heels, threw back his head and wiggled off to an aisle at the far corner of the room. Maurice shouted after him, "And bring a black t-shirt, *s'il te plait.*" The satellite radio channel had moved on to the Eagles ... *"They stab it with their steely knives—but they just can't kill the beast ..."*

They waited, listening to Carl curse while he dug through stacks of things unseen. In a few minutes the Asian man pranced toward them holding a large object resembling a suitcase in one hand and a black wad in the other.

"*Levez-vous s'il vous plait,*" Maurice ordered, indicating his desire for Wally to stand. Without pause, Maurice began unbuttoning Wally's shirt and stripping it off. No time to object. "Turn, please," Maurice ordered, manhandling Wally's shoulders steering him in the desired direction. "Arms like thees," Maurice instructed, lifting Wally's arms out like a scarecrow on a pole.

"Ooh ... look at you, honey!" Carl cooed. "Not bad for a boy your age," he said, batting his fake eyelashes. On the radio the Eagles sang: *"You can check-out any time you like—But you can never leave!"*

"Carl ..." Maurice pleaded patiently. "Excuse please, monsieur ... he ees 'armless." Wally contemplated all of the lyrics to *Hotel California*.

The chest plate reminded him of the Batman movies. He was shocked at how snug it fit, how comfortable it felt, but mostly how natural the texture was. It clamped below his neckline and around his outstretched arms like a sleeveless shirt. When Maurice snugged the Velcro straps down the side of his rib cage under his left arm, it felt like the prosthesis had actually become part of his body, no restriction of movement, no pinching around the décolletage or the waist. Wally found he could bend normally with the device on.

"Put the shirt, please *mon ami*," Maurice said, retrieving the wadded up mesh t-shirt from Carl's hand.

Wally squeezed the stretchy black t-shirt over his head and pulled it down around his waist. All the wrinkles disappeared when the shirt stretched over his bulked up chest. He was stunned at the transformation. The six-pack in his stomach rippled and the pectoral muscles seemed huge ... were huge.

"*Et la texture se sent très naturelle,*" Maurice pointed out, touching Wally's new chest. "It ees latex composite," Maurice explained; like real flesh

"Sit, please," Maurice said guiding Wally into the chair. "Aye 'ave make le bat a man ... with ees joker. Aye 'ave make le pirate a madhatter ..." Maurice took one final appraising look at Wally's features and pronounced, "Aye shall make you into Monsieur Bourne."

Wally wasn't entirely sure what the guy was babbling about except he did understand that last part, about turning him into Monsieur Bourne.

As per Wally's insistence, the two men provided a step-by-step running tutorial on how-to as they progressed through each step. Carl began with cotton balls and witch hazel, cleansing Wally's facial skin. They reminded him to shave before beginning this preparation.

Maurice began with a latex mask, which provided a structural pallet from which he would build. "Apply the spirit gum like thees," Maurice explained, "far down the neck so the latex cannot be noticed up close."

Wally watched as his age and identity began to morph into another, much younger face with detectable nuances even at the early stages. Carl worked the forehead, cheeks, nose and chin. The stuff looked and felt like real skin as near as Wally could tell. This must be what receiving a skin graft was like, he thought, absent the pain, of course.

It was after three in the afternoon when Maurice and Carl finished the renovation of Wally Stroud. Over the course of the final hour of work, Wally'd been forced to sit with his back to the mirror. As the two makeup-men applied the final touches, they stepped back, stood side-by-side and evaluated their work. "Ees perfect, no, mon ami?" Maurice said to Carl.

Carl grinned, raised his left eyebrow and walked around behind Wally. "What do you think, sugar?" Carl asked lasciviously, spinning the chair around so Wally was staring into the mirror. Wally was speechless. "Here," Carl went on, and stripped the protective apron from around his neck. "Stand up, sugar."

Wally stood. He was staring, not into just the face of Jason Bourne, but at his entire image. Matt Damon, body and face, moved every time Wally did. Wally edged close to the mirror and touched places on his face. He turned his head one way then the other, marveling at how real the human hair wig seemed. He feared instantly he would never be able to reproduce the perfection he was gazing at, but Maurice and Carl assured him with all the pieces carefully precut by them, all Wally really needed to do was glue everything in place carefully, just as they taught him— like a paint-by-the-numbers canvas—and he could achieve the very same result.

Nothing in Wally had changed physically, yet he felt somehow—empowered. "This is more than I imagined," he said, transfixed by what he saw before him. He leaned in to the dressing table mirror and inspected the work closer. "Extraordinary," he uttered.

"You one handsome boy, sugar," Carl agreed. "If Maurice wasn't here—" he completed his thought with a series of eye-flutters, giggles, and hand wringing.

Maurice indulged his boyfriend's carrying-on with the roll of his eyes, as if he'd heard it all before. He mumbled something to himself in French, shook his head sardonically, and slapped his huge quads. All Wally got out of it was, *mon ami.*

It required slightly more than two hours for the makeup artists to convert him as he'd asked. Now he asked them to reverse the process and save or replace each piece of latex so he would be able to reproduce the effect when he was ready—for his acting debut. But before they progressed too far, Wally produced a snapshot of Dan Dolan and pressed the two for recommendations to make him look something like the man in the photo.

"Look the face," Maurice said pointing. "Ees already very like you, no? Let your face grow a leetle beet thee whiskers, and put thees with the glue," he said, handing Wally a thin mustache piece, "and put thee golf hat, also … yes?"

Betrayed

When Wally reemerged from his incarnation as Matt Damon, he held the lip-merkin under his nose and turned his head from side to side. He tried to imagine the total effect with a couple days' growth and decided it would be close enough for his purpose.

~~~~

At the end of it all, they stood looking at the collection of materials, much of it stacked in the chair in which Wally'd been seated. Another large collection of bottles and baggies was piled to one side on the makeup table.

Maurice charged off without explanation and returned with a black duffle. The bag contained mesh foldout pockets made specifically to hold the bottles of glue, ointments, cotton balls and brushes. He and Carl began carefully transferring everything Wally needed into the bag, making one final explanation for the use of each article, as it was stored in its individual place. Even in the aggregate, the items contained in the bag struck Wally as remarkably light considering, ironically, the gravity of their effect.

Carl appeared genuinely sad for the afternoon to be ending as he went through the process of totaling what Wally owed. When he'd finished his calculations, he slid the itemized bill in front of Wally and began to explain. "The chest plate is not nearly as expensive as that human hair wig, Sugar."

But it was not the prices of the physical articles that shocked Wally. On the last line Carl had written, Artistic Instruction, and itemized the expense at one thousand dollars.

Wally stared several moments at the amount. Then he looked up at Carl.

Without apology, Carl said, "We're queer, honey … but we ain't cheap!" He giggled and went on. "And the bonus is … we don't need to know nothin' 'bout what the production is you're performing in, know what I mean?" Carl batted his eyelashes, pursed his lustrous ruby lips, blew Wally a kiss and turned his cheek, a coy gesture. Wally then understood the unease he'd suffered over these guys having any curiosity as to the 'why' behind what he asked of them had been wasted energy.

"Fair enough, Carl," Wally agreed, shrugging. He laid thirty-seven one hundred dollar bills on the counter.

Carl's eyes grew as big as saucers. He pulled his finely manicured, purple painted fingertips with little rhinestones embedded to his cheeks and exclaimed, "Oh, my, Wally, sweetie, if you don't need that receipt, I think Maurice and me might be able to give a little discount."

"Don't need the receipt."

Carl reached down, grabbed the stack of hundreds and handed two back to Wally. "We're good," Carl announced.

Wally agreed.

R.P. McCabe

CHAPTER 27

It was six-thirty when Wally emerged from the narrow staircase at street level. He was allowed to check out and leave the *Hotel California* after all. The lot where he'd parked his truck was his immediate worry. By his calculation, he was over on the half-day fee. The lot was the type where you insert the fee into a mail slot that matches a number painted on the space your vehicle occupies.

He deposited the duffle bag behind the driver's seat and locked the door. Traffic was heavy at that hour. Wally had no more appetite for driving in San Diego's crazy rush hour traffic than he'd had earlier that morning for the Tijuana traffic jams.

Stuffing another five bucks into the payment-box, he noticed a white chalk mark like a pox on the rear tire of cars parked in the spaces opposite him. No doubt his own vehicle was afflicted. He pushed several times before the folded bill slid it into the slot. Legal again, he could disregard the cancerous chalk-mark.

The two ninety-nine cent tacos from his early lunch at Taco Bell had long since ceased to stanch his hunger. Wally thought he remembered an Italian restaurant where he and Poppy had eaten years before. On India Street, as he recalled. Maybe he could find it.

Back to the corner of Beech and Columbia, west on Beech toward the harbor. The street swept upward in a gentle incline from Harbor Drive; back up the hill heading away from the water. Walking downgrade offered a stunning panoramic view of San Diego Harbor.

The sun was low against the horizon and dramatic silhouettes had begun to form. Even the bumper-to-bumper traffic hysterically attempting to evacuate downtown San Diego with their blaring horns and toxic exhaust couldn't detract much from that view. Wally slowed his pace to a near shuffle taking in the spectacle. The déjà vu began slowly.

The thing about anxiety attacks is a severely depressed person never knows what tiny reminder, a song, a scent, a sound, a familiar shadow—a flash of sweet memory showing up uninvited—will trigger the powerful neurotransmitters in the brain that will send them bounding pathetically out of control, transforming one into the visage of a mortally wounded animal.

That evening the tall masts of the Star of India, her huge sails furled onto her crosstrees and booms offered sharp contrast and a mixed metaphor against the backdrop of the F-22 Raptors being put through successive touch-and-goes by the young Navy top-guns over on North Island, Naval Air Station. Could there possibly be anything more awe-inspiring, Wally thought, innocent of what was coming. The chest-crushing, thunderous explosions of the Raptor engines obliterated one's senses—even the air one breathed, the concrete upon which one stood, skyscrapers vibrating and quivering like the reed of a saxophone being blown in one long, elegant, shrill note; the notion that annihilation, or the crush of the cosmos themselves was about to obliterate all of mankind? All the while, the Star of India bobbed peacefully in her birth bearing the proof of her obsolescence or perhaps just a reminder of how simple things had once been. It was in that moment Wally saw her face once more; she was still locked inside her car.

As if in syncopation to the chest-crushing detonation of jet engines, Wally's brain exploded under the full weight of Poppy's suicide all over again. He stumbled, reached for the edge of a concrete planter box overflowing with freshly planted petunias, geraniums and purple alyssum on which he could steady himself. He tried to control the powerful emotions, but it was no use. His eyes brimmed, and then overflowed uncontrollably. His body began to tremble; his breathing became shallow and irregular. His heart was racing so hard he could feel it trying to erupt out of his chest—and his head, blood gushing frighteningly through his cortex. He managed to keep from falling and seated himself on the edge of the planter. As another Raptor made a low turn to the south shooting out over the Pacific, Wally turned his eyes to the sky. "Poppy ... we would have found a way." Then he broke down and bawled like an injured child.

It was several minutes—three or more, maybe—before he was able to bring himself under control. A young woman placed her hand on his shoulder and wanted to know if he was all right—did he need help? He was unable to speak. The urge to find the little restaurant where he and Poppy'd shared an evening together no longer interested him. Instead, he turned back up the street and returned to his truck. He remembered driving passed a La Quinta Inn on Columbia. Four blocks south he doubled back to find it. While he was checking in he eyed a Peter Piper Pizza down the block. The desk clerk said they delivered.

Wally found his room and ordered a medium three-item pizza. The order clerk said it would take about forty-five minutes; plenty of time to find a liquor store. The pizza arrived fifteen minutes after he'd downed his first glass of wine.

He pushed the pizza box into the center of the small round table with the bottle of wine and plastic glass. While he ate, he dug out a local directory and opened it to used car dealers. On a note pad he recorded three whose addresses sounded close to the La Quinta. Finally, he'd polished off half the pizza and all of the wine. Bill Maher was riffing on what a fuck Dick Cheney was when Wally passed out.

R.P. McCabe

CHAPTER 28

Perhaps it was the entirety of the previous day; maybe the anxiety attack acting like a pressure relief valve on a dangerously full gas drum; maybe it was the wine—maybe it was all of that and more, but Wally didn't wake at the *hour of demons* that night. In fact, by his standards, he'd overslept because it was nine-thirty before he was dressed and vacating his room. He drove the few blocks to Harbor Drive and found a café near East Village hanging on stilts out over the edge of the bay. The waitress turned a heavy ceramic coffee mug on the table upright and filled it with a strong black brew without asking whether he wanted it or not. Wally smiled, nodded and asked for milk and Splenda. He ordered a light breakfast. "Food'll be up in a few minutes," the waitress pledged in a rattly voice hoarse from years of smoking.

In a few minutes a slice of wheat toast and a single lonely egg was staring back at him like a giant orange eye—an equally lonesome slice of bacon rested at its side.

Out in the channel a white sloop tacked back and forth with a huge genoa drawn tight and pulling hard afore a full mainsail. Wally watched, admiring the skill of the person single-handing the sailboat.

Elaine, as attested by the white nameplate pinned above her breast, hovered over him. "Tabasco?"

He ate and watched the lone sailor make his or her way up the channel against the backdrop of the carrier USS Constellation with its compliment of F-18 strike-fighters bristling on the flight deck across the harbor.

Wally pondered what he'd set in motion toward fulfilling his *operation*. Any notion he'd once held the idea was just some mental occupation diverting his focus from the nightmare his life had become was falling away rapidly. He was as caught up as a whitewater rafter bucked by roiling rapids out of his boat being tossed and tumbled, dragged along; dashed against obstacles unseen and beyond his control down a raging river. But he was getting closer. He could feel it in his marrow. Colin would come through for him. Of that he had little doubt. He pushed aside the bitter brew of black coffee and headed to the cash register.

Elaine scurried over. "Everything okay?" she croaked.

"It was," Wally answered without elaboration. He guessed Elaine in her late forties. She looked hard. Dull blonde hair exposing even darker roots the texture of straw, the beginnings of what would become heavy wrinkles creased around her mouth from a lifetime of sucking on cigarettes. The fact her life hadn't been easy was written over the entirety of her presence. Wally dropped a five-dollar tip in front of her.

"You don't need to do that, mister."

Wally ignored the offer to return his money. Flipping open the list of car dealers, he asked Elaine for directions. "Just get me in the vicinity," he said.

"This one's only a few blocks from here." Elaine pointed to the second address on the list.

Relying on the waitress's directions, Wally drove back north on Harbor Drive and turned east one block onto West Grape to get back to the PCH. From there he drove north again a short distance until he found West Laurel. The sales office sat tucked back under an elevated section of I-5 at the corner of Kettner.

A middle aged Hispanic man who identified himself as George pounced on him just as his foot hit the pavement. "Got about anything you could be looking for," George announced, and Wally thought of Snake Oil. There was no discernible accent. He would have preferred dealing with a real Mexican or at least a guy who called himself Jorge.

Wally detested car shopping, but appreciated George, like Snake Oil, had to make a living. He tried to affect friendly, explaining what he was looking for. "Just be a work car. Need something mechanically reliable ... good gas mileage, know what I mean?"

George showed him three different cars. Wally couldn't get interested in any of them. "I want a car nobody'll notice," he mused. "Don't want to worry about car thieves ... *entiendes*?" But George didn't speak Spanish.

"Consider an older Toyota?" The salesman headed toward the rear of the lot. Wally followed. "Just took this one in," he was explaining, arriving at an unattractive minty-green 2003 Toyota Camry. "It don't look like much, but it's a one-owner car with low miles." He reached over and opened the driver's door. "Older fella owned it. Passed away. Son didn't want the hassle of selling it. Lemme buy it off him." George eyed Wally assessing the car. "Make ya pretty nice deal."

Wally eased around the perimeter of the Camry. It did nothing for him. Exactly what he was looking for, a car that wouldn't leave any impression.

"Son told me the old man hardly drove it the last twenty-four months," George added.

"You checked it out mechanically," Wally wanted to know, "breaks ... A/C?"

"'Bout as much as I could," George admitted.

"Can I drive it?"

"I'll get the key."

The salesman trotted off toward the office while Wally slipped behind the wheel. The seat was comfortable. He turned and regarded the back seat; plenty of room for the cargo he had in mind. He was beginning to think if George-the-car-salesman didn't want too much for the heap, he might be able to end his car search right here.

"Here you go," George said sliding into the passenger seat. "Make sure it has enough gas."

Wally guided the key into the ignition and turned it far enough to activate the electrical system. The gas gauge registered less than a quarter tank, more than enough for a test run.

"Head down Laurel here to the PCH and make a right," George directed. "In a few blocks you'll be able to cut back under the freeway and come up onto I-5. Give ya the feel of it in traffic as well as how she runs on the highway."

The Camry had plenty of power. "What size engine?"

"V-6. Can't find a more reliable engine. Economical, too. Twenty-six, maybe twenty-eight miles to the gallon on the road."

Wally turned under the freeway and swung into the on-ramp joining I-5 South. He hammered the accelerator as he nosed into traffic. The car answered without faltering. In a few seconds he was coasting along with the other speed violators at seventy-five.

"Whatta ya want for it?"

George hesitated, perhaps calculating both the real answer to the question as well as what he guessed he might be able to get Wally to agree to.

Wally interrupted his deliberations. "It'll be a cash deal," he said without taking his eyes off the road.

George hadn't responded yet when Wally turned at the First Avenue exit.

"Make a right on Cedar and you'll run into the PCH," George directed, pointing toward the intersection. "I'd like to get twelve out of it."

"For a six-year-old plain-Jane?" Wally exploded. "Thought you said you wanted to sell it." Wally's attitude turned unfriendly in a flash. It was a new failing he seemed unable to control: Piss him off and it was all downhill from there.

"It's a nice car," George whined, "low miles, good economy. S'what people are looking for."

"What people?" Wally spit out combatively. "You have a stash of buyers the rest of the car world doesn't know anything about?" The remark was harsh, confrontational.

In a different time in his life, before—Wally knew, he would not have been so acerbic. But this wasn't that other time and he wasn't that Wally Stroud any longer. *Life's a toilet, Georgie-boy. Not careful—just might get pissed on!*

The two men were silent when Wally made the right turn onto the PCH.

George fidgeted in his seat, turned sideways to partially face Wally. "What would you want to give me for it?"

"Nothing," he replied. "Not interested anymore."

"But—"

Betrayed

"But … nothing!" Wally said contemptuous, cutting the man off. "I offered you a cash deal … friend. You tried to fuck me. I'll go find somebody who really wants to sell a car today and I'll make him...or her a cash offer."

George, whose face was now pyretic over his dark complexion, exhibited a collection of little white balls of spittle at the corners of his mouth. He was in a catatonic state when Wally came up to the corner of Laurel. "Okay," he blurted out. "Best price … nine thousand … cash."

"Seven, take it or leave it," Wally countered, never taking his eyes off traffic.

"You can't be serious," George argued in disgust.

"Should've thought about that when you tried to gouge me," Wally said. "Not a penny more." And his manner offered not one ounce of mercy.

"But I won't make anything on the sale at that price," George whined.

Wally turned onto the used car lot and drove to where the car had originally been parked. He turned off the engine and slid out in one swift motion. "Too bad," he said turning the knife in the wound he'd inflicted, "rides nice." He slammed the driver's door and moseyed in the direction of his pickup.

"Wait," George pleaded with him. "Can't we discuss this?"

"Nothing to discuss," Wally shot back, his demeanor as frosty as he felt deep in his core. "I said I'd give you seven and you weren't interested."

"But I dropped all the way from twelve to nine. Can't you work with me?"

"Nope," Wally replied truculently, and kept moving away.

"Goddamn, man! I've got a family to feed just like the next guy."

At that plea Wally stopped. Clearly he was not the person he'd once been, but there were elements of that man still alive deep inside. He stared at the pavement, turned slowly. "Eight thousand," he said in a manner that heralded to the car salesman if he wanted the sale he'd better accept the offer without further negotiation. "And you have until I get behind the wheel of my truck to take it or leave it," Wally finished, validating George's acuity.

"Cash … right now … today!"

"Fair enough," Wally deadpanned. "Let's do the paperwork."

As it turned out, George owned the lot. He was also the only salesman and his own cashier and title clerk. It was noon by the time he'd finished the documentation. George wanted to know how Wally intended taking physical possession of the car.

"I'll take it now," Wally said without explanation. "Be back later for my truck."

"I go home at eight. Better be back before then." Now George's demeanor offered no further civility.

He handed Wally a large envelope containing all of the documents.

The instant George finished taping the paper plate to the rear of the Camry Wally sped off. He pulled into the first Quick Stop he saw and filled the tank.

Retracing his route of the previous day, he cut to the 805 by way of E Street. At the entrance gate to Allied Storage he punched in his security code. The electronic sensor buzzed and the gate retracted. Wally drove through, continued along the front row of doors to the end building and made a left turn. He stopped in front of his garage, got out and unlocked the door then eased the Camry into the space.

The same Hispanic guy who'd ignored him the day before greeted him in the office. He declined his offer of assistance. "Waiting for a taxi," he said. "Cab company said about twenty minutes."

Five minutes into his wait the front door swung open. Wally looked up to find the Salvadoran girl from the day before come in carrying three large white plastic bags draped over one arm and a Hermes-Orange handbag slung over her opposite shoulder.

To his surprise, the young woman recognized him. "Señor, Estroud?" she called to him, tilting her head in his direction. Clearly she was surprised to find him sitting there. She smiled and continued toward the counter. At the service desk she unloaded the bags and set her orange purse to one side. "'Ector," she said politely, "there *ees* your *lonsh*." Then she turned and ambled toward Wally.

Her gold spiked stiletto heels with dainty ankle straps clicked, castanet-like against the shiny concrete floor as she made her way across the lobby. She wore loose-fitting, white cotton peasant pants that stopped mid-calf and shimmered transparent when she passed between Wally and the front windows. Her hair was pulled back in a long pony tail that fell not from the nape of her neck, but closer to the crown of her skull like the flowing tail of a show horse. A bright turquoise blouse was open to the soft golden fleshy fold of her cleavage where a large abalone shell from her drop-necklace nested. The loose-fitting blouse fell below her waist, eliminating any possibility more than her well-shaped thighs were visible through the cotton pants. Wally stood. A wisp of Jasmine or Vanilla wafted up around her. Even in his ghastly mental state, he could appreciate the stunning femininity of this lovely young woman.

"Chu needed someting more, Señor Estroud?" Xochille asked earnestly.

"No ... miss—?" Wally paused for the young woman to complete her name.

She didn't get it.

"I'm sorry," Wally said. "I don't know your last name."

"Ees Barbosa. I am Xochille Barbosa."

"Nice to see you again, Miss Barbosa," Wally said, proffering his hand. He encountered a surprisingly robust grip. "I don't need any help, thank you. Just dropped off my car. Waiting for a taxi."

"'Ector...ee 'as call a taxi for chu?"

"I called one myself. But thanks for offering."

"Okay den," Xochille said, her straight white teeth gleaming at the center of her friendly smile. "Ees nice to see chu again. Chu needed someting, chu can calling me, jes?" Xochille smiled broadly. Wally found the challenge of her thick accent charming.

"Thanks," he said. With that Miss Xochille Barbosa turned and retreated behind the counter where she retrieved her own *lonsh* and disappeared.

Betrayed

There was ample afternoon remaining when the taxi dropped Wally at the used car lot. He climbed behind the wheel of his pickup without going into the office. As he backed the truck around, he bumped the horn two short bursts and jabbed his hand high out the driver's side window when he pulled west onto Laurel.

The lot owner appeared in the doorway of the sales office but didn't return the wave.

He drove to the same QT where he'd fueled the Camry earlier. While he waited for the pump to fill the tank, he ticked through the remaining items on his list. He was determined to complete the grueling task he'd undertaken over the last two days; stockpiling the supplies on his operations list.

He pulled out of the QT in search of the Home Depot near Qualcomm Stadium. Between HD and Target, Wally knew he'd find most of what remained on his list. It struck him as sadistically humorous how such innocuous items as he sought would lend themselves to creating hell on earth for two unsuspecting criminals.

"I'm getting there, Popp," he said under his breath while he drove north up I-5.

In this way, in increments both measurable and not, Wally was forfeiting his moral compass, never one momentous moment of decision; just one small step after another, inexorably sliding toward nihilism and the total conquest of the human being he'd once been.

CHAPTER 29

Wally didn't make it back across the border until after eight o'clock that night. Another grueling day—but productively gratifying. Check marks went down his list: disguise, car, tubing, painter's hoodie-footie, ratchet straps, muriatic acid.

The instant he was inside the house he dropped his bags in the middle of the floor and called the Dolan's; normalcy, he reminded himself.

"Just walked in, Fo."

"I can warm up leftovers for you," she offered.

"No thanks. Just wanted to let you guys know I made it back in one piece. Gonna grab a shower … call it a day."

He flipped his phone closed, hauled his bags up to his bedroom.

The solitary confinement distinguishing Wally's reality was no longer bearing down on him as it once had. Replacing the loneliness was this obsession gradually consuming his life, having the effect of exchanging despair for his grandiose hallucinations. Trouble was, the longer he dwelled in this fantasy world, the stronger his belief it wasn't a fantasy at all. It was merely a matter of precise execution: no more a fantasy than a mission into a Vietnamese jungle with the specific objective of bringing back an enemy officer for interrogation.

Wally slow-drizzled Johnny Walker into a tumbler of ice cubes and took a sloshy sip. He located a box of crackers, sliced off several chunks of cheddar and delivered it all to the table where the Scotch was getting colder by the minute. He treated himself to another nippy swig before retrieving a lap-blanket. Flipping off the lights in the house, he felt his way back onto the terraza where he slumped deep into his favorite chair. The glow of stars supplied plenty of light for sipping Scotch and nibbling.

Wally's immediate thoughts drifted to Colin and the tranquilizer. He had a strong urge to call the kid; update progress. But he knew; too aggressive—too much spotlight—red flags would begin to appear—if they hadn't already. No, he needed to remain patient. Colin wouldn't let him down. "Just give him time," he told himself.

A movie was playing in his head constantly these days. The scenes were becoming more and more vivid. Details were being added. The operation was expanding in ways he couldn't have imagined just weeks earlier; taking on a life of its own; supplanting his real life. What was coming into focus struck *him* as appropriate justice. He would internalize and visualize and mentalize until there was nothing left but the doing of the thing.

A damp breeze blew off the ocean. He pulled the blanket higher onto his chest and considered if he *was* going insane. Maybe going wasn't the right gerund. Maybe he already was insane. Possible. For if he went through with what was living in his brain like a lesion—then what? Why think about consequences now?

Four months into the process of attempting to understand how to grieve. He'd done what he could to intellectualize what was happening to him. He'd bought the Kubler-Ross book. Identified the stages. Wally had no trouble understanding his collapse—his broken psyche: denial, anger—toward the criminals whom he held ultimately responsible—toward Poppy, too, for having done such a thing to him. He'd tried in desperation to bargain with a deity he did not believe existed, but to whom he was willing to give a chance if He decided He could change what had happened. Ultimately, he thought he'd accepted things for the reality they were, and slipped away quietly into a kind of resigned, psychotic exile where he thought he might continue to slide deeper until he finally slipped into oblivion himself, only to discover that it was still not over.

Grief, such as coursed through his being, was not of a kind that followed prescribed guidelines or recognized progressions—or maybe it did and the insanity he feared in himself was indeed a deeper consequence of a grievant's inability to cope? He found himself revisiting the various stages over and over—not in any transparent order. The one stage he'd finally grown comfortable with, the one stage offering at least a possibility of catharsis was the stage in which Wally'd decided he *preferred* to dwell—anger. His deepening *anger* toward Pace and Taylor, the oversight agencies, Commercibank, the credit card companies, the FBI— The longer he brooded over the entirety of what happened, the angrier he became.

Wally had become dangerous by now. Not just to himself, but to the institutions and people in his path to whom he attributed his misery. He was clever. He was resourceful. More frightening than all of that—he didn't fear death or retribution in an afterlife—and now he was committed.

The night was crisp and clear as crystal. The sea was dotted with lights from close on shore to beyond the horizon. Distant twinkles would flicker then disappear, then flicker again. Experience told him he was seeing small vessels below the curve of the earth's surface, perhaps one hundred miles at sea considering how high above the water he was. Each time the swell of the Pacific lifted the boats back above the curve of the horizon, their lights would flicker, making them visible a few moments before they fell off the edge of the earth once more.

R.P. McCabe

To the south a Carnival Cruise liner was leaving Ensenada Harbor. The cruise ship was lit up like a floating city. Wally watched her make for open water knowing a small crew, perhaps no more than three, was all that manned the bridge, while vacationers ate and danced and drank without a care in the world. It had been so long since his spirit had known that kind of serenity he realized he'd forgotten how it felt. He took another long dram of Scotch and acknowledged he would never know such carefree joy again.

The combination of fatigue and 80-proof-whisky gradually crawled up from his feet to his brain and sought control. He slipped in and out of consciousness. Each nod of the head lasting longer and longer. Each fitful attempt at fighting off its control, weaker and shorter until at last he succumbed to the inevitable.

The auroral green numbers on the digital clock of the microwave read two thirty-seven when he draped the damp lap-blanket over a bar stool in the kitchen on his path stumbling upstairs to bed.

~~~~

For a second consecutive night the *hour of demons*, those dismal hours between three and five a.m., passed without the voices jolting him awake. Maybe it was the alcohol, though that had never worked before—even when he'd tried to get drunk enough to pass out and stay that way.

At five-thirty he rolled over slowly—confused. He lay perfectly still on his right side staring through the open French doors out across the quiet Pacific. His only moving part, his left eyelid, opening—closing—opening once more, until it remained so. Gradually his brain engaged: The sun was spring-time-bright, velvety-golden and soft. It was dead calm outside. Even the endless Pacific swell crashing incessantly on the black craggy lava flow that bled off the side of the golf course below his house was barely audible.

He didn't want to move. His piss hard-on was rod-stiff and his kidneys hurt from holding it in. If he rolled over he knew he'd have no choice but to get up and take a leak. The sheets were warm; womb-like, he imagined. In any event, he didn't relish leaving them just then. There were no ugly voices in his head reminding him of the hell he was living or the apocalypse he was intent on visiting upon the two men who'd forced Poppy to fly away from him. He fought the urge to allow the anguish of it all to come flooding back.

He forced himself to roll into a sitting position on the side of his bed and stared aimlessly out over the empty ocean. There was a slight crispness to the air in contrast to the warmth of the Egyptian cotton sheets he'd abandoned. Finally, he rose to a standing position, his piss hard-on collapsed to half-mast. He walked fully nude out onto the terrace of his third floor bedroom, stretched like a cat and yawned. By the time he was standing at the guardrail looking out over the edge of the steep hill below, his hard-on had become fully flaccid and now he needed to piss in the worst way. He walked to the north side of the terrace where he was certain he could not be seen and let it go over the edge. It was a subtle pleasure he doubted anyone would appreciate.

145

Betrayed

But he didn't really give a shit. The act felt liberating to him—good enough. He watched the long stream fall in an expansive arc nearly seventy-five feet before splattering as spray onto the boulders below.

He went to his closet, pulled on a pair of khaki shorts and a red pullover. After he shaved and brushed his teeth he returned to the closet, dug out his white and brown saddle golf shoes and a gray Ping golf cap. Sliding into the soft cleat shoes he flopped the cap onto his pate and skipped down the staircase.

Wally set the teapot on the stove, broke two eggs into a skillet and punched the down lever on the toaster. By the time the eggs were ready, two pieces of toast were jumping into the air and the teapot was hissing. Turn off the fire. Set a cup to steep. Smear *I Can't Believe It's Not Butter* onto the toast. He nibbled while he slid his eggs onto a plate and finished building his cup of tea.

Sipping hot tea, sopping up egg yolk with his toast, deliberately enjoying breakfast. He'd made his mind up nothing was going to stop him from having one peaceful day. Maybe the pretense of normalcy had secreted itself inside him in a way he hadn't understood. So many unknowable effects were working on him it wasn't out of the question. While he savored a second cup of tea he flipped open his phone, hit the autodial and pressed the speaker button.

Three rings sounded. "Yeah?" A hoarse voice croaked.

"Still interested in that round of golf we talked about the other day?"

"Beginning to think you'd never get around to it," Dolan said. "You've been on the run ever since you got down here." He paused. Wally could make out Dolan sipping. "Getting things under control?"

"Making progress," Wally said. "How long before you're ready?"

"Pick you up with my cart after I eat."

"I'll be hitting balls on the range." Wally closed his phone and headed into the garage to dig out his golf clubs. They'd spent the last year relegated to being used as a rack for hanging things on or leaning gear against.

When he pressed the electric garage door opener, the heavy copper door creaked as it began retracting into the ceiling. The bright morning sun was growing more intense and now it splashed straight into the open garage.

He liberated his golf bag from its burden and pulled it out into the open, brushed the cobwebs from around the base of the bag. The irons needed to be washed. Wally found two sleeves of new balls in a pocket and several used ones he figured he'd need when he encountered the holes along the ocean—several required shots out over water or across deep craggy ravines. He shouldered the bag and headed off in the direction of the clubhouse.

CHAPTER 30

More than a week had come and gone since the day Wally'd received the call from Colin on the golf course. The weather continued unseasonably calm and warm; the exact opposite of Wally's condition. The *hour of demons* returned to haunt him all week and he was once more suffering from sleep deprivation.

Staying lost in a bottle of Scotch or red wine was easy enough, but maintaining the illusion things were all right in front of Dan and Fortunada was becoming tougher. Fortunada especially was suspicious Wally wasn't as okay as he wanted them to believe, but so far she'd respected his need to keep things to himself. Dan apparently hadn't muttered anything to her about Wally using his car and the Sentri Pass.

~~~~

Wally couldn't think about Pace and Taylor without being reminded of the hundreds of frustrating hours he'd searched in vain trying to discover where the money they'd stolen had gone. He knew how the two swindled him and the other investors, but he was never able to actually find the money. Wherever it was, there had to be a lot of it; he'd made calculations of his own.

Lately the words of the comptroller, Leon something-or-other, he'd tracked down months earlier were heavy on his mind. The story he speculated about to Wally was as vivid as if he was standing right in front of him repeating what he'd originally said: "Yeah, they regularly take trips to go scuba diving down in the Cayman Islands—" or words to that effect, the man had said. "I'd bet they have an offshore bank account," he'd concluded.

Wally'd wondered just how difficult it was to create an offshore bank account. What he learned was the mystique surrounding offshore accounts was mostly a lot of urban legend. Opening one of those offshore accounts involved little more than opening an account at any bank. The principal difference was you had to get on a plane and go where they had offices. To justify the distant travel, you have to have a compelling reason. On the surface, Wally couldn't find it any more difficult than that.

Across the Internet large numbers of international banks openly advertised the benefits of restricted access to account information. Surprisingly, the fabled Swiss Banks openly advertised more cooperation with the U.S. government in an effort to assist in the control of the flow of funds to international terrorist groups. For what Wally had in mind, that fact eliminated them.

The idle time Wally found himself faced with while he waited for Colin to find the tranquilizer spawned a new level of lunacy. But if he were to incorporate this inspiration into his plan, he'd have to open his own offshore account.

The bank that caught his imagination was The Central Bank of the Netherlands Antilles. Netherlands Antilles Bank had the entire package: secrecy, electronic access, a sound governmental foundation and stable currency. The bank had been chartered more than a century ago. Beyond deposit security the next most important factor to Wally was located on the jurisdiction page of their website: no treaty requiring disclosure of transactions or records with the U.S. Government.

He navigated his computer to the websites of Aeromexico and Mexicana Airlines. Mexicana had two flights a week into Cancun. The same flight made the Monday and Friday turn around out to Grand Cayman and back. He booked a Monday reservation out of Tijuana.

Friday morning he drove to Ensenada, made a brief visit to his friend Director Garza at Bancomer, who provided Wally with a letter of introduction he could present to the director of The Central Bank of the Netherlands Antilles on Grand Cayman. Garza was also able to release access to the money from the insurance check Wally'd deposited.

Later that day Wally checked weather conditions and temperature for Grand Cayman before he packed the clothing he thought he'd need. He'd never been to Grand Cayman but he and Poppy had traveled to the Caribbean many times. There was a sameness about all of the places they'd ever visited: The most perfect beaches and elegant lagoons or the highest mountain tops with the billion dollar views were all off limits, owned and heavily guarded by the rich, famous or infamous, magnates of world commerce, rock stars, drug lords or dictators of the poorest nations in the world, whom you never caught even a glimpse of and would likely be shot if you did. Below them were the equally unapproachable keepers of the island kingdoms, landowners and business owners—the ethnically superior. And finally the Creole half-castes or expats who provide the ultimate fantasy vacation for the tourists: steel band groups, dive charters, sailboat skippers, tour guides. You imagine what your vacation fantasy would be; you'll find an islander providing the service. And more hotels, bed and breakfast places and pensions than could ever be filled even when Florida goes on spring break. Wally really didn't expect he'd find much different about Grand Cayman—except the fabled international banks.

R.P. McCabe

That evening over drinks with the Dolans, he told them he'd be gone a few days the coming week; more business in the States. He didn't bother to elaborate and Dan and Fortunada, by then accustomed to Wally's comings and goings, thought little of the announcement.

Wally's flight departed General Abelardo L. Rodriguez International Airport in Tijuana at seven o'clock. Monday morning. It was a direct flight to Cancun. He was at the airport for check-in by five-thirty that morning. Inside the waist of his jeans he wore a money-belt in which he carried his cash in U.S. dollars and pesos. His single clothing bag was slung over his shoulder, just another tourist.

He stopped in front of the Mexicana Airlines counter and laid out his Internet confirmation along with his FM-2 immigration card. The young Mexican woman at the ticket counter was stunningly attractive. She spoke to him in English and he responded in passable Spanish. The young woman smiled, typed some numbers onto her keyboard and asked if Wally wished to check the bag. "*No gracias*," he said. Within a few moments he had a boarding pass and the clerk gave him directions to his gate. There were two concourses with six gates each. Seating was open. The flight would be only half full.

They boarded on schedule; no delays and no obnoxious practices like those at U.S. airports; but then terrorists didn't seem hell-bent to blow up Mexican citizens the way they wanted to get at Americans.

The five-hour flight across Mexico's jungle covered mountainous interior was bumpy. The pilot had the buckle seatbelt sign turned on most of the way. Many of the passengers seemed to take that as a suggestion rather than an implicit instruction, and bounced freely between seats up and down the aisle. Wally remained belted into his window seat, and ate the scrambled egg burrito that was served for breakfast and chased it down with a glass of orange juice.

During the middle part of the flight he'd managed to drift in and out of fitful dozing. He couldn't actually sleep. When the flight attendant brought the midday snack Wally ordered a Scotch.

The pilot began his descent out over Campeche. The plane was low enough coming in over the Yucatan Peninsula for him to identify the Mayan ruins at Uxmal and Chichen Itza. His mind drifted back nearly twenty-five years to a time when he and Poppy had visited Isla Mujeres near Cancun and had rented a car and driven to both of those places. He pulled his window screen down, turned his plastic glass slowly in his hands, stared at it as if it were a fascinating jewel and finally took a long slug. He never saw the ruins of Tulum off to the south as the pilot banked for his landing approach into the airport at Quintana Roo.

Wally was the only passenger from Tijuana booked to fly on to Grand Cayman. He was forced to deplane but required to remain inside the international gate. Presently other passengers began to filter in. By the time boarding was called, it looked like the forty-five minute flight to Grand Cayman would be about half full.

At the gate a prickly Mexican customs agent was rechecking documents. Wally gave the imperious little man his FM-2 immigration card. The agent looked at the picture on the card then up at Wally's face and then asked in Spanish why he was going to Grand Cayman. Wally answered him in Spanish: "*A visitar un amigo*—to visit a friend." The pompous minion smirked, handed back the card and waved him on.

The short flight across the Caribbean gave Wally little time to dwell on the madness of what he had in motion. He'd by then made the transition from simply cosseting demented fantasies in his futile effort to escape the constant grief tearing at him, to living in his psychosis; a character in one of those Tom Cruise *Mission Impossible* movies. But there was a commitment and momentum behind it all now. He'd come too far to consider turning back.

Wally paid close attention to the layout of the island from the air as the pilot circled for approach. He hadn't anticipated just how small the island was—not at all what he'd expected to find. He'd had an image—maybe like the skyline of Shanghai or Hong Kong in his mind— elegant, uber-modern skyscrapers for miles. But from the air Grand Cayman Island seemed more like an oversized fishing village than an international banking center. Owen Roberts International Airport was located in the heart of George Town, no tall, impressive skyscrapers, or clusters of highrise office buildings creating a skyline. Yet the place was considered one of the offshore banking meccas of the Caribbean. So, where were all the banks, he wondered?

Clearing Customs was about what he'd expected, what he'd experienced around the Caribbean on previous vacations with Poppy. The crisply white-uniformed officers were friendly and could not be accused of invasion of anyone's privacy on any level. They welcomed everyone coming off the plane as if they were from the Chamber of Commerce. He suspected every inhabitant of these tiny Caribbean islands understood the source of their wealth. Visitors welcome! That was the message. That was the feeling.

It was not lost on Wally places like this were one reason people like Bud Pace, Carl Taylor, Bernard Madoff, Texas billionaire Allen Stanford and hundreds of other criminals just like them got away with it. They found banking partners protected by a friendly government that made it possible to operate in secret: the perfect shield. Even if they got caught; well, do your time, the bulk of your wealth would be here waiting for you when you got out and retired to paradise. Live the lifestyle of a king.

There was a line of taxis at the curb out front. Wally waited for the next one to pull forward. A driver got out, offered to take his shoulder bag. Wally waved his offer away. The nametag pinned to his clean white shirt read Robert. "Where to, Meestah?" the coffee-colored driver asked, in musical patois.

"No reservation," Wally said. "What do you think? I want to stay close to the banking district."

"I know, Meestah," the driver said, smiling at Wally in the rearview mirror. "I know a nice place ... close to the ocean, close to the business," he said, looking over his shoulder, pulling away from the curb.

"Not too pricey," Wally cautioned.

The taxi driver laughed, his brilliant white teeth gleamed in the rear view mirror, light green eyes flashed. "Everything expensive here, Meestah," he said unapologetically. "Where I take you, no 'orrible."

A steel band played reggae music on the car radio as the driver turned west out of the airport. In a few blocks he drove through a roundabout and spun off the northeasterly arm onto a wide, clean street. On the front of one tall building an elegant metallic sign read Cayman National Bank. A few blocks further on another elaborate edifice boasted an equally imposing notification: Butterfield Bank.

"I expected to find a bank on every corner," Wally said, to himself as much as to the driver.

"Plenty banks, Meestah," the man said, turning his head, casting the sound of his voice over his shoulder. "Big banks, little banks ... we got plenty banks. You need find a bank, Meestah?" the friendly driver offered.

"I have a bank," Wally said. "Maybe you know it: The Central Bank of the Netherlands Antilles?"

A new reggae song came on the radio and the driver adjusted the sound a bit louder. "I take you there if you like, Meestah," he said checking his side mirror.

"I need to find a room first," Wally said, his head pivoting like a bobble-head doll.

"No problem, Meestah," the driver said. "We got plenty 'otel."

In a matter of minutes the wide street had veered back west toward the ocean. Robert drove straight into the heart of the only cluster of tall buildings that existed on the island and still none were higher than three stories. Through gaps between the buildings, Wally was beginning to catch snippets of the open roadstead he'd seen from the air located at the west end of the island. There were six cruise ships at anchor and dozens of mega yachts bobbed gently to the breeze. From the air Wally saw Grand Cayman Island was shaped like a guitar and laid in an east-west configuration that broke down the lumpy sea swell and trade winds along the western edge, the bottom of the body of the guitar.

In a few more blocks the taxi emerged from the cluster of tall buildings like a deer edging into an open meadow and turned onto another wide street running north and south along the waterfront; on one side, the Caribbean Sea, on the other, shops, restaurants—art galleries.

Robert drove north several blocks before he pulled into the entrance of the Comfort Inn & Suites. Wally chuffed. Robert said, "Marriott just over there, Meestah," pointing up the street. "Mo money!" He laughed easily.

"This is fine," Wally said. "Wait until I know if they have a vacancy," he said to Robert, sliding out the passenger door.

"Plenty rooms, Meestah," Robert assured him.

The taxi driver's prediction proved accurate, though Wally suffered some sticker shock. The price of a night's stay at this Comfort Inn & Suites, two hundred-fifty dollars, was about double any he'd ever stayed in before. It's not a vacation he reminded himself and accepted the reservation.

Betrayed

Wally handed the taxi driver a twenty and told him to keep the change. Robert thanked him and gave him a business card. "Call me, Meestah," he said, "when you ready. I know this bank," he concluded, referring to The Central Bank of the Netherlands Antilles.

Wally found his room. It had a spectacular view of the emerald green Caribbean. He no longer cared to look upon things of beauty and closed the curtains. He unpacked his clothes and hung things in the small closet. He'd reserved the room until Friday morning checkout. The room would be his cell until then.

There was a small box safe bolted to the floor inside the closet which he made use of to store the cash he carried. He checked his wristwatch against the alarm clock provided in the room. He'd conceded another time zone to easterly travel. It was after five o'clock local time. He paced around the room, unsure what he would do next.

He read the instructions on the phone, picked it up, and dialed nine for an outside line. A clear tone came on. He punched in the numbers as he read them from Robert the taxi driver's business card.

On the fourth ring Robert answered. "Hello, this is, Robert. How can I help you?" he asked very businesslike. The sound of another reggae song was clear in the background.

Robert was the only name that appeared anywhere on the card, so Wally said, "Robert, this is the man you dropped at the Comfort Inn & Suites a short time ago. Do you remember?"

"Oh, yes, Meestah," Robert sang through the phone. "I never forget nobody. *Comment voulez-vous que je peux vous servir?*"

"I'm sorry?" Wally said.

"How I can help you, Meestah?"

Wally thought for a moment. "What time in the morning do the banks open?"

"Oui, monsieur," Robert replied. "Nine o'clock … more or less."

"Good," Wally said. "Can you pick me up in the morning and take me to my bank?"

"Certainly, Meestah," Robert answered. "Nine o'clock. I will wait in the front for you."

Wally placed the phone back in its cradle and thought a few moments. The silence was crushing. He needed a bottle of Scotch.

CHAPTER 31

Wally'd moseyed along Seven Mile Beach, the walk along the waterfront at the west end of Grand Cayman Island. His halfhearted search hadn't yielded a source for Scotch. He'd settled for a couple of island rum drinks in a tiny, palm-thatched joint called Rudy's Nut Hut.

The next morning he slipped on a pair of double pleated olive-green slacks with a black silk shirt. It was as formal as he'd dressed since Poppy was still alive. When he walked by the check-in counter in the lobby the young man who'd checked him in the day before had been replaced by a lovely cappuccino-skinned girl of perhaps thirty. She had jet-black hair that fell in tight ringlets over her shoulders and she had the same soft green eyes he'd noticed in Robert the taxi driver. The girl smiled and said, *"Bonjour, monsieur."*

When Wally pushed through the front doors, Robert the taxi driver was waiting for him. *"Bonjour,* my friend," Robert chirped. "I see you are ready for *'le beesneess'* today."

He ignored any effort at conversation and gave Robert a friendly nod. Robert waited for Wally to climb in and slammed the door closed.

Robert jogged around the front of his taxi and hopped in. He didn't wait for instructions. He looked in the rear view mirror, made brief eye contact with Wally, checked his side mirror and pulled into the slow traffic driving north.

"Le bank not far, Meestah," Robert assured Wally as he deflected the turn signal. He adjusted his car radio when a new reggae song began. Robert made no endeavor to probe Wally's business. His attention was focused, more-or-less, on what was in front of his car, and the music, to which he bobbed gently in his seat, mouthing the words along with the singer on the radio.

Wally made eye contact with him in the rear view mirror again. Robert smiled displaying his brilliant white teeth.

They circled through a series of roundabouts: left here, right there. Suddenly, without any warning, Robert pulled to the curb in front of a nondescript stone façade edifice with no

Betrayed

windows; Livingston Suites, a simple sign announced. It looked more like the outside of a courthouse than a bank.

"You want me to wait, Meestah?"

"This is the bank?" Wally asked, looking out the window but not getting out of the taxi.

"Oh yes, Meestah," Robert said. "You go inside, find le office. It is there, inside."

"The office?" Wally repeated.

"Oh yes, Meestah, oui."

Then it began to occur to Wally; why there was not a bank in evidence on every corner. They were all here; the big international banks, but they didn't maintain conventional buildings with vaults, *(he was wrong about that)* at least not all of them anyway. These were satellites, obviously connected to the institutions wherever they were ultimately domiciled. Wally thought of a question he could never quite seem to wrap his mind around: Where, physically, did banks house all those hundreds of trillions of legal tender in all those different national currencies? Sure, a code here, password there, hit the key and your money moves into or out of your account. But where do they store all the hard currency behind the transaction? Where are the giant warehouses with all those bank notes? Obviously, he figured, the money doesn't exist. It's all just debits and credits to accounts, worthless paper—that supports or destroys a person's life. Jesus, Wally—focus, he thought.

He said, "No need to wait. I can give you a call when I'm ready."

"Excellent, Meestah! You call, I come fer ya."

Wally began to slide out of the car. Robert jumped out of the driver's seat and raced around to open the door for him. He handed the driver a ten this time and told him to keep the change.

"*Merci*, Meestah," Robert said. "Very generous, indeed. You call. I come right away." He pushed the door closed while Wally stood on the sidewalk, looked one way up the street, then in the opposite direction.

Wally finally mustered the courage and pushed open the giant doors to the Livingston Office Suites. Inside he found a sumptuous circular cavern with a step-down from the entryway to an expansive shimmering navy-blue marble floor. Fifty feet up in the center of the domed ceiling was a prism skylight that bathed the interior in soft deflected sunlight. In the center of the stadium-sized vaulted opening was an enormous pond with a fountain that pumped water all the way up to the ceiling, and allowed it to artistically make its return journey to the pool below, running down over an elegant sculptured monolith. Around this was a wide walkway one traversed to locate the specific office suite sought. When Wally walked over and read the masthead on the wall, the picture became clearer. The Central Bank of the Netherlands Antilles was in suite #105. There were only eight other suites in the building that from the outside appeared relatively plain and deceptively confined, but on the inside revealed a lavish expanse of elegant offices. Clearly, the offices descended into the depths of the earth rather than soaring skyward. They were occupied by: Alexandria Bancorp, Ltd., Bank of China, Dresdner Bank,

154

Queensgate Bank & Trust Co, Ltd., Bank of Bermuda, Do Banco Lisbon, Ltd., Bank Danamon Indonesia, Banco do Estado do Rio Grande do Sul S. A. Banrisul.

The vestibule was elegant in every appointment, and as he strolled by the front of each glass-fronted lobby it was apparent he'd find similar affluence inside each of the bank offices. Suite #105 was around the backside of the circle. Wally stood in front of the door and read: The Central Bank of the Netherlands Antilles embossed in the glass doors in stylish gold lettering.

As prepared as he was ever going to be for an introduction to offshore banking, he took a deep breath, pushed the door open and stepped into the lobby. A heavy-breasted strawberry-orange-headed young woman stood from her desk and walked toward him. In heavily accented English she asked how she could help him. When Wally explained he wanted to open an account, she took some cursory information from him and asked him to have a seat.

The sheer heft of the place was intimidating. The walls were covered with rich walnut panels of heavy, dark grained striations. The floor was dressed with a navy blue carpet that had to be two inches thick considering how deep Wally calculated he'd sunk when he stepped onto it. It felt like what he imagined walking on cotton might feel like. In a large circle in the center of the expansive lobby floor was a Coat-of-Arms in red and gold and white and blue. Along the bottom of the emblem, inscribed inside a strip of blue banner that was outlined in rich gold threads were the words: *Koninkrijk der Nederlanden* (Kingdom of the Netherlands), which, as Wally would learn, is a sovereign state of Holland, encompassing the Caribbean Islands of: Aruba, Curaçao, Saba, Saint Eustatius, Bonaire and the southern half of the island of Sint Maarten. It was abnormally quiet, he thought; more like a morgue than a bank.

A triangular block of dark granite with lavish gold lettering identified the receptionist as Aafje Janssen. Aafje's malleable, poetic pronunciations of English words made Wally want to simply sit and listen to her speak.

Pieter Van Hoof appeared almost before Aafje Janssen set the desk phone back in its cradle. He was a squat, pudgy man with a black close-cropped full beard falling out of a ring of thinning hair that was all that was left of what, at one time, covered the entirety of his skull, which was now immaculately bare and shiny and startlingly round on the top—and a disarming smile.

Van Hoof led Wally through a door and down a short, wide staircase behind Aafje's desk. The capacious inner suite of offices was no less impressive than the outer and equally elegant in its appointments. There were three interoffice doors. The walls were covered in the same imposing dark-grained walnut used in the lobby. The carpet from the lobby floor, however, had been replaced with stunning white Italian marble—probably more because the dark navy carpet would have turned the space into a dungeon, than for the wear characteristics of marble. Two double doors at one end obviously led into a very large space. The elegant name plate on the doors read: Senior Vice-President Finn Diextter.

Van Hoof escorted Wally to one of the smaller offices with Van Hoof's name engraved on the door, which in no way, other than sheer volume, seemed to suffer any lack of extravagance. Wally felt exceedingly uncomfortable to be there.

Betrayed

"I was just about to have a cup of tea," Van Hoof said. "Would you like to join me?" He went on, making it crystal clear he intended taking tea whether Wally joined him or not. The man's accent was pleasing to the ear but not as musical as Aafje's.

"Thanks, yes," Wally said.

"Jasmine, China Green, Earl Gray?" Van Hoof offered.

"Lipton's okay," Wally said, not understanding what he'd just revealed to Van Hoof about himself.

Van Hoof smiled amiably. "I have an excellent English black tea."

"I have a letter of introduction, Mr. Van Hoof," Wally said handing him the letter from Director Garza.

Van Hoof accepted the letter from Wally, leaned back in his chair and read it. "This is a beneficial gesture," Van Hoof said, setting the letter aside.

"Here's a copy of my current statement," Wally said, clumsily holding the document out to Van Hoof, as if to justify his worthiness to have an account with Van Hoof's bank.

Van Hoof took the time to study the document. Wally thought he detected a slight uptick in Van Hoof's demeanor as he dwelled over the balance in the account.

A soft tap at the door informed them that the tea was ready. An older black man, so black his skin glistened purple, impeccably dressed in a black suit and white shirt with tie, delivered a tray with two cups of tea, unprocessed cane sugar, milk and butter cookies. Van Hoof instructed the man in French to place the tray on a small table between the two elegant maroon leather wing-backed chairs in the far corner of his office.

"Please," Van Hoof said to Wally, gesturing for him to move to one of the chairs. "We can speak while we have our tea," he said, excusing the server.

Van Hoof was tidy and precise in his movements. He tasted his tea, peered up at Wally and said, "I hope the temperature is correct for you. Sometimes he serves while the water is still too hot for my taste."

"Mine's fine," Wally said.

Van Hoof smiled. "How can I help you, Mr. Stroud?"

"I want to open an offshore account with your bank," Wally said stiffly.

"I see. And what would be the purpose of this offshore account?"

Wally fumbled for a way to explain his purpose. "I'm … anticipating some future business transactions outside the U.S. I want the money to *remain* outside my home country. I'm a U.S. citizen," he explained. "Your privacy policies appeal to me."

"I think I understand your concerns, Mr. Stroud. Let me explain briefly how our system of banking works."

Pieter Van Hoof went into considerable detail about the mechanics of the banking system of the Central Bank of the Netherlands Antilles, emphasizing the bank's reputation for maintaining the anonymity of, and protecting the privacy of, its clients. At the end of his tutorial, Van Hoof concluded by pointing out the wide range of services provided by his bank.

"Maybe we can discuss some of those services after I make the deal I'm working on." Wally said.

"How long are you here, Mr. Stroud?" Van Hoof asked.

"Until Friday," Wally said draining the last of his tea. "I have a flight to Cancun on Friday."

"How much will you be depositing with us today?"

"Ten thousand," Wally responded without giving it a thought.

"Ten thousand … dollars?" Van Hoof repeated. He was unable to mask the astonished look on his face.

"Pounds Sterling," Wally replied, observing that revelation had little calming effect on Van Hoof.

"Pounds … Sterling," Van Hoof repeated.

Wally sized up the situation. "It's temporary. The business deal I'm working on involves a lot of money."

"Do you mind me asking how much is a lot?" Van Hoof wanted to know.

Wally fidgeted. "As much as I have in my Mexican bank," Wally replied. "Maybe more. I'm not sure yet." He was grabbing at straws. He wanted Van Hoof off his back.

"I see," Van Hoof said. "That would be a more appropriate amount for our type of services. Have you an idea about when this business deal might be completed?"

"Soon," Wally said. And this time he sent his own silent message to Van Hoof—open the fucking account or I'm out of here baldy.

Van Hoof seemed to read Wally's thoughts. Well, the gist of them anyway.

"I'll have the documents prepared for you," Van Hoof promised. "If you will be kind enough to return tomorrow, shall we say … one o'clock? We can complete the paper work then."

~~~~

Robert the taxi driver was true to his promise. Aafje Janssen placed the call and told Robert in French his passenger, Mr. Stroud, was finished with his business. Robert was waiting at the curb when Wally exited the huge front doors of Livingston Suites.

"I need a bottle of Scotch," Wally said sliding into the back seat of the taxi.

Robert grinned and bobbed to the reggae music coming from his radio. Several blocks from Livingston Suites he pulled to the curb in front of a liquor store that looked more like Tiffany's Jewelers than a purveyor of spirits. "Find anything you lookin' fer in there, Meestah," Robert promised, bouncing around to open Wally's door.

Robert had not exaggerated. Nor had he exaggerated the day before on the drive from the airport when he'd declared everything on Grand Cayman Island was expensive. Wally gave the grizzled-faced older man behind the counter four twenties for the 1.5 liter bottle of Johnny Walker and received very little change.

CHAPTER 32

Wally'd been gone since before daylight Monday morning when his return flight touched down in Tijuana early Friday evening; he'd gained three hours traveling west. Except for the layer of grime over his truck, it sat unmolested where he'd parked it. He tossed his bag in the back seat and pulled to the exit. The end of July was closing in.

He followed the *Zona Rio* getting out of downtown Tijuana and onto the toll road to Ensenada. The forty-five minute trip south along the Pacific Ocean was peaceful. He was tired. He was always tired these days. He'd clung to his room the entire week on Grand Cayman. He tried to stay drunk. Even that had not worked. He was forced to live with his demons, accepting that they were never going away. Sleep, in the conventional sense, was a past experience. Utter collapse at unpredictable moments from exhaustion was the rest he relied upon. He drove slowly. Cars zoomed by, horns blaring; one guy flipped him off—a low-rider with California plates.

Wally'd kept his phone turned on all week. He'd have known if Colin attempted to call. He'd told Colin he was driving south of Ensenada for a few days, tasting wine from that region. It was as good a lie as any. It apparently worked. There were no messages on his voice mail.

Darkness was complete when he wheeled his truck into the carport at his beach house. The lights inside the Dolan's house lit up the inside of the rooms. He saw Fortunada and Dan stand up and peer out into the blackness toward his house as he grabbed his tote out of the passenger-side door. He waved knowing they could see his silouette.

He went straight up to his bedroom and turned the lights on rather than illuminating the main floor of the house; his way of saying to his friends, "Not tonight."

~~~~

Saturday morning he felt lethargic. The day progressed in slow motion. The shower, the comfort of being in his own space helped but didn't generate much enthusiasm for anything beyond the meager breakfast he'd prepared and the glass of cranberry juice he was nursing.

Toward the end of the morning Dan Dolan walked up onto the main floor terraza and shouted into the house, "Anybody home?"

Wally was scrunched down in his big chair with a golf magazine on his lap. "Hey Danny Boy," he said with no display of energy. "Come on in." He closed the magazine and stumbled to his feet.

"Stay where you are," Dolan insisted, and crossed the great room. "How was your trip?" he asked settling himself into a chair across from the one Wally had just evacuated.

"Something to drink? Got more of this cranberry juice," Wally offered holding up the glass of rubicund liquid.

"Pass," Dolan said.

"Long," Wally answered, meaning the trip.

"Get everything done?"

"Banking mostly," Wally said. Then continuing to construct the web of lies, "Doctor's appointment," he added, no further information.

"Everything okay?" Dolan's curiosity was palpable.

"Sure," Wally said, not feeling up to pretense at that moment. "I'll tell you about it sometime." He sipped some juice.

"Went to this woman proctologist once," Dolan reminisced. "Real gentle … small, slender fingers … but long. Know what I mean?"

Wally laughed. "You're a whore, Dolan."

"Yeah … I know," he agreed grinning widely. "Fo's got dinner planned tonight."

"I'll be hungry," Wally promised.

"You look tired. Need anything?"

"I'm good," Wally said standing. He was merely going to return his empty glass to the kitchen, but Dan Dolan received the gesture as a cue the visit was over.

"No need to rush off," Wally said unconvincingly.

"Get some rest," Dolan suggested showing himself out. "Usual," he added, shouting back, "sundowners after four if you're interested."

Wally wasn't in the mood for drinks or dinner. But there it was: normalcy.

~~~~

It cooled enough during the night Sunday to cause the warm, humid air to condense. Wally awoke Monday morning to everything dripping wet, as though it rained during the night, but it hadn't. Heavy droplets still clung to the eves of the house, periodically dropping in big splashes onto the tile. Everything smelled of clean wet dirt and the air felt crisp.

Betrayed

He couldn't hold back any longer so around nine-thirty he phoned Colin.

"'Sup, Uncle Wally?" Colin answered cheerfully, "been thinking about you."

"You get my last email?"

"Yeah. Discover any new vineyards?"

"Historical," Wally lied. "Santo Tomás surprised me."

"Got your stuff," Colin said, absent any fanfare.

The near outburst caught in Wally's throat. "Great," he said as subdued as he could keep it.

"*Great!* You gotta be kiddin' me," Colin objected.

"Hey, no lack of appreciation," Wally interjected immediately, "I can only imagine it must have been a pretty difficult thing for you and your friend. Just that it started to slip to the back of my mind," Wally lied again.

"You still interested in this stuff?"

"You bet!" This time he allowed some of his angst to come through as enthusiasm. "Damn critters are as big a nuisance as ever."

Wally could hear the tenor in Colin's voice change. "My friend went a little overboard with this stuff, but I think it'll do what you have in mind ... lot more, probably." And then, "Definitely, a lot more."

"No such thing as being ... *over prepared*."

"Look, Uncle Wally," Colin said. Wally heard the switch-up in his manner once more. "I really don't want to drive this stuff down to your place."

"Of course not," Wally agreed feeling relieved. "Can you hang on a day or two until I can come up to you?"

"No problem."

"What's your schedule look like?"

"You know me," Colin said.

"Next couple of days then," Wally promised.

"Give me a call the night before," Colin said. "We'll meet at my condo. That's where I'm storing it."

"I really appreciate this, Colin."

"Just be careful with your ... project." Colin laughed softly. "Not sure how long you'd be out if you shot yourself in the foot with this stuff."

"Hey!" Wally shouted, "Any way we could load one of Dick Cheney's shotguns with that shit?"

Colin laughed louder. "Call me," he said. "I gotta run."

"Next day or so," Wally assured him stifling the sincere urge to ask if he could come and get it right then. *Patience*, Wally, he reminded himself—*normalcy*.

That afternoon over cocktails he continued his web of lies with the Dolans; told them he'd be going up to San Diego to attend a Padres game with Colin. He narrowly escaped Dolan inviting himself along.

Wally spent the entirety of that following day online; fingers dancing across his keyboard, his eyes glued to the monitor. Spread over the top of his desk were organized lists of supplies, nearly every item with a checkmark next to it by then. Once he got his hands on the tranquilizer—he'd be ready to move. *Finally*! For the first time in months he experienced a feeling that was close to contentment.

He'd by then reduced the operation to a written script. He went back over it again, every step, from beginning to end. For one moment, ever so brief, he wondered if he could really go through with what he saw laid out before him. Any remaining reservation evaporated quickly.

The day ended with drinks and dinner with the Dolans: *pretense*—now more than ever.

~~~~

That next morning he pulled his truck over in front of the Dolan house around nine-thirty. He honked the horn and shouted to Fortunada up on the balcony.

"Making a grocery run," he claimed. "Need anything?"

"Won't think of anything until you're long gone," Fortunada said giggling, her face red from some exertion she'd been up to.

"I have my cell," Wally shouted. "Call if you think of anything." He waved and drove on.

~~~~

It was nearly dark by the time he returned. He made a show of unloading the few items he had in the backseat of his truck.

Fortunada shouted over to him. "Some shopping trip!"

"Ran into old friends," he lied. "Had a late lunch … drank a little wine."

Wally had, in fact, drunk some wine. But the man he'd spent the day with, Tomas Garza, was not an old friend. Garza owned the most prominent funeral home in Ensenada. And Garza was politically connected; knew all the right people; doctors, hospitals, important officers in the Federal Police.

"You gonna be hungry for dinner?"

"I will!" he shouted. "Let me get this under control and I'll be over."

Wally put the dry goods he'd picked up as cover into the pantry before running upstairs.

He flipped open his phone and hit Colin's number on the speed dial while he peeled off his shirt.

"Hey, Uncle Wally," Colin answered. "Thought you'd changed your mind."

"Nah," Wally replied. "Just a couple of chores I wanted to finish up before I headed your way." Colin could not know Wally's trip to see him had to coincide with the Padres game. In any case, it set a good pitch for Wally not appearing to attach anything more than a crazy idea with a few mischievous animals to the serious matter of the tranquilizer.

161

Betrayed

"So, I'm thinking I could drive up tomorrow."

"Make it around one?" Colin replied. "I have a meeting in the morning."

"That would work out fine," Wally said.

"Cool. One o'clock, my place. Listen," he hedged, "if I get hung up it won't be for lo—"

"I'll be waiting," Wally said. "Take your time."

"It's an important meeting."

"Like I said, I'll be waiting."

CHAPTER 33

At the *hour of demons* Wally kicked the blankets back and crawled out of bed. The voices, which for so many months had been contradictory, confusing, terrifying in what they sought from him were calmer; seemingly satisfied he'd fallen into agreement with the strongest of them. He walked out onto the terraza and stared out over the calm Pacific considering the rage bottled inside of him and his unalterable commitment to shatter the lives of the people responsible. Finally, he was in lock-step with the tormenting voices. And they seemed—mollified for the moment. It was as good a rationale as any, he figured.

At four-thirty he gave up any hope of sleeping and went downstairs. He switched on a lamp and lit the fireplace. A gentle, warming glow spread across the large room illuminating corners and creating shadows across which danced flickering images. The warming air quickly began to dry the space.

It was a mere three-hour drive to Colin's condo in Escondido. Their meeting wasn't scheduled until one p.m. He wandered into the kitchen and put the water to heat for his tea. Poppy'd bought one of those electric hot water pots that made the task faster, but Wally still preferred putting a teapot on the stove the old fashioned way. He just liked the routine. Early mornings didn't seem the time to be worried about efficiency of movement. He rather relished his aimless meandering, shuffling around, waking up slowly, organizing his thoughts.

He glanced to the buffet where his shrine to Poppy sat. "I know, I know, Popp," he said. "It's faster with the electric pot." He set out a mug and hung a black pekoe tea bag over its rim. It was then Wally realized his anger toward Poppy was beginning to subside or, at least morph into something softer; he couldn't be sure. He stared at her image. He loved her—in spite of what she'd done.

The teapot began to spit tiny droplets of water from its spout that jumped out and landed hissing on the hot cast iron burner. Wally turned off the stove before the water reached a full boil. "Too hot to drink, anyway," he grouched to himself. He finished putting his cup of tea

163

together and groped his way into his favorite chair in front of the fireplace. He rested his feet on the hearth and slumped down into one corner of the deep chair.

He sat motionless, lost in the mindless dithering of his morning's routine. Soon enough the caffeine caught hold and he resumed the familiar stream of consciousness dedicated to his chosen purpose. The time was close. He felt a tightening in his stomach muscles when he recalled the words he'd used with his squad in the jungles of Vietnam: "*Move out!*"

Colin was coming through just as Wally'd known he would. There'd never really been any doubt he would. Still, Colin was exceptionally bright. Wally wondered what the kid suspected, but hadn't asked. He figured he'd learn the answer soon enough.

It was ten-thirty when he was locking up, walking out to toss his tote into his truck. Fortunada Dolan stepped out onto the balcony of her home and shouted down to him. "Drive careful! Say high to Colin for us! Have fun!"

Wally waved, climbed into the cab of his truck and drove away.

~~~~

Otay Mesa was the border crossing he'd be using from here on. Traffic through Tijuana was normal that day; crazy taxi drivers cutting him off, flashy new pickups with shiny spinner hubcaps speeding here and there; horns blaring. In the Sentri lane at the border he pulled his golf cap down low, held his pass up to the scanner and glanced away toward his console just as the camera flashed. The result was the same as his previous experience. The officer eyed him and waved him through without so much as a hard stare. Still, he wondered if he could be as casual when it came time for the real performance.

He pulled through the control gate in the far right lane and edged onto the 905 north. A few miles up the freeway he drifted into the off ramp for the frontage road and continued a couple of miles to Allied Storage. The place always seemed quiet. He never ran into large numbers of cars or people rummaging through open storage lockers. But he'd never approached the place on a weekend either.

He punched in the access code and drove to his garage at the end of the row of buildings. The stacks of supplies he'd stored at the front of the storage space required a few minutes to organize. Duffle bags would organize things the way the makeup bag had organized his disguise.

He switched vehicles. The Camry needed to be driven to recharge its battery and Wally needed to get to know the car better.

At the Telegraph Avenue off ramp in Chula Vista, he drifted into the exit lane and drove straight into the Canyon Plaza Strip Mall on the north side of the street. He could see the Starbuck's sign at the east end of the mall where he thought he'd remembered it.

Back on the freeway he sipped slowly from the small hot chocolate he'd bought. At Interstate 15, he cut northeast. Colin's condominium was actually situated in the community of

San Marcos, a suburb of Escondido. From Interstate 15 Wally turned west on Highway 78, a two-lane, windy canyon byway that spilled him into the heart of downtown San Marcos.

He turned north on Twin Oaks Valley Road for a short distance before turning left onto Mission. Colin lived in a trendy low-rise condo complex not far from Cal State, San Marcos. Wally'd been there only once before.

He was a half hour early—if Colin was on time. Wally chose a space where he could see the front of Colin's condo and backed into it. There was a fair amount of foot traffic, mostly young women ... mostly nice looking young women. Or maybe it was that everyone is beautiful when they're twenty and you're sixty-five. Wally could appreciate why Colin liked it here.

A young woman in her early twenties crossed the parking lot. She glanced up and smiled as she strolled by. Her short hair was jet-black with tips of bright turquoise and she wore a tattered Levi mini-skirt that could not have been any shorter without giving up a clear view of everything it was apparently intended to hide—or advertise, as the case may have been. An indefinable tattoo was visible just at its hemline on her inner right thigh. It did the trick; Wally strained to get a better look. Her medium-sized breasts bounced around in so many different directions under the thin silky fabric of her emerald-colored blouse it was pointless to speculate about a bra. And if the freedom of movement of the perky orbs was not sufficient to answer that question, then the imprints of her naked nipples were there to elucidate the point. Wally thought she was cute as hell, though he pitied her father.

When Colin pulled into his parking space Wally'd been waiting forty-five minutes.

He watched while his nephew uncoiled his tall, lanky frame out of his white Crossfire Roadster. The top was down and Colin's black hair was tousled like a movie star on a set. Colin stood up and did a quick recon of the lot. He didn't notice Wally in the Toyota.

Colin was wearing a pair of jeans with an Urban Legend t-shirt under an open blazer with its sleeves pushed halfway up his arms. Wally knew the kid was coming from an important meeting. Stockbrokers and television news anchors still wore suits and ties; apparently not so for private computer consultants like his nephew.

He tapped the horn and Colin searched in his direction. This time Wally was climbing out of the Camry. Colin spotted him.

Colin waved and started in Wally's direction. "Now that's a seriously ugly piece of crap!" he shouted approaching Wally.

"I wish the hell you'd stop holding back how you feel about things," Wally replied grinning. "My economy wheels so I don't have to drive that damn gas-guzzler everywhere," he lied again.

"I could get behind that," Colin said, "but why'd you have to buy the ugliest thing you could find? My HOA might fine me for letting you park it!"

Colin was on him by then. He clenched Wally in a bear hug he had no chance of escaping. For as rangy as the kid appeared, he was strong—or maybe he (Wally) was getting old.

"Don't be too critical," Wally joked. "That's part of your inheritance!"

Betrayed

"And I guess I'll get some orange 'sans-a-belt polyesters' and a pair of 'Pat Boone white bucks' … maybe a pea-green 'Lacoste' sport shirt … oh yeah, make sure you throw in a white belt to go with that ensem, will ya!"

"I'm amazed you even know about those nice clothes considering this stuff you're running around in!"

"God … you are an old fart!"

"Guilty as charged!" Wally agreed.

"Come on," Colin said leading away toward his condo. "You aren't gonna believe the shit my guy got you." Colin was actually excited about his acquisitions, which greatly surprised Wally.

Wally followed him.

"You're gonna be a regular goddamn, Marlin Perkins," Colin was saying.

"How do you know this stuff?" Wally mused incredulously. "You're too young to have ever seen *Wild Kingdom*."

"Saturday Night Live," Colin confessed. "Did a skit with a sucker fish attached to Marlin's forehead once. Saw it in reruns."

Wally followed his nephew shaking his head. Colin was the real deal. His was a star destined to shine bright, Wally felt certain of it.

Colin inserted his key and opened the heavy blue door slowly. A "meow" was instantly followed by the appearance of a pink nose. Colin used his foot to block the bottom of the opening.

"Didn't realize he was still alive," Wally said.

"He's old," Colin acknowledged, reaching down to pick up the furry cat. "I don't let him out anymore. Not sure he could protect himself. Hey Midnight," he continued, nuzzling the large tabby, scratching behind its ears, "you hungry, boy?"

The old cat meowed his appreciation for the affection or the promise of food—or both.

"Come on," Colin said, letting Midnight jump out of his hands close to the floor. "You're gonna wanna check this shit out."

As they entered Colin's office Wally registered a corner desk against the two far walls. Three large flat screen monitors were black and silent except for the colorful whirligigs gyrating in various geometric shapes across each screen.

"Orderly confusion," Colin justified, looking at the top of his desk. "I wouldn't allow anyone to touch it. I know exactly where everything is. Your supplies are over here," he said, pointing to the opposite corner of the room where a stack of boxes rested very orderly, one atop the other.

Colin walked to the corner and removed the topmost box from the stack and set it down on the floor in front of them. He pulled the flaps open and removed a large gunmetal-gray pistol with a long barrel on it that looked something like a Glock 22 with a silencer attached to it. It struck Wally as incredibly intimidating just looking at it.

R.P. McCabe

"Here's your dart gun," Colin said, handing the pistol to Wally.

"It doesn't look like it would be very light, but it is." He held it out at arm's length, and then retracted his arm slowly turning the pistol from side to side inspecting the weapon, acclimating to the sensation of it in his hand. "It's … more than I thought it would be," he admitted, "scare the hell out of anyone."

"I thought you said you had coyotes to get rid of?" Colin engaged his uncle straight in the eyes.

Wally looked up, caught off his guard. He lowered the weapon, ignored the probe. "Let's see what else you have for me."

Colin attempted to maintain eye contact. Wally could sense the wheels turning in his nephew's head. Colin finally gave in and grabbed the next box. "Like I told you on the phone," he continued, "I got you what you'd need … not necessarily what you had on your list." Again there was an engagement of the eyes that made Wally go a little queasy.

The kid was dropping a lot of hints. Maybe it was his imagination? Clearly though, Colin seemed suspicious.

Colin flipped open an aluminum case padded inside and divided into small compartments. It held six vials of a milky colored liquid with red rubber tops on the bottles. Next to those were six more vials of the same size containing a clear liquid and capped with a similar rubber top in blue.

"The red tops contain the tranq cocktail," Colin explained. "The guy that got this for me says it's strong enough to take down a full-grown male baboon in seconds." He looked up at Wally once more. "Plenty strong enough for what you need, right?"

"What about the bottles with the blue caps?" Wally asked pointing, ignoring the innuendo.

Colin let the question hang a moment. He knelt in silence staring into the open case as if in deep contemplation. Finally, he reached in and selected one of the blue-capped bottles. "This is the antidote," he said. "You can wake the animal up with this in about two minutes. There are some sterile packaged hypodermic needles in the box.

"I had this guy I know, Kyle, provide precise instructions on how much to administer based on the weight of the animal. You'll find that here," Colin said, unfolding a sheet of paper. He tucked it into the side of the case. "You can adjust the dose depending on the size of each animal. Kyle says a cocktail of tranquilizers is a better way to go than just the Ketamine. He knows about that kind of shit. But you have to be more precise with the dosage."

Wally reached down and picked up the case. The value of what his nephew placed in his hands was overwhelming. "You've done right by me, Colin," Wally said softly.

"What bothers me is the animals don't get the drop on you before you can knock them down. Maybe you'd let me give you a hand with this?"

"They're just coyotes," Wally objected before the words had even cleared Colin's lips.

"I figured you'd opt out."

Wally shifted about turning around, glancing over the array before him on the floor.

167

Betrayed

Colin started to address what he suspected then stopped. He'd come to regret that decision. "Okay, Uncle Wally," he said more upbeat. "I get it. If there's anything—"

"You've already done everything you can," Wally said, cutting him off.

"These are the darts," Colin said, holding up one of the feathered needles. "There's a small tubular cylinder that attaches here," he said pointing, "after you fill it with the tranq. The impact causes this plunger," he pointed again, "to inject the juice instantly. According to Kyle, the gorilla's on his ass in seconds." The two men laughed uneasily.

"You see the size of that dart needle?" Colin continued. "Be like getting hit in the ass with a six-penny nail."

A look of anguish screwed across Wally's face in acknowledgment of the pain he knew the needle would inflict on anything but the toughest of hides.

The two men began repacking the items in their respective boxes. It took longer to recapture everything than it did to open them.

"You don't have to refrigerate the tranq or antidote, but it does have to be kept in a cool, dark place."

"Noted," Wally acknowledged. "Let's get everything out to my car. We can leave the tranq until I'm ready to leave."

When they came back inside Colin went to the refrigerator and poured them both a glass of iced tea. "So, how've you been?" he asked, turning to his uncle. "You look bad, Uncle Wally. You lost more weight?"

"Don't sleep so well some nights." Wally pulled out a chair at the kitchen table and sat down. "Couches go nice in here," he said, noticing his and Poppy's furniture. "I try to keep busy. You know how it is," he said, shifting back to the subject. Wally hoisted his glass draining a long swallow.

"Yeah," Colin agreed. "I do know how it is. It's on my mind a lot, too." Colin paused. There was an awkward moment. "Any word on the investigation?"

"Nothing new," Wally said without elaboration.

Colin shook off the downbeat tempo, went perky. "Well, you're all set with your critter project, so maybe you can get your mind on different things."

"Kind of looking forward to the hunt," Wally agreed, following his nephew's up-tempo.

"How'd your meeting go?"

Colin brightened. "I think this Siemens contract with NASA has the potential to go big for me. I mean … an international company built around the project."

"You ready to handle something on that scale?"

"Intellectually … sure," Colin said. "But I'll have to find capital. It'll take hardware and people … both expensive for a start-up."

"Any chance for help from Siemens?"

"Doubtful," Colin replied, "not how they roll."

"Wish I could help, Colin." Wally spun the empty tea glass around and around between his fingers in its puddle of sweat on the table. "Even before—" Wally stared aimlessly at the bottom of the glass. "This would have been out of my league even back in the day," he admitted.

Colin smiled. "I know, Uncle Wally," he said affectionately, "and I love you for thinking about it that way. Thanks!"

"Well, you'll find your way. But not if I don't get out of your hair." Wally stood. "Thanks for the help with this kid. I know you're busy."

"Cool it, Uncle Wally! That's one of the perks of what I do and why I do it the way I do … like my freedom."

CHAPTER 34

Wally worked his way back to the Escondido Freeway. Rush hour was beginning to ramp up.

He intended to leave the gun and tranquilizer stashed in the trunk of the Toyota. As long as the weather continued moderate, the tranquilizer would be safe enough hidden there. He planned to insulate it under the duffle bags.

Traffic grew heavier. It was six twenty-five by the time he pulled into Allied Storage. They closed access to the units at seven o'clock. He pulled around to his space, pushed the door up and switched vehicles.

He stood assessing how much space the equipment and supplies were going to require. The costume and makeup gear was all stored compactly in one duffle. Two more duffels would do the trick. He could visualize what he needed now.

He locked the garage and drove back to the access gate. It was five-after-seven. As Wally input the code to be let out, the young Salvadoran woman who worked there walked out the main door and turned to lock up. She smiled and waved to him. He waved back and continued toward the outlet onto the frontage road. While he waited out the oncoming traffic, he watched in his rear view mirror as the girl walked out to the street. She was headed for the bus stop.

He rolled down the driver's side window as she drew near.

"Buenas tardes, Señor Estroud," she said.

"Good evening, Xochille," he said. "You remember my name?"

"An why no? Chu remembers mine, no?"

"Only one of you. You must deal with lots of people every day."

"No really."

There was an awkward moment before Wally asked, "Catching the bus?"

"Jes," she replied simply.

She had on a smart navy-blue pantsuit that was conservative by comparison to what he'd seen her wear on the last occasion. Her petite, curvy frame appeared androgynous. Not feminine

170

enough for his taste. She wore the buttons open at the top of the jacket revealing a white silky blouse covering the rise of her breasts. Her heels were at least six inches high and open-toed. Wally speculated she might be self-conscious about her height.

"Could I give you a lift?"

"Is no necessary, Mr. Estroud. I am accustom to ride de bus."

"It's no trouble. Besides, I need to find a motel to stay the night. I have business tomorrow. Don't want to bother driving across the border."

"If chu gets back on de freeway here," she said, pointing to the intersection up the street, "chu fine a La Quinta Inn near to de E Street exit."

Wally'd seen it many times. "I know where it is," he said, shaking his head. "Should have thought of it myself."

Xochille smiled. "I living not far from der. Is how I knowing."

"That settles it," Wally insisted. "Hop in!" He leaned across the front seat to open the passenger door. "I can drop you at your house before I go check in."

Xochille started to refuse, glanced up and saw her bus pulling away from the stop. She watched it drive off and then turned back to Wally, back to the bus one last time. "Okay," she said, shrugging her shoulders and smiling.

Xochille walked around the back of the pickup and pushed the passenger door open the rest of the way. "I appreciate de ride, Señor Estroud," she said smiling. "De nex bus is no for forty-fi minutos ... an I no like to staying in de dark." Before she could close the door the cab of the truck filled with the soft scent of lilies.

"It was my fault you missed it in the first place. Really, it's my pleasure."

The E Street off ramp was only two miles north of where Wally entered the freeway. He gave his signal and edged into the exit lane.

Xochille indicated he should continue west on E Street a mile. The atmosphere tensed after the girl climbed into the cab of the truck. Except for brief indications of directions there'd been no conversation during the short drive. At a stop signal, Wally saw a Chinese Buffett on the corner. Suddenly he was hungry. Without any forethought he said, "You hungry, Xochille?"

The girl began to fidget nervously, "I will have some food at my home, thank you."

"Come on," Wally pressed. "You like Chinese food?" He thought he could detect the girl blushing.

"I don't know is proper, Señor Estroud."

Ah, Wally, he thought! "I'm sorry, Xochille. I thought it would be nice to have some company while I had dinner. I wasn't thinking. I hope you'll accept my apology. I assure you, it was only a friendly gesture."

It was silent for several seconds. The goddamn red light was taking forever.

"I sorry, too, Señor Estroud. I tinking maybe you tinking someting."

It was silent again for a few moments.

Betrayed

"My wife—Poppy," Wally said softly, staring straight ahead. He hesitated slightly before going on. "She always said I was like a bull in a china shop. Needed to pay closer attention to what people might think about things I say or do." He turned and smiled at Xochille. "Don't get me wrong, you're pretty enough—"

The light turned and he started to accelerate through the intersection.

"I liking comida Cheena," Xochille blurted out, cutting him off.

Wally grinned.

"Chu nice man," she said. "But in my country, girls like me haves to be careful."

"So, you really, *really* hungry?"

"I hungry enough," Xochille replied.

Over dinner Wally learned Xochille's family in El Salvador consisted of her mother and father, a younger brother and baby sister. Her entire family, including her, worked and saved when she was growing up to earn enough money to send her to America. Her dedication now was to send every penny she could save back home so eventually both her younger brother and baby sister would be able to come and join her.

Observing the amount of food she packed away, Wally marveled she could maintain such a petite size.

~~~~

Wally awoke early feeling curiously at ease. The short dose of normalcy over dinner the night before, maybe? He grabbed a quick shower and checked out. The Chinese buffet had worn off. He didn't bother to search any further than the Denny's restaurant next door. The waitress added a couple of buttermilk pancakes he conceded he didn't need, but simply wanted.

There was a Target store just off the freeway not far north of where he was eating. He headed straight there from Denny's. The store was just opening for the day when he arrived. A few customers were milling about. Mostly, employees shuffled around trying to give the impression of being busier than they actually were.

Wally asked one desperate, pimply-faced youngster where he would find duffle bags. "Luggage," the kid replied. "Aisle 26." He pointed in a direction while he kept right on walking away. Wally shook his head as he watched the kid; jeans hanging half down his ass, tattoos up both arms.

Aisle 26 yielded an entire wall of duffels in a large variety of sizes and colors. A stroke of genius came to him. His makeup bag was black. He chose heavy-duty bags in navy, forest-green and saddle-brown. He bought the extra one just in case. By glancing at each bag's color he'd know exactly what was inside.

It was close to eleven when he pulled through the entry gate at Allied Storage. He drove to his space and unlocked the door. He backed his pickup close to the open door and lowered the tailgate. It provided the perfect work surface where he could unpack and repack each and every

172

piece of equipment and the supplies he'd assembled. This phase required careful consideration. What would be needed at each moment during the operation; combined weight; ease of access; economy of movement. He knew how critical it would be to limit his efforts—as few steps as possible. And everything that went in had to come out. Not a speck could be left behind once the job was finished. There'd be fatigue and fear to deal with. He considered for the thousandth time, every possible aspect of the plan; visualized each separate movement so it felt like he was performing the act right then and there. It had to be visceral in order to lodge deeply into his subconscious.

He packed and repacked the bags. It was all there, finally: every last piece. Then he took time to practice the physical movements over and over. He'd bought extra gas cartridges for the dart gun. Again and again he fired it with a dry dart standing at the tailgate of his truck and aiming at a watermelon he'd bought just for that purpose.

It didn't take him long to develop a feel for the weapon. The gun was nearly silent when it fired. Only a distinct click and swooshing sound was audible. Within a few shots he was hitting the melon every time. He moved the bags from the car to the truck—then back again. He repeated each movement several times. Then he returned to the pistol and took more shots, ingraining the feel until his muscles and senses could remember without him thinking about it. He checked his watch, understood precisely the time he was consuming. There'd be no second chances.

CHAPTER 35

When Wally crossed back over the border into Mexico that day, he stopped at the customs declaration office. He declared two cases of wine and two 1.75 liter bottles of Johnny Walker Red, paid the absurd 90 percent import duty, smiled up at the surveillance camera and had his resident visa validated. He tucked the paid customs receipt with his and the agent's signature on it neatly between the stamped pages of his visa.

The trigger was pulled. He made the short drive to his home in somber silence, his brain racing, orchestrating the few remaining details. By the time he was backing his truck into his carport, he'd made the firm resolve to "*move out*" before sunup next Wednesday, August 19th.

Fortunada Dolan waved to him from the third floor balcony of her home. He waved back and shouted to her as he got out of the truck. "Laid in some new supplies for Danny Boy," he yelled, hoisting one of the Johnny Walker bottles over his head.

Fortunada grinned and shook her head. "Just what you two need," she shouted back. "You just missed him." She pointed in the direction of the golf course. "Said he was gonna play nine."

Wally gave thumbs up with his free hand. "Why don't you guys come over for a sundowner?"

"Just say the hour."

"Five-thirtyish," he yelled opening the passenger-side door of the truck.

"What can I bring?"

Wally extracted one of the cases of wine from the rear seat. "Didn't forget you, Fo." He pointed toward her with the case of wine. "Found an interesting looking Old Vine Zin."

"Woo-hoo!" Fortunada yelled, dragging the sound out like a song.

"Bring some nibbles," Wally suggested, heading toward the open garage door. "I'll throw on a pot of spaghetti."

"Done and done."

Wally took only a few minutes to unload his truck. Inside he threw open the expanse of French doors on the main terraza and collapsed into a chair. He closed his eyes; breathed in the fresh salt air and let his head fall backward. He lifted his face to the warm sun. There were few sensations as satisfying as sitting quietly ... listening ... crashing waves ... warm ... no distractions. The only intruding sound, besides the constant crush of waves, was the shrill whistle of a Ferruginous Hawk in the distance soaring over the inhospitable contours of the Sonoran Desert. Serenity or resignation settled over Wally. There was only one voice in his head now. It came from deep within his distorted psyche. He communed with the distant bird of prey—I'll be hunting soon, too, my friend.

Dinner was cozy, uneventful. Sunset was a spectacular show. Conversation never drifted beyond the Padres game Wally never attended and Dan's unwitnessed tales of golf greatness earlier in the day. The three of them got *"tuned-up,"* as it were, on the supplies Wally'd brought back. When the evening ended they all swore they would not do *that* again—until the next time. They laughed together. That's where the night ended.

~~~~

Wally spent Saturday up in his library. His fingers pecked, non-stop, across the keyboard of his laptop throughout the day. He took few breaks except those required for deep contemplation. His focus was hyper-sharp and yet he felt he was in suspended animation.

At four-thirty his concentration was broken by the sound of Dan Dolan's voice echoing up from the main floor.

"Pour yourself a Scotch," Wally shouted back. "Be right down."

He finished typing the last sentence of the document. Wally stood, stared for a moment at the pages the copier spit out during the day. The page he was looking for was near the top of the stack. He pulled a number ten envelope from a box on the shelf and sealed the single-page letter inside.

"You comin' down?" Dolan shouted up, sounding irritated.

"Sorry," Wally said descending the stairs two steps at a time. "I was just finishing something on my laptop."

"Shit," Dolan complained, "you live in front of that damn thing."

"Where's Fo?"

"Decided to drive up and spend the weekend with her niece."

Wally went for a glass and ice, and poured himself a Scotch. "Want something to snack on?"

"Fo made dinner for us. All we gotta do is warm it up."

"Great," Wally said, "but I need a little something while I drink."

"Why not? Got any mixed nuts?"

"I do." Wally found the nuts and filled a bowl. He laid the sealed envelope next to it.

Betrayed

"What's that?" Dolan pried.

Wally took a short nip of Scotch. "You know Dan," he began, "you and Fo are the only people I maintain any kind of contact with these days … except, Colin, of course. But he's clear up north. I mean right here at home … regular basis."

"And?"

Wally scooped a handful of nuts and popped a few into his mouth. "What the hell would you do if something happened to me?"

"Simple," Dolan said, picking through the nuts for the cashews. "I'd leave your ass for the buzzards to pick your bones or get you to Val Mar Medical … if you were still sucking air."

"You know, Danny Boy," Wally chuckled, "that's one of the things I really appreciate about you. I'm pretty sure you mean that."

"Half serious," Dolan said dryly. "Fortunada'd go bat-shit on me. Never let me get away with it."

"I'm saved. Thank you, Fortunada!" Wally held his drink up in salute before taking another slug: *normalcy*. He went on. "Seriously, I made some notes to help you out … phone numbers … people to contact … that kind of stuff."

"Where's this coming from?" Dolan became more seriously engaged.

"The biggest thing would be if I up and died on you—"

"Okay! What's this shit about?" Dolan's voice got deep; sounded annoyed.

"Look, Dan," Wally said. "I'm just trying to figure out how to be alone and not be a burden on people I care about." He turned and looked at his friend. "Think about it. I know it's a simple thing, but what the hell do you do if I drop dead on you?"

"You ain't gonna fuckin' drop dead."

"Well," Wally responded stopping to sip some more Scotch, "that's probably true … but just in case—"

"This have anything to do with that doctor's appointment you told me you had in Phoenix?" Dolan was worked up.

Wally liked the way Dan remembered minutia. "I almost forgot about that," he lied.

"Well," Dolan demanded. "What about it?"

Wally played him like a fish on a line. The hook was set. He'd let him run. Dan was tired of the game now. "Yeah … about that." Wally popped a few more nuts into his mouth, had another shot of Scotch. "Short version … I got this heart thing."

"What heart thing? You never mentioned no heart thing."

"It's minor," Wally explained. "All the stress I've been under. I get these episodes. Doc says they'll probably go away with time."

"You ain't gonna die from that," Dolan insisted.

"You're right," Wally agreed. "But it got me thinking if something ever did happen, it wouldn't hurt to leave you with a little guidance … don't you think?"

Dan Dolan grabbed another handful of nuts, settled back in his chair, popped several into his mouth and followed with a healthy slug of Scotch. "You ain't gonna die," he concluded.

"Okay. I won't!" Wally laughed. Some of the tension dissipated. "But if I did," he hammered instantly, "you should know all the arrangements have been made right here in Ensenada and all the details you need are here in this envelope. Something happens, don't do shit. Open the envelope and follow the simple steps."

"Fuck you," Dolan said.

"Sorry, I forgot … you can't read. Let Fo follow the instructions."

Awkward silence.

"So, what'd she make us … for dinner?"

"Not sure I'm gonna let you have any of it now."

"Is it that rice and bean thing I like?"

"You really are an asshole," Dolan said, and clinked his glass against Wally's before having a final sip. "Yeah … it's the rice and bean thing."

~~~~

Wally's depressed stupor had been replaced by the nervous energy of purpose. During the days he sat glued to his laptop—typed in feverish bursts, then killed hours searching for specific details on the Internet before returning to the word document he was preparing for Colin. Unlike Dan Dolan's one page instruction sheet, he was detailing for Colin everything he'd learned over the past months about PPI—what he hoped Colin would complete for him should something happen to him before he could carry out what he had planned. The thing was turning into a novella, but it was critical to the operation. He bore down and went on, even when what he had to put on paper left a sickening, vacant feeling in his solar plexus or the metallic taste of bile in his mouth, he kept typing.

Late Sunday afternoon he took a break and pulled out the black duffle bag that contained his disguise. He carefully laid out every piece on top of his bed and examined it, fixing the image in his mind of how the two makeup artists in San Diego had employed each device. He held the latex face piece in his hands and recalled how they'd smeared spirit gum over his face and then sculpted the rubbery material onto him to create a whole different person. He slipped the chest plate on; Velcroed the thing closed around him and pulled the tee shirt over it.

Around five Fortunada called. Said she'd brought back takeout Chinese for all of them. Wally left everything where it was and trotted over. Fo looked up at him when the staircase spit him out into her kitchen. "Wow! That's a look," she exclaimed, noting the scraggly growth on his face and neck. "You growing a beard or just forget to shave for a week?"

He actually enjoyed the meal from the cardboard boxes. They didn't make an evening of it. Wally ate and ran, saying he was expecting a call.

Betrayed

By eleven o'clock the black duffle bag had been meticulously repacked. Wally was ready to use its contents and believed he could. He slept fitfully. All night he was up and down, got very little rest. He spent as much time standing out on the terraza staring out over the placid Pacific Ocean as he did lying in bed trying to sleep. For the moment, he was no longer suffering the *hour of demons.*

Monday was a listless struggle. Work grudgingly crept forward on the letter he was preparing for Colin, but he was having trouble concentrating. He wanted to finish as much as possible before it was time to go, but unless the operation was successful, most of what he was laying out for his nephew would amount to useless information; details that might be interesting, but nothing of consequence. If he pulled off what he had planned, he'd have time to add the finishing touches after the fact. He paced the upper level of his house, but didn't show himself. He was far too keyed up to have to sit with Dan and Fortunada for the moment. Wally purposefully awaited telling Dolan he'd need the car and Sentri Pass soon. Didn't want him to have time to think about it. Wally knew Dan would grumble and carry on, but if he hit him at the last minute, Dolan could only opt to do it or not do it—there'd be no time to argue or rethink his agreement to be complicit in whatever it was Wally had planned. He felt positive when given that situation Dolan would cave.

Monday'd been a bright, you could even call it hot, day. Wally had Dan and Fortunada over for sundowners. They passed on dinner.

"Your eyes are red, Wally," Fo observed, "you sleeping okay?"

"Not well last night," he confessed.

"Too much time in front of that damn computer," Dolan predicted.

"Maybe." Wally yawned and stood.

Fortunada got to her feet and began collecting glasses. "We'll get out of here so you can turn in early."

"I'm gonna do just that, Fo," Wally said. He didn't add he intended downing enough pharmaceuticals to ensure he would not see daylight until well after sunrise. If there was no other way, and there was not, he would have to force rest upon himself. "Sorry to bag out on you guys."

"I'm still recovering from my weekend," Fortunada claimed.

"Couple of wimps," Dolan declared gaining his feet. "Won't be long I'll have to put you both in the home."

There was the shuffling around of the evening's end, a hug and a peck on the cheek, a slap on the shoulder. Finally—silence.

~~~~

Wally turned off the lights and ascended the stairs. Just as he swallowed an overdose of sleep aides his cell phone rang.

"Hey, Uncle Wally," Colin said cheerfully. "You weren't in bed yet were you?"

"Just getting there."

"Want me to hang up?"

"No ... no, of course not. What are you up to?"

"Working ... wondering if you've bagged any lions or tigers yet?"

"Still getting organized," Wally lied. "Need to practice a little with the dart gun before I try the real thing."

"Good idea. Any trouble at the border?"

"I'm not in jail."

"Just making sure. Okay ... gotta get back concentrating. I was just thinking about you ... wanted to check up on you."

"You're a good kid, Colin."

"And you're a good old fart, Uncle Wally."

"Touché!"

"Let me know when you have your first safari. Can't wait to hear how you do with that stuff."

"You won't need to wait long," Wally said—and *that* was not a lie.

"Gotta go. Good night, Uncle Wally."

"Night, Colin."

Those words were the last conscious recollection Wally had until eight-thirty the next morning.

~~~~

Wally awoke feeling sluggish, dope hangover. He shuffled downstairs, opened all the doors to the terraza before commencing to make his tea. It was bright, sunny again. While the water heated he made himself two pieces of toast.

Little by little the caffeine began to take hold. The fog in his brain was clearing. As Wally became alert, he felt somewhat rested but not calm. He found himself feeling resigned and recalled the similar feelings he'd had as a young soldier; no way backward—only gaining the ground in front of you—making it back from the mission in one piece.

The day progressed for him in slow motion. He studied his food, stirred the yoke of his egg with a piece of toast, lifted the bread a little and watched the yellow substance drip back onto his plate before following the toasted bread with his eyes into his mouth. He paid attention to the flavors.

When breakfast was finished, he went upstairs and pulled out a small tote. He was painstaking in his selection of a pair of comfortable slacks. It was hot where he was headed, no need for heavy clothing. His Doc Martins settled into the very bottom of the bag; clean underwear and socks followed.

179

Betrayed

For lunch he made himself a ham sandwich and drank a cold Pacifico out on the terraza. The hawk could be heard whistling off in the distance; its quest for food an endless devotion to its existence.

After lunch he straightened the house, washed and put away the dishes, made orderly the pillows on the couches and chairs. He looked around, ensuring everything was in its place, just in case this was the last time he'd ever see the place.

He stood for a long time in front of the urn and gazed lovingly at his favorite picture of the girl of his dreams. How the hell the wonderful life they'd shared could have come to this was beyond his ability to reconcile. They'd been kind to others. They'd worked as hard as anyone he knew, harder than most it seemed to him. It just wasn't right. Wasn't fair. But none of that mattered. What happened to them came without warning, like an avalanche down a mountain. Until spring came to melt it all away, there'd be no way of measuring the destruction buried beneath the aftermath.

When everything in the house had been put right, Wally lay down on his bed and stared out across the quiet ocean. He could not close his eyes.

At four-thirty he flipped open his cell phone and pressed the speed dial for the Dolans. Fortunada answered. "Hi, Wally," she said cheerfully. "Comin' over?"

"Sorry Fo, can't make it this afternoon. Had a little something come up."

"Anything we can help with?"

"Nothing like that … isn't a big deal … Danny Boy around?"

"Sure," she said.

Wally waited. "Whatta ya need?" Dolan demanded in his charmless manner.

"Your car and Sentri Pass in the morning," he answered without giving Dolan any warning. "Leave it out tonight, just like we discussed. I'll be back in a couple of days."

"I knew you were up to something over there these last few days."

"Put it out tonight," Wally said, ignoring Dolan's attempt to draw him into any exchange.

"So you're just not gonna be sm—"

"Gotta go, Danny Boy," Wally said, cutting him off mid-word. "Stop grousing about it. Put the car out tonight."

Wally hung up before Dolan could respond. He stood back from the window in his office eyeing the Dolan house. Dolan's arms flailed as he stood in front of Fortunada in a rant of silent pantomime.

Aimlessly Wally went down to the refrigerator and poured himself a tall glass of cranberry juice. He turned the TV to MSNBC … *Hardball* with Chris Matthews.

When dusk faded to full darkness, Wally lit the fireplace. It wasn't cold. He was merely trying to squeeze in every sensation that meant anything to him. The black duffle bag and overnight tote were staged at the front door, ready to go. In the bathroom upstairs the jeans, shirt and tennis shoes he intended wearing on the road were laid out. It was difficult to pull his eyes away from the photo of Poppy. He fidgeted as if he suffered a nervous twitch pulling his eyes from the fire to the photo then back to the fire over and over.

At ten o'clock he turned off the fire, the lights and went up to his bedroom. He went to the window facing the Dolan house and searched the street below. The black Honda Accord sat out as Dan Dolan reluctantly promised it would.

Wally went back into his bedroom, set the alarm clock just in case, though there was no real danger he'd sleep. From this point forward he couldn't afford a single lapse. He was no longer merely thinking about what he might do. The deed was now *in play*.

~~~~

At two a.m. he got up and went into the bathroom. Unbelievably, he'd actually dozed off twice for brief periods. He turned on the hot water in the shower before beginning to take off his clothes. He dropped everything into the laundry basket, tested the water was running hot. He hadn't shaved for a week and the whiskers down his neck were irritating. When he stood in front of the mirror after toweling himself off, he decided the neck whiskers could go without damaging the effect.

Slipping into his pants, Wally headed down to start his water heating. While the kettle sat on the burner, he carefully applied spirit gum to his upper lip and affixed the lip-merkin. When he stood back he was astounded at the transformation the simple device made. He went into the bedroom and retrieved the baseball cap he intended wearing and pulled it on. When he looked in the mirror he was relieved. If you didn't know Dan Dolan or Wally Stroud, he felt confident anyone could confuse the two.

The teapot gave its first bursts. Wally descended the stairs buttoning his shirt as he went. While the tea steeped he went back upstairs, smoothed his bed, folded his towel and double-checked everything. He'd gone through these checks four or five times in a futile attempt to quell his nerves.

~~~~

At three twenty-five he stepped out his front door and set his bags at the curb. A chill breeze blew off the ocean. In the onyx sky of early morning, uncontaminated by city lights, the stars shown as crispy flakes. Chiron, the Centaur, could be seen unleashing his eternal arrow and the Milky Way was so dense it seemed like powder in the distant cosmos.

Wally looked up the street toward the Dolan house. The Honda was still sitting in the driveway. He glanced about. No reason for stealth. It was a nervous twitch. Acknowledgment of what was in motion. He moved toward the car and opened the door slowly. The interior light came on. He slipped in under the steering wheel and groped around with his right hand under the front edge of the seat. Keys ... the Sentri Pass in its cardboard envelope—and under that, though he hadn't asked for it—Dolan's passport. He smiled, retrieved everything and set the Sentri Pass with the passport in the console in full view.

He fumbled around to find the ignition switch and inserted the key. The car turned over quietly on his first try. Wally slowly backed out of the driveway without turning on the headlights and allowed it to drift toward his house. In front of the entrance he pulled to a stop, left the lights off and placed his two bags in the back seat. At the highway entrance, he pulled around the northbound leg of the cloverleaf and headed toward Tijuana.

Twenty miles north at Rosarito Beach, Wally pulled into a Pemex gas station and parked near the restrooms. He paid the nickel fee to get rid of the cup of tea he'd consumed.

Before getting back on the road he took time to open the trunk of the Honda and confirm there was nothing inside. As Dolan promised, the car was clean; rear seat was the same except for his two bags. He positioned them so they would be in full view when he got to the border.

It was approaching five o'clock when he found himself winding his way through Tijuana. The morning rush hour was getting under way. Street vendors and newspaper hawkers were already on the corners. While he waited for the light to change at the Glorietta on Paseo de Los Heroes, the guy in the car in front of him bought two burritos and was still making change when the light went green. Every car in the line hammered the horn.

Wally wound his way up onto Otay Mesa and past the airport. Traffic was heavier than he usually faced, but he needed to get across and be on his way by seven-thirty.

The Sentri lane offered an express crossing. The trick was getting through the bumper-to-bumper traffic to get to the Sentri lane. Forty-five minutes later Wally was watching the cars ahead of him being signaled through to the other side. Occasionally the Border Patrol officer would step out of his booth and look into the windows of a car before waving it through. Wally's hands turned damp on the steering wheel. He rubbed his palms on the thighs of his jeans.

Two cars back from the gate his stomach began to quiver. He pulled the golf cap down low and extracted the Sentri Pass from its holder. He cupped the card in his left hand as the car in front of him pulled forward. The car was waved through with little more than a slow down. Wally inched forward into the slot and presented his pass to the scanner. As he did, he looked down at the console as the flash popped. Looking up, he pulled to the gate. The customs officer walked out of the booth and took the card from him. "When you scan your card, Mr. Dolan, you need to look toward the camera," the officer said.

"Sorry," Wally replied. "I sneezed just as I put my arm out."

"You need to declare anything today, sir?"

"No, officer … just have a couple of bags with my clothes." Wally was sweating profusely and his nerves failed him.

The laconic Border Patrol officer eyed him and snooped at the bags in the back seat, handed Wally back the card. "Be sure to look toward the camera next time, Mr. Dolan. Have a nice day." He turned, walked back into his booth and waved the next car up without looking at Wally again.

Wally was shaking so badly he took the first off ramp and found a place to pull off the street. He crawled out of the Honda, leaned against the driver's door and bent forward from the waist hyperventilating. He thought he might vomit. It required several minutes for him to regain control. He would drive half way to Yuma before fully recovering.

Traffic was immediately lighter on the U.S. side. On the 905 Expressway he found no slowdowns. Allied Storage wouldn't open the gate until seven o'clock so he pulled into a Burger King. No order. Direct to the restroom. He relieved himself before taking a look in the mirror. The shirt was soaked and dark in large circles under his armpits. He looked like shit.

The water running in the sink never turned warm. The situation felt dire. He splashed cold water onto his face and rubbed his head until it was wet. When he went for the paper towels there were none. He stood in front of the wall-mounted dryer and did his best to smarten up his appearance.

The spasms in his stomach were severe while he stood in front of the order counter deciding if he should bother to try eating anything. He forced himself to order a breakfast biscuit with a tiny piece of sausage. Diet Coke to wash the goo down.

At seven he pulled through the gate of Allied Storage. He parked beside his unit and backed the Camry out. Quickly transferred his two bags before stowing the Honda safely in the space. The exchange required only a few minutes. It was seven-fifteen when Wally let himself out of the Allied facility and backtracked south along the frontage road toward the border crossing on Otay Mesa. Before entering the empty southbound lanes that would funnel down to the border, he turned off onto the toll-road that would carry him around most of San Diego County's rush hour traffic, out through El Cajon and eventually deposit him onto I-8 several miles east of the metropolitan area and its heavy morning commuter traffic.

Wally settled in for the six-hour drive. He was still recovering from the scare at the border when he descended the east slope of the Tecate Summit into the Imperial Valley. By the time he began to see signs for El Centro, he needed to piss in the worst way.

His brain finally shifted gears, refocused from his panic at the border to the operation that lay before him.

On the east side of Yuma, Wally pulled into the Shell service station at Fortuna Road. It was eleven in the morning. He was running right on schedule. He topped the Camry's fuel tank and bought a hot dog. Food was essential to sustain his energy.

CHAPTER 36

The last sign post he passed put the Hwy 85 turn off at Gila Bend ten miles ahead. Twenty-five miles north of Gila Bend he was driving along side Lewis State Penitentiary; one of Arizona's maximum security prisons. His palms became clammy.

Forty miles beyond Lewis Prison, he followed a long bend, stretching east to the entry lane onto I-10. When he saw the first sign telling him the 35th Avenue off ramp was 2 1/4 miles ahead, Wally checked the dash clock again; two-ten. In a few moments he was easing over into the exit lane. He turned south on 35th Avenue and drove a few blocks to the intersection of Buckeye Road.

One block east of 35th on Buckeye he made a left turn into a rundown dirt and gravel parking lot closed in on three sides by clapboard structures with sagging roof lines and a sign that proclaimed the place: Sunrise Motel. There were thirty individual units. The blistered navy blue paint showed evidence that at some point in its past the place had seen a variety of colors; white, red and green flecks peeked through from below the curled, cracked edges of blue paint like the speckles on a blue tick hound. Its current incarnation in dark blue was covered with the grime of emissions from thousands of passing diesel trucks and swirling dust. It was exactly the kind of place Wally wanted. The only consciousness of its existence to anyone was with the truck-stop whores who utilized it solely for its convenient proximity and cheap hourly rates. Even the trucker "Johns" seemed oblivious of the place in the light of day.

Anyone who'd known Wally Stroud over the last thirty-odd years would have flushed at the idea of the guy staying a night in a sleazy dump like the Sunrise Motel. What they couldn't know, because Wally guarded his history like a state secret, was he'd grown up with surroundings that made the Sunrise Motel look, frankly, not bad. It wasn't entirely unlikely when he was a child his family would have stayed the night in a place exactly like the Sunrise.

He pulled up into the lot and checked inside the office. He figured the toothless relic he found there to be eighty-years-old or better. Even the visage of the old man carried with it echoes from his past. The stench of the hoary man's breath was rancid, even standing across the counter from him. Wally prepaid for three nights with cash. Talbot asked no questions. Talbot. That was his name. "Just Talbot," he'd said to Wally, was glad to have a guest staying more than an hour.

Wally checked out his room before he removed the California plates from the Camry and replaced the rear plate with one from Arizona. A month earlier he'd paid a street urchin five dollars to remove the plate from the back of a beat up minivan parked along a side street on the north side of Ensenada one afternoon, while he sat and ate a couple of tacos at a neighborhood stand.

~~~~

Wally still had the image of Talbot in his head and the odor of the old man's desiccation in his olfactory glands as he sat parked in the lot at Encanto Elementary School watching the offices of PPI. It was coming up on four p.m. He was early, but he didn't want to miss the ballet that would take place when Pace and Taylor decided to call it a day. It was by then two months since he'd put eyes on the two men. He needed some indication habits hadn't changed, and, perhaps, to reestablish a firm visual connection to the hatred he felt toward the two men. He thought about it not for the first time. If they'd changed their pattern, chances were they really were going to walk away free because Wally doubted he'd ever be able to bring himself to come this far again. It was now or never. If they followed their familiar routine their lives would—change. If they did not, he would pack his bags, go home and forget about it, try to find some way to move forward with his life.

He snarled a menacing grin. "Little game of Russian Roulette, and you scum-suckers don't even know it," he said, softly, his eyes locked on the front of the office building like a leopard in a tree waiting for its unsuspecting prey to glide beneath.

At four-twenty Bud Pace appeared, as if on cue, and slid into his Range Rover. He started the vehicle and sat several minutes. Wally figured he was waiting for Taylor. He was disturbed when Sonja Bienvenidos came out and climbed into the passenger seat next to Pace.

"Shit," he grumbled under his breath. "What's this? Out in the open?"

He pulled onto Osborn Road behind the mist-green Range Rover and followed at a distance. Pace drove at an unhurried speed, completely unaware he was being followed. When Pace turned south toward downtown, Wally recognized the familiar route. Pace was headed to the Adams Hotel. At least you're loyal to the Adams, Wally thought. Now he calculated instead of a couple of quick drinks, these two might be off for a round of sport-fucking.

Pace guided his vehicle into the underground entrance and pulled a ticket stub out of the parking machine. Wally followed them in. By the time he found the Rover, Pace and Bienvenidos were already walking toward the elevators. Wally pulled into a space several cars away. He watched Pace and Bienvenidos shuffling impatiently, waiting for an elevator. The body language didn't say sport-fucking. Pace walked in small circles and checked his watch twice.

Betrayed

Wally used the pause to locate the security cameras in the underground garage. There was one at the elevators and one at the end of each row of cars. The coverage wasn't spectacular, but he'd marked their respective locations. After Pace and Bienvenidos entered the elevator, he swung out of his car and walked over to the Rover. He looked the car over, front to back. Then he peered into all of the windows on the driver's side. He still wore the lip-merkin and dark stubbly growth on his face. He kept the golf cap pulled low and felt the cameras could not accurately identify him. He eased around to the rear of the vehicle careful not to touch anything he knew would set off the alarm. The area behind the rear seat was empty. In fact, the whole of the interior of the vehicle was spotless: no papers, folders, briefcases, kid's toys. Pace had an eleven-year-old son—nothing. Keep cooperating, Buddy Boy, Wally thought, walking back to his car.

Wally crawled in behind the steering wheel and closed the door. It was dark enough in the space he'd chosen for concealment. He reached across the front seat and opened a manila folder. Sifted through several sheets of paper until he found what he was looking for: the wiring diagram of the electrical system for the Range Rover. The next page down was a blow-up of the alarm system on the vehicle. He'd studied the diagrams so often he didn't need the printed layout but he forced himself to go over it again anyway; everything was for keeps now. He looked up toward the elevators, waiting.

When Pace and Bienvenidos finally reappeared it was nearly five-thirty. He let Pace make the first turn toward the exit before pulling out of his space. Wally gave plenty of room at the pay booth. By the time he pulled forward to pay his ticket, Pace was already turning the corner, heading north on Second Street. At Van Buren Pace made a left and cut back over to Seventh Avenue. Wally was positive they were headed back to the office instead of to Bienvenidos' condo.

As Wally was pulling into the Encanto Elementary School parking lot, Pace and Bienvenidos were just walking through the front doors across the street. There were still a few employees' cars in the PPI lot. Taylor's Maybach was still there, too. Wally knew from previous surveillance some employees might burn a little after work oil, but by six p.m. they should all be gone. The routines he'd observed months earlier were, more or less, confirmed. No more than ten minutes after Pace returned to the office, three female employees and one male Wally recognized came out. One by one they each opened the driver's door of their cars and within moments the parking lot was empty except for Pace's Range Rover, Taylor's Maybach and Bienvenidos' Caddy. It was six-o-five.

Wally fretted some. He hadn't prepared to handle three people. Bienvenidos created a complication. He'd waited and planned for months. He was ready to get on with what he felt he had to do. The stress of waiting was too great to let this linger. He considered his options and decided day-after-tomorrow, Friday, was a go—one way or the other. He'd be parked right where he was now and if Bud Pace and Carl Taylor followed the old routine of drinks at the Adams before heading home, their lives would change to a nightmare they could have never dreamed. If Bienvenidos went with them, it would be an outing she'd regret the rest of her life.

Wally counted her just as culpable as the other two anyway. She'd lied to his face and misled him on many occasions. He'd let her go because he considered Pace's fate was going to be just punishment for her as well, but if she ended up in the wrong place at the wrong time—destiny, maybe. If you believe in that sort of thing.

On the drive back to the Sunrise Motel Wally found a Boston Market and pulled in. He ordered a meatloaf and mashed potato dinner. The young girl at the register asked what he'd like to drink and he added a small Diet Coke to the ticket.

He sat near a window in a booth and chewed the food slowly. He'd lately developed a condition that could make it impossible for him to swallow. At times his esophagus would constrict when the food went down. It was a painful experience, his breathing would become difficult, not to mention the embarrassment if the food came back up, as it sometimes did. The dinner he was eating just then didn't seem to incite the problem. Or he was managing to control himself. He was sure the meatloaf was delicious but he couldn't taste it. He went on, forcing himself to eat. The food was critical to maintain stamina.

It was getting dark by the time he pulled into the Sunrise again. There were two other cars in the lot, beat up clunkers. Wally unloaded everything from the Camry. He wanted a bottle of Scotch in the worst way, but he denied the urge.

He opened his ditty bag and went to the bathroom sink. He inspected the fake mustache, turning his face from side to side before he leaned in closer to the mirror and gently lifted one edge of the mesh base from his upper lip. It pulled, but was not painful. He worried the theatrical piece loose and returned it to the side pouch of his bag. It hadn't been uncomfortable but he was glad to have it gone.

He took out his razor and began to remove the stubble on his face and neck. The razor pulled at the long hairs. He turned on the hot water in the shower and let the old pipes warm up before stepping in. Hot water ran down the length of his body in a futile effort to rinse away the fatigue and stress. The adrenaline abated enough by ten o'clock for exhaustion to overwhelm him.

He awoke to rowdy voices coming from the room adjacent to his. The clock next to his bed told him it was three-o-six a.m. One voice was a woman's, which Wally could hear clearly. It took him a few moments to realize it must have been one of the hookers who prowled the truck stops along Buckeye Road treating a customer to a little porn sex. He listened to the pounding and moaning and heavy breathing until it ended abruptly, about two minutes later. He could hear the woman ask, "How was that, baby?" The reply was heavy, muffled breathing.

Wally was wide-awake by then and there was little chance sleep would return. He lay in the lumpy bed hoping he wouldn't be eaten alive by bed bugs. As soon as that thought crossed his mind he jumped out of the bed, turned on the lights and ran a complete inspection of his body and the sheets. He didn't find anything. But once the thought found its way into his consciousness, he imagined he felt things crawling on his skin the rest of the night.

~~~~

Betrayed

By seven-thirty Thursday morning Wally had all of his bags safely back in the Camry. He wasn't taking any chance a nosy cleaning woman might look into one of the bags or steal something without him noticing it.

He found a truck stop café down the street called Big Bertha's. He pondered the clientele he saw coming and going, recalled the escapade in the middle of the night that had awakened him and decided he'd drive back to the freeway and find a Denny's. He was marking time. His nerves were on edge. The sugar from the hot cakes and syrup at Denny's gave him a kick-start for the day. He would burn out from its false energy too fast, but he'd deal with that when it came.

He tried not to but he couldn't stop himself from driving by the home where he'd lost the love of his life. The impact was more than he'd anticipated. An auction date was posted on the garage door by the bank. He didn't linger. If the emotions boiling to the surface were not enough, the risk of being seen by a neighbor was sufficient motivation for him to get the hell away from the place.

At noon he drove back to the Sunrise Motel. His room had been straightened but no clean towels had been provided nor were the sheets changed on the bed. He wasn't sure that was because he had prepaid for three nights or that was the regular standard of service. The place was depressing, even to him, and he couldn't wait there. It was so hot outside he began to fear the tranquilizer might be ruined. He found a Safeway grocery store and purchased a five pound piece of dry ice, which he shoved into the duffle bag next to the aluminum chemical box. Wrapped in thick white butcher paper, the solid carbon dioxide gave off its cold while it slowly evaporated. Wally was satisfied it would do the trick.

He spent the early part of the afternoon in a Borders bookstore at the Biltmore Shopping Mall. He hadn't been back to the place since—that day. He went to the fiction section, found the latest James Patterson novel before launching a search for an empty club chair among the many strategically located around the store. He left the book lying on the seat of the chair and went off to the coffee shop where he ordered an iced mocha.

It was after four p.m. when he jerked awake. He looked around, disoriented and confused at first. It only took a few seconds for reality to return. He hadn't gotten past the first three pages of the Patterson novel. The iced mocha sat in a watery puddle of sweat, discolored and unappealing, all of its ice gone. He looked around slowly, wondering if he'd made a spectacle of himself when he noticed an old man across the aisle, his head drooped forward as if he was about to receive a sword to the back of his neck. The Biltmore accommodated lots of older types. Wally hated being identified as one of them, but just then, blending worked.

He walked the Patterson novel back to its place on the shelf and made his way out into the hot parking lot. It was the hottest part of the day. For years Wally had been able to ignore the scorching Arizona summers. But that day he felt drained, and the searing heat made things worse.

He drove back toward the Sunrise Motel, several miles across town and a world away from where he was when he'd pulled out of the Biltmore parking garage. He set the air-conditioning unit in the Camry at full blast and felt blessed the traffic emptying out of downtown was headed in the opposite direction, although he was in no hurry to get back to the roach-nest.

The same Boston Market he'd stopped at the day before was perfectly adequate to satisfy his need for food. It was directly in his path; required no more thought than when to put on his turn signal. That day he chose fried chicken and barbecued beans with a mixed vegetable and homemade country biscuits. It occurred to him there was probably some subconscious proclivity to the foods his mother used to make when he was a child, though they looked and tasted nothing like the meals served up by the Boston Market. None of what he chose to eat was food Poppy ever fed him. He ate slowly and allowed the disconnected meanderings of his mind to distract him for a time.

He picked up a drumstick with his hands and bit into the crispy chicken leg. Both his mother and father would have fully supported what he was about to do; maybe his mother more than his father, but both of them, nonetheless, would have considered his intent wholly justified. They were, at their core, violent people, because their own histories had been violent.

Wally's mother's people were Cajun swamp folk from southwestern Louisiana. His dad's family had been oil-field roughnecks from western Oklahoma. The two had met during WWII while his dad was stationed as a prison guard at a POW camp in Lake Charles, Louisiana, where hundreds of German POWs had been incarcerated during the war. His mom had been a waitress in a nearby café. Both his parents seemed genetically predisposed to settling differences with violence and for a good part of Wally's early adolescence that was how he settled differences, too. He'd spent more than a few Saturday nights in jail for knocking some rival on his ass. His military service and Nam had done little to change that mind set, but little by little, as he'd gotten away from the environment of his youth, and especially after Poppy Zinsser made her way into his life, Wally began to understand that educated society didn't function that way. *"Educated society,"* he said derisively under his breath. You educated fucks are about to receive a different kind of education, he thought, before taking a bite out of a buttered biscuit.

There was a subtle undercurrent that a casual observer having known Wally Stroud over the course of his adult life would have never guessed. Certainly, men like Bud Pace and Carl Taylor never suspected that by doing what they'd done to Wally Stroud, they would be opening the flood gates that could call forward those suppressed tendencies to violence. All those years Wally'd been content to live as a gentler man—tamed, as it were, by Poppy Zinsser. But Poppy Zinsser was no more. And as far as Wally was concerned, she was dead at the hands of Bud Pace and Carl Taylor. With her went any protection the two men might have had from that visceral white-trash-kid who'd pulled himself up from poverty where grievances often got settled in a back alley. They'd defrauded and caused the death of the wrong person, kicked him back into the black hole he'd spent a lifetime clawing his way out of. *Bad idea!*

CHAPTER 37

Back at the Sunrise Wally unloaded the three duffle bags from the car into his room. He scanned the parking lot before locking himself inside. It was eight p.m. and his was the only car in sight. He opened the makeup bag, removed each item and laid it out on the bed. The spirit gum, Q-tips, latex patches, powders and creams, he set on the side counter near the bathroom sink. The clothing he'd selected, including the shoes, were removed from the bottom of the bag and laid out on the single hardback chair in the room. When everything was assembled, Wally stepped back and took stock of the core items in his disguise before he carefully replaced each piece in the bag and set it with the other two on the floor beside the bed.

He slipped out of his shoes and took off his jeans. The undersized window air conditioning unit was barely able to maintain a comfortable temperature. Wally pulled aside the top cover on the bed and lay down. He laced his hands behind his head on the pillow and stared into the peeling paint of the ceiling. He remained in that position for nearly an hour before deciding to overdose on the unidentified sleeping pills he'd picked up at a corner drug store in Mexico. No way could he allow himself to lay awake all night with the reality of what was going to happen the next day facing him.

In spite of the pharmaceutical assist, he awoke early Friday morning. He felt groggy, a little unsteady, and his mouth tasted like the bottom of a birdcage. He splashed water on his face and dressed in the same clothes he'd worn the day before. He looked at the bags on the floor and decided against leaving them there. He grabbed his keys and stepped out the door with one of the bags over his shoulder. It only required a few minutes to transfer the three bags back to the car. Besides, it was good practice.

Before he pulled out he stepped across the lot to the office. Talbot was behind the counter with a chipped coffee mug sitting on a nasty-looking stained piece of paper that looked like it had done service as a coaster more than once.

"Mornin'," Talbot said without ceremony.

"Morning," Wally echoed. "Tell your housekeeper not to bother my room this morning."

"Everything all right?"

"It's fine. Just tell her to leave it alone."

"Your room, mister. Won't hurt her feelins' none."

Wally didn't bother with a thank you. Social graces meant nothing with Talbot. He was better off making clear what he expected and leaving it at that.

He drove the few blocks to the Denny's near I-10 and 35th Ave. His brain still felt like it was in slow motion when he took the first sip of coffee. He'd loaded it with Splenda and milk so he could tolerate the taste of it. He needed the caffeine. As long as he masked the flavor adequately, he could get it down. He made no show of appreciation for the food. The Grand Slam disappeared matter-of-factly while he suffered another cup of the black liquid.

By nine a.m. he'd paid his bill and was driving back to the motel.

Once more he unloaded the three duffle bags into the room. It was a pain in the ass, but he knew all too well the price he'd pay for carelessness. He unzipped the bag with the tranquilizer and placed his hand on the outside of the aluminum case. It felt cold to the touch, but he'd stop for another piece of dry ice just to be sure. He locked the door and then stepped to the bathroom sink to shave. When he finished he took off his clothes and jammed them into a plastic trash bag.

He stepped into the shower for a quick rinse. Wally toweled himself dry and slipped on a pair of briefs before stepping in front of the mirror once more. Taking up the same makeup brush Carl, the gay Asian guy had used, he began brushing the areas where latex was to be applied. Wally studied each piece carefully; held it close to the spot where it should be attached. The latex felt cool and doughy. Before the mask could be attached he had to use putty to shape his nose and forehead. He filled in areas along his jaw line, too. The foundation was ready. He smeared spirit gum onto his face and applied the mask the makeup artists pre-formed for him. His hands trembled slightly; no screw-ups. Like every other phase of his operation, there would be no do-overs. His new, younger face began to appear. Wally became more and more confident with his work.

The application took more than an hour to complete. He stepped back for a look then closed in slowly to the mirror checking key points around his eyes, near each ear and the corners of his mouth. He tightened an edge around one eye.

When Wally pulled on the human hair wig and saw his image in the mirror, he breathed a sigh of relief. "Yeah," he whispered to his own image. He slipped the wig back off and smeared more spirit gum around the edges of his hairline. He worked more confidently now. Finally he glued on the rubber skullcap that would seal his own hair away from the inside of the wig. When it was firmly in place he applied more gum to the top of the rubber cap and glued the wig in place. He felt confident the wig could not easily be dislodged.

Next, he slipped on a thin nylon t-shirt that hugged his torso. Over that he fitted the chest prosthesis. When it was fastened snugly, he pulled on the black stretchy pullover, which made it look like real body muscle. Not only did the device alter his appearance, it gave an illusion of strength. A little intimidation would go a long way.

It was nearly two o'clock by then. Wally couldn't sit in the parking lot of the elementary school for two hours without drawing attention. He pulled on the thin jumpsuit he'd picked for the ordeal that lay ahead. He went on, slipped his feet into the tennis shoes, pulled each foot up onto the front of the chair and tied them. He stood staring for a long spell in front of the bathroom mirror—a young man of thirty-five years, anybody might guess, a strong likeness to Matt Damon. In any case, the image he saw didn't look anything like Wally Stroud. He lay down on the bed and stared at the ceiling.

At three-thirty p.m. Wally reloaded the duffle bags into the Camry and drove toward Encanto Elementary School. In route he made a quick stop off for another piece of dry ice. He parked in the same spot in the lot he had a day and a half earlier. All he could do now was hope Pace and Taylor would follow the routine he'd observed so often in the past. He watched and waited; four-thirty came and went. Wally was sweating heavily. He started the Camry and turned on the AC unit. They should have showed before then. He was growing impatient. Sonja Bienvenidos finally came out of the building, punched the electric door lock on her key ring, got into her Caddy and drove away. Wally waited.

Nearly a half hour more plodded by before the two men he sought finally appeared. They were talking animatedly about something and walked toward Taylor's Maybach. Wally hadn't counted on that possibility. On every single occasion he'd observed the two they'd always driven away in Pace's Range Rover. Taylor reached into his pocket and then threw up his hand. He was saying something and pointing back toward the front of the building. Then Pace held up his keys and motioned toward his Rover. Taylor shrugged, came around the rear of his Maybach and walked to the Rover with Pace. For the first time in the minutes since the two men made their appearance, Wally breathed.

He watched as Taylor got into the passenger seat of the Rover. "See you boys on the other side of the moon," Wally said to himself. A simpering grin spread across his counterfeit face. He pulled out of the parking lot ahead of the Rover and watched them in his rearview mirror. He drove the same route he knew Pace always drove to the Adams Hotel. Exactly as expected, each time he turned, within moments Pace's vehicle appeared behind him. Wally sped up to ensure he arrived at the Adams ahead of his targets.

He retrieved the parking stub and continued around to the section in front of the elevators. It was the exact route Pace had driven on every occasion including, two days earlier with Bienvenidos; a creature of predictable habit for which Wally was sadistically grateful. He took the first two open side-by-side spaces and backed his car in, partially overlapping the space on the side of the oncoming traffic. When Pace turned the corner and come toward him, he eased his car out into the lane. Pace came to a full stop while Wally backed up a short distance, but not enough to permit him to get by. Then he pulled out again, maneuvering the Camry into the correct space. He repeated the drill a second time. As he calculated, Pace became impatient and pulled the Rover into the vacant space next to him. Wally waved to the two men who didn't bother to hide their annoyance. He pretended to fumble around his front seat as though he was searching for something misplaced. Pace and Taylor walked off to the elevators and hit the up button.

Wally watched the two get in and waited for the doors to close. He waited several more minutes, gathering his nerve. Finally he looked around, taking care to notice if anyone was sitting in a nearby vehicle. It was eerily quiet with the occasional screech of tire rubber against concrete as a car someplace inside the garage went around a corner. The place was hot and stuffy with the smell of overheated engines and burnt oil.

His hands were trembling when he opened the bag on the seat next to him and retrieved a box of rubber gloves. Five gloves slid onto each hand. It was a clumsy operation but he'd discovered when making dry runs a single or even double glove could break, risking a palm or fingerprint without realizing it. He was taking no such chance.

He reached down into the footwell of the passenger side and retrieved a flat metal bar with a slight hook on one end and a pair of needle nose pliers. One more quick recon and he slipped out the driver's door. He left the door open to obscure the fact he was standing next to the door of Pace's Rover. Without hesitation he shoved the metal bar down into the window slot. The car alarm went off. No panic. A quick pull upward and the door lock released. In one fluid motion he opened the driver's door of the Rover, dropped to one knee, pulled a tab at the side of the dash: fuse box. He shined a small light at the box with one hand and grabbed the exact fuse with the needle nose pliers and pulled it out. The alarm stopped sounding. He closed the door to the Rover and got back into his Camry. He waited more than two minutes to ensure the alarm did not trigger a visit from security.

When he felt safe, he got out of his car and pulled the brown and blue duffle bags from the back seat. He went to the Rover and tripped the master lock on the driver's door. Now he had full access to the Rover. Wally slid the two bags into the back seat and followed them in, closing the door softly behind him. It was quiet inside. It smelled of one of those scents they spray in at carwashes; some flowery lavender shit. He wrestled the two large duffels to the compartment behind the rear seat. A moment to glance up and down the rows of cars before moving again. When he was satisfied the coast was clear, Wally slipped out of the Rover and back to the Camry.

He checked both hands. The gloves were intact. He slid a beige colored blanket aside and picked up the dart gun. In the shadowy light it looked enough like a Glock 22 with a silencer that he was confident having it shoved into your face would cause you to piss yourself. He opened the breach and checked the dart that was in the chamber. He'd armed it with the tranquilizer before leaving the motel. He clicked the safety into place and returned the weapon to the seat. Next he inspected the two syringes he'd filled and double-checked that the plastic covers were secure over the needles. Everything was perfect; ready to go.

Betrayed

Finally, he removed the keys from the ignition of the Camry and tucked them in the pouch inside his pants. Another quick scan. He opened the door and slid out again grabbing the gun, syringes, and blanket. Quickly, smoothly, Wally locked the door of the Camry and slid quietly into the back seat of the Rover. He pushed the bench seat back as far as it would go in order to maximize the space on the floor directly behind the front seats. He placed the Glock lookalike on the floor where he could access it quickly, then slid one syringe into the side pocket of the rear door. Couldn't risk damage in case he needed a backup. He carefully placed the other syringe on the floor next to the gun.

He was scared. It was incredibly hot in the parking garage and his disguise added to his misery. Ready. He reached across the driver's seat and pressed the master door lock. Clicking sounds came from all the correct places as the electric switch engaged the mechanisms. He smoothed the blanket over the back seat, then got down into the footwell and dragged it over himself. He'd made certain the blanket was the same fawn color as the upholstery. The effect was as good as he could hope for. He would only need them *not* to notice he was there for a few seconds once they were inside the vehicle. The darkness inside the parking garage was his friend. He pulled the thin cloth the rest of the way over his head, turned on the small light he carried, found the syringe, removed the plastic needle cover and tucked it into the pouch with his car keys. Finally, he positioned the syringe in his right hand holding it like he was about to stab something instead of poking it and placed his thumb on the plunger. He turned off the light and lay still on his side.

It was stifling, hard to breathe—miserable. Discipline he had not employed since he'd laid on his belly 40 plus years in his past—in another lifetime really, on a rotting, insect-infested steaming jungle floor in Vietnam waiting for a different kind of enemy—surfaced like curd in a sour jug of milk. He could only prey Pace and Taylor would decide to make an early evening of it. Oddly enough, he sensed his fear subsiding. That, too, was a forgotten defense. Fear was being displaced by his acceptance that if death was necessary to accomplish what he was after— he was ready to accommodate that necessity.

CHAPTER 38

For thirty-seven wretched minutes longer Wally lay perfectly still, his body fluid and strength oozing out of his pores in the footwell of Bud Pace's Range Rover. Suddenly he felt the muted thud followed by the sound of the door locks answering the electronic signal of the switch when Pace hit the button on his key ring. Wally stiffened slightly as the passenger door opened. Taylor got in first. Almost immediately followed the sound of the driver's door being opened.

"You headed to Sonja's?" Taylor asked, pulling the passenger door closed.

Pace scooted into the driver's seat. "Begged off tonight," he replied, slamming his door.

At the sound of the closing door, Wally jerked to a kneeling position and stabbed Carl Taylor at the base of his neck with the syringe, hitting the plunger with his thumb as the needle slid into flesh. Taylor grabbed at the painful spot and screamed. Too late.

Pace was so stunned he sat for a split second too long. Wally raised the barrel of the gun into his face. "You make one fucking wrong move, I'm gonna blow your head right out that window." Bud Pace froze. Carl Taylor was already twitching, slumping in his seat. "Your friend is fine," Wally said. "Just a little relaxer so I don't have to watch two of you at once. Put both your hands on the wheel and keep 'em there." Pace eased his hands onto the top arc of the steering wheel while looking into the barrel of the gun.

"What do you want?" Pace demanded. "Just take our wallets and go."

"Shut up," Wally said, "and listen. We're gonna go for a short ride. You do exactly as I tell you; you and your friend here will see your families tonight. You get cute, I'm gonna blow a hole in the back of your head first and his next. We clear?"

Pace didn't reply.

Wally stretched forward and stuck his mouth close to Pace's ear. "I asked if we were clear?" he whispered menacingly.

"We're clear," Pace said.

Betrayed

Wally sat back in the seat a few moments. He was breathing heavily. He took several deep breaths, glanced around to make certain no one was watching. Things seemed quiet outside the Rover. "Start the engine and get the AC on full blast." Pace hesitated. "Now!" Wally repeated, all the promise of a bad ending in his gesture if Pace failed to cooperate.

Pace shoved the key into the ignition and started the Rover. The AC was already on.

Wally sat a few moments allowing the cool air to blow onto him; the evaporation helping cool his body. "Pay attention," he said to Pace. "You're gonna drive back to your office—"

"We don't keep any cash in that office," Pace scoffed, cutting in abruptly.

Wally knew better than to accept any disobedience from him. He placed the muzzle of the Glock lookalike just behind Pace's right ear and pressed it hard enough against his head to force Pace to bow forward. Very calmly Wally said, "Shut-your-fucking-mouth. I'll tell you when to talk." Wally slid forward on the seat and leaned close to the back of Pace's head. He was close enough to feel the heat of his own breath reflected into his face off of Pace's skull as he spoke. "Don't make that mistake again. Understand?" He spoke softly, slowly, enunciating each word. "Understand?" he repeated grinding the barrel of the gun hard into the flesh of Pace's head.

"I got it, I got it," Pace said. "Don't get nervous. I'll do whatever you want." Pace glanced over at Carl Taylor who was now completely unconscious.

Wally caught the squint. "Stop worrying about him. He'll be awake again in a while."

"I want you to pull out of this garage and drive straight back to your office. Only thing you need to do to stay alive. Understand?" He glared back into Pace's eyes in the rearview mirror. He figured Pace was struggling to recall if he recognized him.

"Forget it," Wally said. "We've never met. Move. Let's get out of here. The parking kid asks about Sleeping Beauty here … he had too much to drink."

Pace pulled the shift lever into reverse and began to ease the Rover out of the space. He followed the exit arrows to the pay booth. The young female attendant seemed to notice Carl Taylor but expressed no interest in his condition. Wally held the handgun under the blanket, keeping it trained on Bud Pace's back.

Pace followed Wally's instructions. He made a right onto Adams St. and drove to the corner. He continued through the light at First Street, neared Second and gave a right turn signal. Wally didn't say anything, just maintained a glaring focus on Pace's eyes in the rear view mirror.

Traveling north on Second, Pace moved his vehicle into the right lane coming up to Van Buren and pulled the turn signal lever down indicating a right turn. It was the wrong direction.

Wally shook his head slowly from side to side as Pace watched his implacable reaction in the rearview mirror. "Let me ask you something, Buddy Boy," he said stone-faced. "You kiss your wife and kid goodbye this morning?"

Pace seemed baffled. "How the fuck do you know my name?"

"Oh, you're famous, Buddy Boy. But apparently not nearly as smart as you think you are."

"What are you talking about?" Pace glowered, feigning ignorance.

"There's a good chance you're never gonna see 'em again, Buddy Boy," Wally said, mocking Pace's phony ignorance. "Didn't I tell you what was going to happen if you got cute?"

Pace objected. "I'm doing exactly what you told me—"

Wally hit him hard in the ear with the barrel of the gun. Pace's head ricocheted off the driver's door window. He instinctively grabbed the side of his head where he'd been hit. A slight trickle of blood oozed from a shallow gash just in front of his right ear.

"Listen, you two-bit, punk! You think I don't know the way back to your office?" Wally yelled the words at Pace who was recovering from the trauma of the blow. "Drive the fucking car to your office, asshole! And the next wrong turn you try to make will be your last!" Pace made no attempt to reply. He looked into the rear-view mirror at Wally, and Wally saw hatred. But he also saw fear in the man's eyes.

Wally knew he could take no chance that either of these men might get the idea they could confront him and get away with it. He knew full well if that happened, he'd be lost; he'd be no match for the younger men. Total control was absolutely essential. He had to dominate and intimidate them; train them, as it were, to obey implicitly. They needed to believe the vision he'd created. They needed to believe the possibility of death confronted them, and perhaps, Wally thought for the first time, it actually did. "Go around the block and cut back to Seventh Avenue," Wally ordered, his voice husky with anger, "and drive *directly* to your office."

Pace removed his bloody hand from the side of his face and accelerated around the corner at Van Buren. Wally didn't blink holding Pace's pupils, boring into his soul in the rearview mirror.

This time Bud Pace guided the Range Rover to Seventh Avenue as he'd been instructed and turned west on Osborn. "Now you're getting the idea."

Less than ten minutes had expired after Wally disciplined Bud Pace when they made the turn into the parking lot of the PPI offices. "Back into the space directly in front of the main entrance," Wally ordered, noting the only car in the lot was Taylor's Maybach.

Pace did as he was told.

"Shut it off and give me the keys."

Pace glared at him in the mirror. Wally responded. "Careful with that temper, Buddy Boy," he cautioned. "We're gonna get out together and unlock the front doors … and please … don't force me to blow your brains all over the sidewalk."

Pace opened his door and settled his left foot on the pavement. Wally matched his movements. He kept the gun behind the door so it would not be visible to a passing car. It was six forty-five. Traffic had thinned considerably. Pace slid the rest of the way off the seat and came around the door toward the front of the office building. "My key is on the ring," he said to Wally.

Wally pulled the car keys from his pocket and tossed them to him. "Hurry up," he said.

Pace walked to the main entrance and shoved the key into the lock. He pushed the door open slightly and Wally heard the security alarm activate.

Betrayed

"Get in there and disarm it," Wally ordered. He recognized hope in Pace's eyes and raised the gun to his face. "You'll be long dead by the time they get here. Disarm it right now." Pace pushed the door open, walked to a wall in the lobby and punched in the code. A robotic voice from the control panel intoned, "Alarm deactivated."

"You're learning," Wally said.

It was quiet and cool inside the building. Wally stood with the gun pointed at Pace while he surveyed the set up. He was still overly hot, tired, operating on pure adrenaline. He was scared and at the same time felt a sense of real power.

"Let's take a walk back there," he said, pointing toward a door leading deeper into the maze of offices. The door opened into a capacious area that must have served as a secretarial pool. There were four desks spaced evenly in the middle of the huge room. Two sat side-by-side while the other two faced them. Each desk was supplied with a computer terminal. Pictures of kids, husbands, boyfriends or brothers clustered around the front edges. The desks were strewn with small stacks of folders on the corners, in/out trays along the tops. Three of the walls were lined with black metal filing cabinets, the tall ones with wire baskets on top of some of them. "This'll do," Wally said. "Let's go get your partner." He motioned toward the door with the gun and Pace began to move slowly back the way they'd come.

Wally stopped him at the front door. "I want you to walk to the passenger door, get your pal's arm around your shoulder and muscle him in here."

"How the hell do you expect me to do that? He's a big guy."

"Or, I could just shoot him right there. Would that make it easier?"

"What the hell is this all about?" Pace pleaded.

"All in good time, Buddy Boy," Wally said, annoyed at the delay. "You gonna go get him, or do I shoot him and forget him?"

Pace shoved the front door open with attitude. Wally could see his prisoner's inability to gain some control in the situation beginning to grate on him. Wally followed close behind to the passenger side of the Rover.

Pace opened the door and reeled backward. "What the hell is that smell?" He grimaced.

Wally detected the foul odor as well. *Sometimes the animal eliminates when tranquilized, the notes had said.* "He shit himself," Wally predicted nonplussed. "Get him inside."

Pace leaned into the vehicle and pulled Carl Taylor's limp arm over his shoulder, jerked upward and out. Taylor groaned and rolled his head toward Pace.

"Hurry it up!" Wally ordered.

Pace grunted something that sounded like, *fuck you*, as he slipped his arm around his partner's waist and began to drag the man toward the doors of the office building. Pace used the staggering weight and the lurching motion to shoulder the door open. He was only a couple of steps inside when he dropped Carl Taylor to the floor. "He's too heavy."

"You're doing fine, Buddy Boy ... almost there," Wally said, gun leveled at Pace, checking through the glass doors to the lot outside gauging whether or not they'd been seen by anyone. It seemed still.

It was abundantly obvious Carl Taylor's bowels and bladder had both been sufficiently relaxed to cause release. His pants were soiled in the crotch and the stench was identifiable.

"Drag him inside."

"He's dead weight," Pace groused.

"He could be," Wally threatened, "if you don't do what I just told you."

Pace glared under black hooded eyes, contempt written across the space between them. "Hold that thought, Buddy Boy," Wally taunted. "Move!" he shouted, gesturing with the barrel of the gun.

Bud Pace grabbed both of Carl Taylor's arms and began dragging him. Dragging proved easier than carrying.

"Just leave him next to that desk," Wally said, pointing to a spot in front of the closest desk.

Pace grunted as he dragged Carl Taylor's limp body toward the desk. "You ever gonna get around to ... letting me," he grunted while he dragged, "in ... on what this is all about?"

"All in good time, Buddy Boy ... all in good time." Wally moved around, careful not to get close enough for Pace to make any kind of move. "Get out both of your cell phones and set them on that desk."

Bud Pace reached onto his hip and pulled the flat phone from its holster.

"Now his."

Pace rolled Taylor slightly onto his side and retrieved his phone.

"Okay," Wally continued, "we need to go back to the car."

"Now, where we going?" Pace demanded to know.

"Just do what you're told."

Pace stepped over Carl Taylor's legs and trudged out to the front doors. Wally stopped him in the lobby. "Get the two large duffle bags behind the rear seat and bring them here."

Pace was confused but continued doing as told. Wally knew he needed to incapacitate the man soon, before he found an opening to try something. The back of the Rover was less than eight feet from the door. Wally hid just inside the doorway while he sent Pace to get the bags.

Pace opened the back of the Rover. He turned, puzzled. "Where the hell did these come from?"

Wally used the muzzle of the gun to motion for him to get on with it. Pace pulled the two bags to the back of the vehicle and hefted them out. They were heavy; one must have been fifty pounds, Pace judged. He set the two bags on the ground and closed the rear door of the Rover. With a bag in each hand, Bud Pace half dragged them into the office building. He was tiring.

"Get them into the office," Wally commanded. Pace glared threateningly at him and hesitated a few seconds before doing as he was told. Wally observed the growing tendency in the man not to respond instantly.

Betrayed

"What's in these?" Pace grunted, moving slowly into the back office.

Wally walked around to the desk where Pace had set the cell phones and retrieved them. Carl Taylor was beginning to show signs of waking up. Wally needed to speed things along. He reached across the desk and with the sweep of his arm, knocked everything to the floor. The computer monitor and phone hung on the side of the desk by their cables. Wally made another full sweep and cleared what remained. Then he stepped back a few feet and ordered Pace to get Taylor up onto the desk.

Taylor was still several minutes from consciousness but he wasn't exactly dead weight any longer. Pace tried to talk to him while he got him to his knees. "You okay, Carl?" No response.

Pace had his back to Wally, doing what he could to position his friend onto the desktop so he wouldn't roll sideways and fall off. Just as he completed the maneuver, Wally deliberately elevated the barrel of the pistol slightly and shot Bud Pace in the back. The dart found flesh just below the deltoid of the man's right shoulder.

"Ahhhh!" Pace whimper-screamed, spinning in circles, both hands flailing over his shoulders in a futile effort to subdue the agony coursing through him from the nail-sized needle stuck in his back. "You sonofabitch," he bellowed at Wally. He spun again and threw one arm downward to try getting at the object of his misery from a different angle. Nothing worked. Before Pace could respond further, he began to weave. His knees started to buckle, and he grabbed at the desk Carl Taylor was splayed out on. Just before he went to the floor, he spun and bore into Wally Stroud's eyes. Wally saw sheer hatred and felt a sense of accomplishment.

As Bud Pace crumbled to the floor, Wally turned his focus to Taylor. He was moaning, rolling side-to-side. It wouldn't be long before he'd be conscious enough to be difficult.

Wally ran out to the Rover and recovered the syringe he'd secreted in the side pocket of the rear passenger door. He jogged back into the office and pulled the plastic protector off the needle. He hurried to Taylor, who was thrashing around, and calmly plunged the needle into the base of his neck. Taylor winced but was not sufficiently coordinated to deflect Wally's hand.

Wally stopped pushing the plunger at about one quarter of the dose. He didn't want Taylor out too long and figured a little of the tranquilizer cocktail at this point would go a long way. Within moments Taylor began to slow his flailing and in a few more he went still, breathing deeply.

Wally stepped back and listened to the silence. He went to the brown duffle bag. The first thing he retrieved was a liter of bottled water. Half of it went down in one long, breathless gulp. When he dropped the bottle from his mouth his chest heaved in gasping, deep, sucking breaths. As soon as his breathing caught up, he drained the rest of the bottle and returned it to the bag. While his hand was still inside he found the aluminum tranquilizer case, pulled it out and set it on the desk beside Taylor's inert body. He casually loaded two syringes with tranquilizer and set them safely up on a file cabinet. At the first sign of any unexpected movement from Pace or Taylor, Wally would bring them quickly back under control.

He reached into the brown bag again and pulled out another water bottle. "Well, gentlemen," he said holding the bottle as if to toast the two torpid bodies before taking another deep swig, "shall we get to work?"

CHAPTER 39

Wally went back out to Pace's Range Rover and locked the doors. He glanced out toward the street. Nothing out of the ordinary—an occasional car traveling east on Osborn—then one coming from the opposite direction. Just traffic. He went back inside and locked the door. The keys dangle from the lock. He leaned momentarily against a wall and closed his eyes, took in several deep breaths, held it, then exhaled slowly. When he opened his eyes again, he inspected his gloved hands. The right hand showed two layers of torn rubber. He smiled.

He pushed himself off the wall, shuffled back into the room where Carl Taylor was lying in his own feces and urine atop the desk and closed the door. The stench was extraordinary. He knelt and opened the navy blue duffle bag and found the box of rubber gloves. Before going on, he replaced the two torn ones on his right hand.

Returning the box of gloves he groped for the plastic bag containing the painter's jumpsuit. Wally tore open the bag, pulled out the jumpsuit and stuffed the empty wrapper back into the duffle before he stood. He unfolded the work garment, leaned against the desk and began pulling the papery-fabric suit on. He zipped it part way, then pulled on the footie covers over his tennis shoes. He set a sock-hood on the desk next to Taylor's head. At that point, Wally stopped a moment and glanced down his front. He looked again at his hands.

Satisfied with what he saw, he picked up the pace. He rummaged in the blue bag and retrieved a nylon tie-down strap fitted with a metal jacking device for tightening a load securely. Looking like a fireman in a HAZMAT suit, he moved around the desk where Carl Taylor was still out cold and straightened him out, as if to place him on a stretcher on his back.

The desks needed to be separated. Wally shoved the desk facing the one Taylor was on about four feet back so he could walk between them. He shoved the computer monitor onto the floor watching its screen shatter and plastic parts splinter. He cleared the rest of the desktop with broad sweeps of his arms sending folders and small-framed photos hurtling across the room.

He was soaked from sweat as he stepped around and grabbed Bud Pace under the arms and dragged him next to the desk he'd just cleared. Pace was roughly five-nine, flabby-soft, but not overly fat. Dragging him up onto the desk, Wally guessed he weighed about one hundred ninety-five pounds. Based on that, he'd judged the dose of tranquilizer about right. He laid him out flat on his back, as he had Taylor.

Wally slipped the hook at one end of the tie down strap under the front edge of the desk, ran the strap up, across Pace's head, which he adjusted sideways so when the prick opened his eyes, he'd be looking right at Carl Taylor. He attached the opposite hook end to the bottom edge at the back of the desk and pulled the strap taut, checked its placement across the side of Pace's head and tightened it down until he couldn't move Pace's head with his hands. Get it so he can't move, he thought, but don't pop his brain out like a fucking pimple.

He retrieved several more tie-down straps from the duffle bag and continued to cinch Pace to the desktop so he couldn't move; one went across the chest, another for the hips. Wally placed a strap across Pace's neck just tight enough so if he did somehow wiggle loose, he'd effectively strangle himself trying to get up. It was merely a precaution. He was positive by the time he was finished, the most Taylor and Pace would be able to manage would be squirming and straining against the straps—and they were both going to be doing a lot of that. It required only a few minutes to render Bud Pace completely immobile.

He went to work on Taylor then. The gained experience from his work on Pace made the job quicker. In a few minutes the task was complete and Carl Taylor's head was pinned sideways so he'd be looking right into the eyes of Bud Pace when he regained consciousness.

Wally stepped back to the duffle bag and retrieved several more tie-down straps narrower and considerably shorter than the ones previously employed.

He went back to Pace and wrapped one of the straps around each arm, as close to the shoulder as he could get it, then tightened each one so tight pieces of the man's flesh were pulled into the jacking mechanism. Trickles of blood oozed from the wounds and made his rubber gloves slippery. Wally didn't see how there could be one drop of blood-flow below the point of the tourniquet. He repeated the process around each of Pace's thighs, placing the straps as close to his groin as he could.

Again, experience from the process allowed Wally to improve the time it took to truss up Taylor the same as he'd done Pace. He was grateful, for the stench from Taylor's released bowels was rank. Maneuvering around the urine soaked crotch and shit-filled pants was ugly business. The clock on the wall read seven-twenty p.m. Wally set a large roll of duct tape on the desk next to Taylor's head. In an emergency he could run a strip of the stuff across anything he needed secured.

Now he stood back, placed his hands on his hips and surveyed his work. His clothing inside the jumpsuit was soaked to the skin. The moisture made him feel a bit cooler. He went to the brown bag, found another bottle of water and took a long pull. He breathed heavily before taking another long hit. The bottle was replaced deliberately back into the bag.

Betrayed

Wally guessed the two men would begin to come around in a few minutes. The final item he pulled from the duffle bag was a heavily padded case from which he pulled a laptop computer. He set the PC on the desk next to Bud Pace's face, plugged in the AT&T wireless network antenna and turned it on. The hard drive began to whir softly and small blue lights illuminated on the front of the keypad, one by one.

Carl Taylor made a groaning noise. Wally glanced at his face and figured Pace wouldn't be out much longer either. When the PC was fully booted, he went online and checked connectivity. All bars on the scale were fully lit. He opened the Yahoo browser and went directly to the website for The Central Bank of the Netherlands Antilles. Pace was beginning to make sounds. He scrolled to the login page for his bank account in the Cayman Islands. Username and password, and his account page opened. Balance £10,000. He marveled at one's capabilities with such a tiny thing as a laptop computer connected to the Internet. He logged out of the account but left the login page open on the screen.

Both men were groaning now; consciousness was returning more quickly as the tranquilizer continued to wear off. Colin's friend, Kyle, warned in his notes that when the tranquilizer began to break down, the animal could come-to rapidly. The tranquilizer is powerful juice. *"But it will break down fairly rapidly in the animal's blood system,"* the instructions had informed. Kyle understated just how rapidly, because it didn't take Bud Pace very long to sense his predicament and begin shrieking. Wally grabbed the duct tape and slapped a piece across his mouth. He turned quickly and treated Taylor to the same dessert.

~~~~

"Well, Buddy Boy," Wally said calmly, turning back to the man he'd come to despise so much, "how was your nap?"

At that moment, Taylor screamed as loud as the tape across his mouth would allow, which was not loud enough to accomplish anything except the popping out of the arteries along the sides of his neck and forehead and to acknowledge the terror gripping him. "Hello there, Carl," Wally said turning his attention. "I don't believe we've had the pleasure; nice to meet you." Taylor's brow knitted. Wally understood. "Very soon now, Carl," he assured his panicked captive, "both you and Buddy Boy here," he went on, turning again to Pace, "will see the entire picture—more clearly than I imagine you'd prefer.

"If you would be," Wally continued, "kind enough gentlemen to bear with me just a few more moments while I finish setting up?"

He went back to the blue duffle, removed a large Ryobi reciprocal saw and an eighteen-inch-long coarse blade. Returning, he stood between the two desks so both men could watch; see exactly what he was doing.

"You boys know what this is?" Wally inserted the shank of the blade into the socket of the saw, tightening the shaft lock. "Of course you do. You boys been in the building trade a lot of years, haven't you?"

Both men struggled to speak and squirmed as best they could in a futile effort to escape their bonds. Tears streamed down the sides of Taylor's face, but Wally could still see defiance in Bud Pace's eyes.

"Look at you, Buddy Boy," Wally jeered, turning his full attention to Pace once more. "Still a defiant little prick, I see.

"Let's see if we can adjust your attitude a bit … shall we?" Wally stuck his face right down onto the desk, his nose practically touching Bud Pace's nose. He wanted the man to look deep into his eyes. And he wanted to see into his captive's soul, if indeed he had one. "You fellas," he went on, "might note that neither your hands nor your legs are bound. Go ahead, lift up a hand and have a look."

Pace attempted to lift one arm but it didn't respond. Now both men tried in vain to move their extremities only to discover the best they could achieve was a hysterical flopping movement; control was impossible.

"You see gentlemen," Wally intoned while completing his ministrations with the reciprocal saw, observing the belligerent look in Pace's eyes, "there has been no blood flow to your arms or legs for quite a long while now; more or less like you slept wrong on your arm and put it to sleep … except worse, get it?" He half chuckled, shrugged his shoulders. There was a loud click when the power pack snapped into place on the saw. He held the threatening tool out in front of him so both men could easily see his index finger close around the trigger. The 18-inch blade jumped to life with a terrifying buzz.

A look of comprehension came into Pace's face, and he pissed himself. "Ah," Wally said softly. "I see you and I are beginning to understand one another, Mr. Pace." Bud Pace emitted sounds from his guts, strained and flailed so hard at his constraints the veins in his neck and face appeared as though they might burst out of the flesh. "Very good, Buddy Boy," Wally encouraged. "Those straps really work … don't you think?" Pace's eyes filled and overflowed for the first time; hatred, rage—ultimately, fear.

Wally set the saw down on the desk so both men could see it. He waited several moments for effect. Then he began to speak. "You boys didn't give a shit about the lives you destroyed with this nasty little scheme of yours, did you?" The men turned their eyes toward each other as Wally exposited. "Are you two even aware how many people have lost everything … their entire life's efforts … not just the fucking money, but every waking morning of every long work day, and every paid obligation, and every deferred gratification … I mean the totality of what life exacts from you just to make it to when you think you might eke out a few brief moments in time for yourself and your family before you evaporate back into the cosmos? Old people who have no chance to recover, too old to get jobs, no way out, not a single fucking alternative except to pray death comes quickly." Wally paused, took a breath, and looked up into the ceiling. "Six of your victims are dead now," he said matter of fact. "Heart attacks, strokes—suicide. But that doesn't bother the two of you, does it?" Wally put his face down close to Bud Pace once more so the man could see into his black, unforgiving eyes. Wally could smell ammonia on Pace's breath. "Not quite so confident any longer ... Buddy Boy?" Wally whispered into Pace's face.

"Okay!" he announced abruptly. "We have work to do, gentlemen. Down to it, shall we?" Wally looked from one then to the other of the two men. "Here's what I know about you two. You've run this fraud of yours now for close to six years. I've gone over thousands of public records and I see you two have cleaned out between seven hundred and a thousand unsuspecting investors." He paused to make eye contact with each man. "You boys following me here?" Wally folded the fingers of his gloved hands together in front of him. "I took the time to add up the recorded value of those projects." He paused again and looked first into Pace's eyes, then Carl Taylor's. "Now ... I'll bet you boys already know the exact amount you've stolen from all those investors. Course, all I can do is make a rough guess." Wally shifted his weight, put his hand on the desk for support, leaned down close to Taylor's face. "Wanna know what I come up with?" Wally snickered and pivoted over into Pace's face once more. "Wanna hear what I think, Buddy Boy?"

Wally unexpectedly stood up and glanced rapidly back and forth between the two men pinned to the desks. The eyes he looked into were indeed clouded with fear, but they also betrayed the fact both men were beginning to understand what this was all about. "Yeah, that's right ... you know I know. The question is: How much of that $500 million, more or less, do you boys have socked away in that little bank account of yours down in the Cayman Islands?"

Carl Taylor's eyes flicked back and forth between Bud Pace and Wally Stroud. Wally thought he was the weaker of the two. He'd be the one to collapse first.

He edged over close to Taylor. "I'm going to take that tape off your mouth, Mr. Taylor. I hope you won't do anything to make me regret that." Taylor had no choice but to look into Pace's face. Pace was trying to say something to him. Pace's agitation revealed disgust that Taylor would even consider giving this maniac any information.

"I wouldn't worry too much about what Buddy Boy thinks, Carl. He's going to play his own role in all of this." Wally reached out without ceremony and ripped the tape from Taylor's mouth. "There ... feel better?"

Taylor didn't respond. He gasped, inhaled deeply taking huge gulps of fetid air into his lungs.

Wally forged ahead menacingly. "Carl," he began, "you don't mind if I call you Carl, do you?" He smiled, went on. "Carl, I'm not interested in how much you boys have in that account." His smile turned to a wide grin. "No ... you see, when you tell me which bank you do business with, and provide me with the access codes and account number, I'll be able to simply log on and your bank will tell me what I need to know."

"You're fucking insane," Taylor growled through clenched teeth. "You can't get away with this. Somebody's going to come looking for us soon and you'll be caught."

"There is some truth in that, Carl. That's why we can't take all evening to play this game."

"I'm not telling you one fucking thing," Taylor said defiantly.

"I'm sorry to hear you feel that way, Carl." Wally shifted his weight, shook his head. "Because, what I have in mind is a little game of … Jeopardy … of sorts. Listen closely to the rules, Carl." Wally smiled and cocked his head slightly so Taylor could see his eyes before he turned and picked up the reciprocal saw. Taylor's eyes grew to the size of quail eggs and shot rapidly back and forth between Wally and Pace. "You answer all my questions," Wally explained calmly, "and I'll just put this back in its case. But if you need a little persuasion … I'm gonna use ole Buddy Boy here as an example of what *you* might expect if you try to lie to me or refuse to tell me what I want to know. Whattaya think?" Wally grinned … a wide ominous grin.

"How does that suit *you*, Buddy Boy? Feel sporting?" Wally said jerking in the direction of Pace.

Taylor didn't respond. He shot a pleading glare at Pace who was clearly giving him signals not to cooperate.

"Shall we give it a go?" Wally asked indifferently pulling the painter's sock over his head so only his eyes showed. "First question … Jesus, I feel just like Alex-Fucking-Trebek," Wally said sardonically. "First question," he repeated. "In which bank in the Cayman Islands do you and Mr. Pace here keep all that money you've stolen from those investors?"

Taylor squirmed and strained against the tie-down straps until his face went bright red from exertion, looked across at Pace, then back to his tormentor. "Fuck you," he replied.

"Sorry, Carl," Wally said turning toward Bud Pace. "That was *not* the answer I was looking for." As the last restive syllable dripped from his lips, Wally pulled the trigger on the reciprocal saw and began hacking off Bud Pace's right arm just below the makeshift tourniquet. Pace's entire body immediately convulsed while he screamed and jerked and shit himself. Pieces of flesh flew from the sharp, coarse blade and then bone fragments from his splintering humerus spewed out along with a surprisingly small amount of blood. In a terrifyingly short instant, Pace's severed arm fell twitching to the floor, its fingers finally going limp.

Pace, fully conscious, was looking down at the stub where his arm had been just a moment before and appeared befuddled, disbelieving of the sight in front of him. Finally he screamed into the duct tape clamped tight against his lips and in the next instant began to hyperventilate.

"There you go. Calm down, Buddy Boy," Wally said unsympathetically to Pace, patting him on the shoulder of his new stub. "See, that wasn't so bad, was it?" Pace was delirious.

"Oh God! Oh God! What are you doing?" Taylor bawled. He was terrified at the sight, but he could not avert his eyes, partially because he was strapped down and forced to look in that direction and partially because he could not believe the insanity he was witnessing. "You're out of your fucking mind. Stop … stop. You're going to kill him. Oh Jesus, God what have you done?"

Wally casually inspected Pace's mangled stub closely noting how the artery wanted to retract backward into the gory wound, then turned to Taylor, pushed the blood spattered painter's sock up off his face and calmly said, "You're wrong, Carl." He moved to the side and pointed at the gash. "See, hardly any blood at all. And for now … it doesn't even hurt much, does it Buddy Boy? Go ahead, tell your friend, Carl. 'Cause he needs a little support."

"Oh, God … oh, God … oh, God," Taylor blubbered.

Pace's eyes were afire with hatred. He was beginning to control his breathing. Wally leaned over and slapped him crisply on the cheek. "Nicely done, Buddy Boy," he allowed. "That's it." He slapped Pace again. Pace began to focus on Taylor once more. Wally then swung back to Carl Taylor who was still babbling out of control.

"Carl," Wally, began, "look what you made me do." Taylor was weeping uncontrollably. "Okay, okay," Wally said, "get yourself under control, Carl."

Taylor was following Wally's every move with his eyes.

"You ready Carl?" Wally went on, leaning down into Taylor's face, obliterating any view of Pace. "Let me ask you again, Carl. Look at me, Carl! Open your eyes. Here we go. In which bank in the Cayman Islands do you boys have your account?" Wally enunciated every word of the sentence individually, softly—with perfect diction.

"You sonofabitch!" Taylor screamed. "You motherfucker! You're out of your fucking mind!"

"There is some truth in that, Carl. The bigger question is: Are you going to tell me what I want to know?"

"Fuck you!"

"Oh, Carl," Wally replied contemptuously. "Wrong again."

Pulling the sock down over his face once more, he walked casually around to the opposite side of the desk Bud Pace was strapped to, paused, stared into Carl Taylor's eyes and without hesitation laid the firing blade of the reciprocal saw against Pace's remaining arm. Pace's torso twitched and jerked reflexively to the torment ripping through his body. He screamed into the duct tape for all he was worth. Again, flesh commenced to fly every which way. The front of Wally's jumpsuit was covered with blood, human flesh, and bone fragments. When the blade struck bone much of the splatter flew across onto Carl Taylor's face. In a frighteningly short few seconds the limp arm of Bud Pace made a distinctively loud thud when it hit the floor.

Taylor's bellowing was too loud. Wally put down the saw, trotted back around the desk and slapped the tape back over his mouth. "You need to get yourself under control, Carl," he cautioned. "After all, it isn't as if they were your own arms."

Bud Pace was in shock, but still conscious. His body had stopped reacting to the trauma. For his part, Wally was pleased at the relative absence of blood. Those articles he'd read on the Internet about the amputation of limbs on Civil War battlefields, without anesthetic, had proven relevant after all.

Wally went back around the desk and picked up Bud Pace's severed left arm, then carried it back around where he tossed the limp extremity onto Carl Taylor's chest. He bent down, feigning great ceremony, collected Pace's right arm from the floor, grimaced as he held it at arm's length out in front of him and deposited it across Taylor's chest with the other arm.

"Look at you," Wally mocked, cocking his head sideways to look into Taylor's terrorized eyes. "There you are with four arms and poor Buddy Boy there has none." Wally bent down once more and put his face close to Carl Taylor's.

Though he'd become accustomed to the foul odors permeating the entire office space, Wally thought he detected the smell of new feces. "Don't you feel just a little bit bad, Carl?"

Taylor closed his eyes, screamed and cried hysterically.

"Come on, Carl," Wally growled, impatiently. "If you're going to continue to be so obstinate, you need to be stronger than that." Wally stood up straight, took up the saw once more. "I'm getting irritated, Carl." He hit the trigger and Taylor flinched. "Wanna try again, Carl?" He reached over with his free hand and ripped the tape from Taylor's mouth. "Tell me the name of the bank."

This time Carl Taylor whined and begged. "Please don't kill us," he pleaded.

"Oh, Carl," Wally explained. "You have the wrong idea entirely. Nobody's going to die here tonight. At least not on purpose, anyway." Wally shrugged. "Now, once more … the name of the bank?"

Taylor closed his eyes. "Please," he begged, "no more."

Wally held the terrifying weapon at the ready, pulled the trigger. Taylor jumped and started to babble something. Wally nudged him. "Go on, Carl, you almost said it."

"Banco do Brazil," Taylor shouted, collapsing into pleas and heavy, gulping sobs. "Let us go! Please let us go!"

"Very good, Carl," Wally congratulated. "And I'm gonna do that soon enough. Hold that thought."

Wally set the saw down and moved purposefully around to the laptop and Googled Banco do Brazil. Several websites were indicated for the bank. He chose the main site. The Banco do Brazil home page opened and he scrolled to the account login page.

"Good job, Carl," he announced. "And what did you say your username is?" But Carl Taylor had clammed up again. Wally repeated the question. "What's your username, Carl?"

No reply.

"Last time, Carl … username?" Taylor did not reply.

Wally stood up. He took up the reciprocal saw once more and without allowing Carl Taylor so much as a second thought, laid it across Bud Pace's right leg and pulled the trigger.

Instantly, flesh flew everywhere. Blood shot out in a wide spray and Wally bore down hard with the saw forcing it quickly to the bone. Pace quivered and twitched and screamed while the saw did its devastation. He was becoming delirious.

Carl Taylor went insane begging and screaming for Wally to stop, but Wally pushed the saw the rest of the way through the femur of Pace's dangling leg. When the saw went to wood, Wally

Betrayed

stopped, looked back at Carl Taylor, stood to one side to make sure the man had an unobstructed view of the mayhem and slid Pace's severed leg off the desk to the floor.

Wally set the saw down, bent toward Taylor and yelled, "Username!"

"*Homerun,*" Taylor screamed without further resistance. "It's 'homerun' you miserable motherfucker! Now let us go." He was bawling like a child who'd just fallen down and skinned her knee. "Oh, God! How is this happening?" he mumbled.

"Carl," Wally chimed in, "God doesn't have anything to do with this. This is your Karma coming home to roost. Password, please." Wally was again crouched in front of the laptop computer, typing *homerun* in the username box on the sign in screen.

Carl Taylor didn't respond.

"Password, Carl," Wally insisted. "Give me the password."

Again, Taylor said nothing.

Wally stood up and for the first time during the ordeal lost his temper. "How fucking stupid are you, Taylor?" He didn't wait for the reply. He jerked the reciprocal saw from the desk and headed around to the opposite side.

Carl Taylor yelled. "No ... please ... no more ... stop ... stop."

But it was too little, too late. Wally fired the saw and sent it tearing into Bud Pace's only remaining limb. Flesh splattered against Wally's chest and across the sock on his face, shot across and landed on Carl Taylor, along with blood and more bone fragments. Bud Pace was unresponsive by the time he lost the last of his limbs. As the saw shredded the sinewy pieces of flesh keeping Pace's leg connected, Wally scraped it aside like trimmings from a roast and tossed it to the floor.

He walked back around the desk toward Taylor in a huff. He held the saw at the ready. "Who's fucking arms and legs do you think are gonna be next if you don't answer me the first time every time? You just ran out of time, Taylor. Tell me the fucking password ... now!" Wally pointed the saw at Taylor's left arm and pulled the trigger.

Taylor screamed, "No, no, no. Stop. I'll tell you. Please ... stop."

Wally took his finger off the trigger and set the saw down. "Much smarter Mr. Taylor. I think we're finally communicating." He crouched down in front of the laptop once more. "I'm waiting," he said.

"*Primadonna35,*" Taylor sobbed, his voice trailing away. His body convulsed three times and he vomited.

"Jesus, Taylor." Wally snarled, his face pinching up in disgust. He grabbed the laptop and moved back to the desk Pace was on. "Not enough you guys shit and piss yourselves. You gotta fuck the place up with puke, too?" He finished typing in the password and hit the submit key. He watched the screen impatiently while a whirligig rotated for several seconds before the account window opened.

Wally stared at the screen in silence. There it was. Just that simple—if you had those two little code words: *homerun—primadonna35*. Those two unsophisticated tiny words were all that shielded anyone from viewing an offshore bank account that said it contained a balance of $425,000,000. Wally was awestruck. He stared at what he was seeing for several seconds before he collected himself.

"Carl," he exclaimed softly. "You boys have done right well for yourselves, haven't you?"

Taylor was coughing and spitting, trying to clear his mouth so he could breathe again.

"Indeed you boys have," Wally declared, ignoring Taylor completely. He was scrolling, moving the cursor, opening windows. He came to the one he was searching for: Transfer Funds. Wally's hands were shaking as he set up the "transfer-from" and "transfer-to" transaction. His brain was swimming in chemical releases that were palpable.

This final reactive bombardment from what was before him, the realization of what he was about to do left him lightheaded; spots floated before his eyes. He shook his head to clear the cobwebs—forced his shaking hand back to his laptop and punched the submit key.

Immediately a window opened and asked for: 'Confirmation Code.'

Wally's heart stopped. He read the error notification at the top of the dropdown box; transfer exceeds limit—confirmation code required. This was something he had not anticipated. He leaned forward, grabbed the edge of the desk and pulled himself to his feet. "Shit, Carl," he barked, "looks like you and I have more work to do."

Taylor was still spitting, trying to get his breath. "What more can you possibly want?" Taylor croaked, his voice hoarse, grave. He pronounced the words deliberately, the disgust he felt unhidden.

"Looks like we need one more code, Carl," Wally said. "You boys ever need to put in a special seven digit code when you move large sums of money?" Wally grabbed one of Pace's severed arms off of Taylor's chest and scraped away most of the vomit next to Taylor's mouth.

Taylor didn't reply. He looked up at Wally, calculating.

Wally smiled. "I would think you'd have no stomach for testing me, Carl." He pivoted and slung the saw up into his hand. "After all, yours are the only arms and legs I have left to cut off. You really wanna fuck with me?" He pulled the trigger. The motor made a high-pitched whine and the saw blade shot in and out in a terrifying blur.

Taylor's lips quivered and he began to speak, *"7491710,"* he recited. Carl Taylor had reached total capitulation.

Wally set the saw down and placed his fingers on the keyboard. The page had not timed out. "Say it again, slowly," he ordered.

Taylor hesitated a beat.

Wally turned toward him and growled, "Say it again, I said."

Taylor repeated the code, *"7491710."*

Wally typed the code into the box and hit submit; again the whirligig and the delay. Suddenly a new window opened. It read simply: transfer complete.

Wally could not believe his eyes. He minimized the current page and opened the login page for his own bank. He pulled up his account and saw a simple notification: Transaction Pending.

Betrayed

His head dropped to his chest and he remained in that position for several moments as though he might be praying. He was not.

Abruptly Wally burst back into action. He shut down the computer, removed the antenna and replaced the components in the padded case. He turned slowly toward Carl Taylor. Taylor began openly pleading for his life to be spared. Wally let him beg for a time, "You're one lucky sonofabitch," he ultimately proclaimed. He jumped back into action and grabbed the dart pistol. He double checked the area again and then shoved the laptop and dart gun into the brown duffle.

After he'd made certain not a single thing was left behind except the tie-down straps, Wally walked back around to face Carl Taylor. "We're almost finished here, Carl," he said. "Won't be long now, you boys will both be back with your families." Wally paused, looked down. "Here's the thing, Carl ... I walk out of here, leave you like this ... guy of your character I figure gets right on a computer, cancels my little transaction and then you call the cops and finally you get some help for your partner here." Wally studied Taylor's eyes. He saw a new wave of fear beginning to cloud the man's pupils.

"I won't," Taylor stuttered, "I ... I ... I swear, I won't! I'll just call an ambulance. No ... no ... cops!"

"And I can believe that, Carl, because, why ... you're a man of such high moral character ... honest ... considerate? You possess such great empathy for your fellow man? Yes, I've seen that from you, Carl." Wally crossed his arms, looked up in mock contemplation, then back down to the floor. He nudged Bud Pace's severed leg with his foot. "You know, Carl," he went on, "I just don't think I believe you."

Taylor was crying again, babbling and pleading with Wally to let him go.

Wally surveyed the devastation he'd wrought on Bud Pace. "There was no avoiding that was there?" he said to Taylor. "You fellas weren't going to give up one dollar even to save your own asses, were you?"

Wally sat in silence listening to the whimpering man.

"I'm not going to kill you Carl," Wally said, "though I imagine there are going to be times in the future you're gonna wish I had. I'm also not going to put you through what Mr. Pace here endured. I didn't do that for fun. It was necessary because you boys loved that money just a little too much." Wally looked down at Taylor who was straining his eyes upward in an attempt to see what Wally might be up to next. "It's the ultimate lie, you know," Wally said. "The money, I mean. It begets so much more misery than joy ... don't you think?"

Wally walked to the file cabinet where he'd set the two reserve syringes and picked them both up. He left the protective cap on one and returned it to the case. He stood behind Taylor where the man could not see what he was doing. Wally slid the needle effortlessly into the base of Carl Taylor's neck and the man screamed.

Slipping the protective cover back over the needle, Wally slid around in front of Taylor. "In a few seconds this will all be over for you, Carl. The betrayal you're going to feel when you wake up ... I assure you, hundreds, maybe thousands, of people have felt at the hands of you and

Buddy Boy there." Wally bent down close to Taylor's face. The man's eyes were already growing glassy and the lids drooping. "Have a nice life, Carl," he said gently, as Taylor went unconscious.

~~~~

Wally finished quickly what he felt he had to do to Carl Taylor. If there was one thing he wanted, it was that these two should live. *That* was to be the price they would pay for Poppy's life. They would go on living with what he'd personally done to them—penniless. The arms and legs he dedicated to the destroyed lives of all of the victims of their schemes.

He carried the two duffle bags to the doorway before returning to stack the severed limbs of Bud Pace and Carl Taylor together in a heap in the center of the room. He stepped quickly to the blue bag and pulled out two one-gallon jugs of muriatic acid, which he drizzled slowly over the stack of human limbs laying in front of him like wood on a bonfire. Acrid fumes began to float upward and mingle with the stench of human feces; sizzling, burning, bubbling sounds were audible. By the time help arrived, the acid would have emulsified the muscle tissue and nerves of the severed limbs, destroying them completely. "They won't be reattaching these to you boys," he said. "Welcome to your new lives, gentlemen." And with that, Wally returned the empty bottles to the blue duffle, opened the door to the office, set the two bags back into the foyer and closed the door behind him.

He moved purposefully but did not hurry. He checked his gloved hands before going any further. Both hands showed tears in several layers of the gloves but no skin was showing. He stopped and opened the brown duffle, removed a large black trash bag and set it on the floor. He unzipped the jumpsuit and wiggled out of it. Everything was rolled up and stuffed into the trash bag. Finally, the gloves came off and were replaced with new fresh ones. It felt glorious to be out of the jumpsuit and out of the stench of the inner office. His soaked clothing felt cool against his body in the fresh air. He looked around one last time. The trash bag was safely in the duffle. There was not a sign anything had been opened in the entryway.

Wally turned the key in the lock and pushed the front doors open slowly. It was quiet—dark and hot outside. The ordeal had taken too long. He needed to get out of there. Taylor'd been right. Somebody was bound to come looking for them soon. He lugged the two heavy duffle bags with him out to the driver's side of Bud Pace's Range Rover. He pressed the unlock button on the key and the driver's door lock clicked up. He pushed a second time and all the other doors unlocked. He opened the driver's side passenger door, removed the blanket he'd used to conceal himself and stashed the two duffels inside the vehicle. Then Wally spread the blanket over the driver's seat before scurrying back into the building. He peeked in one final time, not a thing there. He left the door unlocked and returned to the Rover. Keeping the blanket under him, Wally scooted in to the driver's seat. He understood he couldn't afford so much as a trace of sweat left behind.

Betrayed

He started the vehicle and took a moment to check his face in the rearview mirror. He was startled when he looked into his own eyes, for he did not recognize the person looking back at him, and it was more than just the physical appearance that unsettled him. He wiped at the sides of his eyes with the back of his forearm, slipped the shift-lever into gear and pulled onto Osborn Road travelling east.

Immediately driving through the light at the intersection of 15th Ave. and Osborn, Wally took Bud Pace's cell phone and dialed 911. The operator came on, asked him to identify himself, his location and the nature of his emergency. "1602 West Osborn. And I'd get there fast if I were you." Then he slammed the phone onto the pavement, out the driver's window. By the time he reached Seventh Avenue, a police cruiser was flying past him moving in the opposite direction, lights flashing, but no siren.

Wally turned south on Seventh Avenue and continued downtown to Adams Street. He glanced at the dash clock. It was ten-thirteen p.m. when he pulled the Rover back into the underground parking garage. Unfortunately, the space next to Wally's Camry was now occupied so he continued down several spaces until he found two open spaces side-by-side.

He slipped out of the Rover and walked to the front of the vehicle so he would remain in deep shadow. He made his way across the fronts of the other parked cars until he reached the spot where his Camry was parked. He pushed the key into the lock, opened the door and sat behind the wheel. Wally caught his breath and for a moment—comprehension. He'd pulled the whole thing off, at least to this point.

He collected himself and started the Toyota, pulled out and moved the car next to the Rover. Immediately the two bags containing proof positive of the horror of the last three hours came back into the Camry. He turned to the front seat of the Rover and retrieved the blanket covering the driver's seat. The only remaining item in the vehicle was Carl Taylor's cell phone on the front passenger seat. He left the keys to the Rover in the ignition, climbed back into his own vehicle and removed the rubber gloves. His hands were white and wrinkled, fingers puckered from being immersed in sweat for nearly four hours; he dried them on his damp trousers.

Wally backed the Camry out and drove to the ticket booth. The attendant took several moments to calculate the charge. "Gotta hit you for a full day," the man said. "Shoulda had it validated." He held the stub up and waved it in the air. "That'll be ten bucks."

Wally produced the bill instantly from the center console. "Next time," he said, and pulled out onto the street.

CHAPTER 40

1602 West Osborn Road, Phoenix: The offices of Perfect Property Investments, Inc., ten-twenty p.m., Friday, August 21—Two minutes after the ominous 911 call was received, the responding squad screeched to a stop in the parking lot of the single level office building. The only car there was a gray and black Maybach. The two police officers crept cautiously inside the building, guns drawn. The front doors were unlocked and a dim light was on inside.

"This is the police!" One officer yelled out. "Anybody in here?" There was a light showing under the closed door of an inner office. Foul smells were coming from inside but no one answered.

The senior patrolman signaled to his partner to cover the opposite side of the closed door. They crept closer with their weapons held at the ready. With his mouth close to the door he shouted again, "Phoenix Police ... anybody in there?"

Nothing.

He signaled his partner. The younger cop shook his head in the affirmative. The officer running the show reached down and turned the knob slowly, then shoved the door open and recoiled. The menace charging out at them was an intensification of the most horrible odor either of the two men had ever encountered, mixed with the toxic smell of some chemical. When they crept inside, the sight before them was sheer horror. It caused the junior officer to retch. Strapped across the top of two office desks were the torsos of two men exhibiting gashed, bloody, oozing stubs. All four limbs of both of them had been ... *removed in a violent manner*, as the officers would later word it in their reports. Blood spatter still dripped from the ceiling and chunks of flesh and bone and more blood covered the clothing of the two victims as well as the fronts of file cabinets and adjacent desks and the floor. The stench was nearly unbearable even to the senior officer who had witnessed a lot of crime scenes in his sixteen years on the force. But this—

Betrayed

Fumes from the gasses being released by what HAZMAT would later identify as muriatic acid was eating away and putrefying the flesh of the severed limbs, which had been piled in the center of the floor. Sucked oxygen right out of the cop's lungs. The younger cop retched again before he could get himself under control.

The first officer in eased over, placed two fingers on the carotid artery of Carl Taylor. "Shit," he shouted. "This guy's alive." He holstered his weapon while his partner stood guard. He moved rapidly to the second victim who would later be identified as Bud Pace. "Jesus! They're both alive!" he proclaimed in utter disbelief. He reached up to his lapel, hit the talk button on his shoulder-radio and called for two EMT units, *code 3*. Then he called it in to the station.

~~~~

By the time Clark Reynolds from the Phoenix field office of the FBI arrived on scene, the parking lot was jammed with Phoenix Police cars, huge ladder trucks; the EMTs had long since transported the victims. The entire parking lot from the sidewalk back to, and including the building, had been blocked off with yellow crime scene tape. The Arizona Department of Public Safety, Criminal Investigations Unit, was already processing the scene. The victims had been transported to St. Joseph's Hospital, just minutes away on Thomas Road.

Reynolds flipped his ID to the uniform standing guard. The cop lifted the crime tape. "Who's got this one?" Reynolds asked, stopping inside the line.

"Detective Garcia," the uniformed cop replied.

Reynolds, a huge man, six feet, four inches, two hundred fifty pounds of solid muscle, had a voice so booming he could call out Placido Domingo or Paul Bunyan. He was a seasoned profiler who led one of the FBI's elite special crimes units. He'd been with the bureau more than twenty years, PhD in behavioral psychology, leading man in his field, author of several books on the criminal mind. He lectured regularly at the FBI Academy in Quantico, Virginia, and answered to very few superiors below the Director himself.

He could be a pensive, stoic man; but he could also be one of the most affable guys you'd ever want to meet, a trait not common in men in his line of work. His reputation was well known. There wasn't a detective with the Department of Public Safety who wouldn't welcome the man's presence at a crime scene. That night DPS lead detective Bill Garcia had initiated the request for his assistance and the call was made.

~~~~

"Hey, Guillermo," Reynolds said greeting Detective Bill Garcia, using his given Mexican name. Reynolds, who spoke several languages, had worked more than one crime scene with Garcia over the years. The two appreciated each other, no interagency bullshit between them.

216

"Hey, Clark," Garcia replied, extending his hand.

Detective Bill Garcia of Arizona's DPS, CIU, was no small man himself at a solid six feet of bulk. Unlike his colleague, Reynolds, Garcia's two hundred plus pounds included a soft middle that was beginning to try to hang over his belt, sloped shoulders and chubby cheeks framing his pencil-thin mustache. His head seemed overlarge for his body, owing, in part, to a crown of profuse jet-black hair, which he wore combed straight back over the top of his broad skull.

The characteristic both men shared was their countenance; both were easy-going guys, always in control might be a better way of putting it.

Reynolds smothered Garcia's hand in his giant mitt and shook firmly. "Must be bad for you boys to get me outta bed at this hour?"

"Bad don't describe it, Clark."

The mere tone in Garcia's voice told Reynolds something extraordinary had taken place. But then, why else would he have been called?

Garcia went on shaking his head. "Two vics, both still alive ... for now, anyway. Perp hacked off all four limbs from both of 'em. Scene looks like Hell and Satan rose up right through the floor to meet those two tonight."

"What do we know?" Reynolds felt sure he knew what the response would be.

"So far not a thing," Garcia confirmed. "The two vics are both in surgery as we speak. No chance to interview them for hours ... maybe not even then."

"Motive?" Reynolds ventured.

"Pissed off, to put it mildly, I'd say. No way to know for now, but have a look. That's why I called *you*."

Garcia led off toward the front doors of the PPI offices. Investigators flashed cameras, carried plastic bags, scurried back and forth from inside to out collecting samples of any item that might provide a lead as to what happened here tonight and who did it. The scene in the parking lot was punctuated by the sounds of radios squawking inside police cars and fire trucks. Hot engine smell rolled out from under idling ladder trucks.

HAZMAT had been called in to determine the nature of the chemical and gasses inside the building. The suited-up investigator leaned at the side of one of the fire trucks removing his protective suit. A SWAT unit cleared the building and stood by. Red and blue lights flickered from car tops casting an eerie gyration of hues across the scene. Reynolds half expected to hear the music from *Close Encounters of the Third Kind* boom out at any moment.

He stopped in the entry lobby. "Think we could have a look without all the foot traffic inside?"

Garcia eased over to the door where the crime had been committed. "Sergeant," he said, gaining the attention of his CI in charge. "Can I interrupt you and your people for a few minutes? Give 'em a break."

The sergeant shot him an irritated glance. "Come on, folks. Intermission."

Betrayed

Four investigators wearing slipcovers over their shoes and heads, hands enclosed in blue rubber, single filed out of the room.

"Only a few minutes," Garcia promised, as the last investigator came out into the lobby.

Garcia stood next to the door with his arm extended inviting Reynolds to step to the doorway. "Not beyond here, Clark, until my people are done. Sorry."

"Not a problem." Reynolds knew the drill. He stopped squarely in the doorway, his mass obliterating the opening.

The FBI agent did not recoil from the scene before him, nor did the stench of the place overtake him. He'd seen and smelled worse—but not often.

He began a systematic visual analysis from the point where he stood, progressing orderly a few feet at a time into the room. As he observed every centimeter of the horrific scene, he made calculations about the kind of individual who'd planned and executed this crime. He was already convinced it was the work of one person—a man. A very clever, determined, well prepared man filled with rage and hatred that went to the core of his being. What happened here was personal; he was sure of that—very personal. Reynolds remained in the doorway for several minutes before turning back to locate Garcia who was outside talking with his sergeant. Reynolds looked down at the floor just outside the office doorway in which he was standing. He went down on one knee.

Garcia and the sergeant saw him kneel and came in. "Find something?" Garcia wanted to know.

"Not much," Reynolds replied using a pen he'd pulled from his shirt pocket to ruffle the fibers of the carpet on the floor. "Did your team process this lobby area?" he asked, addressing the sergeant.

"Yeah," the sergeant answered. "But the two uniforms that discovered this mess had trampled through here ... the SWAT unit, and then the EMTs and fire units had to get in, too."

"Nothing you could do. Not a big deal," Reynolds conceded, extending his arm, touching the carpet gently with the pen. "You won't find much anyway. Your perp staged up here." Reynolds pointed out a number of anomalies on the floor just outside the doorway to the inner office, again just inside. "My guess ... large bags. Fairly heavy, too. Maybe 36 inches long. Probably duffle bags."

Garcia and the sergeant were crouched down with Reynolds looking closely at the area to which he was referring. The marks were faint, but the patterns were there, even a couple of brown and blue fibers had transferred to the carpet fibers.

Reynolds went on. "You'll find two areas somewhere near those desks where there won't be any blood spatter. Pretty sure you'll find matching fibers. Might give you an outline of the bags. Ought to give you a better visual of their size."

"Shit," the sergeant said. "You saw all that from this doorway?"

"Just theory, sergeant," the FBI profiler confessed. "Asking myself what I'd need to pull off a crime like this? How would I get ... *my tools* ... in and out quickly?" Reynolds stood, walked toward the front doors, pushed one side open and looked at the sidewalk out front. "He'd have had a car parked right there," he said, pointing to the space where four hours earlier Wally Stroud forced Bud Pace to park the Range Rover.

"But look," Reynolds went on, returning the pen to his shirt pocket, turning to face the two police officers, "you're not going to collect enough physical evidence from this scene to tell you much you can't already see. This … *person* planned this like a pro, though I'm betting when we catch him we're going to find out he isn't. He will have left you next to nothing to go on."

"Any ideas, Clark?"

The sergeant broke in before Reynolds could answer. "Look, we got a lot of work left here tonight, even if we don't turn up a single clue," he said, pointing toward his team. "How 'bout I get my people back in there while you guys solve this thing?" It was not a sarcastic indictment, just the calloused reality of what he had in front of him before this night would be over.

"Sure, Harold," Garcia said extending his arm, gesturing for Clark Reynolds to follow him outside.

Sergeant Harold Crawford gave the signal and his team filed back inside the room where one of the grizzliest crimes the State of Arizona had ever seen had been committed.

CHAPTER 41

From the parking garage of the Adams, Wally'd driven in a psychotic haze, reliving, disbelieving, almost out of body, what he'd just done, back to the Sunrise Motel. He sat motionless in the driver's seat of the Camry staring at the door to his room. "I did it, Poppy," he whispered not with any jubilation, rather dismay—shame. "I … I—" He was unraveling. Tried to clear his head and checked around: a paranoid tick. The place seemed empty. There was a light on in Talbot's office but the rest of the place was dark. He sat dazed for several moments before opening the door and sliding out of the car.

In the stifling heat he leaned against the side of the vehicle sliding back toward the trunk. He retrieved the small duffle bag with his change of clothes and the black makeup bag. He let the trunk lid down softly and put his weight on it until he heard the latch click. Then he stepped deliberately to his room, slipped his key into the lock, hefted the two bags in front of him and edged himself into the opening. He dropped both bags next to the bed and stood in the soundless shadows.

The weight of silence swept over him like the smooth, quiet water of a high mountain stream just before the tumultuous currents below its surface drag it irrevocably over the precipice of a bottomless cliff, sending the sum of its totality into an oblivion of mist that evaporates into nothingness before it can find itself and be made whole again. Slowly, Wally crumbled to his knees, dropped his face into his hands, his thorax heaving—and wept until he couldn't see how there could be any tears left, and yet the streams down the sides of his face went on.

Eventually he climbed back to his feet, gasping for breath and switched on the lamp next to the bed. He did what he could to collect himself. He picked up the black bag and stepped to the bathroom. Flipping the light switch Wally leaned close in to the mirror. Methodically he began removing his disguise. The wig came off first. Release of tension on his head, around his brain; as if the blood flow was being returned to his cranium. Next he tore off the stretchy pullover t-shirt and ripped at the Velcro straps down his side to get the chest prosthesis off. Frenzied.

Panicked. Make it all go away. He tossed his phony chest to the floor while his real one heaved. A blue bottle cap protruded from under the flap of the black bag. Wally grabbed, pulled out another bottle of water and downed it without taking a breath. When he was finished sucking air he placed both hands on the front edge of the sink and once more leaned in close to the mirror. He wasn't aware he was weeping, but a fixed flow of liquid leached from the corners of each eye in sturdy streams down the sides of his face, and hung in droplets along the bottom of his jaw.

He began at the edge of his hairline to pull away the latex. Long strings of adhesive stretched and pulled out from his skin along with the rubber. He dabbed at the edges with a cotton ball soaked in witch hazel.

Presently the face of Wally Stroud reappeared in the mirror, but the human being behind the face was no longer that man. Got to pull yourself together. He stared into the dark, sallow eyes peering back at him.

The money created a complication he hadn't anticipated. Pace or Taylor's families, the cops—somebody would come looking for where it went. Well, he had anticipated that, he allowed, but not this. Not what he thought he saw on his laptop. Maybe it was an illusion. Shit! That was the last thing he could afford to think about right now. Gradually he was beginning to think again. He realized what he'd feared all along; he would not escape what he'd done. It was simply too horrifying. Even if he could come to live with it himself, the authorities, society— nobody was going to excuse this. All that was left now of his life was a little time. How much he couldn't be sure. It would take them a while to zero in on him, he figured, but they would come for him. A little time—that was all he had left now. There could be no justification for the kind of viciousness he'd visited on Pace and Taylor. He'd be seen as worse than them. *"What the hell were you thinking, Wally?"* he said to the face in the mirror. He hung his head, stepped to the side and turned on the hot water in the shower. He let it run while he stripped off his shoes and clothing. He wanted desperately to be Wally Stroud once more, but it was far too late for that. Wally knew from lifelong experience, sometimes when you get into a situation so deep there seems no way out, the only solution is to get in deeper; finish what you started.

Inside the stall he let the scalding water bake his skin before turning on some cold. He soaped and scrubbed his body until his skin felt as if he'd peeled it away. He scrubbed his hands over and over until he understood he'd never be able to wash away what he'd done. The remarkable thought creeping into his consciousness was he felt no pity, even now, for Pace or Taylor; only sadness at how disappointed he knew Poppy would be in him if she were still alive. He'd succumbed to his demons—done the unthinkable.

He turned the squeaky handles of the shower and stepped out onto the flimsy bathmat. As he wobbled toward the bed he patted his raw skin with the rough towel. He drew back the blankets and collapsed, half wet, into the sheets.

~~~~

Betrayed

Wally jerked awake and sat upright as a rail. The lamp next to the bed was still on as was the light over the mirror in the bathroom. He listened. No sounds. He grabbed his watch from the nightstand. Three a.m. He'd been passed out nearly four hours. He scrambled out of bed and pulled on the clothes he'd set aside for the drive back.

Movements were sluggish, like having a hangover. He went about gathering up clumps of latex, miscellaneous bottles, tubes of cream, the false chest he'd worn—all of it—and crammed everything back into the black makeup bag. No time for order. The concern was how fast he could clear out. When he thought he was ready, he made a double check of the entire room; even corners he'd not been in. That's when he noticed the California license plates for the Camry sitting on the chair.

He stopped long enough to find a screwdriver and slipped outside. He waited in the shadows. Nothing moved. Quickly to the rear of the car, remove the Arizona plate—switch. At the front bumper he went down on one knee and fastened the second plate.

He hurried back into the room, zipped the stolen license plate and screwdriver into his clothing bag and jogged out to the car. He stepped back to the door to the tiny room one last time, stuck his head inside and made a quick appraisal, then tossed his key onto the bed, slid his hand across the light switch and pulled the door closed.

He dove behind the wheel of the Camry and backed slowly out of the Sunrise Motel. Gravel crunched under the wheels of the car, made popping sounds when he cramped the tires for the turn onto Buckeye Road. Still no activity from the Sunrise. Why would there be? Paranoia. He turned west to the light at 35th Avenue, made a right turn and drove north to I-10. The dash clock read three thirty-three and it was still 100 degrees outside. A few stoplights north he turned left into the westbound on-ramp of I-10 and fell in with the big rigs deadheading back to L.A. Groggy utility workers in a hurry to get to the nuclear power plant at Tonopah zoomed passed. He wasn't the least tempted to push the speed limit as they all did.

Wally peeled off I-10 at the Arizona 85 off-ramp toward Gila Bend. Still dark. There was little traffic on the road at that hour. He cruised along quietly, his mind a blank for the moment. Lewis Prison slipped by for the second time in as many days. There was no shiver up his spine, just the conviction he was not going to end up in a place like that. He began thinking about the bags in his back seat. He had to get rid of their contents.

On the west side of Gila Bend he pulled in to the Love's Truck Stop. It was still dark but a gray smudge at the eastern horizon heralded the arrival of morning. He pulled to a vacant spot at the side of the building where there was still plenty of light from street lamps and signs, and turned off the engine. Except for a few eighteen-wheelers whose drivers were nowhere to be seen, the place was ghostly.

Wally sat for a few minutes thinking again about the bags in his back seat. He looked around once, then decided on coffee. His stomach growled, but eating was out of the question. He went inside the convenience store where a heavy-set Navajo clerk said good morning to him. Wally returned the greeting and shuffled to the coffee display. The lights seemed overly bright, but the strong smell of fresh brewed coffee was pleasant, even a little inviting.

"Gonna be a perdy day," the fat woman behind the counter said as Wally walked up to pay.

"Looks like," he said evenly, and set down two one-dollar bills.

"That's one-nineteen," the cashier said, and handed Wally back his eighty-one cents. He flipped all of the coins into an ashtray that held several pennies.

"Have a nice day, mister."

Wally went back to the Camry, sipped from the hot brew and stared at its rear door a few moments. The cool pre-dawn air was rejuvenating. He absorbed the chill prickle against his face and arms, inhaled several deep breaths and held it in. Finally, he set the coffee cup on the roof of the car, opened the rear passenger door and pulled out the black bag. At the trunk he slid the key into the slot. The bag fit snug under the overhang behind the rear seat.

Next he grabbed the blue duffle. After he'd pushed it into the trunk he stood staring at it for several seconds, looked sideways, then reached in and unzipped it. He spread the loose sides apart looking in. What he found forced a recoil as if he'd discovered a rattlesnake inside. Reflex—furtive glance toward the big rigs.

The reciprocal saw was covered with blood. A vision came into his brain and he saw himself holding the saw, pushing down on it, forcing it through bone and flesh that was spewing red. "Ah, Wally—"

Stumbling back beside the Camry, he reached for the coffee cup; steam danced up from the opening. He took a cautious sip, looked up into the lightening sky. One of the truck drivers down the line fired his engine. Wally set the cup back on the car top and grabbed the brown bag. He worked it into the trunk next to the blue one. No need to unzip it. He knew well enough what he'd see. He rested his hands on the edge of the trunk lid and leaned his forehead against them. Several moments elapsed before he slowly backed away and let the trunk lid drop under its own weight.

Wally edged back to the driver's door and in one smooth motion, retrieved the coffee cup and slid back in under the wheel. When he pulled onto I-8 West the gray smudge at the eastern horizon had begun to glow soft pink in the side-view mirror. Forward, Wally, he told himself—the miserable bastards deserved it. Get back to Mexico and finish what you started.

Fifty miles west of Gila Bend he found the turn off to the tiny town of Tacna, Arizona. He pulled in and parked behind a dumpy looking roadside café. There were three big rigs parked parallel along the frontage road, breakfast hour. Slop was about to be added to the contents of the trash dumpster which stood not more than ten paces from where he'd parked. Without hesitation, Wally got out of his car, opened the trunk and recovered the trash bag from inside the brown duffle. He crossed to the dumpster, held the trash bag upside down and slung its contents across the nasty garbage which was about half way up from the bottom or half way down from the top depending on one's perspective. An array of wadded up rubber gloves, a painter's hood full of—red paint. He wished the white jumpsuit didn't stand out so much, but a few greasy trash bags on top of it would obliterate everything. Nothing he'd added to the refuse looked out of place amongst its other contents. Half the debris inside the dumpster was contained in bags, the rest was uncontained slosh flung quickly for convenience by kitchen help who could give a shit about how clean they kept the inside of the dumpster. The black trash bag he tossed in partially covering the jumpsuit. It landed crumpled, but obscured most of the white garment.

How to get rid of the evidence had come to him in a rush a few miles west of Gila Bend when the first sign notified drivers the next stop was Tacna. Tacna, Arizona. Last stop to nowhere. Only fucking UFOs could find a reason to visit the place. Now he was trying to think ahead about places coming up. He began systematically planning where he'd get rid of what.

Dateland was his next stop. It was a major truck stop along I-8 Wally'd pulled into before. Just like Tacna, the place was full with a breakfast crowd. He drove straight around the side of the building and found the enclosure for the trash dumpster. It was open. When he looked in, he saw it was nearly empty but for several cardboard boxes of empty plastic oil bottles, trucker junk. He wasted no time sprinkling more remnants of his crime over the debris in the bottom of the dumpster.

When he'd lightened the bags of the easy evidence to get rid of, he pulled the Camry around to a small, unused picnic area at the side of the restaurant and parked. Transfer the laptop to the front passenger seat. The money briefly crossed his mind. The dart pistol and the aluminum case with the tranquilizer he removed and slid into the spare tire compartment. That emptied the brown duffel bag. He crammed it into a corner of the trunk.

Wally was feeling faint—food. He hadn't eaten since breakfast yesterday. Inside the restaurant he ordered a single egg with two strips of bacon and some toast of sourdough bread. He felt the need for something cold to drink—tall glass of skim milk, please. When he took the first slug of the ice-cold liquid, he could trace its progress down every inch of his esophagus until it emptied into his stomach. The food was a wise choice. With each bite he felt strength returning.

He paid cash with a twenty and left the fiftyish woman with a gravelly voice and the smell of cigarettes on her, a five-dollar tip, which got him a weary smile and a moribund thank you.

For whatever reason, he could not bring himself to simply drive away. Instead, he pulled around back to have one final look inside the dumpster. The lid had been pulled down in the time he'd taken to eat. He tipped the edge of it up and looked inside. Wally smiled when he saw the contents of what had to be at least a thirty-gallon trash can, dumped, uncontained over the existing waste. A couple ends of something recognizable to him still showed through here and there; they would soon be buried in some unknown landfill, no longer a threat of any kind to him.

He stopped again in Yuma where he filled up with gas and made another deposit to a random trash dumpster. He did the same in El Centro. He was making good progress getting back to Mexico and getting rid of the evidence along the way. There was nothing left in the black bag but the chest prosthesis.

Just as he was about to pull onto I-8 from Fourth Street at El Centro, he found the solution to his problem standing next to the stop sign, holding a hand printed message scribbled on a piece of cardboard that read: Vietnam Vet—Need help.

The ragged looking homeless man had a large roll of miscellaneous junk tied together resting against the fence a few feet away from where he stood. Wally pulled around into the Valero gas station adjacent to the off ramp and called the guy over.

"How you doin'?"

"Little hungry," the man admitted.

Wally went around to his trunk and pulled out the black bag. There was nothing left inside but the chest plate. He handed the bag to the man. "Might be able to use this," he said.

The homeless man accepted the gift. "Thanks, mister," he said, a weary befuddled look of disappointment on his face.

Wally had no idea what the man might do with the chest plate, but he felt certain in a very short time it would either be employed in a regular regimen with the rest of his belongings, maybe traded to another homeless person or discarded behind a building or in a ditch somewhere with other trash that would gain no more notice than to be collected and thrown away.

"Spare a little change, mister? Awfully hungry," the man said. His eyes were sunken deep into the sockets of a crusty, filthy skull, his thin, cracked lips flaccid from the absence of teeth behind them.

Wally produced a twenty and pressed it into the man's hand. "Eat something before you buy the wine."

The man looked back at him through vacant eyes. "Yeah," he said, simply, and turned away with his new bag and—pillow. When Wally pulled around to get back onto the freeway, the homeless man was sitting on the chest prosthesis, which was nestled down into the powdery dirt near the intersection, holding up his cardboard sign.

All he had left in the trunk now was the blue bag quelling the reciprocal saw. The blade was there along with its plastic cover, the power pack and more empty water bottles. He had a different idea for disposing of the saw. The empty water bottles could be thrown in any trash container at any time.

At nine forty-nine that Saturday morning in August Wally was coasting down the western side of Tecate Pass gaining the suburbs of San Diego quickly. He made the transition off I-8 onto the 125 South. In a short distance he was maneuvering into the left lane to catch 94 West. Traffic grew a bit heavier in this stretch, but when he took the off ramp to the 805 South toward the International Border at San Ysidro, the traffic immediately dropped to the occasional odd vehicle.

Wally guided the Camry into the second to the farthest right lane and drove a few miles before he saw the familiar signs for the Palm Avenue off-ramp. It was ten forty-two a.m. when he punched his security code into the entry gate at Allied Storage.

Betrayed

He guided the Camry to the end building and pulled around the corner. He sat a few minutes. Unmoving—didn't get out of his car; just sat there. Presently, he reached over to the glove box and grabbed the key to the door.

With the garage door open Wally dragged out the blue duffel and spread it open. He removed the reciprocal saw and set it under a water bib near the door. While water ran slowly over the saw he rinsed the blade, its cover and the power pack. Returning his attention to the saw itself he rolled it side-to-side, rubbing his hands over it, removing visible traces of blood until the saw casing was clean. He inspected the tool to make certain there were no traces of blood or flesh.

Each duffle bag was given a quick rinse as well, making sure to wash away the obvious splotches of blood and flesh on the blue and brown bags. He set them out on the pavement to drain, while he organized his remaining gear.

Finally, he switched the two cars and left the Honda idling while he locked the storage compartment. Then he gathered the duffle bags, folded the brown one, and crammed it into the blue bag with the reciprocal saw. They were all that was left of his supplies and gear, *evidence*, he'd compiled for his, *operation*.

CHAPTER 42

St. Joseph's Hospital, Phoenix, Arizona, Saturday Morning, August 22—Megan Pace, like Lara Taylor, had been sitting vigil next to her husband's bed all night long. The team of doctors who'd saved the two men's lives had been candid with the women about what lay ahead for their husbands and them. It would be several days before the immediate danger of infection would pass. The wounds had been badly contaminated.

The amputations were located on the limbs such that prosthesis was going to be a challenge. Reattachment would have been an option had not the—if the limbs had not been mutilated with acid. Rehabilitation would take years and complete recovery was likely to be a matter of definition. Much was going to depend on the will of the men to go on living with their new circumstances. Lara Taylor required a sedative. Megan Pace, stoic, stood listening to her fate.

Around seven that morning Sonja Bienvenidos stuck her head into Bud Pace's room. Megan Pace looked up. "What are you doing here, you bitch?" Megan hissed. Sonja Bienvenidos looked haggard. Her hair was tangled, looked wiry; her eyes were red from crying, the lids and under-eyes blackened by running mascara.

Bienvenidos remained outside the door but asked, "How is he?"

"How do you think he is? Look at him," Pace's wife spat acidly, pointing at her husband lying on the hospital bed, four heavily bandaged stubs showing red splotches from the seepage of blood where his limbs once were. He looked like his body was in a short cardboard box with only his head sticking out: a caricature of a magician's act where a member of the audience volunteers to be placed in the box and cut in half. But there was nothing funny here. And this was all unspeakably real.

Bienvenidos broke down and sobbed uncontrollably. "The police have been questioning employees all night long," she sputtered between sobs. "That's how I found out. Is he going to live?" She choked so badly she could not go on.

Betrayed

"That's the bad news, you slut," Megan Pace barked. "He probably will live. And then what? What am I supposed to do with … this … this—" Megan Pace's eyes were brimming with tears, too, while she gazed upon all that was left of Bud Pace, "*That!*" she screamed pointing at what remained of her husband.

Sonja Bienvenidos slid backwards and let the door close. When she caught her breath she was sitting on the floor outside the room, a nurse asking her if she was all right.

Megan Pace had called the nursing station for help. She stood misanthropically arrogant over Bienvenidos watching the nurse minster to her without emotion. "Who did this?" she demanded, not a trace of sympathy in her voice.

"How in the world would I know that?"

"You fuck him on a regular basis!" Megan Pace accused unapologetically, disgust dripping off her tongue. "Did you think I didn't know? You think I don't know you follow him around on his business trips like some kind of nymphomaniac-groupie, having your romantic dinners and fucking the nights away in plush hotel rooms while I sit home with our child … his son? You're as stupid as you look right now. You think you're his first? You think you're special? And now you mean to tell me you know less than I do about his business?"

Sonja Bienvenidos covered her face with both hands and crumpled like a beaten puppy. The nurse helped her to her feet and deposited her in a chair down the hall, which was where Detective Bill Garcia found her a half hour later.

He'd left his card at the nurses' station with a request someone call him if anything developed. The nurse on duty considered this a development and called. The nurse recounted the altercation between Mrs. Pace and the young lady in the chair. Garcia listened.

Garcia approached Sonja Bienvenidos. "Ms. Bienvenidos?" he began. She looked up, red-faced, red-eyed.

Garcia stood up straight, looked from Bienvenidos to the door to Pace's room, to the nurses' station, back to her, then opened his mouth to speak, but no words came out. He sat down in the chair next to her and said nothing for several moments. Then, "I think you neglected to tell me some things last night?" he said gently.

She shook her head yes, but did not reply verbally.

"We need to talk about that."

"Now?" she whimpered.

"I'm afraid so."

Bienvenidos' eyes remained downcast at the floor, her head hung on her chest, her long, stringy black hair obscuring her face.

"How long were you having the affair with your boss?" Garcia waited patiently for Bienvenidos to gather herself.

"Two years," she whispered finally. "More or less. About that."

"Why didn't you tell me last night?"

She fidgeted and picked at her cuticles. Her voice was a snivel when she answered. "I was scared."

Garcia took his time. "Do you have any idea who would want to harm Mr. Pace or Mr. Taylor?"

"No," she blubbered. Then she went on. "But the company's in trouble. A lot—a lot of people," she continued haltingly, "a lot of people have lost a lot of money."

"Has anyone made any threats?"

"I don't know. Not that I know of. Nothing like this."

"Like what then?"

"Hundreds of them are threatening to sue us."

"Did either of your bosses ever have any physical confrontations with any of their clients that you know of?"

Bienvenidos shook her head in the negative.

"I'm going to need a list of all of your investors, Sonja."

Bienvenidos made no reply, continued to scrape at the cuticles of her fingernails while Detective Garcia questioned her. Her long, stringy black hair fell forward across both sides of her face hiding any glimpse of what might be working its way across her mind.

Garcia went on questioning the woman for nearly an hour but learned nothing that would provide a lead.

CHAPTER 43

Crossing the border into Mexico had been routine. Wally feared it might be one of the few routine things left in his life.

It had grown to be Saturday afternoon by the time he pulled Dan Dolan's Honda to a stop in front of his (Wally's) house. He left the engine idling while he slid out the driver's door and collected his two bags and the laptop. He set them down outside his front door and returned to Dolan's car. It had been seventy-two hours since he'd taken the car from his friend's driveway. He reached down with his right hand to ensure Dolan's passport and Sentri Pass were under the edge of the front seat exactly where he'd found them.

When he got out of the car in the Dolan's driveway, he looked up to find Dolan looking down at him from the third floor balcony. "Get done what you had to?" Dolan wanted to know. His countenance was chilly.

"Done," Wally answered with some attitude, no elaboration, no attempt to melt the freeze. He turned and walked back toward his own house without looking back.

A new and different kind of nightmare was now upon him. He could spare little attention at the moment over Dan Dolan's feelings. Wally's failing in all of his planning had been that he never expected to actually get his hands on the money; certainly not the millions of dollars he saw in Pace and Taylor's offshore account. He was exhausted. He was scared. He couldn't think any longer. He needed time to stop. There was a palpable tick-tick-ticking inside his head.

Wally collected the bags at the front of his house and moved them into the foyer. He left them where they lay and went to the kitchen, filled a tall glass with ice and returned to the liquor cabinet. Grabbing the quart of Johnny Walker Red, he filled the glass to the top. It was the first alcohol he'd allowed himself since Wednesday. A long, deliberate swig drew down, as if he were taking a pull from a glass of water. Wally dropped the glass from his lips and looked into the eyes of his dead wife's photograph. The liquor seemed to find its way to his brain instantly and he felt lightheaded. He set the glass on the buffet, leaned against its edge and wept quietly.

230

The only audible sounds besides his heavy breathing were the muted sounds of collapse as breakers crashed onto the black lava flow beside the golf course below the house. Wally didn't understand that exhaustion was finally in full grip of not just his body but his mind, too. He straightened, tried to collect a cohesive thought. All that was possible was a feeble attempt to quiet the voices of indecision inside his brain. Without any imminent threat, the adrenaline that had sustained him since the night before was subsiding rapidly. He was physically incapable of warding off what was happening to his body. His limbs felt thick and foreign to him. Suddenly, he was in severe pain, but he wasn't sure where it hurt exactly. His feet and legs didn't want to function. He wasn't sure he would make it up to his bedroom.

He groped his way over to the staircase and began to drag himself one step at a time upward. When he gained the top step, he stripped nude, stumbled out of the puddle of garments around his feet and crawled in between the clean sheets on his bed. It was the middle of the afternoon and warm outside, but he trembled uncontrollably as though he were freezing to death. His last conscious impression was of the clean smell of the Egyptian cotton sheets.

~~~~

At the *hour of demons* Wally's eyes flashed open. Still in his mind was the vision he'd had of being in a room of blood and gore and horrible smells and human limbs lying akimbo about the room; and then he remembered—it had not been merely a hellish dream. He rolled out of his bed to be greeted by a body so sore he could not identify which parts hurt the worst. He limped into his bathroom and fumbled with his hand along the wall until he found the light switch. He pulled his medicine drawer open and rummaged around inside it knocking over bottles until he found the Advil. He spilled four two hundred milligram tablets into his hand and shoved them into his mouth. The pills hung dry in the back of his throat, able neither to go down nor come back up until he scooped a handful of water from the faucet into his mouth and swallowed.

He shuffled into the water closet and relieved himself before searching for something warm to put on. An old sweatshirt slid over his head and soft flannel lounging pants up over his legs. The need for food felt overpowering. He wasn't hungry. He was starving. Conscience or no conscience, he needed to eat.

He edged his way down the stairs holding tight to the handrail. In the great room he fumbled for a lamp and switched it on. Over the fireplace mantle he felt around for the remote. Point. Press. The flame whooshed to life, the familiar ochre glow spreading across the expanse of the room. When he turned back toward the kitchen he was greeted by a friendly army of shadows dancing against the walls and ceiling.

Presently, the teapot was hissing and spitting, while he fumbled between the refrigerator and stove calling forth anything that sounded good for the omelet that was building. It wasn't a pretty concoction, but it was growing large. Smelled good.

Betrayed

He buttered a couple of pieces of toast, then settled down in front of the fireplace with the steaming food on a lap tray and began to devour the fusion of eggs, onions, mushrooms, serrano peppers and bacon. A shiny bead of sweat spread across his forehead, the hot chili pepper in the omelet. When he finished eating he sat back gazing into the flickering flames and finished his cup of tea. There existed an eerie sense of normal. But it was not possible for *anything* in Wally's life to be ordinary or routine—especially not normal—ever again.

He pushed himself up out of the chair and set the tray on the countertop. The food—and eight hundred milligrams of Advil—was having an impact against the assault of pain on his body. Not much was going to relieve the angst from the jumble of bewildered thoughts working their way through his brain. He retrieved his laptop, still lying in a heap with the other two bags in the foyer, set it on the kitchen counter and plugged it in. His hands were trembling when he pressed the power button to boot up the computer.

He pulled up the site for The Central Bank of the Netherlands Antilles and scrolled to the login page. Quivering fingers hovering above the keyboard, he hesitated before inputting his username and password. Another waffle. Click the submit box. Brush the sweat across the forehead with the back of his forearm, and right click. The whirligig spun and the hard drive purred. Within seconds his account window opened. Again he vacillated, rubbed his sweaty palms on his thighs. An unsteady index finger lingered over the mouse while he stared at the command that would display his account balance. Click, the sound came from the mouse. He jerked back quickly as if the touch had shocked him. The window opened. Balance: £263,843,841. The transfer had automatically been converted to Pounds Sterling.

Wally stumbled off the stool, grabbed the sides of his head in his hands like a bowling ball and wobbled around in unsteady circles repeating the words: Holy shit! Holy shit! Holy shit!

Suddenly he stopped, hurried back to the computer, stared at the screen again. Same information: Current Balance £263,843,841; (more than four hundred million U.S.) the transfer from the Banco do Brazil plus his £10,000. He was addled. For several minutes he couldn't hold two cohesive thoughts. Then realization came at him in a hysterical rush. In an instant the burden he carried over what he'd done to Pace and Taylor was replaced by the panic over what to do about the money. His first thought at least was pure; the money did not belong to him; it wasn't his—well, more than a million of it is mine, he corrected himself. Wally calmed down allowing his panic to be replaced by a sense of urgency to secure the money before anyone could recover it. He'd worry about what to do with it later.

He turned to the plasma TV across the room. Where's the fucking remote? His fingers went on trembling to an extent that made it difficult to press the correct buttons to get the damn thing on and find *CNN Headline News*. A nice looking woman Wally didn't recognize was reading down the breaking stories for the hour. She went on to international news; Marines were making a little progress in Helmut Province, Afghanistan. He continued to listen, waiting for her to get to the top national news stories. The topic of midterm elections and the Tea Party was leading that coverage. Immediately following was the reference he was certain was going to be there: The grizzly crime committed in Phoenix, Arizona where two victims suffered the amputation of all of their limbs. Then came what he needed to know: *"Police and FBI investigators have few leads in the case. Both victims are in critical but stable condition and have been placed in medically induced comas, making it impossible for authorities to learn the details surrounding the incident ... etc., etc."*

Wally was shuddering. Medically induced coma. That was a break he hadn't counted on. Okay, calm down and think. Soon enough somebody's going to find the bank transfer, try to trace it.

The morning news from San Diego wouldn't be on for another hour. He flipped off the TV and returned to the computer. The page had timed out and a drop down window was presented to sign back in. He didn't bother. Where's the website for Mexicana Airlines.

Wally went to the reservation page. Found a flight from Tijuana to the Cayman Islands. He could wait another day and book the same direct flight he'd flown before. Or he could leave in a few hours and connect through Guadalajara. Better than waiting around. He'd be in Cancun to catch the same Monday flight from Quintana Roo to Grand Cayman he'd flown a few weeks earlier.

Lucidity. It occurred to him if he could break the chain of evidence—well, there'd be time to contemplate all of that later.

The urge to return to his account page was powerful. No matter how many times he called up the page, the account balance remained the same: £263,843,841.

Adrenaline was flowing again. Wally charged upstairs and pulled out his khaki colored Bill Blass shoulder tote and began stuffing it with clothes.

By seven o'clock he was behind the wheel of his GMC pickup headed for the airport in Tijuana. He'd been back from Phoenix less than twenty-four hours. No time for niceties with the Dolans, Not psychologically fit for that anyway.

He pulled into the long-term parking lot at the airport and headed for the terminal. It required only a few minutes at the check-in counter to receive his boarding pass.

Wally sat fidgeting impatiently while he waited at the gate. Colin hadn't learned anything yet or he'd know it. No sooner had the thought crossed his mind than his phone rang. He checked the caller ID.

"Hey, Colin," he chirped, attempting to sound cheery. "Pretty early on a Sunday morning for you, isn't it?"

"Where are you?" Colin demanded. He made no attempt to mask the anger in his voice.

"Jesus, Colin," Wally exclaimed feigning surprise. "Who put the bee in your bonnet?"

"Where are you?"

"Here at home," he lied, "in Baja. Well, to be accurate, I'm out to breakfast but I'm here at home. Why? What are you all jacked up about?" It was all Wally felt he could do to maintain the charade.

"Have you seen the news?"

Betrayed

"No. Why?"

"Where've you been the last couple of days?"

"Right here, kid. Why the third degree?" Soon enough, Wally acknowledged, Colin was going to know the truth. But it could not be now. Not now.

Colin was silent several moments before getting into the details of what he'd learned about Phoenix, Friday night. Same sketchy information Wally heard on CNN.

As evenly as he could maintain, Wally lied to his nephew. "Well, I'd like to tell you I feel bad. But I don't. Sounds like somebody finally had enough and took matters into his own hands."

"And you know nothing about it? You had nothing to do with it, Uncle Wally?"

"Not unless you could beam me over and back, Scotty."

"I'm not stupid, Uncle Wally. What's next?"

Colin knew. It was clear. But he wasn't positive about what he knew; or perhaps it was that he could not allow himself to accept the truth of what he knew. But Wally couldn't concede yet. Still a lot of ground to cover. No time for this just then.

"Look, I've been right here in Baja," Wally went on lying. "Haven't been back across the border. How the hell could I have anything to do with anything?"

The lie would hurt later, but for now, lying was all he had. At least it was all he could think.

"Hey," he went on, changing the subject. "Glad you caught me, though. I'm gonna drive down to San Quentin a few days. Not sure about cell coverage down there."

"You don't sound interested in what went on in Phoenix." Colin was confused, but Wally knew that wouldn't stand.

"What do you want me to say? They got their comeuppance. 'Bout time."

Colin was silent several seconds. "I know you did it, Uncle Wally. I want to see you ... face-to-face," he demanded.

Wally stopped denying it. "I can't right now, Colin," he said emphatically. "And you need to stay away from me and don't call me anymore for a while. Who knows how the cops might investigate this. I'll get back to you ... soon."

"We're in real trouble, aren't we?" Wally heard the uncertainty in Colin's voice; like a lion trainer in a circus backing away from a dangerous cat sitting on a perch.

"We're not in any trouble at all," Wally lied. "I'll call when I get back."

"Just like that. A thing like this goes down and you're trotting off on holiday?"

"Four or five days ... week more or less,"

"Pretty hard to swallow, Uncle Wally."

"I'll call you in a few days." Wally decided not to talk about it any further.

When the call was disconnected he hung his head on his chest and stared at the phone. Overwhelming shame. What his nephew was going to learn about him. How he'd used and lied to him, but by then the lies had become, at least partially, protection.

If Colin knew anything about what happened and what was about to happen and didn't go straight to the authorities, he'd be in serious trouble. It was bad enough he'd involved the kid to help him get the tranquilizer. He sure as hell was not going to involve him any further—at least not until he could create a shield of safety for him. After that—Colin was going to have some life-changing decisions of his own to make.

~~~

The flight was full. Open seating. Wally slipped into a window seat three rows back in coach. In less than twenty minutes the plane was airborne and the stewardesses went to work. Food was served and they were constantly around to take drink orders. Wally bought several shot-sized bottles of Scotch. He noticed how the head stewardess kept an eye on him.

He peered down from thirty-seven thousand feet at the lush subtropical mountains of Central Mexico looking like one giant Chia Pet and drank the Scotch straight, trying to divine what his next move should be. The only thing perfectly clear to him was he could not undo anything he'd done. He could be sorry. He could take responsibility. He could go to prison the rest of his life. But he could not reverse any of it—or the consequences piling up.

The pilot banked hard over Lake Chapala, which was visible in spite of the gray sludge in the air. Wally could just make out the tiny artist colony of Ajijic through the smog as the pilot continued to glide. Wally knew people who lived in Ajijic. But that seemed like some kind of cruel illusion at the moment.

He deplaned into a somber airport; the walls were as gray as his mental state. Or they were gray because of his mental state. The gateways were short and dimly lit with little foot-traffic other than his fellow passengers who quickly dispersed in different directions. He'd been fed in flight and felt no need of food. He found a men's room before setting off to locate his connecting flight.

An hour dragged on before the flight was called. The plane was full. Several couples from Southern California headed to Cancun or Cozumel. Wally sat in an aisle seat next to a young couple obviously on honeymoon. They were occupied with each other so he laid his seat back, propped his head on a pillow and did the best he could to pretend sleep. He overheard their naughty innuendos and let his mind drift to his and Poppy's honeymoon in Acapulco more than thirty years before. He could recall every second of each day they'd shared at the Las Brisas Hotel; colorful hibiscus florets floated on their private swimming pool each morning.

It was dark when the plane landed at Quintana Roo. He caught a taxi to town. The driver dropped him in front of the Cancun Puerto Juarez Hotel. The ferry terminal with service to Isla Mujeres, a tiny island that lay just five miles offshore from the big hotels on the strip was just a short walk up the street. Wally had taken Poppy to Isla Mujeres twenty years earlier. Somewhere between Guadalajara and Cancun, Wally felt her slide into the seat with him. It was more likely the warm presence of the young newlywed in the seat next to him, but the transference felt real enough. Poppy's presence was so strong he couldn't ignore it and he longed to go backward in time, to hold her, to walk with her, to listen to the sounds of her laughter and feel the warmth of her breath against his face. His Monday flight to Grand Cayman didn't depart until three in the afternoon. He'd have time to go in search for her. It was as though she was drawing him, like a magnet, back in time, back to Isla Mujeres.

Wally's mind was trying to defend itself; block out the reality of the horror he'd created last Friday night. He wanted to go back to being that gentle person he thought he was. There was so much conflict within him he simply could no longer process it all. Poppy. Beautiful Poppy. He could let his mind go there—she might actually be there waiting for him; out on Isla Mujeres. Maybe he'd find her there. He *would* find her.

The handsome young Mexican man behind the shiny granite counter said in faultless English he had the perfect room for him, a late cancellation. Wally completed the paperwork and padded away to the elevators.

Out of the shower in his fully darkened room he stood completely nude in front of the tenth story window looking across at the dim lights twinkling on Isla Mujeres in the distance. His heart ached with the memory of her. So young. So beautiful. So happy. He permitted himself a moment's reflection on what he'd done. His heart was hardening against the deed. He would cut their fucking heads off if it would bring her back. They should consider themselves lucky.

But it was images of Poppy twenty years in the past, strolling ankle deep in the warm surf along the quiet beaches of Isla Mujeres consuming him in those hours. He thought the pain of loss should become easier with time. But the cruel loneliness and agony over his inability to reverse what happened were the emotions he lived with day in and day out; death is so final. He closed his eyes and could imagine the warmth of her tanned, smooth, velvety-soft skin next to his. The aching inside went on.

~~~~

He was up early waiting at the ferry dock. On the early trip each morning one rode with the working people who lived on the mainland and traveled back and forth to the tiny island. Wally sat quietly in a starboard window seat listening to the chatter of store clerks, hotel maids and restaurant waiters, and watched the welter of the azure water rippling off from the bow wake of the small ferry boat. Twenty minutes after the boat pulled away from the mainland it was approaching the dock on Isla Mujeres.

The tiny village on the island looked pretty much as it had twenty years earlier. He stepped ashore and allowed the hawkers to swarm him with jewelry, scarves and Mayan figurines of Ixchel.

In the time of the Maya, legend had it, the island was one of the four territories that made up what is today the state of Quintana Roo. The island was supposedly the sanctuary of the Love Goddess and was adorned with elegant stone statues of her nubile form, bare to the waist. Her mystical significance was being celebrated in the current era by hundreds of curvy, heavy breasted ceramic statuettes you could buy for fifty pesos. *Isla Mujeres* means Island of Women. Wally and Poppy had hiked to the ancient temple of the Goddess on the south end of the island. He set off in that direction.

In his mind he spoke to Poppy while he trod up a street one block from the ferry terminal and turned south. "You know what I've gotten myself into, don't you Popp?" He breathed heavily while he hiked and said these words in his head. "I have to finish it. I *have* to finish it! But today—today I need you to come back to me." He walked past shops of Talavera pottery, clothing stores with cotton garments, colorful hand-embroidered designs, shops of leather goods, women's handbag shops with every knock-off label one could imagine. There was every storefront and consumable a tourist could want: t-shirts, jewelry, watches, shoes, and kayak tours to paddle around the island; fishing charters if that was what you thought you needed.

"I know you're here, Poppy," he said. "I can feel you. Please be waiting for me at the Temple."

But Poppy was not waiting for him at the Temple. Still, he stood in the tower on the very spot where they had stood together all those years in the past and he thought he could feel her spirit fill him. He remained for a long time staring out toward Cuba, absorbing the energy he felt coming to him from her. "Oh, Poppy," he said. "I miss you so much."

He turned away finally and walked, his eyes blurred, back toward the north end of the island. It was nearing ten o'clock when he arrived in the village. Every step he took. Every turn he made. Every thought he held was an echo of them together there; so long ago it might as well have been in a different life.

He found a restaurant with four small outdoor tables on the sidewalk and ordered a torta and a bottle of Pacifico. The waiter brought the beer while Wally waited for the sandwich. His thoughts were a jumble of incoherent madness, grief, regret. The streets were alive with tourists. He watched them coming and going, but he didn't see them.

He finished his beer and sandwich and went on. It was a warm tropical day. Just outside of the shallow bay formed in the crescent of the north end of the island, the Caribbean Sea rushed northward through the Yucatán Channel at twelve knots, curling north and east around Cuba, heading toward the Florida Keys. The trade winds arriving at the beach had drifted on those warm tropical currents coursing across the Caribbean and now lavished silky warmth on the golden bodies lying like driftwood over the powdery white sand.

He found a seat in the curve of the trunk of a young coconut palm that had been blown over by some long-passed hurricane, yet managed to maintain a hold on life and now presented an elegantly bent trunk that formed a perfect "U" as it struggled to fight its way back from annihilation.

He gazed out across the water, holding in his mind's eye an image of him and Poppy standing together somewhere near this spot in another life. They'd kicked off their shoes and walked barefoot in this same warm white sand, turned and kissed spontaneously. They'd giggled then over the absurdity of an ancient couple lying nude on the beach, her walnut colored breasts elongated, sagging to the sides as though they'd been pinned to her chest but wouldn't stay, a copious gray bush at her pelvis. The old man's penis was little more than a large peanut peeking out from his own bristled scrub of gray. The old couple held hands, clinging to each other, clinging to the last of life itself. The arrogance of youth had prevented him from appreciating what that old couple had in their lives that he was never going to have in his own.

Wally considered Bud Pace and Carl Taylor for one brief moment. Perhaps that was it on one level, he reckoned, the arrogance of their youth. Most of their investors probably seemed to them useless relics, burdens on the Social Security system. And then he began to remember finding Poppy that afternoon in her car; how she looked, the expression on her face, how her skin felt when he put his lips on hers in the futile effort to breathe her back to life, her limp body in his arms. Wally fidgeted on the palm trunk and looked away across the empty horizon. "You boys have just begun to pay for what you did," he said to no one. He slipped off the trunk of the coconut palm and headed west along the beach.

CHAPTER 44

Customs took a half hour. Almost as long as the forty-five minute flight out to the Caymans would take. Wally's shoulder tote was opened and searched while he waited impatiently. Then the sullen-tempered officer took his Mexican Immigrant card and grilled him about why he was travelling to the Caymans in the first place, as if he were committing an illegal act. How long did Wally intend staying? The prickly customs officer even looked over his round trip ticket on Mexicana. The guy was as imperious as the snotty prick he'd dealt with on his previous trip.

They were hardly airborne before the pilot was descending to Grand Cayman. Wally glanced out the window of the plane. They were approaching the single runway at Owen Roberts International from the same direction as weeks earlier. There were fewer cruise ships anchored at West End.

When the plane ground to a full stop, Wally and the other passengers grappled to recover their carry-on bags from the overhead compartments. They waited while the stairs were rolled into place on the tarmac.

Passengers followed blue lines painted on the asphalt to the terminal where the friendly customs officers were waiting to welcome them. Clearing customs on Grand Cayman was quick and pleasant. The Mexicans could learn from their island neighbor.

Having visited the place recently made getting around faster ... more relaxed. Wally strutted confidently to the taxi line and took the next cab pulling forward. "Comfort Inn & Suites at West End," he said to the skinny old man driving.

The driver jogged 'round to close his door and then back to the driver's side. "You know George Town, Meestah?"

"Was here once," Wally said.

Familiar island music played on the radio. His driver maneuvered around the huge roundabout exiting the airport. Wally recognized the same route, Robert, used. He reached into his pocket and removed his wallet. Rummaged through business cards he carried in the folding side until he found Robert the taxi driver's card and slipped it into his shirt pocket.

The taxi emerged from the small cluster of three story office buildings and made the familiar right turn onto the street paralleling Seven Mile Beach. Wally saw the Comfort Inn sign up ahead. Out in the harbor mega-yachts bobbed at anchor among the cruise liners. The driver pulled into the guest entrance, shoved his car into park and hustled around in time to assist Wally retrieving his bag from the back seat. Wally gave the man a twenty as he had Robert on his previous ride from the airport, told him to keep the change.

Checking in proved easier as well. Comfort Inn had captured his information in their computer system from his previous visit. Information was quickly reverified and the reservationist handed him his plastic key-card. "Would you like assistance with your bags?" he asked. Wally declined and ambled toward the hallway where the man said he'd find his room.

His small terrace faced west, overlooking the ships and yachts in the harbor. Wally closed the curtains, shook out his clothes and hung them in the closet. Again, he used the box safe bolted in the bottom of the closet to secure the cash he carried. Finally, he dropped onto the bed, laced his hands behind his head and stared into the ceiling in complete silence. Gradually, the appalling knowledge of what he'd done leached back to the forefront of his brain. Any thoughts of a moment's peace were gone.

Drink maybe; get the edge off. He rolled up from the bed remembering the beach dive he'd found on his first trip. It wasn't far. He traded shirts and changed into shorts.

The waning sun was beating straight into the west-facing entry of the Comfort Inn. Still warm and humid outside. He jaywalked the wide street to get to the walkway along the ocean. Trudging north along Seven Mile Beach. After fifty yards he was soaked in sweat. What little breeze there was came from behind him and did little to cool anything. The place was further along than he'd remembered. Before long he saw the familiar sign: Rudy's Nut Hut. Hippie-windsurfer-beachcomber-funky little place; palm-frond roof, windsurfers leaning against the walls, fish nets with cork floats strung about, reggae music drifting out the open windows.

He poked his head in as if testing the water in a shower. The *Hut* housed six tables. Two were occupied; windsurfer kids in their twenties ... early thirties ... sun-bleached hair, wetsuit bottoms still on, baggy t-shirts over their tops. Bob Marley was declaring, "Power-to-the-People" over the sound system, supported by the fresh scent of saltwater and boiling shrimp brine. The hood from a 1956 Chevy hung upside down from the ceiling and an ancient rusted Coca Cola sign fronted the counter across the small open room. Wally captured one of the tables. They were all window seats. The rum drink he ordered was too sweet. He pushed it aside and called for a glass with the rum straight over ice. "Yes. Fill the glass," he told the waitress.

More than an hour drifted by to the thump of Reggae beat and humid air. By then Wally was nursing a second glass of rum, not caring much about the effect it was beginning to have. He stared aimlessly out across an empty sea. It was surreal what he felt; so much normal all around him. Ironic. He'd declared sentence on Pace and Taylor ... carried it out, soon sentence would be declared on him. But before he could allow that to happen, there was the money to figure out. He had ideas. But would there be any way in the real world to make them happen?

The visit to Isla Mujeres lingered in his mind, too. As angry as he'd been at Poppy for leaving him the way she had, the visit to Isla Mujeres reminded him how much he loved her. He finished the rum and then wobbled slowly back along the waterfront toward the Comfort Inn.

~~~~

He passed out for a time. But it proved no more effective than any other pharmaceutical he might have tried. Up early next morning, feeling like shit. Looking like shit. He fumbled around to find the business card of the taxi driver. "Nine o'clock out front," they agreed. "Meet you there." He hadn't bothered explaining to Robert he'd used his services before. No interest in familiarity or recognition of any sort. Simply that he knew what he was getting. The guy knew where he needed to go and performed without making it necessary for Wally to do more than get in—get out—of his taxi on his first trip to Grand Cayman.

He flushed his eyes repeatedly with Visine in an attempt to wash away the telling neon red. He slipped on a smart pair of double-pleated slacks that hung better on his skinny frame than they had in years. Silk shirt open at the collar; casual but not tourist-slouch.

Wally stood staring into the bathroom mirror a long time. It wasn't the clothing. It was the face squinting back at him that was puzzling. Familiar, but Wally couldn't place where he might have seen it before.

When he walked past the check-in counter in the lobby, the young man who'd checked him in the day before had been replaced by the same cappuccino-skinned girl who worked the morning shift on his previous stay. Her eyes were the softest yellow-green. She should have been a model. Instead she was a desk clerk at a Comfort Inn. "Life's fucked," he mumbled going by. The girl smiled and said, "*Bonjour, monsieur*," just as she had once before.

When he pushed through the front doors, Robert the taxi driver was waiting for him. "*Bonjour*," he chirped and opened the rear door of his taxi as though it was a shiny limousine instead of a tired 1998 Citroën. Wally climbed in.

Robert scurried around and slid behind the wheel. "Where would you like to go, Meestah?"

"Netherlands Antilles Bank," Wally replied.

"I know this place Meestah," Robert said. He adjusted the volume on the radio, made eye contact in the rear view mirror. Quick double take of Wally as though something glimmered in his memory and then he pulled onto the street. "Le bank not far, Meestah." He flicked the turn signal, adjusted his car radio when a new reggae song began to play.

Wally recognized the street. He knew there'd be two roundabouts before his driver banked left a few blocks to the Livingston Suites office building.

Short ride. He sat motionless in the back seat when the Citroën pulled to a stop. He was tempted to tell Robert to drive back to the motel and begin again.

Betrayed

"Monsieur?" Robert said standing beside the open passenger door.

Wally slid out and dug in his pocket.

"Shall I wait, Meestah?"

"Call you when I'm finished."

"*Oui monsieur*," Robert said sensing more tension than he wanted any part of. "I wait for your call."

CHAPTER 45

At nine-thirty Monday morning, August 24th, sixty hours after Wally had committed one of America's grizzliest crimes, he pushed open the giant doors of the Livingston Suites office building and entered the capacious vestibule that had intimidated him on his first visit, little more than one month earlier. He found it no less intimidating in that moment. The constant burden of what he had done, and the business still before him, compounded his feelings of fear and anxiety. He could barely say, *"two hundred sixty-three million pounds,"* and he was about to walk into Netherlands Antilles Bank and ask a total stranger to help him hide the money. Wally was treading in deep water he realized could easily drown him if he wasn't careful. What the hell was he going to say if they wanted to know where the money came from? He'd become a victim of his own success.

He made his way around to Suite 105. Stood a long beat. Deep breath. Ahead, he stepped into the lobby. Aafje Janssen stood from her desk as she had before and walked toward him. "May I help you?" she offered, in that perfectly inflected singsong accent.

Wally identified himself. He could see the moment of recollection in her eyes. Aafje seemed embarrassed she had not recognized him without the prompt. "I have some new business to conduct," he said.

Aafje returned to her desk and sat down before her computer terminal. Her fingernails clicked audibly while she typed. Wally stood in front of her like a truant waiting to be punished. Within seconds, Aafje looked up at him as if she were seeing him for the first time, her sapphire eyes ablaze against her silky, peach-colored complexion and asked if he would excuse her a moment. She invited him to have a seat. "I'll be a moment, please," she said. He began to sweat.

Nearly two minutes elapsed before Aafje reappeared through the door behind her desk, followed by Senior Vice President, Finn Diextter. Diextter was an impeccably well-groomed man of about forty, Wally guessed. His hair was black and shiny, combed back over the top of his head like Count Dracula. His face was strong with angular, chiseled, stern features that did not convey conviviality. His shoulders were broad, imposing. Diextter strode confidently around Aafje's desk toward Wally with his hand extended.

"Finn Diextter, Mr. Stroud," he said, as if he'd known Wally all of his life. "I'm Senior Vice President of the Central Bank of the Netherlands Antilles." His words carried the bearing of the Prime Minister of a nation. The man was commanding, yet the baritone voice was inflected with that same soft accent Wally heard in Aafje Janssen's spoken words.

Wally's fear grew. "Wally Stroud," he responded simply. "Thank you for seeing me."

"My pleasure, Mr. Stroud. Please, step this way." Diextter stood to the side, gestured. Wally slipped through the elegant door behind Aafje Janssen's huge desk for the second time and descended the elegant wide staircase. At the landing, he was directed to the grand double doors he'd seen before with Finn Diextter's name engraved on them in imposing gold lettering. Diextter invited him to have a seat in a plush, venerable wing-backed chair at the far corner of the spacious office, behind which an entire wall library was filled with expensively bound reference books Wally did not recognize.

Diextter closed the door. "May I offer you something, Mr. Stroud, coffee, juice—a drink perhaps?" He didn't wait for Wally to respond before he went on. "If you are hungry, I can have breakfast prepared for you."

"Thank you. I ate before coming," Wally lied. He really wanted a glass of Scotch but could not bring himself to say it. "Would a cup of tea be too much trouble?" Wally ventured, more out of a need to engage with the man than any real desire.

"Nothing is too much trouble, Mr. Stroud," Finn Diextter assured him. Wally finally had his fear sufficiently in check to notice the slightest air of deference from Diextter. Diextter walked to his desk, leaned across the front side, pressed a button and said, "Aafje, would you be kind enough to have two cups of—" He paused and turned to Wally quizzically. "—English Black?—tea prepared and brought to my office?"

Wally nodded his approval.

"Immediately, Mr. Diextter," Wally heard Aafje reply.

Finn Diextter crossed to where Wally sat and seated himself in a chair as posh as the one Wally occupied. The Oriental rug on the floor felt rich beneath his feet. Severe anxiety boiled up inside once more.

"Now then," Diextter began, deep baritone, "how will I be of assistance to you, Mr. Stroud?"

Wally hesitated. Guilt on so many levels oozed from his demeanor. He had no idea how to discuss with this stranger what he needed, or hoped could be done. For all he knew, the guy would call the FBI and have him arrested. "I'm not sure how to explain what I need," Wally admitted feebly.

Diextter reached over and picked up what looked like a TV remote and said, "Why don't we do this?" He pressed a button on the device. A strip in the floor retracted and a screen glided soundlessly up out of a slot about six feet in front of them. It was roughly sixty inches across,

Wally guessed. On it was displayed his account balance and details of the only two transactions he'd ever performed in the account; his original £10,000 deposit and a transfer deposit on Saturday last from Banco Do Brazil in the amount of $425,000,000, which Netherlands Antilles had converted to Pounds Sterling upon receipt. The print on the screen was so large Wally had no difficulty reading every detail without moving; £263,843,841.

Wally stared several seconds, astounded still by the very idea the money was there. No alternatives. He realized he'd already taken the plunge. He knitted his fingers together, leaned forward in the chair with his elbows supported by the large overstuffed arms and looked Finn Diextter squarely in the eyes. "I need that money to disappear in a way that it can never be found, no matter who might gain access to your account records." A bead of perspiration broke across his forehead, and he knew if this were a police interrogation, he'd be nailed.

"I see," Diextter replied calmly. "Let me be candid with you, Mr. Stroud. I need to know if this money is in any way tied to illegal drugs or any terrorist organization."

Wally shook his head in the negative. "Absolutely not," he assured Diextter, with authority.

"Bank robbery?" Diextter asked seriously.

"No!" Wally guaranteed him.

"Have you committed a federal crime of financial fraud in the United States for which you are under investigation by the FBI or the IRS in which *this money* is the subject?" Diextter asked these questions unapologetically, very businesslike.

"I assure you, that is not the case," Wally said honestly, knowing full well he was splitting hairs. But the guy hadn't asked *how* he came by the money. He only wanted assurance it wasn't drug money or a bank robbery or Wally wasn't under investigation by the Feds. He rationalized he could honestly say no to all of those questions, at least in that moment.

There was a light tap on the door. "Ah," Diextter said, setting the remote down on the arm of his chair. "That will be our tea." He lifted himself and strode to the door. When he opened it a short black man wearing a handsome white chef's coat over black tuxedo slacks stepped into the room. He did not bother to ask where Diextter wanted the tray placed. He crossed to the two chairs, arranged the table between them and presented a sterling silver tray: coarse brown, unrefined cane sugar, milk and real cream, four crisp butter cookies coated in heavy granulated sugar and two cups of tea served in white Bone China. Must be the standing order in the private kitchen, Wally concluded. It was a virtual déjà vu and he thought momentarily of Pieter Van Hoof's bald head.

The manservant stepped to the side, bowed slightly and asked, "*Y aura-t-il tout autre, M. Diextter?* Will that be all, Mr. Diextter?"

Diextter remained at the open door, his hand on the knob. "*Ce sera tout pour l'instant, Jean.* For now, Jean," he said in velvety French, without ceremony.

The black man quietly crossed the room and Diextter closed the door after him.

"Please," he said, coming back to reclaim his chair, "prepare your tea to your liking." He picked up the cream and added a splash to his cup.

Betrayed

Wally doctored his with the sugar and added some of the cream to his, too.

"Please, help yourself to a biscuit if you wish." Diextter carefully selected one of the cookies without hesitation, sipped from his tea and sat back.

"I'm sorry it is necessary … the crude questioning," Diextter offered with a slight hand gesture. "But if the answer to any of those questions would be yes, it would be entirely possible our privacy barrier could be pierced by your government. We live in a … dangerous world." Diextter smiled. "It is my duty to inform you of all the possibilities."

"Fair enough," Wally said holding his teacup with both hands. "I can guarantee you I haven't done any of these things."

"Good," Diextter said. "Then I'm completely confident we can help you. Go ahead, explain to me what it is you wish, let me see what we can do."

Wally began cautiously to explain what he hoped could be done. "At the core of it, Mr. Diextter, shortly, and I'm sorry I cannot be more specific than that … shortly, someone is likely to come looking for this deposit."

Diextter stopped him. "How is it you believe anyone will be able to locate this account, Mr. Stroud?"

Wally thought for a moment, and then said, "They're going to follow the transfer from the Banco Do Brazil to this account number."

"That is correct," Diextter conceded. "It will be a relatively straight forward process for the owner of the account on the other end. They will be able to identify the money was transferred to this account; but it is highly doubtful they will learn any more unless you have committed a crime." Diextter paused, observing Wally closely. "Even then, it would require such crime be of a certain … *specific* nature … before our government would require we surrender information about you." He sipped quietly from his cup, watching Wally over its rim.

Wally squirmed in his chair. He could feel his hands trembling so he set his cup down. It was obvious he was hiding something significant.

"Mr. Stroud," Diextter said, "you've told me where you did *not* get this money. I really don't want to know where you *did* get it—unless you've lied to me about the questions I asked you earlier."

"Yes … I mean no, no I didn't lie to you." Wally paused and looked down at the floor. "I need this money to disappear so no matter what your bank might be forced to disclose about me, it can't ever be found. It doesn't belong to me—but it doesn't belong to the people who will come looking for it either."

"I see," Diextter replied evenly. "What of…whomever it does belong to?"

Wally searched for the correct answer. "They don't know it still exists … *yet*." He tried to explain. "It's like this money was lost and I found it. But … people … certain people … know it's been found and—recovered. I'm pretty sure they're going to try to get it back."

Finn Diextter picked up his teacup, reclined thoughtfully into his chair. They sat in silence. Diextter fixed his gaze on Wally and held him. Wally waited, scared out of his wits. He needed to piss in the worst way. "You assure me, you are in no way involved in any of the criminal acts I specifically asked you about?"

"On my word. None of those things. This was ... personal ... quite personal—between me and two ... individuals."

The two men sat in quiet contemplation or anxious anticipation depending upon the chair in which you happened to be occupying.

Presently, Diextter spoke. "It appears you play, shall we say, a precarious game *Monsieur* Stroud." He finished his tea and returned the cup to the tray. "You require an ally. Allow me to explain how we are already protecting you," he continued. "The first thing to understand, Mr. Stroud, is that while it may be relatively easy for someone to see a transfer was made from one account number to another account number, there is no way for anyone to obtain the private information regarding the name and ownership of our account number short of government intervention." Diextter went on. "That is very difficult, even for your IRS or FBI—as long as they don't come to our government with claims such as those I discussed with you. Even in that case, a long period of time is going to be consumed in the process." He added almost as an afterthought, "It could take years. And, if they were successful at requiring us to relinquish information, they would not be allowed to go on a fishing expedition. They would only be allowed to look at this specific account." He paused. "As to any private entity being able to access the information ... you need not concern yourself."

Wally persisted. "Can you make it all disappear?"

"I can," Finn Diextter replied absolutely. "If you insist there *never* be any way to find this money ... I can make that happen." He sat erect in his chair, fingers interwoven into a temple with its spire pressed against his lips. "The method," he went on to say, "has its caveats, but if it is a complete erasure of any trace of the money you're after—" He smiled knowingly and added, "in theory the transactions *could* individually be traced ... if someone were willing to devote say, fifty or perhaps seventy years to such a project with no certainty of success. Know anyone like that?" Diextter asked, smirking.

Wally waited impatiently. In a few moments he asked cautiously, "Can you tell me what you have in mind?"

"Yes," Diextter replied simply. He looked sideways at Wally but engaged him eye to eye. "It would work like this, *Monsieur*. We can establish a new account. A number only. Different from the Swiss accounts of which you have no doubt heard. Your name will appear nowhere. Neither, for that matter, would the name of any other person or entity, merely a number. Once we have created this new account, we will establish secret access. No one but the person in possession of the number. One serious caveat is this number will be the equivalent of a *bearer bond*—irreplaceable, unchangeable. Whoever is in possession, owns it. For that reason," Diextter cautioned, "you must take great care should anything happen to you, that information be transferred only to an individual whom you want to gain ultimate control over the account, for there will be no other way." Diextter slid forward in his chair. "Do you understand the implication here, Mr. Stroud? If that access key is ever lost, this fortune will sit here in this account until the end of time."

Wally thought he did understand, and it sounded like more than he could have hoped for.

"Now then," the banker continued, "once the numbered account is in place," Finn Diextter's eyes twinkled as he explained the next step to Wally, "I will personally establish an automated journey, sending every pound out of your current account, close it out." He grinned and went on. "When I'm finished, your money will be split up, deposited in hundreds of other international banks around the world that will have automated triggers to cause it to be retransmitted the instant the first transaction is complete to yet another international bank. This process will repeat itself thousands of times in transactions of varying amounts until one by one, each of the final transactions around the world will have one final transaction that will deposit the money back here into your numbered account. Never," Diextter pronounced with an air of pride, "would anyone be able to connect the money in this account to you or any real person." The banker sat back in his chair, tugged at the cuffs of his long-sleeved white shirt and smiled with satisfaction.

Wally sat mesmerized, watching the handsome banker. "You can do that?" he asked, unable to conceal his dismay. "And the money would come back? It's safe?"

"There are fees, of course," Finn Diextter said.

"What kind of fees?" Wally was instantly suspicious.

"Substantial fees," Diextter admitted unappolgetiacally. "This is a highly complex transaction. It will require a great deal of preparation to put all of the automated triggers in place."

"But you can do it?"

"Yes," Diextter pronounced with authority.

"How much?"

"Two million," Diextter replied without flinching.

"Dollars?" Wally half shouted.

"Pounds," Diextter corrected him. "Right off the top," the banker told Wally flatly. "The instant the button is pushed to initiate the transactions."

"That's outrageous," Wally complained raising his voice.

"It's an optional service, Mr. Stroud. You can leave the account just as it is. There are still substantial protections to you already in place." There was a taste of arrogance in Diextter's countenance Wally didn't like.

Wally sat quietly, doing his best to assimilate what was being proposed. Foremost in his mind was Colin. He was also considering the gravity of what he'd done to Bud Pace and Carl Taylor. The cops would be working tirelessly right at that moment to get at him and this money.

"It costs money to establish the kind of ... *anonymity* ... you want for yourself, Mr. Stroud," Diextter added.

Wally continued to consider the whole idea. Finn Diextter waited patiently.

Finally Wally asked, "So how long will all of this take?"

"A few days," Diextter replied jovially.

"I have a return flight on Friday. Can it be completed by then?"

"Cancel your commercial flight, Mr. Stroud," Diextter said emphatically. "We'll fly you home in our corporate jet. We can have the new numbered account in place. You will be in possession of ... your secret number. The web of transactions will have been initiated. However, the transactions themselves will take a few days to complete. You will need to be patient. These things take time."

"I see," Wally said. He glanced at his watch. He'd sat with Finn Diextter now for a little over an hour. It was coming up on midday.

Suddenly, Wally pushed himself up onto his feet and looked down into the surprised face of the banker. He stuck out his hand. "Let's do it."

Diextter rose and shook Wally's hand. "We'll get started immediately," he said. "In the mean time, I'll order our lunch."

Wally was still feeling severe anxiety. And he had to find a restroom at that instant, or piss his pants.

"You should relax, Mr. Stroud," Diextter said, knowing full well the man before him, Wally Stroud, had never known the kind of wealth he was currently in possession of. "You are one of our more prominent clients. Try to enjoy your status."

"I need to use the restroom," Wally said.

"This way," Diextter said, smiling. He opened his office door and indicated where Wally would find the sanitary facilities.

Betrayed

CHAPTER 46

Four o'clock Monday afternoon, August 24ᵗʰ, Phoenix, Arizona. Department of Public Safety, Criminal Investigations Unit, Office of Detective Bill Garcia—Garcia used his cell phone to dial his colleague, FBI Agent Clark Reynolds. He was on his way to his last call for the day. The phone rang several times before Reynolds picked up.

"Guillermo," Reynolds answered, reading the name off of his caller ID, "How's that list coming?" he asked, referring to the Investor/Client list from PPI.

"It isn't," Garcia deadpanned.

"What's the problem?"

"Employees are playing CYA. Without the boss, nobody wants to say shit. They're either claiming no access to the information or they don't have the authority to give the information out. I'm gonna have to get a warrant. Chaos over there, Clark; they're all scared shitless."

"They better be!" Reynolds said.

"Don't think that's it," Garcia speculated, "… our perp, I mean. Something else has 'em spooked. Upper level management types know something they don't want to talk about. Something here we don't know yet."

"Whoever this guy is, Bill, he's getting a big lead on us. He'll either strike again, or flee."

"I'm headed out to see Señorita Bienvenidos right now. Anybody knows anything, it's her."

"Remind her what happened to her boyfriend could happen to her we don't find this guy soon. Maybe that will get her attention."

"Why I'm going after her," Garcia agreed. "She's scared … real scared. She knows something she's not giving up."

"No need to let her know … odds are this was a one-timer. It was revenge, Bill … against something specific."

Garcia could practically hear the wheels turning in the FBI agent's head.

250

"Maybe they owed the wrong people money … somebody wanted to make an example. This kind of rage isn't just about money. Your vics know this guy … or whoever it was sent him after them. And they know why. So what are these two into? Drugs? Gambling?"

"All possible," Garcia agreed. "But I gotta have a shred of something to know where to look. I got friends on the force in Vegas. I'll have 'em run our guys. Maybe they turn up something over there."

"Worth a shot," Reynolds said. "Any word from the hospital?"

"Same," Garcia reported, grunting as he turned in his car seat checking oncoming traffic. "We won't get anything there for several days. You want to be around when they wake these two up?"

"No thanks," Reynolds said. "You can have that pleasure."

"Can you imagine?" Garcia reacted.

It was easy for Clark Reynolds to imagine. He'd treated many vets after Vietnam and Bosnia who'd had limbs blown off; many were multiple amputees. "Our perp knew just what he was doing, Guillermo. He imagined the nightmare he was creating for those two and did everything he could, including calling for help to make certain they lived to have to face the very moment we're talking about.

"Squeeze this Bienvenidos woman, Detective," the FBI agent urged. "We don't get a lead on this guy soon, he's gone."

"I'll keep you informed." Garcia promised.

CHAPTER 47

Robert was waiting beside his Citroën out front of the Livingston Suites office building a little after four. He scurried to open the door. Wally fell heavily into the back seat. "You want to see some sights, Meestah?" the taxi driver offered, climbing back in behind the wheel.

"No thanks," Wally said. "Just take me to my hotel."

Robert grinned at him in the rearview mirror and pulled into traffic. At the corner he turned right and Wally could see opalescent wavelets sparkling at the end of the attenuated street, like looking down the wrong end of the barrel of a telescope, three story buildings rising along each side of the narrow boulevard creating a tight, shaded corridor. It was merely minutes before the taxi was depositing him at the Comfort Inn.

A new face at the front desk.

Wally trudged through the lobby to his room, shed his clothes down to his underwear and collapsed across the bed. Anxiety and adrenaline utterly depleted him then. And there was the sleep deprivation; there was constantly that. His body'd finally shut down. It was seven o'clock when he woke. Those three hours were the longest continuous sleep he'd had in days.

He could feel the shroud of depression surrounding him. Food held little interest, though he felt pains in his stomach. The hot shower he climbed into offered no relief from his misery. At nine o'clock he went out in search of a bottle of Scotch.

He scuffed along the waterfront, heading north. Not a breath of breeze. Humidity hung heavy in the night air. Sweating heavily. He mindlessly brushed the buzzing mosquitoes from his ears. Taxi drivers honked horns to get his attention as they drove past but he waved them off. Every beachfront bar and hangout was pulsing with loud reggae music and swaying, half naked bodies. Not a scene that held any interest for him.

He'd wandered about a mile when he came upon a corner market catering to tourists who'd suffered lapses in memory or bad planning; the ones who neglected to pack one thing or another they discovered they couldn't live without for a week. The small store offered a hodgepodge of mundane items from dental floss to flip-flops and sunscreen—lots of sunscreen. He didn't find Scotch, but there was a grand selection of Caribbean rum. He grabbed a liter of Seven Fathoms Premium because the girl behind the counter said it was distilled on the Island.

By the time he'd tramped back to the Comfort Inn, he was ready to make his own evaluation of the Seven Fathoms. He poured it straight—over a glass of ice. No interest in the characteristics of the rum or anything else for that matter. Wally simply wanted to be anesthetized to the agony he felt in his life. He poured a second glass and reclined on his bed staring into the ceiling. By the third glass of Seven Fathoms he was beginning to let go of his troubles and appreciate the finer nuances of the amber liquid providing his deliverance. He attempted to pour a fourth glass but only managed to drizzle a fair amount onto the side table instead of over what was left of his melted ice.

He passed out around midnight. At nine-thirty in the morning he awoke slowly, still in his clothes, lying atop his unslept-in bed. No memory of the night before, not even having walked to the market to find the liter of rum sitting open, half empty, on the table next to his bed. The ache in his head seemed an unfair exchange for the profound loss of memory.

He rolled to a sitting position … sat several minutes doing his best to hold on to his world before attempting to gain his feet and make it into the bathroom. He had to brace himself against the wall behind the toilet while he pissed. Clawed his way to the sink. Searched his eyes. Couldn't recall the whites being that particular shade of crimson ever. The rum, or his psychosis? He reached for the Visine and began multiple flushings.

Hot shower. Change of clothes. The room wasn't spinning quite as fast. The state of his reality dribbled back. The bank guy, Diextter, was going to solve his money problem—if he didn't outright steal the money. He waivered in his buoyancy over the matter of making the money disappear. No option but to trust this, Diextter. It was only a matter of time before the cops would come looking for him. They'd figure the whole thing out and come after him.

Once he'd gotten food into his stomach, Wally was having moments of clarity. The soft breeze off the Caribbean had returned. It was comfortable out.

He shuffled back to his room at the Comfort Inn, took out his laptop.

Wally estimated there was going to be more than two hundred million left, even after the investors he'd found to that point were made whole again. He explained his idea for Colin to borrow from what remained of Pace and Taylor's stolen stash to start that international company they'd talked about, the one with Siemens and NASA. But Wally hoped Colin might find a way of locating more of the lives Pace and Taylor had devastated and, in time, return as much of the money as was possible. The idea was cockamamie, hopelessly idealistic. He admitted that. But it was the only plan he could imagine that didn't make him feel he really was worse than Pace and Taylor. He'd never expected to find even his own money much less the fortune he'd stumbled into. Perhaps some of it *was* Pace and Taylor's and Colin would never find all their victims. That was likely, he reckoned. It mattered only to Wally that Colin try—if that was his choice, of course.

Betrayed

Wally went on refining the confession he'd written to Colin, hoping to find absolution in his words. The act of contrition in his notes lifted some of his burden. It wasn't much, but he'd try to do what good he could before—what? Colin would finish what Wally'd started or he wouldn't. No control. The haze of confusion that was his torment remained.

Everything he'd told Colin was written in anticipation of being caught by the cops—arrested, put away in a cage the rest of his life. And it wouldn't be any cushy, private cell like Bernard Madoff's. He'd be tossed in with murderers and rapists and child molesters. That nightmare was with him every moment. His only solace came in knowing they'd never find that money. Pace and Taylor were doomed to the exact circumstances he'd intended. If Colin couldn't find all of their victims, he'd surely find many; it was as much as he could hope for.

Wally had been desperate to ensure Pace and Taylor could never touch the spoils of their fraud, but the notion it would end up confiscated by the system, the same system that turned its back on him and Poppy, the same system that refused his every effort was equally repugnant. None of the people's lives that had been destroyed would ever see one penny of help from any of them. That's how the system worked. He'd seen first hand. They could go fuck themselves. He'd never surrender so much as a hint about that money. The system would never have put Pace or Taylor away for what they'd done; but he understood no matter what he considered justification, that same system would surely put him away until the day he died.

Wally'd conceded any possibility of rationalizing his pain away and gone out to walk. He'd explored north and south along the waterfront. He cut up one street and headed toward what amounted to the center of George Town. A few blocks in he stumbled into an exotic fish shop out of boredom ... and because, besides selling saltwater fish, they had two tables out on the sidewalk where they would bring you a cup of cappuccino. Pet fish and coffee—only in *touristlandia*, he mused.

Cruising aimlessly about the little shop Wally studied the bright colored blennies and sergeant majors and mollies and guppies and sea anemones—striped clown fish, while waiting for his coffee when the epiphany hit him. He'd laughed out loud. The pretty Creole girl behind the counter making his coffee looked over and smiled. He was standing in front of a small aquarium reading the particulars about the nondescript little critter inside. When the girl looked again, Wally was tracing a small pattern against the glass with his finger, but the tiny gray cephalopod either didn't notice or was bored by humans.

Outside on the sidewalk Wally sat drinking the cappuccino, and owing to the vision that came to him inside the shop a few minutes earlier, thought he may have found peace within himself for the first time since committing the horrendous act back in Phoenix. He actually smiled. What he'd seen in his mind's eye was the final act in his—operation. He would beat the system. They'd never have the satisfaction of making him pay for anything he'd done. He was going to get away with all of it.

He began to notice people walking by and found pleasure in the simplicity of observing them.

Suddenly, he was starving. He paid his tab and headed back to the waterfront. Rudy's Nut Hut. It was afternoon by the time he'd retraced the path to the cozy 50's retro joint. All but one of the tables was taken. A steel band was laying down another reggae riff over the sound system. Wally had no knowledge of the group but they sounded great. He ordered a cold beer and a small bucket of fried calamari. By the time he was ready to call it an evening, it was dark outside and he'd consumed a lobster dinner and had moved on to straight rum once more. What amounted to glee in his warped world proved short-lived. Once more the urge to be anesthetized overwhelmed him.

CHAPTER 48

Thursday morning Aafje Janssen called his room. Wally was still drunk but he understood her message; he should come to the bank for a three o'clock appointment with Mr. Diextter.

At seven minutes after three, Finn Diextter looked across his desk at Wally. "You look quite … tired, Mr. Stroud," he said. "Are you sleeping well?"

"Not well," Wally confessed.

"Perhaps we can ease your worries," Diextter suggested. "Would you like to watch your money … disappear?"

Wally had spent nearly the full day Tuesday with Diextter setting up the specially numbered account. Frankly, it seemed suspiciously complicated … not to mention, scary—and somehow illegal. But at this point, what the fuck did he care about legal? Diextter said once the numbered account was in place, every document that could connect the account to Wally would be shredded, then and there. Wally knew, were the money to be stolen by these people there was no recourse. It would simply be gone forever, nothing he could do about it. Then he permitted himself a bit of irony; maybe Mr. "*Slick*" would want to check with Bud Pace and Carl Taylor about stealing money from Wally Stroud. He had plans for this money; at least most of it anyway. He looked back at Diextter. Made no attempt to hide his apprehension.

Diextter didn't wait for his reply. "This way." He guided Wally to the same corner of the office where they sat on Tuesday. Motioned for Wally to take a seat, then pointed the remote, pressed the button. Once again the giant screen levitated itself out of the floor like the space shuttle being rolled onto the launch pad. Wally could feel the sweat across his forehead and his palms were damp. Once more, his account information appeared on the screen. "Ready?" Diextter asked, looking to Wally with confident anticipation.

Wally shook his head, yes.

Diextter engaged him gravely. "Last chance, Mr. Stroud. Are you absolutely positive this is what you want?"

256

Wally shook his head. "Do it!"

Diextter set the controller down and glided to his desk. He reached across, paused a moment, looked back over his shoulder at Wally. His eyes glinted demonically as he pressed the submit button on his computer. While Wally had his apprehensions, Diextter was clearly basking in his element.

Instantly, two million pounds was subtracted from Wally's account. It happened so fast he didn't see it at first. In an instant twenty million more was gone, then ten million more and eight after that … another fifteen million. "Where's it all going?" he wanted to know. Within seconds his account balance went to zero.

Diextter perceived the alarm in Wally's voice. "Just a little holiday," he said casually.

"And *you* have total control?"

"Not anymore," Diextter admitted. "That was all taken care of *before* I pressed the button. Your money will be received and automatically retransmitted by hundreds of banks involving thousands of transactions around the world over the next several days. Even the amounts you saw leave here in each original transaction will be broken down into different amounts over and over again. The process will repeat until the final transmittals—"

"Back to my new account?" Wally completed the explanation himself.

"All but that first two million pounds," Diextter reminded him. "We take our fees right off the top, as I told you."

"Fair enough," Wally said, "as long as it all ends up the way you've promised."

"Mr. Stroud," Diextter objected, sounding insulted, "how long do you think we'd be in business if we did not … perform as promised for our clients? I assure you," he went on to say, "by next week, you will access your account number, which I remind you again, only you possess, and you will find a balance of, £261,843,841." Diextter made a grand gesture with his arms. "Manipulate it as you wish. No one, except someone *you* allow will ever see it." Finn Diextter smiled warmly, walked over to Wally, proffered his hand. "I promise," he said as Wally feebly reciprocated.

Wally stood. "Then I guess I won't be seeing you again after today?"

"Only if you find you require my assistance."

"I doubt you'll be hearing from me."

"Then I insist," Diextter said, "we share a farewell drink. Celebrate." He crossed to the opposite corner and pulled open the front of the bookcase to reveal an elegant bar with cut crystal glasses. "My personal pleasure," he confessed, reaching for an ornate bottle of cognac that read '18 year-old' in gold letters across the label. He poured a generous portion into two crystal snifters and handed one to Wally. "*A votre santé*," he said. To your health.

Diextter set his snifter down and poured again. He held the bottle at an angle toward Wally, offering him another. Wally accepted. "Our pilot," Diextter went on while he poured, "will file a flight plan as soon as you tell me where you would like us to fly you. Have you ever flown in a G5?"

"Never flown in any private jet," Wally admitted.

"Then you are in for a treat," Diextter bragged. "I'll send a car to your hotel to collect you tomorrow."

"What time?"

"Not before lunch. And you will want to preserve your appetite. Your meals will be prepared in flight."

CHAPTER 49

1602 West Osborn Road, Phoenix, Arizona, Offices of PPI—Thursday, August 25th—The west wing of the office building where Bud Pace and Carl Taylor had their limbs hacked off was still isolated by crime tape. No one was allowed in that area. The police needn't have worried. No one *wanted* to go anywhere near the scene.

Sonja Bienvenidos closed her office door at the opposite end of the building complex that Thursday afternoon and convened the meeting she'd called with the other three portfolio managers. She was the senior employee now.

She sat down behind her desk. No one spoke for several seconds and then they all tried to speak at once. "Hold on ... calm down," she ordered, taking control. "To state the obvious, we're in some serious trouble here," she began. She paused and glanced from one to the other of the three men in front of her. "Howard is gone." She exhaled the words with a deep breath instead of speaking them. "He left a note on my computer. Just said he isn't having anything more to do with this mess. Told me I could deal with it. Didn't even leave me a way to contact him." That revelation dropped the whole PPI debacle squarely in her lap.

Ray Glish growled, "Without a Comptroller, who's going to write payroll checks ... pay the fucking bills?"

"We have bigger problems than who," Bienvenidos said. "Not enough in the operating account to cover payroll. And none of us has signing authorization anyway."

"So get what we need from one of the other accounts," Chip Lawrence said, sounding very much like he'd just given her an order.

"Bud and Carl are the only ones who can sign on those accounts."

"Un-fucking-real," Ryan Andrews chimed in.

"Are you telling us we have no way to run this company?" Glish said, placing a very fine point on their situation.

Betrayed

"I'm telling you Bud and Carl hold the purse strings on everything. Even Howard didn't have access to anything except the operating account and there isn't enough in the operating account to pay *our* salaries much less meet payroll. Shit! All the bills are coming due. We're in serious trouble here, guys."

It was stone silent several uncomfortable moments.

"How the *fuck* are we supposed to make our house payments ... car payments?" Andrews complained, speaking to the real issue all of the participants in the room were concerned about— their own skins.

"That's not our biggest problem," Bienvenidos said, cutting short the three account managers who had begun to grouse amongst themselves. "That DPS investigator, Garcia, says they're worried as hell whoever did this to Bud and Carl could come after *us*." They shifted uneasily in their seats, protested aloud, attempted to dispute even the notion. Bienvenidos quieted them. "Listen. It's game over." She looked directly into the faces of each of the managers. "We were already under investigation by the SEC before this happened to Bud and Carl. It was only a matter of time—"

Glish interrupted her angrily. "We were all promised a parachute! Bud and Carl personally told each one of us if the time ever came, they were going to take care of us."

"Well, just how in hell do you expect them to do anything right now, Ray?" Bienvenidos raised her voice for the first time.

"Easy for you to say," Andrews argued, "you have a special arrangement with Bud, but we sure as hell don't."

Bienvenidos glared at the guy but didn't defend herself.

Glish backed down. "This isn't getting us anywhere. What are we going to do, Sonja?" He placed the burden of coming up with a solution squarely on her shoulders.

"First things first," she said. She'd given a lot of consideration to that very question. Not on behalf of her co-workers, but with regard to saving *herself*. "We have to accept the reality of closing the doors," she informed them, "and breaking the news to the employees." She ran her fingers down the length of a pen, flipped it to the other end and did it again—over and over, pounding the point or the butt end into a note pad each time she flipped it. "We're stuck, too, so I hope you guys have a nest egg you can use until Bud and Carl—" She looked off into space and shook her head. It was quiet again a few moments while she composed herself. "I'll try to talk to them the instant I can," she said looking down at the scratch pad on her desk.

"DPS and the FBI want the client lists," she continued the bad news. "They already know a lot. When they read the SEC complaint ... no telling what's going to happen next. This ... *business model* might not have been our doing, but we all knew about it and we all accepted substantial financial gains from it."

The three men glanced deliberately around at each other and then back to Bienvenidos.

"Goddamnit!" one of them bawled.

"Sonofabitch!" shouted another.

"The cops think this guy might come after us, too," Bienvenidos repeated.

"We gotta start thinking about protecting ourselves and our families," Ray Glish said, standing, pacing about the office.

"That's the point," Bienvenidos agreed. "We're the only ones left with any kind of authority. I say we close the doors. Shut the company down … right now. Send the employees away today. They can file complaints about their pay or whatever they need to do. We can't do anything about it anyway."

"Then what?" complained Chip Lawrence.

"Well Chip," Bienvenidos went on sardonically, addressing him specifically, "I don't know about you, but I'm going to give the cops everything they need to try to catch this guy. Then I'm going to get the hell out of town before this creep comes after *me*." She paused several long, emotional seconds, breathing heavily, fighting back tears. She continued, her tone husky. "I saw Bud in the hospital … I'm getting the hell out of here and you guys better think about it, too." There was terse finality in what she said.

"You realize every property we're involved in is going to collapse." Lawrence pointed out the obvious. It was not a question.

"If we took every penny of revenue those dumps are generating we still couldn't pay the bills," Bienvenidos countered.

"We could pay ourselves!" Lawrence argued.

Everyone in the room stopped and looked around at each other. It was true. They could take what rents could be collected from the properties under their control and at least *they* could get paid. Maybe they could scrape by until their bosses could make a bank transfer.

"They think it was one of our clients?" Andrews asked, flinching at the possibility.

Nobody said anything during a long silence.

"And how long do you think we could play that game?" Bienvenidos wanted to know, addressing Chip Lawrence.

"You know," Ray Glish interrupted them, "the minute the cops start talking to these investors, they're gonna expand this SEC thing."

"And you guys are willing to add to what we're already facing for what, a couple of paychecks?" Bienvenidos was incredulous.

"They're gonna hold our feet to the fire for more information," Chip Lawrence fretted.

"Shit, at least we got feet," Ryan Andrews said without thinking. The other two men looked at him. Bienvenidos was glaring a hole right through his face. "Sorry," he said, "that just slipped out."

Bienvenidos refused to listen to anymore. "Go back to your offices," she instructed them. "Clean out your belongings and get your people out of here. Fill them in. They're on their own." She pushed back from her desk and stood.

"What about you?" Glish asked, standing.

Betrayed

Bienvenidos paused, looked down at the top of her desk. "I'm gonna give the cops everything they want, and then I'm running for it. I saw Bud in the hospital," she said. Tears finally spilled from her eyes.

She picked up the phone and dialed Detective Bill Garcia.

CHAPTER 50

Wally used what was left of Thursday to pack. Occupation. He was ready to be done with it all. He could think of little else but to be back in the relative peacefulness of his home along the Pacific.

To wear on the flight home he'd set aside a pair of soft, faded-out Levis, a well-worn, long-sleeved khaki shirt with which, for some reason, he especially identified himself, and his brown Doc Martens. Colin's sense of style was finally wearing off. In any case, he decided to take Diextter's advice about enjoying his celebrity status with Netherlands Antilles Bank.

Whether or not it was true in fact, it was true in substance. He was at that moment a man of privilege, even if the balance of his life was filled with entropy. Wearing clothing that expressed how he felt about who he was aboard their fancy private jet was his idea of taking advantage of his status.

~~~~

Sleep was no more attainable his final night on Grand Cayman than any other. The night remained his enemy. Wally imagined it would be so the rest of his life. He must have dozed because his eyes opened in a fog of confusion around the *hour of demons*. The room came into focus slowly, ceiling, walls, doors opening out onto the balcony. Everything was a muted shade of gray. Outside there was a waning half moon etching a glittering silvery highway across the quiet Caribbean, throwing a blush of light into his space: sort of a reverse of the Da Vinci Glow. The beauty of it felt nothing short of obscene. The silhouette of the bottle of Seven Fathoms on the table tempted him. He'd finally pushed himself out of bed and shuffled out onto the balcony. He sat there slapping at the occasional buzz of a mosquito until the gray streaks of morning began to lighten the sky. Wally was in a constant state of toxic loneliness and now that he was near the end of his ordeal, life had begun to feel attenuated.

Betrayed

He *waited* impatiently for morning to advance. Jump in the shower. Dress and *wait*. His two bags were packed and *waited* by the door. There was nothing to do but stare out across a vacant ocean and—*wait*.

At eight-thirty he'd waited as long as he could stand. He headed out through the lobby and told the girl at the desk he'd be back in plenty of time to check out. She promised to have his final bill when he returned.

He strolled along the side street he'd taken two days before walking toward the center of George Town. He was only going a few blocks.

He waited on a street corner for the one car in sight to pass. On the sidewalk, halfway up the block an island-girl was setting up the two tables in front of the exotic fish shop. She was still setting out sugar packets and table settings when he walked up. "Can I be your first customer?"

She smiled, displaying startlingly white teeth. "Ja mon, tek de table ya like." She was a Rastafarian version of the Creole girl who'd waited on him before.

Wally stuck to what he knew about coffee and ordered a tall cappuccino with a warm muffin. The girl's bright emerald eyes twinkled and the mop of dreadlocks on her head twirled out, around and across her face as she spun and bounced off to the coffee bar.

Wally noted the name of the place: Rupert's Exotic Fish. He left the table and went inside. Scooted back to the tank holding the tiny gray cephalopod. Once more read the essentials about the shy little creature.

When the Rasta-girl announced his coffee and muffin were ready, Wally announced his intention to buy the tiny octopus.

"Ja understand da neture 'o da little fella?"

"I do," Wally said. "I'll need a way to carry him easily on the plane."

The girl thought a moment, then grinned. "I kin put 'em in dis coffee cup," she said, pointing to the largest cup size they offered—sixteen ounces. "Da lid fit good'n tight."

"That ought to work fine."

"Ja got ta chenge him watta in twenty-four hours," she cautioned.

"I'll be sure and do that," Wally promised.

"Solt watta."

"Right from the ocean," he said.

The girl looked puzzled. "I give some instruction tek wid ja."

Wally agreed and bore his coffee and muffin out to his table.

~~~

It seemed a long day by the time the black Mercedes finally arrived. The terminal he was driven to was surprisingly inelegant. A single tattered customs desk where his papers were checked without ceremony was all that adorned the tiny room. No one looked in his bags. The paper coffee cup from Rupert's Exotic Fish was of even less interest.

R.P. McCabe

On the tarmac he was met by a fashion model doubling as a private stewardess—Wally's interpretation. Briggita stood five-seven in her designer heels. The legs descending to the ground from under the knee length black skirt could only be imagined in their entirety, but the shape of her calves and the curvaceous hips and thighs that showed through the dress gave prurient promise. The loose fitting, plain white silk blouse she wore was unbuttoned enough to reveal no cleavage, but displayed the top edge of a sensuous lace camisole which concealed her tastefully moderate-sized breasts. Her complexion was that of finely polished white porcelain. Delicate features. Startlingly shiny gloss of crimson lips. Shimmering pearl hues of eye shadow. Eyes as close to gray as they were blue. When she turned to escort him up the steps into the G5, he found it impossible to take his eyes off her long elegant neck as it disappeared into the upward sweep of her sleek platinum-blond hair, which she wore pulled tight into a bun.

Inside the cabin of the private jet, the contrast between its elegance and the terminal he'd just walked out of was stark. It was enough to temporarily draw Wally's attention from Briggita as she invited him to choose any seat he wanted.

The cabin had been customized to seat eight with the remaining seating area converted to four private sleeping berths. The seats were of some expensive plush fabric in a tawny faun color that was in perfect balance with the dark walnut wood-paneled forward bulkhead that separated the cockpit from the main cabin. Liberal use of wood trim with gold fittings throughout appointed the interior.

The main galley was forward, fitted out like any fine restaurant, complete with crystal glasses and china dishes. The flatware was sterling, of course. There was a small service galley in the rear of the plane where domestic chores could be accomplished out of sight of passengers. Aft of that was space for storing more baggage.

The pilot stepped out of the cockpit cabin and introduced himself; estimated four hours flying time depending on weather and head winds. Nothing unusual on the radar, he assured Wally.

Alexander Knight was in his early fifties. Said he'd been flying for Netherlands Antilles eight years. He sported those refined features that seem reserved for the affluent or famous. Tasteful streaks of gray were beginning to show at his temples under his perfectly sculpted crop of black hair. He was as handsome as Briggita was pretty and his uniform was an elegant male version of what she wore. Wally was impressed, but suddenly found himself feeling superior in his jeans and work shirt.

"Once we're at altitude," the pilot explained, "the place is yours. We have a full bar. Briggita will prepare anything you'd like." He gestured toward her and she smiled at Wally.

He failed to grasp the full extent of service.

"I have a menu, Mr. Stroud," Briggita said, crossing the cabin to join them. She handed Wally a leather bound folder. "I'll organize your dinner whenever you'd like." She smiled at him and returned to her preparations in the galley.

Betrayed

The pilot excused himself and climbed back into his cockpit telling Briggita to prepare the cabin for takeoff. Wally settled into one of the easy chairs facing forward. Briggita came to him and showed him where the lock was to disable the swivel on the plush chair. Wally spun to face full forward and locked it in place before pulling his seatbelt around. As surreal as was this whole business of the private jet, it was still flying, and Wally never learned to like flying. Briggita collapsed the table against the side bulkhead and latched it in place.

The pilot left the cockpit door open and Wally could hear him and his co-pilot going through their pre-flight check. Briggita finished stowing everything as the G5 began to pull away from the terminal. She smiled at him again, and then clipped herself into the front-most passenger seat.

Knight taxied the G5 to the single runway, spun it around in a full circle, hit the throttle without delay. In spite of his dislike of flying, Wally could not argue against the thrill of being crushed back into the soft, deep cushions of his seat by the thrust of the G5's powerful engines. It was a distinctly different experience from commercial flights. The sense of speed was awe-inspiring. It felt like what he imagined a rocket sled must feel like. The plane didn't bounce and bump like commercial flights either. They shot into the air in one smooth arc like an arrow fired from a bow. It was only a couple of minutes before they were at cruising altitude: 26,000 feet. A little green light appeared on a panel above the cockpit door followed by a pleasant ding sound.

Briggita unclipped her belt, swung Wally's table back into position and told him he could remove his seatbelt and unlock the swivel on his chair. He chose to keep the seatbelt in place. Briggita offered to make him a drink. Wally opted for Scotch on the rocks.

"Do you have a favorite?" she asked.

"I usually drink Johnny Walker Red."

Briggita smiled. "May I recommend you try Johnny Walker Blue?"

Wally smiled back and admitted he'd never heard of Johnny Walker Blue.

"Then allow me to introduce you," Briggita said. She seemed erudite without being snotty. Wally enjoyed listening to her malleable voice.

While Briggita fetched the Scotch, Wally popped the lid on his coffee cup to check on Rupert. That was the name he'd given his little friend. The tiny cephalopod was curled up into a ball in the bottom of the cup. "Sorry for the inconvenience, Rupert," he said replacing the sealed lid on the cup.

Briggita served the Scotch. She stood by, knowingly, while he hoisted the glass and took his first sip of Blue. While Wally'd spent a lifetime enjoying the best red wines and what he'd always thought was good Scotch whisky, he'd never tasted anything matching its elegance. "I've never even heard of Johnny Walker Blue," he repeated, lowering the glass.

"It's a boutique class whisky," she explained. "You won't find it in any regular liquor outlet. But I'm sure you'll agree," she added, grinning modestly, "it would be well worth the effort to find."

~~~~

Finn Diextter had been right about the experience Wally was in for with regard to flying aboard their G5 jet. Briggita prepared a salmon fillet stuffed with delicate cheeses and crabmeat with unique fresh herbs sprinkled atop a tangy white béchamel sauce that had been seasoned with the faintest hint of rosemary and lemon. She'd introduced him to a bottle of French Chardonnay that, like the Johnny Walker Blue, he'd never heard of, but would never forget.

Captain Knight checked on him several times inquiring as to his comfort or any additional needs. Wally didn't get that Briggita was prepared to provide any service he would have enjoyed. As much as he'd wanted to continue wallowing in his stupor, that brief time locked in the elegant fantasy world of the G5 cabin with Briggita waiting on him hand and foot offered no option but to acknowledge his prurient musings toward his exotic hostess. That would have been enough, even had Wally understood the fantasy could have been realized but for the asking. He hadn't enjoyed a real hard-on in over a year except when he had to piss first thing in the morning once in a while. It was highly doubtful he could have performed—even with Briggita.

Subtracting the three-hour time difference, it was nearing midnight when Knight landed the G5 at Tijuana's General Abelardo L. Rodriguez International Airport. Prestige has its perks. The sullen customs official inspected Wally's resident permit, tossed it back to him and walked away as if it had not been worth the effort to be awakened at that hour for such a trivial exercise.

In the brief expanse of time it took him to walk from the terminal to his pickup, the fantasy of the G5 disappeared like a mirage in the desert. In fact, once he was paying the parking attendant and pulling out onto *Avenida La Frontera*, the entire week in Grand Cayman already seemed a figment of his imagination; an event that may or may not have actually occurred but for the hard evidence of the special account number he now owned—and little Rupert, of course.

Wally wasn't physically tired. The hours in flight seemed to evaporate with Briggita attending him like a handmaid, but the weight of his depression shoved all of that aside the instant he'd cleared Mexican customs. He drove home, not in a state of confusion, for he'd worked out the final details of his operation as precisely now as he'd planned the attack on Pace and Taylor. It was that he'd grown tired of it all: the pretense, the lying, the deceptions—especially where Colin was concerned. He was anxious now to button things up. Couldn't have much time left, he figured. How far behind could the cops be?

CHAPTER 51

It was close to three a.m. Saturday morning when Wally pulled his truck in front of his beach house. He pressed the garage door opener, left the vehicle running and slid out. In a corner of the garage, near the washer and dryer, he found what he was searching for: a three gallon plastic bucket. He returned to the truck, tossed it into the empty passenger seat beside him and made a "U-turn."

Wally backtracked to the corner of Paseo Bajamar, turned down the lane below his house. The waning half moon—the same waning half moon that flooded his hotel room with soft gray light just the night before on Grand Cayman Island—was beginning to set for the morning. He grabbed the bucket; jogged across the cool, damp grass of the golf course to an outcropping of dark lava rocks sloping gently into the gurgling breakers. A brisk breeze blew spindrift from the waves crashing only a few yards away.

Inching his way closer to the water. Plenty of moonlight to navigate by. Besides, he knew this spot. He and Poppy had spent many sunsets with a bottle of wine sitting on these very boulders. A tide pool was what he sought. Dip the bucket, drag. He pulled it back, swished it around several times before jettisoning its contents. Make sure it's clean ... uncontaminated. A few strands of slimy, fresh kelp ought to provide a well-deserved treat. He carried the makeshift aquarium back to his pickup and retrieved the paper coffee cup from the holder.

Unsnap the plastic lid. The tiny gray ball in the bottom was motionless. "Sorry it was such a long day, Rupert," Wally whispered sympathetically to the little octopus. He swirled the cup. Rupert unfolded his delicate arms and jetted in the circle of his prison. "I'm really glad you're still with me, little guy."

Wally secured the bucket behind his seat so it couldn't tip and submerged the coffee cup. Rupert washed out in a swirl and disappeared into the kelp. "*Now*, we can both go home and settle down."

Wally awoke mid-morning. He'd managed a few hours sleep. Downstairs he scanned inside the bucket on the counter. Smell of low tide ... seawater and three clumps of kelp. He agitated the seaweed until little Rupert, rousted from a knotted cluster, jetted across to the safety of an unmolested leaf. "Good for you," Wally said to his friend.

Saturday morning was mundane—unpack—dirty laundry in clothes hamper. There were still his clothes from Phoenix lying around. The entire pile was headed straight to the washer.

Wally was disengaging. Calm after the storm. No longer the deed before him ... only the implacable reflection of its hideous consequences and the intolerable knowledge he'd gone through with it. He rummaged in the refrigerator for something to eat. A few pieces of processed sandwich ham and a small chunk of Gouda cheese satisfied his urge. He checked again on the tiny octopus and slid the bucket to a corner of the counter.

Back upstairs he booted his laptop and buckled down. By early evening he was tossing a small filet mignon on his barbeque grill. Copies of his notes to Colin were sealed in envelopes. Everything tucked orderly into his safe. He'd confirmed one final time, each document he knew Colin would require—made certain it was in the exact order the kid would need. Now the *deed* was finished. No loose ends. Tidy. The way he liked things. All that remained ... play out the final act before the cops could get at him.

He pulled the cork from a bottle of Silver Oak Cabernet and poured himself a taste of the elegant red wine. He rolled the spicy dark currant colored liquid over his tongue allowing its pleasant nuances to bathe his taste buds before permitting it to slide slowly down his throat.

In a saucepan on the stove he'd poured a liberal portion of the rich wine in with a cube of butter and crushed two cloves of garlic. A generous handful of Shitake mushrooms simmered, sautéed in the buttery wine sauce.

The filet enjoyed its allotted two minutes on each side atop the hot grill. On a warmed plate he poured the sautéed Shitakes, along with a portion of the rich juice, directly over the top of the thick steak. Topping it, he crumbled several chunks of goat cheese before heading out onto the terraza where he'd set up a place setting for one. He poured himself another glass of the Silver Oak. The sun dipped below the Pacific; shadows were coming quickly.

Tomorrow, Sunday, he'd find a way to make things right with Dan and Fortunada. Monday he reserved for calling Colin and mending that fence. The lying was done, behind him—simply maintain the façade. Normalcy. Finally.

He'd prepared the steak as tribute to Poppy. It was one of her favorite recipes—because she knew how much he enjoyed it. He'd done his best to appreciate it in her memory, but it simply was not the same without her. He'd wished he could tell her *nothing* was the same without her. Well, he thought, wasn't that what he was doing?

He chewed the tender last bite of the blood-juicy filet slowly, chased it down with the final sip of the rich red wine.

CHAPTER 52

St. Joseph's Hospital, Phoenix, Arizona, Saturday morning, August 27th—Megan Pace and Lara Taylor listened while the two doctors explained what was about to take place. Two psychologists were in attendance as well. The doctors explained physiologically their husbands were doing remarkably well—considering what they'd been through. Neither had not lost a critical amount of blood in spite of how it had seemed. The tourniquets had prevented that. Both men were strong and in good physical condition before—the doctor who was speaking stopped, glanced over to one of the psychologists—*what happened to them*. "We've been exceedingly fortunate no secondary infections have presented."

The doctors explained how they planned to introduce a drug through their IV drips that would bring Bud and Carl out of the coma. They were going to be confused, disoriented, have no sense of the time elapsed.

One psychologist added, "The critical moment will come the instant Bud and Carl realize their circumstances." It was vital, all of the doctors agreed, they, Megan and Lara, remain calm, in control, reassure their husbands everything was going to be all right.

"Fear will assault them first," one of the shrinks was explaining. "Followed by their revulsion of themselves," the other added. "Then it will hit them hard how *you* see them. They won't accept what you're saying at first … that they can count on you to stand by them … that they are as loved as they always have been … nothing is going to be any different. But they absolutely must hear those words from *you*. Do you understand?" Both psychologists were emphatic.

"The other challenges they face," the team of doctors went on to explain, "will come into focus over the next several hours. We'll explain things slowly. They'll be trying to process too much information as it is. Their bodies are healing nicely," they concluded. "Now we must begin the process of healing their minds."

Stating the obvious, one of shrinks said, "That will be a far greater task than the physical healing, and regardless of this conversation, we will have to take our lead from your husbands, how they react to their circumstances. We have no choice for now but to go forward at their measure."

A nurse approached the group. "We're ready, doctors." They nodded to her and the meeting began to break up.

Pace and Taylor had been moved from ICU to rooms in the psych ward. They were on the same floor, but had been located at opposite ends of the hall.

Detective Bill Garcia arrived a few minutes late to the procedure. A PA had called to let him know the two men would be brought out of their comas that morning. Megan Pace told the doctors the detective was to be allowed to speak to her husband the moment it was possible.

Garcia was breathing heavily as a nurse led him into the room. "Sorry I'm late," he said, addressing Megan Pace.

The psychologist said, "And you are?"

"Detective Bill Garcia, doctor … Criminal Investigations, DPS."

"Detective," the doctor replied, acknowledging Garcia. "Not sure how much you'll be able to learn this morning."

"We have to try," Garcia insisted, leveling a piercing stare at the psychologist.

Megan Pace agreed.

"We can try," the doctor acquiesced.

Bud Pace's head rolled to one side. The room went silent. In a few seconds the stub of his right arm moved; Pace had been right handed. Several more seconds elapsed before his eyelids opened slowly and then fluttered open and closed several times. He began to try to focus. Finally his eyes remained open, puzzled. He was looking, dazed, straight up into the ceiling. His state of total confusion was obvious to everyone in the room.

The psychologist nudged Megan Pace to her husband's bedside. "Speak to him, Mrs. Pace," the doctor whispered, nodding toward her husband.

"Bud, can you hear me? It's Megan," she said tentatively, a little embarrassed. She looked up at the others watching her.

Pace's brow knitted. "Meg?" he replied softly.

"Bud," she began again slowly, "you're in the hospital."

"Hospital?"

"Yes, St. Joseph's. There's been …" Megan Pace looked up as if to ask what she should say next, "an accident."

"… kind of accident?" Pace asked, becoming more alert. "Loren!"

The psychologist stepped to the opposite side of Pace's bed, across from Megan Pace. He looked into her eyes. Then he turned to connect with Pace. "Bud, I'm Dr. Clarence Jackson," he explained gently. "Your son is fine. He can't wait to see you, Bud. Would you like that?"

Pace rolled his head sideways to look up at Jackson, as if to seek clarification.

Betrayed

"You were viciously attacked by someone," Dr. Jackson went on. "Do you have any memory of what happened?" Bill Garcia stepped close to Megan Pace's shoulder. He listened intently. There was cruel silence in the room.

Pace jerked his head to the right violently. "Where's Carl?" he yelled. "Where's Carl?" he yelled louder.

"Carl is safe, Bud," Dr. Jackson assured him. "He's here, too; just down the hall."

"Why ... why are we here?"

Dr. Jackson looked over at Megan Pace. Their eyes met once more, locked for several seconds. Dr. Jackson turned back to address Pace again. "Bud," the doctor hesitated, "do you recall anything at all that happened to you?" Bill Garcia moved even closer to the bed watching Pace's reactions, listening to every word being spoken.

A hideous look of comprehension screwed across Pace's face, like the gathering smut-black pall of a category five hurricane. Suddenly, the colostomy bag and catheter bag hanging on the side of his bed began to fill with feces and urine simultaneously. Without warning, Pace began screaming from the core of his being, a sound both huge and grotesque. He flailed from side to side, the noises coming out of him were hellish; all four of his stubs gyrated out of control. Both Dr. Jackson and Megan Pace cosseted Bud Pace as best they could to no avail.

Dr. Jackson motioned urgently to the nurse and she introduced a powerful sedative into the IV tube. Within seconds Pace began to calm down, conscious, but incoherent.

Bill Garcia spun on his heels and shot out the door. He raced down the long hallway, made a quick left at the far end to Carl Taylor's room. The scene there was different.

Taylor had awakened slowly, gained some focus, turned his head and casually examined the stubs of his arms. Several moments of brittle silence ensued before he looked up at his wife, Lara, and said simply, "I am so sorry." Then he fixed his gaze somewhere up in the ceiling, tears streaming down each side of his face and never spoke another word. He was there physically, but he'd disappeared psychologically.

Bill Garcia raced into the room, out of breath, fully expecting to find a similar hysterical scene in progress. Instead, the psychologist was speaking softly to Taylor, asking him questions, attempting to test his cognitions. There was total hush in the room. Carl Taylor's mind had left the existential world.

Lara Taylor wept quietly and stroked her husband's hair.

"Does he remember anything?" Garcia asked softly.

Lara Taylor said nothing, watched her husband's glazed eyes staring into a place none of them could know. The doctor walked to the side of the room with Garcia. "I think he remembered everything, Detective. And quite frankly, it was more than his psyche could handle. His mind seemed to snap. He told his wife he was sorry ... never uttered another word."

"What do you think? Will he come out of it?"

"Time, Detective. The first thing we need to do is simply give him time. He could be trying to process his situation or he could have totally shut down his brain; too much for him to handle. It's hard to tell right now. We need to give him time. Let his wife be with him, try to reach him."

"We talking hours here ... days ... what?"

"No way to know," the doctor answered honestly.

"Can I talk to him?"

The doctor looked across to Lara Taylor, who was paying no attention to the two men. "Mrs. Taylor," the doctor interrupted her, "may I allow Detective Garcia to speak to your husband? Just for a moment."

Lara Taylor did not speak or look to the doctor. She shook her head slightly in the affirmative, continuing to stroke the head of her catatonic husband.

"Mr. Taylor," Garcia began, stepping in close, leaning down closer to Taylor's ear. "I'm Bill Garcia, DPS, Mr. Taylor. I'm trying to find out who did this to you and Mr. Pace. Is there anything you can tell me about what happened? Did you recognize whoever did this? Was he one of your clients?"

Nothing. Carl Taylor's eyes were open, but totally vacant. The man was not there.

Garcia backed away from the bed slowly. Clearly, he was not going to get any help from either man for the moment.

~~~~

Sonja Bienvenidos had called Garcia the day before to say he wouldn't need to get a warrant to access company files. She was having the client list he'd asked for prepared. It would take her the weekend. He wouldn't get even that until Monday. The perp was getting all the time he needed to cover his tracks. Eight days already elapsed and Garcia still didn't have one solid lead.

On the walk back to the parking lot he dialed Clark Reynolds. "Guillermo," Reynolds answered. "How'd it go?"

"About what you'd expect."

"That good?"

"Even better," Garcia said. "Taylor has slipped into a *real* coma and Pace was screaming so bad he had to be knocked out. He went insane right before our eyes."

"Can't say as I can blame the guy. Did you get *anything*?"

"Nothing."

"We've got to develop something substantive in this case, Bill. What about that client list?"

"Monday."

"Unfortunately, your guy could be in Rio by Monday."

"You read that SEC file I emailed you?"

"These guys are a piece of work," Reynolds said. "They're lucky the perp didn't kill them."

"I guess," Garcia agreed. "Instead, he sentenced them and their families to hell on earth."

Betrayed

"The suspect is on, or connected to, that investor list, Bill. We need to get our hands on it … let your people narrow it down by the percentages."

"Like I said, Clark … Monday."

CHAPTER 53

Monday morning, August 29th, Phoenix, Arizona. Department of Public Safety, Criminal Investigations Unit, Office of Detective Bill Garcia—Garcia's cell phone rang. The caller ID identified Dan Jenkins, CSI: Phoenix Crime Lab.

"Garcia here."

"Detective Garcia," Jenkins repeated jovially. "Dan Jenkins, Phoenix Crime Lab. We've crossed paths a few times … just never ended up working one together."

"Luck of the draw, I guess. I remember you. What can I do for you, Dan?"

"Might be what I can do for you," Jenkins said. "Been thinkin' about your dismemberment case."

"Figured it out for me?"

"'Fraid not," CSI Jenkins apologized. "My own case load's over the top. Besides, I wouldn't want this one up *my* ass. The politicos gotta be bringin' heat to find this guy."

"They all think we use Ouija boards!"

"Better thee than me!" Jenkins asserted immediately. "Listen, Detective Garcia, it took me several days to figure out why your vics sounded familiar. When the news started getting into this SEC complaint about this PPI outfit, I finally remembered what it was. Could be nothing. Thought I'd pass it on."

"Right now I'll take a, '*could be nothing*.' Whatta ya got?"

"Case I worked … about nine months back," Jenkins continued, "suicide … woman by the name of, Stroud … Poppy Stroud. ME ruled it straight forward, no foul play."

"Think there's a connection?"

"Possible," Jenkins said. "Like I told you … could be nothin'. This … PPI company," he went on, "your two vics … husband of the suicide victim … let's see here … Wally … Wally Stroud … took it real hard. Told me the story about how they'd lost everything. The wife went

275

off the edge. Went for a drive in the garage. The husband comes home and finds her. This guy was seriously blown apart."

"Motive, all right." Garcia mused. "But from the looks of this SEC complaint, he wouldn't be alone."

"Agreed, but this guy took it hard, Bill, harder than most. Know what I mean? Just a thought I had."

"Well, at this point I have less than nothing to go on," Garcia admitted. "Got an address on the guy?"

Dan Jenkins read Wally's address to Garcia along with other notes. "Worth a look."

"I'll have a talk with him."

"I'll email you a copy of the file," Jenkins offered.

"I'll look into it Dan. Thanks."

CHAPTER 54

**St. Joseph's Hospital, Monday morning, August 29th, two days after Pace and Taylor had
been brought out of their medically induced comas. Taylor remained catatonic. Pace
remained sedated, but was beginning to have moments of cognition**—Megan Pace was by
her husband's side when he awoke that morning. He rolled his head sideways and looked at her.
His eyes were glassy, unfocused. He furrowed his brow; made an effort to connect the blurry
image in front of him with a name. "Who's there?" he said in a whisper.

"It's me, Bud ... Megan."

"Me ... gan?"

"Yeah, remember me? Your wife ... Megan." Her tone offered scant kindness.

"Megan?" he repeated more assertively.

"Bud," she said leaning close to his face, "listen to me. Try to understand what I'm saying
... can you hear what I'm saying?"

"Megan?" he repeated weakly, seeming to try to connect.

She leaned closer. "Bud, try to understand what I'm asking." She spoke to him again. "Do
you know who I am?"

"Megan," he repeated, as if on cue.

"That's right, Bud ... your wife, Megan. Listen to me, Bud ... listen. You've got to help
me." She paused, allowing him time to process what she was saying. "I need to know where you
and Carl have our money stashed, Bud ... the access codes." She cast a cautious glance toward
the door. "I only have a few thousand dollars left in the bank. The insurance company wants our
deductible paid before they'll start paying the hospital."

"Megan?"

"Come on, Bud ... you gotta help me with this. We're in trouble ... things are beginning to
fall apart. I need some money, Bud. Come on ... focus."

Betrayed

Pace rolled his head back, scanned the nothingness of the ether. He might have been trying to remember something. There was a brief procession of facial contortions, but little more than shadows of confusion in his watery eyes.

Megan Pace buried her face in the sheets at the side of her husband's head, despair and a sense of hopelessness coursing through her.

Pace mumbled something. Her head shot up. "What was that, Bud?" She fumbled through her purse, pulled out a notepad and pen. "Come on, Bud … I need you to tell me again."

Silence several moments before Pace tried again. His voice was so faint she couldn't be sure what he was saying. "Bud," she coached, "it sounded like you were trying to say, *run*. You want me to, *run*?" She bent closer to his lips.

"*'omeone.*"

"Bud, I can't understand. Say it again—"

Silence.

Then, "*'ome … run,*" he whispered again a bit more forcefully.

She wrote it down on her notepad and the light came on. "*Homerun!*" she cried much louder than she'd intended, then lowered her voice. "Is that it, Bud … *homerun*? What is that? What does that mean, Bud?"

More silence. Pace finally struggled to speak again. "*'Ser na'*—" came out of his mouth before his voice faded.

She wrote the sounds on paper … stared at what she'd scribbled several confused moments. "*Username!*" she pronounced, unable to conceal her optimism. "That's it, isn't it, Bud?" she whispered, close to his ear. "*Homerun* is the username."

Megan Pace went on grilling her husband, taxing him hard. She was exhausted. Her husband's state of fatigue had to be ignored for the moment. It wasn't that she was heartless, but she'd known for the last three years Bud Pace cheated on her regularly. Who knew how long it had gone on before that? She'd learned to swallow her dignity in exchange for the lifestyle he provided her and their son, Loren. But that was obviously over. He could get one of his girlfriends to wipe his ass the rest of his life. She hadn't signed on for that, and she sure as hell was not going to subject Loren to that kind of life. Right now, she had to stay focused. She needed that information. She'd wrung from him the crucial data written on her pad: Bank of Brazil—username: *homerun*—password: *primadonna35*. She stopped and leaned back in her chair, took several deep breaths. She looked down again at what she had deduced from her husband's babbling. She couldn't imagine the password significance. Probably another one of his girlfriends, she predicted contemptuously.

The shocking-pink Kate Spade carry case sitting on the chair in the corner held her laptop. She was growing desperate.

She'd called her husband's office on Friday to tell them she needed money only to be informed, by a secretary she didn't know, the comptroller was gone, and the company was being closed down by senior managers.

278

She insisted she speak with Ray Glish. The conversation generated abject fear. By the time she'd finished the call, she was frantic about what to do next. She desperately needed money to pay the bills. What was left of her world, her son's world, the situation with her husband, the insurance company, the hospital—her life was tumbling down like a castle of sand. This was the most critical situation Megan Pace had ever faced.

Wally Stroud could not know the ripple effect of his horrific act of revenge was at that moment washing across the family of Bud Pace like a tidal wave, just as the consequences of Pace's Ponzi scheme had drowned him and Poppy and hundreds of other families.

After a few attempts on the Google Search Engine, Megan Pace found something called Banco do Brazil. She tried the site. Found a login page. She filled in the spaces, double-checked before she hit the submit button.

Her heart thumped as the whirligig on the screen began to spin, verifying her access information. Within seconds an account page opened. She was stunned. Before her was an account in a foreign country that responded to the access information she'd wrenched from her husband.

She navigated the site looking for the *account* page. When she found it, it showed one recent transaction. Bile came into her mouth as she reviewed the details. She was sure she was about to vomit. The transaction was dated the night of the attack. Withdrawal ... $425,000,000. Current balance—zero.

The terror currently overwhelming her trumped any revulsion she felt toward Bienvenidos. She took out her cell phone and dialed her.

Sonja Bienvenidos looked at her caller ID, caught the call on the second ring. "Mrs. Pace," she answered, fully expecting to learn Bud Pace had died. What else could bring Megan Pace to call her? "What's wrong?"

Instead, Megan Pace confronted her about the bank account. She wanted to know who withdrew all the money.

For several seconds, dead silence between the two women.

Bienvenidos finally said, softly, "Some of us knew there was an account, but we had no idea where, how much was in it ... and not one of us had access ... unless it is someone inside the company I know nothing about," Bienvenidos hurriedly added. "But I can assure you ... I don't know anything more than that."

The silence that followed spoke ruthlessly of the cruelty, or karma, that would continue to unfold in the lives of Bud Pace and Carl Taylor.

Betrayed

CHAPTER 55

Wally awoke to a gorgeous, bucolic Monday morning. Even early the air felt warm and dry as the sun crept above Baja's Sierra Juarez Mountains.

Dan Dolan had finally, reticently, but nevertheless, caved to Wally's cajoling and repeated sycophantic acts of contrition over his unexplained absences. The entire incident with the use of Dan's car in what Dan was absolutely convinced involved something sinister. Dolan voiced the hope it had not involved that business abuzz on the news over the two guys in Phoenix. Dan and Fortunada either decided, or learned, it was less frustrating to simply maintain a myopic view of goings-on, regardless the lame explanations Wally offered.

He'd lubricated them with several drinks Sunday evening before finally coaxing them into letting him throw a pot of pasta on the stove. It was a simple but symbolic gesture. By the time Dan and Fortunada went stumbling amiably down the street toward their house, Wally was satisfied he'd made a good start in the repair of the damage he'd inflicted on their friendship.

It was nine-thirty when he bounded up the stairs to his library, unable to restrain himself one minute longer. His laptop was booted. He opened the login page for The Central Bank of the Netherlands Antilles. The page that opened didn't look anything like his original account page. No name identification of any kind. A box requiring a single number. No username. No password ... simply—the magic number. He looked at the open folder on his desk, copied the number Finn Diextter provided him back on Grand Cayman.

The page momentarily shaded out. The hard drive flickered a few seconds. A new page opened. The account balance showed: £258,650,000. It was sufficiently early in the day Wally didn't panic over the shortage. Diextter warned him the transactions would take time to complete.

He sat back slowly in his chair contemplating the portentous significance of what he saw on the screen. The tacit anxiety he'd harbored toward Finn Diextter disappeared.

280

Wally, by degrees, turned sideways from the heavy walnut bistro table serving as his desk and gazed out across the cerulean wavelets dancing upon the calm Pacific Ocean. The blue before him spread to infinity. "Those motherfuckers are going to go right on paying for what they did to you, Popp," he whispered. He leaned back, turned once more to the screen. He stared until it finally timed out.

Pull the lid shut on the laptop, clamber downstairs. Standing in front of the bar, looking at the image of himself and Poppy, he retrieved the bottle of Johnny Walker Red, his constant companion.

"Pretty early for Scotch," he admitted, staring into the image of Poppy's eyes. His hands were shaking. He needed a little tune-up—all there was to it. He flashed momentarily on Briggita and his first experience with Johnny Walker Blue.

Out on the terraza sipping Scotch, Wally considered how best to initiate the conversation with Colin. It wasn't acceptable he have one more out-of-step word with the kid. And he needed to stop calling him the kid. Colin was a lot of things. "The kid," was not one of them … and yet—

"You were gone a long time," Colin intoned without salutation when he answered.

"Nice to talk to you, too," Wally replied. "Catch you in the middle of anything?"

"No! And I am glad to hear from you. Where have you been?"

"Good," Wally answered, ignoring Colin's question. "Nice get away," he added, deciding for the moment to continue the deception. The atmosphere was so thick between them it was palpable. Wally understood Colin had finally figured out the broad strokes.

"We need to deal with this, Uncle Wally."

"It's been dealt with, Colin," Wally parried. "So! Fill me in. How are you doing with that big Siemens venture?"

There were several long moments of silence on the phone. When Colin finally spoke, his tone was flat, his words perfunctorily staccato. "Local stuff is going great. The offer to go global is on the table. Haven't figured out how to put that together, but they tell me I have time to work on it. Things this big move slowly. Who knows?"

"Who knows?" Wally repeated.

"What about with you, Uncle Wally?" Before Wally could answer Colin went on. "I'm sorry I got in your face about the stuff in Phoenix. Just that—"

"I know, Colin. I know." There was a long pause. "It's done. It will resolve itself. I haven't followed the news. Any new developments reported?"

"You know the media," Colin said. "Been over a week. They don't even mention it anymore."

Wally thought—that's because they're zeroing in on me and they don't want to tip their hand.

"So when you comin' up?" Colin wanted to know.

"Soon," Wally promised. "I need to catch my breath. Feeling tired lately … more than my normal tired."

"You doing all right?"

"Yeah … yeah. Sure. Just a little under the weather," he lied. "That's all. Fatigue, I think. Probably working a little too hard at keeping things off my mind. Know what I mean?"

Again Colin said, "We need to deal with this, Uncle Wally."

"Been dealt with, Colin. Leave it alone. Focus on your work. Things will take care of themselves."

"Are you out of your mind?" Colin didn't know anything for certain, true. But the big picture was clear enough. His Uncle Wally couldn't possibly have done this himself. But Colin was convinced he'd set it up—like a hit—hired some crazy to carry out the act itself. And his uncle had used him to get the tranquilizer they needed to subdue these guys. His Uncle Wally was behind the whole thing, Colin was sure of it.

"I was," Wally said calmly. "But I feel better now."

"I need to come down there. Right now. Today!"

"Don't do that, Colin, and that's an order. Don't even think about doing that. Everything is fine. I have things completely under control and if you just keep *your* suspicions under control, and that's all they are, suspicions, everything is going to work out perfectly."

"You can't know that."

"I *do* know it, Colin. Trust me."

Colin's options were limited. The issue of trusting his Uncle was out of his control. If Wally was behind the gruesome crime in Phoenix, there was little he could do. Of more concern, his involvement. He could pretend he hadn't known what his uncle was up to, but he admitted to himself he felt certain, at least after a point, he had been complicit in whatever his Uncle Wally had done. Now he realized what *whatever* was. "I don't have any choice but to trust you, do I?" Resignation.

"Things will work out, Colin. Just hold tight a little longer. You'll see."

CHAPTER 56

Wally was puzzled. No mention in the news about the money. The cops hadn't come looking for him—yet. What was going on? More to the point, what had not happened yet? Whatever the answers to those questions, he was not delusional. The dots had not been connected, but surely that would not be the case much longer.

He dropped his empty glass into the sink, went out into his garage and retrieved the blue duffle bag with the reciprocal saw and miscellaneous paraphernalia from his operation. He'd made certain not one item of evidence remained outside that bag except what he'd left in the trunk of the Camry. He'd made adequate explanation to Colin in his letter. He went to his truck and tossed the bag into the back, crawled into the driver's seat and pulled down in front of the Dolan house. Fortunada appeared as if summoned onto the upper balcony.

"Making a grocery run to Ensenada," he shouted up. "Bring you anything?"

"Oh," she replied, fingers to her lips in contemplation, and then hands placed on her liberal hips. "I think you might. Hold on." Fortunada disappeared inside. "Mind picking up a couple of tomatoes and a head of iceberg lettuce?" she shouted down on her return.

"Not at all," he signaled. "That's it?"

"Gets me through 'til next week."

Wally stuck his arm out the window and waved when he pulled the truck around and drove away.

In Ensenada he turned onto Mexico Highway 3, headed toward San Filipe. But before he was out of the city he turned off into a barrio of black corrugated tarpaper shacks, cut through with deeply rutted dirt streets. No stop signs or benefit of other municipal services. The neighborhood had a name, but only the locals would have known it.

He'd become acquainted with this shantytown when his beach house was being built. Several men who'd worked for him lived here. Wally sometimes drove them home on Friday evenings so they wouldn't have to spend hours waiting for busses to get back to their families.

283

Betrayed

This was not a place into which any inexperienced gringo would venture. While the abject poverty did not, of itself, make the place any more dangerous than any other unknown neighborhood, the spectacle of ramshackle existence would simply scare the hell out of people who were not accustomed to the realities of how large segments of Mexican society exist.

Wally wound down and around several narrow streets before finding the taco stand he was looking for. He parked around the corner from the lean-to that protected the outdoor kitchen with its small plastic tables and chairs. Before heading off to have a couple of tripe tacos, he stepped around to the rear of his truck and lowered the tailgate. He pulled the blue duffle bag out onto the lowered gate, unzipped it enough so the tools inside were visible, and walked away.

He was hungry and polished off three of the pig-gut tacos, a delicacy he'd learned to appreciate. He took his time, washing the burn of the serrano peppers off his lips with an orange soda.

Wally was relying on the principal of the *hormigitas (little ants)* to clear away things that should not have been left lying about if they possessed any value to their owner. Like the insects for which they were named, these poor kids would happily relieve anyone careless enough to leave useful possessions unattended, and without remorse on their part or their parents, since those belongings were considered the crumbs left behind by society, tiny morsels they were entitled to since you hadn't expressed more concern for their security.

By the time he returned to his truck, the blue duffle bag was gone, and with it every trace of its contents. None of what was in the bag would ever be found. Of that, there was not the slightest doubt in his mind.

The day had cascaded to early evening by the time Wally pulled his truck into his driveway. He walked the lettuce and tomatoes to the Dolan house. Begged off the invite for a toddy, blaming it on being tired after his long afternoon in town.

Around seven-thirty he set up the docking-port for the iPod Poppy'd kept loaded with music. He hadn't used it in nearly a year and struggled to remember how to make the damn thing work. Presently, he figured it out and the system began playing songs in rotation. He scrolled the playlists looking for a specific song. When it scrolled up, Wally set it to loop until he was tired of listening to it. He'd save actually listening until later.

Close to eight o'clock, as the waning sun was beginning to cast deep shadows, he went upstairs and retrieved his laptop. Coming downstairs, he ignited a small flame in the fireplace purely for ambiance. The French doors onto the terraza stood open. Wally went to the wine cellar for the bottle of Brunello di Montalcino, which he'd saved for this very special occasion. He removed the cork and poured two ounces into his glass. He swirled the wine in the goblet while he waited for the laptop to boot.

When the whirring had finally stopped and the machine was ready to function, Wally went online and opened the link to his offshore bank account. He typed in the secret number. The screen opened to his account information, which, by then, showed a balance of the correct amount; £261,843,000.

The sheer weight of that sum of money still stunned him but he was becoming more accustomed to looking at the digits by then. He reflected once more on the lives Pace and Taylor had destroyed in their quest to that hoard.

He settled back into his chair sipping the elegant red wine, toasting the victims of the elaborate fraud whose lives had been destroyed by these two criminals. "Won't be long now folks." At least that was what he hoped.

Then he opened the Google Search Engine and typed in the words: *Blue-Ringed Octopus*. A list of search results opened to the word—cephalopod. Wally selected the one whose description matched the animal he wanted to know about: enough venom in a single animal to kill twenty-six men; as deadly as the King Cobra, no antidote; leaves no visible sign of a bite.

"Okay, Rupert," he said under his breath. "Let's get you settled." He held the particulars posted on the aquarium back on Grand Cayman firmly in his head. It was the details about the tiny creature he wanted to clarify. All-in-all, Rupert seemed well suited to take care of himself. Wally savored another sip of the Brunello, draining what was left in his glass.

He shut the laptop down, scooted forward out of his chair folding its screen onto the keypad. It was nearly nine o'clock and dark outside. Dancing flames inside the fireplace and the dim table lamp next to Wally's chair lit the great room.

He grabbed the keys to his truck—tucked the laptop under his arm—and ambled out the front door. The big truck rolled out the driveway, around the circular lane back up onto Paseo Bajamar, made a left turn going north toward the narrow lane that dropped down to the golf course below his house.

He parked along side the fairway. Same spot he often used when going down to sit on the rocks with a bottle of wine at sunset. He collected the laptop from the passenger seat and strolled casually over the craggy lava flow running into the sea. Just below the putting green the rocks formed steep crevices with jagged cliffs dropping precipitously sheer, thirty feet straight down. The water below was deep and constantly battered by the ceaseless onslaught of crashing breakers. The waning half moon, still high above the horizon, glowed like a half apricot, bright enough to cast night shadows. Wally walked out to the farthest point along the jutting cliffs, smashed the laptop several times against the rough lava boulders. The screen shredded and broke into pieces. The keypad popped open exposing its innards like the entrails of a gutted fish. He flung the disparate parts out into the roiling breakers. Checked around. Nothing. A few plastic shards. The laptop would never be recovered by a crime lab or the FBI. It's hard drive would never be mined for data that would convict him—worse yet, find the money he now controlled.

Contemplating his scrupulous attention to detail, Wally shoved his hands deep into his pockets, regarded the copper-streaked highway the half moon was engraving across the Pacific. The air turned damp and a little chilly standing close to the water. Spindrift reached up to him when the thunderous rollers smashed against the rocks below, sending spume high into the air. He stood there a long while recalling evenings Poppy had stood next to him, her arms entwined about his, snuggling close against his side to stay warm.

285

Betrayed

After a time, Wally hiked back to his truck and guided it home. Inside his house the cozy comfort of the flickering fireplace dried and warmed his bones. From the buffet top he picked up the photo of him and Poppy, set it on the lamp table next to his chair. Then he turned on the iPod and returned to take up his seat in front of the cozy fire. This time he poured his glass half full of the Brunello and switched off the lamp. Outside, below the hill in the glow of moonlight, the endless breakers of the Pacific Ocean arrived every few seconds in a reverberating collision against the craggy lava boulders.

As Wally settled back to sip the Brunello, the song he'd searched out began to play softly. The opening lines of Irving Kahal's lyrics backed up by Sammy Fain's 1938 big band verily slid over Bing Crosby's cool, crooning voice like an oyster off the half-shell in his 1944 top 40 version of the song—Wally's favorite recording of it:

I'll be seeing you
In all the old familiar places
That this heart of mine embraces
All day through.

In that small café,
The park across the way,
The children's carousel,
The chestnut trees,
The wishin' well.

I'll be seeing you
In every lovely summer's day,
In everything that's light and gay.
I'll always think of you that way—

Wally cradled the picture of him and Poppy in one hand, cosseted the stem of his wineglass in the other—attempted to sing along with Bing: *I'll be seeing you … in all the old familiar places … that this heart of mine embra—.* He gave up and wept silently from the depths of his being. He pulled the photo close to his heart, slumped deeper into the big chair. The song played over and over so many times he lost count.

The bottle of Brunello sat empty next to his wineglass. It was around midnight and Crosby had been singing, nonstop, close to three hours.

Wally balanced the photograph on the arm of his chair, scooted forward and raised himself out of it. In the kitchen he switched on the light. He pulled the makeshift aquarium over so he could better see inside. Swishing the leaves around brought Rupert out of hiding. The little cephalopod was no longer gray. As equipped, he'd adapted to his surroundings to hide himself,

286

so now he was a light burnt sienna color and the tiny irregular circles on his mantle were easily visible.

Wally put his fingers close to the piece of kelp Rupert was hiding in and nudged the little guy. The tiny cephalopod responded by jetting across the bottom of the bucket to one of the other pieces of kelp. Wally smiled and spoke softly to the innocent little creature.

Again he pursued Rupert with a flick of his finger and once more the octopus jetted away to hide as best he could. By the time Wally harassed Rupert the fifth time the rings on his mantle had begun to glow a throbbing neon periwinkle color. Rupert had had enough nonsense.

At that point Wally reached into the bucket with both hands and picked the tiny cephalopod up in his cupped palms. Almost instantly he felt the first sting. It was slight but he was expecting it to be so. He continued to agitate the creature observing the blue rings pulsate in his anger while he felt at least three more stings, after which he returned Rupert to the peace of his aquarium.

Wally gazed affectionately into the bucket. "Seems like a really shitty way to repay you for your services, Rupert," he said, "but you and I are fated for the same journey tonight." And with that he took the bucket, stepped out onto the terraza and flung its contents far down the slope of the hill in front of his house. He took the extra moment necessary to return the bucket to the garage before casually reclaiming his spot in front of the warm, glowing fireplace.

He held the photograph of Poppy out in front of him once more and searched the image of her eyes. "It just couldn't be any other way, Popp. Not without you in my life." With that, Wally pulled the photo close to him and folded his arms around it across his chest.

In a few moments his hands began to tingle slightly, nothing unpleasant. He held one hand up to his face and studied it. He couldn't detect anything and he knew where the sites of the stings were. *(I'll be seeing you … in all the old familiar places.)*

Wally whispered the words along with Bing again. In a few more moments he felt the numbness in his extremities; all-in-all, not a disagreeable experience.

(That this heart of mine embraces …)

Several moments went by before he detected the tightness in his breathing. Feeling tired. Closed his eyes a few moments. The rise of his chest began to feel heavy. His lungs labored to fill with air. He gazed one final time into Poppy's eyes, pulled her close to him, squeezed her tight. Wally's heart rose gently to its final beat. *(I'll be seeing you …)*

CHAPTER 57

Eight-thirty a.m. Tuesday morning, August 31st, Phoenix, the address of Wally and Poppy Stroud as shown on Dan Jenkins's report regarding the suicide that had occurred there; a foreclosure sign was tacked to the gate at the courtyard entry—Before going into his office that morning, Detective Bill Garcia pulled his Crown Vic to a stop in front of what used to be the Stroud's home and got out to read the notice. He wrote down the bank name and contact information.

Sonja Bienvenidos had emailed PPI's investor list to him toward the end of the afternoon the previous day. A couple of hours earlier, Dan Jenkins followed through, sending over his report on the Stroud suicide. Garcia finally had a few concrete leads. He'd looked down the list and found Wally and Poppy Stroud's names. They'd invested more than a million dollars with PPI—apparently wiped out. When he added the details of what he'd learned from Jenkins's report on the suicide of Poppy Stroud to what he saw on the PPI investor list, he wondered how many other train wrecks he was going to find. But Wally Stroud certainly had motive.

Garcia knocked on the door of the neighbor's house to the east. No answer. He tried the house on the west side. An elderly woman came to the door in her robe; hair bundled in some kind of a piggy-pink colored rubber wrap. It looked like one of those megaphone-shaped cones veterinarians put around the neck of an animal to prevent it from chewing on a wound. The thing began at the nape of the old woman's neck but clearly would not have prevented her from chewing on any of her wounds. It swept upward from there, capturing her silvery-white hair, which was still puffed and quaffed as though she'd just come from the hair dresser. The device somehow managed to leave her face isolated. The apparatus was apparently intended to preserve "the do" while she slept. Garcia had to admit the thing seemed to work.

"No, I don't have his forwarding address," she said. "But I know he moved to Mexico right after his wife … passed. Is Wally in some kind of trouble?" She seemed agitated over not being able to provide exactly what Garcia asked for. "I used to have her mother's phone number if you would like me to see if I can find it?" She fretted. Her tensing neck muscles created a twitch.

"I'd appreciate that, ma'am."

"Here you are, Detective," the woman said, walking out toward him. "Is everything all right? Is Wally in some kind of trouble?"

"You think he should be?"

"Oh, gracious no!" she objected. "Why, Wally Stroud is one of the kindest, gentlest … most upstanding gentlemen you'll ever meet."

"You knew them a long time then … the Strouds?"

"More than ten years," she bragged. "Bought our houses almost on the same day." Suddenly her thoughts caught up with her and she cast her eyes downward. "It's so heartbreaking what happened to them. And poor, dear Poppy … she was so kind."

Garcia sensed he wouldn't learn anything meaningful from the woman. "Just a follow up about his wife," he said, offering nothing further on the matter.

"I see," the neighbor lady said. "It was so awful. Well, I hope that number is still good."

"You've been a big help. Thanks."

He sat in the front seat of the unmarked white Ford with the air conditioner pumping out cold air. It was already 105 degrees at eight-fifty that morning. He dialed the number the woman gave him.

Jake Zinsser answered on the fourth ring. Garcia identified himself, explained he was doing routine follow up on all of the PPI investors. Having a little trouble getting hold of Wally. Did he know how he could be contacted?

"Lives in Mexico," Zinsser divulged without hesitation. "This about those two guys I seen on the news?"

"Just need to talk to all of their investors," Garcia said.

"Wally didn't do it," Jake said emphatically. "Bastards got what they deserve, though."

"Oh …?" Garcia responded in that police-sort-of-way, suggesting maybe a suspect just revealed something incriminating about himself.

Jake Zinsser could have given a shit. "My daughter's *dead*, ain't she?" he growled into Garcia's ear. "I hope the hell they both die!" Garcia could hear Jake breathing heavily on the other end of the line.

The detective let the vituperative outburst pass. "You got a phone number where I can reach your son-in-law, Mr. Zinsser?"

Jake set his phone down. Garcia heard him fumbling in the background. Jake returned and read Wally's cell phone number.

"Have you spoken with your son-in-law lately?"

"Not since he moved away … right after everything happened. He ain't been back since."

"He hasn't been to visit your family?"

"Nope."

"That's a long time without any contact, isn't it?"

"We ain't what you'd call a close family."

"Okay. Thanks," Garcia said, terminated the call and immediately dialed Wally's number. Wally's automated voicemail picked up right away saying the phone was not active at that moment. "Mr. Stroud, this is Detective Bill Garcia with the Arizona DPS," he said, identifying himself on the voicemail. "Would you please give me a call when you get this message?" Garcia gave no reason for his call.

Back at DPS headquarters he dialed the number for Commercibank's mortgage department. The ditsy minion who answered the phone refused any personal information regarding the original property owner over the phone even after Garcia identified himself.

He motioned over a subordinate. "Do a credit background on this guy, would you?" He handed the information to the young cop. A pair of investigators was assigned the tedious process of following up every investor on the list. It would take them weeks just to isolate the ones who might be real persons of interest, longer to get through the entire list. He was hamstrung for personnel. Arizona's blistered economy and state budget crisis reached all the way into his office. He had no choice but to work with the resources he had.

When he got back from lunch Wally Stroud's credit report was sitting on his desk.

He read it carefully, then dialed Clark Reynolds. After their usual catch-up he recounted the Jenkins report on the Stroud suicide.

"Just back from lunch, read the guy's credit report."

"And?"

"Listen to this," Garcia said to Reynolds. "Maxes out all of his credit cards ... two hundred Gs, plus (all cash advances), then he buys himself a brand new pickup truck (paid cash with two credit cards, forty-plus grand) ... turns the homestead in for voluntary foreclosure ... collects the life insurance payout on his wife. Yeah. They'd owned the policy so long the indemnity clause against suicide had expired. Company had no choice but to pay out (another two hundred fifty Gs). And then he makes an exit stage left to Mexico." Garcia paused. "Nobody's heard from him since. Father-in-law says the guy hasn't been around to visit any of the family."

"Gives the world the finger," Reynolds ruminated, "commits credit fraud, pockets close to a half mil and takes his leave to Mexico. Guy could live a nice life down there on that kind of dough," Reynolds observed.

"Banks won't chase him," Garcia conjectured. "He took chump change from nearly a dozen different cards. He only gets tagged if he tries to file *BK*."

"They might chase the truck?"

"In Mexico?"

"Some do," Reynolds pointed out. "He has plenty of motive, we see he's clever enough. This could be our guy. Circumstance fits the profile. Problem is ... it's all anecdotal. We need to talk to this guy. We need more."

"Left a message on his cell but no response."

"Okay. The agency has a good relationship with the Mexican Consulate in San Diego. Let me see what they can do to get the Police in Tijuana to let you and me go down there and pay an official visit to Mr. Stroud."

"What do you think?"

"They've worked with us before. Meantime, I'll check his passport … see if it's been scanned recently. He can't get into the US without a passport scan. We place this guy crossing the border any time close to the event, he becomes our prime suspect"

"I've got a team running the investor list from PPI," Garcia said. "I'll let you know if we turn up anything interesting. How long you think it'll take to find out if the Mexicans will let us in?"

"It's a time of *cooperation*, remember?" Clark Reynolds laughed. "I'll be in touch."

CHAPTER 58

Six o'clock Tuesday evening, August 31st, on the terraza of the Dolan home in Baja, Mexico—"Wally did say he was coming for sundowners tonight, didn't he?" Fortunada Dolan asked her husband, who was about to pour his second Scotch.

"What he said Sunday. But you know that squirrely bastard. I never know anymore what he's up to one minute to the next."

"You talk to him today?" Fo asked, dabbing her lips with a napkin.

"Tried him a couple times. Phone's turned off."

"Truck's there," Fo mused, leaning forward so she could see over the railing.

"He's there all right," Dan grunted.

Fo picked up the phone and dialed. She heard the default to his voicemail.

"Maybe you should walk over."

"Shit, he's fine," Dolan argued. "Only problem with that asshole, you can't tell when you can count on him anymore."

"Dan …" Fo sang the rebuke in a rising crescendo. "Now, how would you feel if you found out tomorrow Wally'd fallen in the shower and hurt himself?"

"He could crawl to a phone," Dolan bickered, grumping in protest.

"D-a-n-n-y!" Fo said his nickname singsong once more. "That's your friend you're talking about …" She rolled her eyes, made that face that told Dan Dolan he would obey her wishes, whether he wanted to or not.

Exasperated, Dolan set down the Scotch bottle. "Oh, all right. I'll go check on the old fart. But he better have a damn good excuse for me having to go looking for his sorry ass."

"*He* always speaks so well of *you*, darling," Fortunada said chuckling, raising her wine glass to her lips. "Get him and get back over here. I've got dinner in the oven."

~~~~

Dan Dolan ascended the south side staircase, his preferred angle of attack, as it were, onto the terraza. The French doors were wide open and the afternoon sun beat inside the huge room with intensity. He could hear a voice singing soft and low—*(In every lovely summer's day)*—. He recognized the voice of Bing Crosby, who, unbeknownst to Dan Dolan, had now been singing his 1940s hit for more than eighteen hours straight. And, of all things, a small flame flickered in the fireplace. Only the balding spot atop Wally's head was visible. It appeared to Dan he was sound asleep; his head slumped slightly forward onto his chest.

Not wanting to startle his friend, he stepped softly up beside the chair to see, yes, Wally'd fallen asleep clutching the picture of himself and Poppy.

Grumpy old Dan Dolan felt sorrow grip him as he rested his hand on his friends shoulder so as to wake him slowly. But he instantly sensed the lifelessness in his touch. "Wally?" he said softly, hoping, but knowing there was not going to be a reply. "Wally?" he repeated just to be sure.

He moved around in front of Wally and gazed down upon him. Bing Crosby continued to croon softly in the background—the fireplace flickered.

Dan took several moments to check the house. He climbed the stairs and entered the bedroom and bathroom. The house was in perfect order. The bed was made and had not been slept in. Their recent conversation about the minor heart issue came to him. Another thing Wally probably hadn't leveled about. Obviously, it'd been more severe than Wally'd confessed.

He recalled the envelope Wally gave him in the event something exactly like this was to happen: premonition or preparation? Maybe both, he thought. He went back in his mind to Sunday evening, just a couple days earlier, when they'd all sat around having drinks, right here in Wally's kitchen. Wally'd cooked up that pot of spaghetti. They'd all laughed a little too enthusiastically as he'd cajoled and entertained them, doing his best to mend fences. He'd looked enervated and drawn, Dan recalled—too tired. Dolan concluded his friend simply decided not to live on any longer—sat quietly in front of a kind fire, soft sweet sound, beautiful bottle of wine—and willed his life to stop. Who can know another's pain, he thought; his loneliness; his utter loss of will to take one more step forward?

"Sonofabitch Wally," he said, feeling a sting in his eyes. "What happened to you just wasn't right."

He left everything just as he'd found it and let himself out by the front door. He walked several paces down the street toward his home before he stopped and turned to look back. Fortunada, watching from their terraza, saw instantly the droop in her husband's shoulders, the melancholy turn toward Wally's house, the way his head sagged and then looked up in her direction. She guessed what must be coming.

Fo was standing in the doorway when Dan mounted the steps to his house. Their eyes met. No words. Dan climbed the two steps and embraced his wife. They stood several moments.

"Looks like a heart attack … what I can tell," he whispered into her ear.

Betrayed

Fortunada's shoulders heaved while she wept. Dan walked her back into their house settled her into a chair and brought her wine glass. Then he went to his bedroom and found the envelope Wally'd given him weeks before.

He grabbed his Scotch. Sat quietly in a chair next to his wife. Long swig—set the glass on the lamp table—tear the envelope open.

Danny Boy,

If you're reading this, I can only imagine you and Fo are upset. Don't be. Please. There are lots of things worse than dying. We've talked about that.

I'm sorry to ask this of you but it will be the last trouble I'll put you to. Don't bother with anything in the house. It will all be taken care of. Just make the following calls in the order I ask:

1. Tomas Garza Funeral home in Ensenada.
646-982-7654—Tell Tomas I have died.

2. Only AFTER Tomas has taken care of things, call Colin. Break the news to him. 310-567-6543—It isn't fair to ask this of you, but I have no one else who can do this for me.

Now then, take another hit on that Scotch you have in your hand and get Fo a nice glass of red wine. Remember me well, my friends.

Dan looked up at Fo through burning eyes, picked up his Scotch and held it up as if to toast his friend. Fortunada was just barely able to hold her glass.

"They just had too much shit land on their heads," Dan said, meaning both Wally and Poppy.

He picked up the phone and dialed Tomas Garza.

CHAPTER 59

Before the failing light of day had given over to full darkness that Tuesday evening in August, after Wally Stroud died, a blue and white late model Dodge Charger, bubble-bar mounted on its cockpit-top flashing in neon bursts of scarlet/cerulean/blinding clear halogen, with the words *"Policía Federal"* painted in black letters on the doors, pulled to a stop in front of the Stroud home. A black hearse followed.

Dan and Fo watched from inside their kitchen, but stayed away from the windows, made no gesture to be identified or singled out for questioning. They guessed the guy in the hearse must have been Garza. He trod confidently with the Federal Police officer to the front door and let himself in. Within a few moments they were back outside standing next to the police car discussing something. The police officer waited while Garza retrieved a clipboard and a fat brown envelope from the hearse. Dan and Fo could make out a document was being considered. Presently, the officer took the clipboard from Garza and appeared to sign it. Garza proffered his hand with the envelope, which the officer accepted. They shook vigorously—more than perfunctory—more like a deal had been struck. The two men concluded with brief conversation while Dan and Fo observed the activity. After a few minutes, the Fed returned to his car, turned off the flashing lights and pulled away.

In a matter of minutes Wally's body was loaded into the hearse, and it disappeared.

~~~~

A little after eight the next morning, Wednesday, a beat up Chevy S-10 pickup pulled up in front of Wally's house and two cleaning girls were let out. They disappeared inside as though they knew exactly what they should do.

Later that same morning, around ten-thirty, a newer model bright yellow Nissan pulled to a stop in front of the house. Dan and Fo eyed the activity. Identified the driver of the Nissan as the one who'd driven the hearse the night before—probably Garza, they continued to speculate. He slid around the front of his car, opened the passenger door and retrieved a shiny black amphora, which he cradled in one arm. In his free hand he carried a manila folder.

The man remained inside roughly fifteen minutes before he reappeared and drove away. At noon the rickety S-10 Chevy pickup returned. The driver didn't get out. Just sat and blew the horn impatiently. The two women came scurrying out carrying their personal belongings, got into the pickup, and Dan and Fo watched them drive away.

There was no further activity at the house the remainder of the afternoon. At four p.m. Dan poured his first Scotch and popped the cork from a bottle of wine for Fo. "What do you think?" she asked.

"Mighty quiet this afternoon," Dan allowed.

"Should we go have a look?"

Dan contemplated the idea, sipped from his Scotch.

"We could say we were just checking to see if Wally wanted to have a drink ... anybody shows up."

"We do it all the time, right?" Fo rationalized. "Let's take our glasses ... just in case."

"Good idea."

The Dolans moseyed up the street. They looked suspiciously conspiratorial. Had anyone been watching, they would have fooled no one. Just in case someone was watching, they decided to try the front door. It remained unlocked.

They stood in the foyer several moments, expecting a police car to come zooming at any moment. When that didn't happen, they shuffled further into the house. The smell of floral scented cleaning liquid hung a little too heavy in the air. The house was completely shut. The fireplace had been turned off, as had the iPod. The chair where Dan found Wally had been returned to its normal spot. The place sparkled. The cleaning girls had done an outstanding job of mopping, vacuuming and polishing. The house seemed—unlived in. Certainly, no evidence a man had died there two nights earlier.

On the bright granite kitchen counter sat a folder. Dan flipped it open. Inside they found six copies of a Mexican death certificate. Fo picked up the top copy. Dan read over her shoulder. The document was officially signed off by Captain Jorge Fernandez of the Mexican Federal Police; the body was officially released by the Mexican government. Cause of death was attested to by Dr. Lopez Ruiz Alarcon; Myocardial Infarction, massive heart attack. No further responsibility left to the family of the deceased.

A brief disclaimer revealed the funeral services had been carried out by the Tomas Garza Funeral Home by prior authorization and arrangement with the deceased himself.

"How the hell he get them to do it all so fast?" Dan pondered.

"I figured this place to be tied up for months," Fo agreed. "Maybe longer."

They eyed each other. Scanning the capacious room, they saw the two urns on the side buffet accompanied by Wally's favorite photo of him and Poppy laughing, holding each other in their arms at some distant happy moment in their lives. Fo turned to Dan, buried her face in his chest.

He let her cry a time before he said, "Come on, Fo. We gotta go home and call the kid."

CHAPTER 60

Colin Craig zipped his Chrysler Crossfire Roadster to a stop in his uncle's driveway a little passed noon the next day. He'd accepted Dan Dolan's call with bitter calm the night before. Called his mother. She'd phone family. Colin and Ellen agreed the news was not entirely unexpected. Better than anyone, they understood how broken Wally was.

Dan and Fortunada shuffled up the street to greet Colin as he stepped from his roadster in the driveway. His hair was a disheveled array of "Pick Up Sticks." The pupils of his eyes were islands of bright blue in pools of red that had once been startlingly white. The jeans he wore, a bit wrinkled, had an abraded tear on one thigh. His long sleeved plaid blue shirt was rolled to the elbows and unbuttoned with a plain black t-shirt underneath. He wore his purple Vans without socks.

"We are so sorry," Fortunada said, reaching out to hug him.

Colin hugged her back. "I know," he said. "Thanks for keeping an eye on him. I know how much he liked the two of you."

"We liked him, too," Dan said more sincere, more subdued than was usual for him.

Awkward silence hung between them a few moments.

"Think I'd like some time to get used to him not being here. Please don't take offense."

"You've been through a lot, Colin," Fo acknowledged.

"You were about the only bright spot left in his life, Colin," Dan offered. "Talked about you all the time."

"He was very proud of you," Fo added. "If we can do anything, just give us a shout. We'd be more than honored to help any way we can, Colin."

"Thank you … thank you very much."

Fortunada hugged him again. Dan proffered a handshake before they retreated.

Colin reached over into the passenger seat, collected a black soft-sided leather carry-all and a matching ditty bag. The laptop was wedged behind the driver's seat. Jockeying the bags, he wobbled inside and locked the door behind him.

He negotiated his lanky frame down the four steps from the foyer into the cavernous main room and dropped his bags next to the staircase leading to the guest rooms.

Colin stood rooted for a time. The eerie aura of immutable tragedy filled the imposing space. His eyes fell onto the two urns sitting side-by-side atop the buffet where not long ago there had been only one. He crossed the room, picked up the photo and brushed the image of their faces gently with his fingertips. Tears stung his eyes. His Uncle Wally's words the evening of his Aunt Poppy's memorial back in Phoenix rung in his head: *"Tears are not weakness, Colin," he'd said. "Tears are messengers of overwhelming grief and abiding love."* After a time, he set the photo back and went to the kitchen. He grabbed a paper towel from the holder and blew his nose. Refrigerator light came on when he pulled the door open, locked his grip around a Dos Equis Lager.

After a long pull, he set the bottle on the counter, flipped open the leaf of the folder he found there. He followed down the document, digesting its details. When he'd finished reading the death certificate, he thumbed through the rest of the papers; copies

The pitching deck was beginning to stabilize beneath his feet, though he had no clue about the tidal wave about to smash into his life; change his world forever, and reconfigure Colin Craig, the man, in ways he could have never imagined, much less foreseen. Composure was working its way back. Maybe the emotional calluses of having dealt with the death of his Aunt Poppy so recently. Maybe the psychological hardening that had been forced upon him as a child at those times when he'd return to the cancer ward for yet another round of chemo, only to learn another of his friends hadn't made it. Or perhaps it was his preternatural instincts underpinning his long-held fear that his Uncle Wally was not going to be with him long once his Aunt Poppy was gone. The terrible sense of loss he'd experienced in those moments taught him, the hard way, even when deluged by incredibly profound loss, as he'd most certainly felt at all of those moments, there'd been no choice, not a single option, but to put one foot in front of the other, pull up his bootstraps; get on with life. Or maybe it was the unalterable fact that the culmination of all of those harsh realities in his truncated youth had hardened Colin Craig into a survivor.

He relocated his personal effects to his room. Upon his return from downstairs, Colin booted his laptop, emailed his mother he'd arrived without incident.

Once he'd hit the send button, he climbed the circular staircase to the upper level of the house. He explored each room—library, office, master bedroom and closet, with a fine-tooth comb. One-by-one each door was closed as he traced his steps back downstairs to the great room. There he locked the French doors leading out onto the main terraza, engaged the storm shutters, which began to roll down electronically, sealing him inside the house, like the burial chamber of a Pharaoh's tomb. He switched on the overhead lights in the kitchen before slipping out to double check the outer utility door into the garage ... locked it from the inside. No one would be walking in on him. Finally, feeling secure, Colin went to the wine cellar, turned on the soft string lights and maneuvered his way under the staircase.

Fingers feeling into the corner, he found the latch. First, the audible solid click when the heavy bolt released, then the door sprung free. He reached around the right side and fumbled until he felt the switch. The small cave-like space unfolded before him bathed in golden ochre hues. From his kneeling position he made a quick survey. Nothing detectibly changed from the first time he'd laid eyes on his uncle's secret hiding place. Stacks of cash still stood in the cubbyholes as before. He recognized a new stack of papers on one shelf, on top of which lay his uncle's passport and other forms of identification.

He slid backward onto his haunches—decided he'd need another beer to get him through what was coming—one wouldn't do it.

Crawling back into the safe, Colin set the Dos Equis to one side, folded himself into a sitting position with his back against the wall opposite the warren of cubbyholes, crossed his legs, took a quick swig of beer, breathed deeply and reached for the stack of documents anchored by his uncle's passport.

Leafing through the passport he found nothing worthy of further consideration and set it aside. The other passport-looking document turned out to be Wally's Mexican Resident documents, which were no more informative than showing Wally'd stopped and paid duty on the extra Scotch he brought back on his last trip to the States. Colin tossed the document with the receipt inside, onto the shelf next to the passport.

It was the letter Wally'd addressed to him he began to read next that caused every organ in his thorax to constrict. It was as if Wally was speaking directly to him. Colin could hear his uncle's voice. What Wally was saying was hammering him in the solar plexus like a battering ram. Colin's hands trembled as he read. Wally was confessing everything he'd done. Wally'd spared Colin only two particulars he knew would serve no purpose: the nightmarish brutality he'd visited on his two victims and the fact he'd engineered his own heart attack, the results of which, in both cases, would be well known by the time his nephew read his confession. The letter was several pages.

When he'd finished reading, Colin let his head fall backward until the crown of his skull rested against the wall behind him, closed his eyes and tried to clear his mind. He fished around for the beer with his hand without opening his eyes and raised it slowly to his lips. He downed what was left in one slow guzzle. He remained in that position for several minutes before he opened his eyes, flipped back to the first page and began to read from the beginning once more. He'd guessed Wally was behind the horrible crime in Phoenix. He understood he'd allowed himself to be used. In his gut, he'd known, more or less, what his uncle was up to all along. But this—all his Uncle Wally was confessing—he was ashamed at how naïve he'd been about the conflict going on inside Wally. He might have done something to stop it. What? Who the fuck would know? Something! He read the letter three more times until he not only fully understood *what* his uncle had done, but he now knew in specific detail *how* and *why* with regard to the more

300

obscure minutia, such as the last time his passport was scanned and the stamped, dated customs receipt and validations on his Mexican Resident documents—*alibi;* irrefutable proof he could not have been in Phoenix when the crime was committed. Except … he was.

By the time Colin read the letter the third time, the numbness in his body was beginning to wear off, replaced by the severe realization he was now faced with a decision more rigorous in its implications than anything he was likely to encounter in his life ever again. He'd been sitting so long he couldn't feel his ass, and his knees ached; his lower back felt stiff and cramped. Colin understood fully, if he extricated himself from that hiding place, did not go straight to the phone, call the FBI and tell them what he'd found, he'd be setting his life on a course he could not yet fully fathom. Well, perhaps that was a bit melodramatic, he thought, since it was arguably late enough in the day to claim it had been too late to make the call just then.

So that was it, he decided. Make no precipitous decisions. "Just let what you know percolate," he told himself; consider what he now understood from every angle.

He replaced everything except the letter where he'd found it and unfurled himself from the safe. The robust locking mechanism gave forth its reassuring click.

Stumbling out of the cellar he grabbed a bottle of red wine. What he'd read was more than sobering. It carried him beyond the emotional state of mourning that existed when he'd begun the process of sorting through his uncle's life. He was stiff—a little sore. He stretched, bent this way and then that. Worked his way into the kitchen and found the corking tool. He poured himself a glass of wine and searched for something to nibble on. The pantry'd been well stocked, plenty to choose from.

A bag of tortilla chips was convenient. The open bag lay next to his laptop. Stuffed a couple of chips into his mouth and hit the space bar. The screen woke up. Colin pulled up the website for Central Bank of the Netherlands Antilles, used the sign-in information Wally provided. Instantly, the site demanded the secret number. Colin had committed it to memory and typed it in. He was stunned when the account balance window opened. Wally'd said in the letter what he was going to find. But the claim, pardon him, sounded off-the-wall, a little too grandiose— £261,840,000—"Yeah, right!" Without knowing the exact number, he knew the conversion to put the sum near a half billion dollars. Billion … with a 'B'. What he saw on his screen informed him he could not take lightly *any* detail in that letter.

Suddenly, what seemed ridiculously farfetched a few minutes earlier became reality. Colin studied the screen intently feeling himself being sucked further and further into the vortex of insanity his uncle had created. He lifted his wine glass slowly, leaned back into the tall barstool and sipped deliberately while he studied the figure before him on his computer screen.

In a burst of energy he signed out of the site—called up the Banco do Brazil website. The account Wally said he'd—*coaxed out of Pace and Taylor*. The login information was there in Wally's letter. An account window opened, showing an account balance of zero. In a moment of portentous insight, Colin knew how, if he was loony enough to involve himself in this insanely genius scheme his uncle had dreamed up, he could, with a stroke of pure ironic revenge, return the money to those investors Wally'd identified. He had to admit, the epiphany was tempting to consider, if not for anything more than the challenge of being able to do it completely undetected. But it was like a string of dominoes stood end-on-end, down the center of a table, wasn't it? Knock one down—they're all going to fall.

Colin signed out of the bank site and opened his email. One short note from his mother: Are you doing okay? He typed a quick reply, closed his email and cleared his browser history before letting the screensaver take over.

CHAPTER 61

September 14th, DPS headquarters, downtown Phoenix—It was moving into the fourth week of the investigation. FBI Special Agent Clark Reynolds had filed the formal request with the Mexican government through their consulate office in San Diego to obtain permission for him and Detective Bill Garcia to cross into Mexico on official police business, to interview Wally Stroud in connection with the heinous crime that had recently taken place in Phoenix, Arizona.

Reynolds produced his ID and was buzzed through the bulletproof door into the inner offices. The uniformed officer at the door guided him down the hallway to Garcia's office.

"Guillermo," Reynolds said as he stood obliterating the open doorway.

"Agent Reynolds," Garcia replied as convivially as any police official of his rank could ever bring himself to do. "Come in, come in." He motioned toward one of the straight-backed metal chairs in front of his desk. "Have a seat," he said, offering a brief handshake before stepping around Reynolds, closing his office door.

"The fucking Mexicans gonna let us go down there or not?" Garcia started in, revealing his frustration over the waiting that had been imposed by the slow response to their request from the Mexican government. He slid around behind his desk and sat down heavily.

"Guillermo," Reynolds remonstrated, "those *'fucking Mexicans'* are *your* people!"

"Not *my* people. You're dealing with *conquistadors* down there," Garcia asserted sardonically. "Smug bastards think they're superior to people like you and me."

"Request denied," Reynolds announced, settling into a chair.

"You gotta be shittin' me!"

"I'm not. But I guess their reasons are sound enough."

"You're bullshitting, right? What legitimate goddamn reason could they have for denying cooperation in our investigation?"

"Wally Stroud died on August 31st—day *before* our request was filed."

"How?" Garcia's voice conveyed doubt rather than shock.

Betrayed

"Massive heart attack, they say."

Garcia sat back in his chair, rocked backward and fixed his eyes on the ceiling. "Doesn't mean he didn't do it," he said less vituperatively.

"I agree," Reynolds said, "but they decided there was no reason for them to invite us into their domain."

"You believe 'em?"

"Here's a copy of the death certificate," Reynolds said, handing Garcia the faxed copy of the document the Mexican Consulate had sent over.

"Goddamnit," Garcia said under his breath, studying the document.

Reynolds crossed his legs, stretched and rested an arm across the back of the adjacent chair. "Your guys turn up anything new off the investor list?"

"Four more dead; all from heart attacks. Doesn't count the Strouds." Garcia said shaking his head. "These guys left a trail of destroyed lives. Nothing that points us in a direction, though."

"If Stroud was our guy, he was smart," Reynolds allowed. "Emptied these guys secret bank account, but makes sure it all takes place offshore. Could take us years to access even the original transaction," Reynolds mused. "If he was clever enough to engineer this whole thing in the first place, that money would already be buried so deep we couldn't track it."

The two investigators sat in quiet contemplation several moments.

"Pace able to give you anything more?" Reynolds asked interrupting their repose.

Bud Pace had been weaned off the pharmaceutically induced euphoria that had kept his brain swimming in a state of sanguine confusion, disconnected from the vicissitudes that marked the rest of his life. Garcia had finally been able to question him. From what he'd learned, they'd constructed the sequence of events that took place the night of the assault.

Megan Pace, after several futile attempts to trace and reverse the transfer of funds out of the Banco do Brazil on her own, had reluctantly turned all of the information about the secret bank account over to Garcia, who in turn passed the information to the FBI and SEC investigators, who had, by then, begun to look into the formal complaint of fraud filed by: Wally Stroud, et.al. against Pace and Taylor.

"Nothing that helps. Says it was a young guy. Muscular looking. Average height. Dark hair. Tranqed Taylor with a needle to the neck the minute they got into his vehicle. Stuck a gun in his face and made him drive back to his office. We have the surveillance video from the parking garage. We can see the guy. Like Pace told us, young, workout-looking type … something of a Matt Damon look-alike from what we can make out. Kept himself between the vehicles so the cameras only got bits and pieces of him. Thorough." Garcia shuffled documents on his desk. "Got the fuse out of the vehicle's alarm and disabled it before anybody came to investigate. No prints. No DNA. Always far enough away from the cameras to prevent us getting more than grainy blurs. Could have been a pro. Somebody paid this guy to hack these two up. Or … maybe we've gone the wrong way. Maybe an ex-employee got wind of the offshore account, sees these guys are about to be in big trouble and decides to get rich quick—we could even see the perp

304

return to the Adams in Pace's Rover and make the switch back to his own vehicle: older Toyota Camry wearing an Arizona plate we traced to a junk yard. This thing was planned and executed by somebody who knew what he was doing."

"And wanted to make a statement," Reynolds interjected, "as well as punish these guys, which is why your speculation about an opportunistic employee is wrong. Nature of the thing. Perp wanted these guys to suffer. The money was secondary."

"Pace says the guy forced him to carry Taylor inside before he shot him (Pace) in the back with a dart. Doesn't remember much after that until our perp starts hacking off his arms and legs. He was awake for most of it."

"Jesus Christ!" Reynolds bushy eyebrows shot upward.

"He's a belligerent sonofabitch," Garcia said shaking his head. "Hospital's having a hard time controlling him. I think they'd just as soon have him back in the coma. Wife can't pay the insurance deductible so he's being shipped to County.

"Wife told me she's taking the kid and retreating to her family in Pennsylvania."

"And we think we got troubles," Reynolds added.

"Yeah, suddenly the girlfriend isn't so interested either. Apparently the guy leveraged every dime of cash he could out of all of his personal holdings and stashed it in his offshore account. He's so far underwater he can't raise a dime to help himself. Neither the girlfriend nor the wife want any part of what's facing him."

"What about the other guy—Taylor?"

"Still zombied out. But his wife is sticking with him. If he comes out of it, she promises to cooperate."

"From what Pace told you, sounds like you won't get much from him."

"Unless he recognized the guy or something about him, maybe."

"A stretch."

"Might be all I'm ever gonna have to work with," Garcia admitted. "Most of what we have is anecdotal at best, nothing hard." Then he shuffled the papers on his desk and pulled up a call record. "Look at this," he said to Reynolds, handing the document across the desk.

"Whatta we got here?"

"Stroud's cell phone records for the past six months. Only regular contact this guy had was a number in San Marcos, California; his nephew turns out."

"And just like that we have ourselves a new person of interest. Why didn't you tell me about this?" Reynolds asked, accepting the sheet of paper, leaning forward in his chair, skimming the information the document contained.

"Checked him out already," Garcia explained in self-defense. "Zero! Not a single thing in this guy's background. He's cleaner than a boy scout and doesn't come close to the description and video we have on the perp. Verified … rock solid verification he was in meetings with some very high-ups of Siemens Corp, working a consulting job the entire week of August 20. Guy's some kind of computer genius or something. No way for him to be there and here at the same time. Anyway, we came up with nothing; not even a whiff of suspicious activity of any kind. Plus he was as cooperative as we could have asked."

"Can you make me a copy?"

"Keep that one," Garcia said. "I got the original.

"Look, Clark … this case has been cold from the start," Garcia continued. "And I don't see it getting warmer any time soon. Doesn't seem right to keep chewing up your time with the kind of rookie grunt-work we have to do now." Garcia lowered his head and ran his thick fingers through his long black hair. "I'll give you a call we find anything."

"Remarkable," the FBI agent pondered, "with all the resources we have, how often these guys slip away from us." He folded the phone record and slipped it into his inner coat pocket. "Stay in touch, Guillermo," he said standing.

"Let's grab lunch sometime. I know some great cheapie Mexican food joints, you're ever in the mood."

"I'll hold you to that."

Garcia walked Reynolds to the door.

CHAPTER 62

Near the end of September, PPI investor, Gary Stoll, pulled from his Globe, Arizona mailbox a curious-looking envelope from The Banco do Brazil. He almost tossed it out-of-hand into the trash as junk mail. When he opened it he couldn't believe what he was looking at; an electronic check in the amount of $875,000, the amount of principal he and his elderly parents had invested with PPI. Appended in the lower right corner were the electronic signatures of Bud Pace and Carl Taylor.

Bill Morrow's widow, Emily, up in Port Ludlow, Washington, found a similar check in her mail in the amount of $900,000; Bill had already died. Rahm and Kerry Tan, of Downey, California, discovered $850,000 in their mailbox; Robert Sully, a retired attorney in Scottsdale, Arizona, now suffering the onset of senile dementia, and in profound need of help, received $600,000; Wilford Gayle of Montgomery, Texas, opened an envelope containing all of the $2,000,000 he'd invested with PPI.

Checks, in the amount of their original investments, began arriving in the mail to the seven hundred PPI investors Wally Stroud dug up nearly a year earlier. Many were puzzled and too frightened to deposit the curious looking instrument fearing yet another scam that might land them in even worse straights. They contacted the SEC to find out if some settlement agreement had been reached since all of the checks carried the electronic signatures of Bud Pace and Carl Taylor.

The SEC, FBI and DPS were all as equally baffled as the investors. The good news for the investors, however, was that every check was being honored; funds being paid into their accounts the moment their banks presented the checks for payment. Bud Pace and Carl Taylor were personally paying back to every investor the money that had been entrusted to them.

When Special Agent Clark Reynolds learned of the checks being received by the PPI investors, he was neither baffled nor surprised.

Betrayed

~~~~

"So Guillermo," Reynolds said into his cell phone, "whattaya say to some of that cheap Mexican food you promised me?"

They met later that day at Carolina's, a favorite cop hangout in South Phoenix.

"What do you make of all those refund checks?" Garcia asked, sliding into a plastic chair.

"Not surprised," Reynolds answered laconically, removing foil from his burrito.

"Not surprised?" Garcia repeated, gawking at Reynolds over the top of his sunglasses.

Reynolds took a healthy bite of the burrito. "Not really," he repeated with his mouth full, studying the stuffed flour tortilla in his hands.

"Enlighten me ... please."

"Perp wasn't after the money. It was about retribution, eye for an eye. Just as I've said all along. Giving the money back is his way of justifying what he did to these guys."

"Got any ideas?"

"Sure."

"You gonna educate me?"

Clark Reynolds took another healthy bite out of the burrito, followed it with a sip of water. He gave a slight nod as he chewed slowly, "Stroud," he said simply. "Wally Stroud." He continued to grind his food deliberately. "Guy was shrewd. Circumstances all broke his way."

"You positive?"

Reynolds casually consumed the burrito. "Can't prove it."

"How can you be so sure?"

Reynolds finished the burrito, wadded the foil wrapper and wiped his hands vigorously with a napkin. "I've continued to work the case on my own."

"Unofficially?"

"You might say," Reynolds admitted. "I started with the scans from his passport. Matched their timing to the phone calls to his nephew. Kid's in it up to his armpits."

"Let's go get him!"

"Not a shred of admissible evidence," Reynolds admitted. "Pretty sure I have it figured out, though. Stroud was smart enough to leave no tracks; paid his way with the cash from his credit card fraud, did all the work himself."

"So how do you figure the kid's involved?"

"Two points. That Toyota in the garage security video matches the description of a car Stroud bought a couple of weeks before the assault. He never got around to registering it but the dealer paperwork showed he planned to title it in the kid's name." Reynolds took another swig of water. "No trace of it for now. Then there's the matter of that offshore bank account ... the refund checks. Stroud's dead. Kid's a computer genius. Stroud passes the ball to the kid, the kid decides to take the handoff and ... *voila*."

"Why? What's in all this for the kid?"

"Well, for starters the refunds that the SEC have been able to track only add up to about $275,000,000. If that original offshore account had $425,000,000 in it, as your vic Pace claims, that leaves $177,000,000 still out there."

"You think the kid stole it?"

"Nope."

"What's the deal then?"

"He's controlling it."

"Can we prove it?"

"Computer genius, remember?"

Bill Garcia considered the situation several moments. "Let's get a court order. Seize his computers. Let your people mine the information out of the hard drives."

"I don't have to tell you, Bill … it'll take more than me knowing it to establish probable cause to support any court order. And just for your edification, we still got the problem with the Mexicans," Reynolds added.

"How do you figure?"

"Colin Craig now resides full time at his new home in Mexico; a four thousand square foot *'beach house'* left to him by his uncle, Wally Stroud. Now operates his consulting business from there."

Garcia grinned, took a long swig from his sixty-four ounce Coke. "Fucker's sharp."

"And suddenly loaded. He's taking his company, *Craig Interface Solutions*, global on the back of a Siemens worldwide contract; big bucks … serious big bucks; nine figures."

"What's our move?"

"For you … none that I can see, for now, anyway. He's international. Now it *is* my jurisdiction."

"Got a plan?"

"Follow the money," Reynolds conceded. "Sooner or later … he oversteps … starts to believe his own press, maybe? Like his uncle, though … this guy's sharp. Money says he makes his uncle look bush-league when it comes to cunning."

"Keep me in the loop?"

"You can count on it."

CHAPTER 63

November 3rd, Special Agent Clark Reynolds pulled his Mexican rental car to the curb in front of a beautiful Moorish styled beach home along Baja's Pacific Coast, where a large black oval placard announced: *Casa Acantilada.*

It was a gentle, warm Indian summer kind of day. The sun was bright—not a cloud in the sky. A cottontail rabbit hopped from one side of the lane to the other followed by the frenzied flurry of a covey of quail that decided to follow. Two fuzzy squirrels stood upright on their haunches atop an outcropping of venerable granite boulders on the opposite side of a vacant lot whistling alerts to the community at large of their potential intruder. In the distance, emerald green breakers crashed against ebony lava flows announcing each new arrival, punctuated by an explosion of white foam and spindrift.

A white pearlized Chrysler Crossfire Roadster with its top removed sat in the driveway.

Reynolds pressed the doorbell. He could hear it echo inside the house. Presently an intoxicating female voice spoke to him over the intercom. "May I help you?"

"I'd like to speak to Mr. Craig, please," he said.

"May I tell him who's here?"

"Clark Reynolds."

"Does he know you?"

"I don't think so," Reynolds replied.

Over the intercom Reynolds heard in the background, "Who is it, Victoria?"

"Some guy … Clark Reynolds or something. Says you don't know him. You want me to tell him to go away?"

"No, Vic. Answer the door, please."

The tall, pretty brunette bounced to the front door in her bare feet wearing cutoff, expensively tattered jean shorts frayed at the legs and a thin, sleeveless white cotton see-through blouse tied in a knot at her belly button that she wore braless. Her ensemble was clearly intended to place her assets unselfconsciously on display.

Colin arrived at the door behind her. Victoria stepped back after opening it. "Colin Craig," Colin announced, proffering his hand. "I know you?"

"No," Reynolds said affably. "Clark Reynolds, Special Agent FBI," he went on by way of introduction. "Could we visit a few minutes?" Reynolds observed Craig didn't flinch; gave not the slightest impression of discomfort ... fear ... furtiveness—and he was good at reading such signals.

"Is this an official visit, Agent Reynolds?" Craig asked, equal affability in his demeanor.

Reynolds smiled, locked onto Craig's countenance. He observed the way the man held his gaze with ice-blue eyes as cold as an Alaskan glacier, and returned his smile with ease. "No," he said, "it's not official."

"You're lucky," Colin laughed mischievously. "Victoria and I were about to pop a bottle of wine. I'd have hated to have to drink it in front of you."

Colin invited Reynolds in.

"Victoria, will you bring an extra glass for Agent Reynolds?"

He nodded toward the terraza. "This way, Agent Reynolds," he said, ushering the FBI Agent out onto a large glass-enclosed landing overlooking first, a spectacular stretch of golf holes meandering like some pastoral meadow north and south along the wrinkled coastline. A craggy flow of black lava beyond that held in freeze-frame precisely where it had ended its molten cascade during the Mesozoic era on its unrelenting journey into the rolling Pacific Ocean, and finally the entire expanse of the Pacific itself. "I can see *Japan* from *my* backyard," Colin said sardonically, mimicking Sarah Palin.

"About as clearly as the former governor of Alaska when she made the ridiculous comment she could see Russia from hers," Reynolds added.

Colin laughed easily. "Have a seat inspector. What can I do for you?"

"I'd be greatly surprised if you don't already know why I'm here, Mr. Craig."

He observed carefully how Colin absorbed the challenge. Not a twitch. No tightened neck muscles. No gnashing of the teeth or flexing jaw. Colin held Reynolds's piercing gaze evenly, his smile remaining friendly without being smug.

"You'd be wrong about that Agent Reynolds."

Victoria appeared carrying an opened, chilled bottle of Chardonnay and two glasses. It was Colin's turn to observe how Reynolds followed the movements of his beautiful friend with his eyes. When she bent down to set the glasses on the table between the two men, her décolletage opened revealing the nipples of her bare breasts.

"Beautiful, aren't they," Colin said.

"Quite," Reynolds agreed. "Is that a tattoo of an iris on your ankle?" he asked Victoria while she poured the wine.

Betrayed

Victoria kept her eyes on the glass she was pouring into. "Nope," she chirped as if the question were quotidian. "It's a vagina." She joyfully sang the meretricious proclamation, informing his question. She finished pouring, smiled innocently at Reynolds, then returned to the kitchen.

Colin looked to Reynolds and shrugged. "She's unique," he said grinning.

"And drop-dead gorgeous," Reynolds added sincerely.

Colin raised his glass toward Reynolds, "Cheers, Agent Reynolds. Now … what's this about?"

"Your uncle, Wally Stroud," Clark Reynolds began without reserve.

"Losing both my aunt and uncle has been … truly painful for me," Colin responded guilelessly.

"I believe that," Reynolds said. He allowed a respectful, silent pause to emphasize his sincerity before he continued. "The thing is," he started to go on—

Victoria returned with her glass of wine and sat down on the opposite side of Colin. Reynolds observed how she linked her little finger into Craig's little finger as he dangled his hand casually off the arm of his chair. She reclined in her chair and crossed her shapely tanned legs gracefully, never said a word.

"The thing is," Reynolds began again, staring at the *vagina* tattooed on Victoria's ankle, "your uncle committed one of the most horrendous crimes in history, stole $425,000,000 from an offshore bank account and so far has gotten clean away with it." Reynolds recited the accusation as a portentous harbinger.

"I wouldn't say that exactly, Agent Reynolds," Colin interrupted. "He *is* dead, remember."

Reynolds paused, looked Colin Craig straight in the eyes, waited a few beats, "And you helped him."

Several seconds of silence followed.

Reynolds continued. "You've altered the bank account of the victims so they can't access their own account and you've manipulated it so it appears they refunded investment losses to their clients."

Colin again absorbed the direct challenge without effect.

"I could lay out most of the details for you," Reynolds goaded him, "but that would be redundant for both of us, wouldn't it?"

Colin sipped from his wineglass. Reynolds detected no unsteadiness in his hands. "That's an interesting hypothesis, Agent Reynolds," Colin countered, his voice as steady and just as infused with good nature as before Reynolds's accusation. They might just as easily have been discussing a movie recently shared as something the gravity of which the conversation they were engaged in inferred. "Did you ever meet my uncle, Agent Reynolds?"

"I never did."

"When I was a boy," Colin said, "more of a boy than I am now," he went on, self deprecatingly, "my Uncle Wally was a picture of strength … lifted weights, serious jogger. He

312

and my Aunt Poppy had a magnificent sailboat. Did you know they sailed down to South America, transited the Panama Canal, spent several years in the Caribbean?" Colin smiled wistfully at Reynolds, but didn't wait for a reply. "Of course, you know that. You're the FBI.

"When my uncle died a couple of months ago he weighed just one hundred sixty pounds. He'd grown gaunt, not quite feeble but horribly withered in his physical capacities. Losing my Aunt Poppy was a blow from which he never recovered." For the first time in his narrative, Colin's voice became grave and he briefly showed emotion. "Sorry," he said to Reynolds, "as I told you, losing them both is a blow from which I haven't recovered." Victoria squeezed his hand.

He collected himself, went on. "I followed the news about the attack on those two men. My uncle and I even talked about it. I had no idea who they were but my uncle did. I'll admit he felt no pity for those two. He even applauded the brutality of whoever it was got to them ... but he wasn't physically capable of ... *executing*, no pun intended, such an elaborate and, clearly, physically demanding scheme. I mean ... come on Agent Reynolds, he keeled over from a heart attack only days after it happened! He wasn't your guy," Colin lied flatly.

"You helped him, somehow," Reynolds declared matter-of-fact. "The Toyota he bought for you just days before the assault, matches perfectly the vehicle we see in the security video at the Adams Hotel where the victims were abducted."

Reynolds observed Victoria tense at his words.

"News to me, Agent Reynolds," Colin lied with uncommon confidence. "My uncle never gave me *any* car, much less the one you describe. I'm certain you already know, no such car has ever been registered to me."

"You've got it stashed somewhere," Reynolds asserted with equal confidence.

"Agent Reynolds," Colin countered still in a friendly tone, "I know both the DPS and FBI have looked into where I was, what I was doing when all of that business took place. You know conclusively I had nothing to do with it. And *I* have proof positive my uncle was right here at this house when that horrible crime was committed ... if you care to get into that. I found a stamped tax receipt from Mexican customs showing the duty he paid bringing back more than his allotted amount of Scotch from a couple of days before that whole thing took place in Phoenix. Be easy enough for you to check the scan of his U.S. Passport to see if he reentered the States, wouldn't it?"

"You helped him," Reynolds repeated in a demeanor that told Colin the investigator was sure of himself but lacked the details—no hard evidence—that could make his speculation anymore than just that—speculation—no matter how certain he felt about his conclusions.

So why then was he there? Colin wondered. Moreover, why was he laying his cards on the table? Why not keep to himself whatever he thought he knew?

"Know what I think, Agent Reynolds?" Colin took the offense. "You decided to come down here on a fishing trip. And if you didn't catch anything, at least you will have dropped a little chum in the water … maybe get a big fish to take the bait by mistake. Problem is, the kind of fish you're after is cautious … doesn't chew on just any bait it finds in the water."

"Well … who knows?" Reynolds responded, spreading his hands in a gesture of faux capitulation. "Maybe the fish gets too sure of itself sometime and then—"

"Could happen," Colin allowed.

The two men smiled at each other; simultaneously drained their wineglasses.

"We'll be meeting again down the line," Reynolds predicted without rancor, setting his glass down and pulling himself up from his chair.

"Well, then," Colin said, smiling and proffering his hand as he stood, "wine's on you next time."

Reynolds nodded graciously. Both men knew they would indeed meet again.

Colin and Victoria walked him to the door. They waited until FBI Special Agent Clark Reynolds drove away before stepping back inside. Closing the door, Colin turned slowly and folded Victoria into his arms, slid his hands down over the curve of her rump. "*A vagina?*" he said incredulously.

"Did you see his face?" Victoria giggled and kissed Colin on the lips.

THE END

R.P. McCabe

AFTERWORD FROM THE AUTHOR

No oversight agency could see any clear jurisdiction over the fraud in this story, which is based on a real Ponzi scheme. And if there is one thing bureaucrats are very good at—it is passing the buck. What better excuse to do nothing than to be able to say, *"It isn't our responsibility."* Or: *"We don't have the authority."* This, in my opinion, is a significant consequence of deregulation; for the agencies that could act to defend the public, it is a built-in excuse to do nothing or pass the buck.

I came to know four individuals who one day were there to take my phone calls, and were dead the next time I attempted to contact them, heart attacks for the most part. The human carnage from this Ponzi scheme was horrific and made all the worse for me because I'd come to know those people personally. This novel is inspired by actual events. Of course, as with all works of fiction, I have taken considerable literary license in the dramatization of this story. I wish to make it clear, while I know of many suicides in connection with Ponzi fraud, the suicide in this novel is fictional. The Ponzi scheme itself, however, is taken directly from the allegations made against the perpetrators in filed complaints with the Arizona State Attorney General, The Arizona Corporation Commission—Securities Fraud Division, The Arizona Board of Realtors and the FBI. The case remains open with all of these agencies, though no action has ever been brought against the two men who perpetrated the fraud.

In the course of researching this novel, I met and interviewed hundreds of Ponzi scheme victims. The psychological impact on this group of people is rarely discussed as an end result of these frauds. The unfortunate fact, a heretofore productive, successful human being may become completely dysfunctional, perhaps even psychotic, or take his or her own life as a direct corollary of a Ponzi fraud is not a consequence for which the criminals will ever be held accountable. But I would caution that clinical depression, despair, grief, even psychosis can be more destructive and a greater cost to society than the loss of the money.

This novel is intended to focus on the human tragedy of all Ponzi schemes: financial fraud in general. The characters in this novel are a composite of the many people I came into contact with during my research. The beauty of writing fiction is, there is no place far enough to run, no hiding place dark enough to conceal the bad guys, and no punishment too harsh to be imposed on them, as long as it can be imagined.

~~~~

The Ponzi scheme is not a new concept. This fraud, which has roots reaching all the way back to the mid-nineteenth century, finally gained national attention here in the U.S. during the early part of the twentieth century when Charles Ponzi, an Italian immigrant, used the fraud to bilk so

Betrayed

much money *(His schemes were so wide-spread and took in so many millions of dollars from investors an actual total amount of losses was indeterminable.)* that the scheme became known across the country. This scheme was to be named for Charles Ponzi and continues to be perpetrated to this day in a variety of sophisticated manifestations that makes Ponzi's original *postage stamp coupon* scheme seem like child's play.

Ponzi schemes come in all shapes and sizes but they all possess these essential elements: a fraudulent investment operation that pays returns to investors, not from any real profit earned by the perpetrators or organizers of the investment, but from the investor's own money or monies added by subsequent new investors. Frequently the success stories of the first investors are used to entice new investment dollars. Ultimately the house of cards must fall. A new Ponzi scheme is identified nearly every week across the United States. A simple Google search will reveal the tragedy of the human destruction these criminals leave in their wake.

Empirical evidence teaches investor losses, worldwide, from such schemes, reach into the trillions of dollars. What troubles me is the lack of focus on the human carnage; families that have been destroyed by the people perpetrating these frauds. I'm not speaking of investors who have lost a portion of their life's savings and could recover. I'm talking about the hardworking people, particularly the elderly who make prime targets for these types of frauds, who work and save for a lifetime only to lose it all to some criminal scheme—no possibility of recovering their lives. We rarely learn about the suicides, the heart attacks or other ailments exacerbated by the devastation wrought by what the criminals did to them. Lives turned upside down.

Even more frustrating to victims is, as many of these cases as have been prosecuted; in most instances there is little or no recovery of victims' losses. And yet there is little outrage over the laissez-faire attitudes of enforcement agencies to pursue these criminals unless the fraud is of such scale, and involves people of celebrity, they can gain fame or notoriety from doing so. We live in a time when news without celebrity is not news at all. We get the state of our lives fed to us in sound bites and if you aren't rich, famous and beautiful … well, who wants to hear it? Even fewer, if any at all, are much inclined to do anything about it. In fact, mostly the situations these victims are left to face get ignored. It's easier to pretend things really aren't all that bad for them, or maybe we are all just praying something like that never happens to us—getting too close might somehow leave us equally vulnerable.

We are a mere decade into the twenty-first century. The American economy and our political system are in shambles. There is a class war underway in this country in which the uber-rich in our society seem determined to wipe out the middle class. Their efforts to own the American working public has created fertile ground for the biggest, boldest perpetrators of the Ponzi scheme in history.

Go no further back than the year 2000. Remember Enron? Here are the essentials: While the term regulation within a commercial and corporate setting typically applied to the government's ability to regulate and authorize commercial activity and behavior with regard to individual businesses, *Enron executives applied for—and were subsequently granted—government deregulation.* As a result of this declaration of deregulation, Enron executives were permitted to maintain *agency* over the earnings reports that were released to investors and employees alike.

This *agency* allowed for Enron's earning reports to be extremely skewed—losses were not illustrated in their entirety, prompting more and more investments on the part of investors wishing to partake in what seemed like a profitable company.

By misrepresenting earnings reports while continuing to enjoy the revenue provided by the investors not privy to the true financial condition of Enron, the executives of Enron embezzled funds funneling in from investments, while reporting fraudulent earnings to those same investors. This not only encouraged more investments from current stockholders, but also attracted new investors desiring to enjoy the apparent financial gains enjoyed by the Enron Corporation.

Subsequent to the discovery of their crimes, Enron had announced there was a critical circumstance within California with regard to the supply of Natural Gas. Due to the fact Enron was then a widely respected corporation, the general populace was not wary about the validity of these statements.

However, upon review, we now know *Enron executives manufactured this crisis in preparation of the discovery of the fraud they had committed.* Although the executives of Enron were enjoying the stolen funds from investments, the corporation itself was approaching bankruptcy.

The Enron executives drove the company into bankruptcy. The loss sustained by investors exceeded 70 billion dollars. Furthermore, this Ponzi scheme cost both trustees and employees upwards of two billion dollars. This total is considered to be a result of misappropriated investments, pension funds, stock options, and savings plans—*as a result of the government deregulation and the limited liability status (LLC) of the Enron Corporation, only a small amount of the money lost was ever returned.* At least the chief architect of the scheme had the courtesy to drop dead from his own heart attack. So how many of the thousands of human lives destroyed by this one scheme alone did you ever learn about?

There is no need to break down the specifics of every Ponzi scheme I uncovered in researching this novel. However, consider the summary below. It includes only the largest Ponzi frauds over the last decade; the ones you heard about on television or read about in a newspaper … or even more likely, the one you learned about when a close friend or family member told you about what happened to *them.*

317

Betrayed

Enron	$70 billion
Bernard Madoff	$67 billion
Allen Stanford	$8 billion
Thomas Petters	$3.7 billion
Nevin Shapiro	$900 million
Gary Allen Sorenson	$300 million
Gaston & Teresita Cantens	$135 million
Daniel Spitzer	$106 million
Douglas F. Vaughn	$80 million
Peter C. Son	$80 million
Frank Bluestein	$74 million
Millennium Bank	$68 million

According to SEC press releases, between January 2009 and July 2010, thirty-one complaints of Ponzi scheme fraud were filed. These complaints involved between *12 and 800 investors in each complaint; potentially nearly 25,000 individuals in one year. And what about their families that were devastated by the effects of the victimization?* It is this demographic on which I wish to focus your attention, the very real faces behind the statistics.

Even more insidious than those complaints that have actually been pursued are those which are never investigated, because they were of a type that did not require an SEC filing. These complaints fell outside the purview of that agency, or were the type that were not clearly regulated by any of the oversight agencies, which in turn were not required under government deregulation to hold these operations accountable.

The biggest, most heinous Ponzi scheme of them all was the Ponzi scheme perpetrated against the American public at large by the giant Wall Street banks that employed the very essentials of the Ponzi scheme in the mortgage derivative scandal that led to the crisis in the home mortgage industry *(the real estate bubble)* and has brought our entire nation to its knees. And yet the criminal CEOs go free. Worse even than that fact, we, the American people are forced to wet-nurse these criminals with more of our hard earned dollars to ensure they keep cashing those obscene bonus checks, while they continue to devastate and pillage our economy.

R.P. McCabe

REFERENCE SOURCES

Journal of Accountancy,—Ponzi-Scheme Losses, Nancy B. Nichols, CPA, PH.D., William M. Vandenburgh, PH.D. and Luis Bettencourt, CPA, PH.D., Feb., 2011

Bella Online, The Voice of Women—Ponzi Schemes and Forensic Accounting, Consuelo Herrera, CAMS, CFE—2011 http://www.bellaonline.com/articles/art49196.asp

Laws.com—ENRON Scandal Summary, Posted by Admin: Laws.com, December 2011 http://finance.laws.com/enron-scandal-summary

Bloomberg Business Week, The Greatest Financial Scandals Ever, January 24, 2012 http://www.businessweek.com/investor/content/dec2008/pi20081215_232943.htm

Wikipedia: Charles Ponzi—Fully Referenced http://en.wikipedia.org/wiki/Charles_Ponzi

The Business Pundit—The 10 Nastiest Ponzi Schemes Ever—By Drea—December 15, 2008 http://www.businesspundit.com/the-10-nastiest-ponzi-schemes-ever/

SEC: Press Release Archives—2009 thru 2010 http://www.sec.gov/news/press/pressarchive/2010press.shtml

ABOUT THE AUTHOR

Photo by Jeff Rovner

"Steve Jobs and I graduated from the same alma mater, though he was in the highest one percent of our class while I've struggled to remain in the middle of the pack!"

After a successful entrepreneurial career, Mr. McCabe turned his attention to writing during the late 1980s. During the 90s he was a featured writer for Enterprise Magazine. In 1998 he graduated from a two-year creative writing program with Long Ridge Writers Group.

R.P. McCabe's debut novel, Betrayed, is a contemporary suspense drama of tragedy and revenge based upon a real Ponzi scheme and its heartbreaking consequences for one couple.

Visit the author website:
www.novelistrpmccabe.com

Follow the author on Facebook and Twitter:
http://facebook.com/novelistrpmccabe
http://twitter.com/#!/R_P_McCabe

R.P. McCabe

Did you enjoy, BETRAYED?
Order your copy of R.P. McCabe's new novel
THICK FOG IN PACHECO PASS
Here is a sample

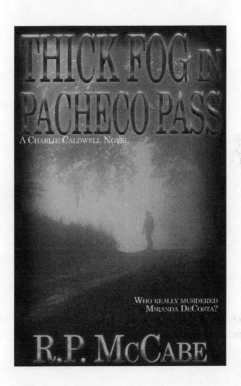

Betrayed

Chapter 1

AT SIX-THIRTY on a cool Wednesday morning in April 1972, I was awake and dressed and shifting along the sidewalk past sleepy storefronts up the wide, mostly deserted, main street of Divina, California. The aura of contentment was in blatant contrast to the fires of dissent burning high across America over the Vietnam War, the Feminist Movement and Civil Rights. The town was slowly waking itself like a puppy stretching and yawning from a long nap. I'd grown up here; graduated high school ten years earlier. The heavy, humid air of the spring morning still held the scent of freshly cut, damp alfalfa, which is always at some stage of maturation on the outskirts of town. Experience told me it would be a hot day.

Several months earlier, the US Army cut me loose after what was euphemistically referred to as a rough second combat tour in Vietnam. I'd made promises to three men who were my brothers. They didn't come home. That's a nice way of saying they'd been zapped. What happened was a lot worse than that, actually, but who needs to hear that shit, right? I'd occupied my time since being back stateside keeping my word to them. War had taught me some things. Two stood out: We are woefully fragile creatures, we humans. And death is profoundly final. Tough, but useful lessons to learn early in life.

We'd promised each other if one of us didn't make it back, whoever among us did would do the deed; sit before mothers and fathers and sisters and aunts and close friends—tell them all the things we'd never be able to say to them ourselves. The way we spoke about, even contemplated, death, as if it were inevitable, a foregone conclusion to what was happening to us was weirdly serene. It would've been bad enough to have to keep that promise to one of them. But when you come up the sole survivor of a squad, the Brass pins a bronze star on your chest, designating you some kind of hero, calls it a rough tour and cuts you loose. Then you're free to figure out how to become a fucking human being again. My first step was keeping the promise

322

I'd made to the guys I fought next to, the ones who died helping *me* stay alive. I constantly have to live with that; why I made it back and they didn't.

I'd decided it was a mistake to allow pride to stand in the way of telling the few people I cared anything about in this world how I felt about them. There was only one person I needed to see and talk to. Then I figured to be gone again—for good I imagined.

While I stared into the huge front window of Viera's Five & Dime, I could still hear the cruel voice of the uppity cashier buzzing in my ears across nearly twenty years. *If your father took his paycheck home instead of to the bar, you'd be able to buy that yo-yo, Charlie Caldwell.* Divina was that kind of nasty little town where everybody knew everybody else's business or made it their business to pass judgment. Kids were easy targets for pettiness toward a parent somebody had it in for or simply felt superior to. My old man seemed to relish making it easy for them to hold him in contempt.

In the reflection of the glass window, I stalked a police car as it crept by, its occupant eyeing me suspiciously. I recognized Jorge Olivera. He was a pimple-faced punk the last I knew. Here he was wearing a police uniform and driving a shiny 1970 black and white Plymouth Fury with a chromed swivel spotlight hanging on the driver's side door above the emblem of a gold badge. The car slowed to a crawl and he ogled me through his side view mirror.

Once the cop car was a block up the street I moved on to the next storefront, which was a place called The Sweet Shop. It was closed, too. A fat orange and white tuxedo cat pondered me with large yellow, curious eyes, lying on its belly in the front window between ruffled pink percale curtains and the glass. I traced a circle on the window with my finger and the cat followed with its nose.

"Name's Simon." The woman's gravelly voice startled me and I spun. She withdrew a key from a worn leather purse and slid it into the locked door. The cat jumped down to greet her.

"You want some breakfast?"

Whether she was talking to the cat or me was hard to tell.

"Won't be open for another hour, but I'll put some coffee on if you'd like."

The morning air was crisp and damp with an edge to it. Why not, I figured? The cat rubbed between my legs, then bounded off after its owner. The dark-haired, middle-aged woman moved purposefully behind the counter.

The inside of The Sweet Shop seemed preserved in a time-warp just the way I remembered it; lipstick-red vinyl covered booths against a worn white linoleum floor. Everything was bright, clean looking, uncluttered, with sharp distinct lines. The counter seats matched and were set atop shiny chrome pedestals like large, juicy, flaming-red lollypops. Each booth table was perched on a matching chrome pedestal. Even the edging around the white Formica tabletops was shiny chrome. Though it was accidental, the décor was 50s retro, including the miniature jukeboxes sitting on each table at the wall end of all four booths. The jukeboxes were strategically located at convenient intervals along the long white countertop as well. The place was as authentic as it gets.

Betrayed

"Don't see many new faces 'round these parts." The woman mumbled the words while turning on the water over a long sink.

"Passing through," I lied, intending to avoid any probing invasion.

I minded the fifty-something-year-old woman while she worked with her back to me. Should've recognized her, but I didn't.

The cat meowed to be fed and rubbed against her legs while she sprinkled coffee grounds into the filter and turned on the tall polished commercial coffeemaker glinting from the far end of the counter. *Shiny* would've been the one word to describe the place.

"Health Department cited me for having him in here last year."

I glanced around the quaint parlor, recalling times I'd spent here in my youth. "Not worried they'll catch him in here again?" I asked, spinning in her direction.

She turned slowly from the coffeepot and locked her dark, puffy eyes onto me. "Not unless some do-gooder turns me in." The way she cocked her head, the grave demeanor of her body language; it was a threat.

Rocking backward from the counter, I held my hands against my chest. "Nothing to worry about from me." My assurance was truth.

"Never know," she went on, dropping her hands from her hips. "Local busy-body turned me in last time." The woman went back to what she was doing, but carried on about being reported. "Before that it'd been a couple years since the inspector even bothered to come out— and then she called first," she said, sliding behind the pass-through window to the grill. "Long drive over here from Merced. That's the county seat."

"People are funny," I agreed. "Some'll let a puppy lick 'em in the face. Others…"

The strong smell of fresh coffee filled the space. A spatula slapped against hard metal at the stove and I heard the sound of gas whooshing into flame.

"Gal 'at turned me in got more'n even she deserved for her troubles, though." The woman's head and shoulders momentarily disappeared from view like a jack-in-the-box.

"How so?" I wondered aloud.

"Found her murdered," she told me as if it were a quotidian announcement. "'Bout a month back now. Bad—real bad." Potatoes rumbled into a metal sink echoing inside the inner kitchen and I heard water splash. She paused as if to consider what she was saying. "Found her necked as an 'ole J-bird. Layin' dead along the edge of a field. Say she was raped and strangled. "Whole town took it real hard."

The profound heaviness of the words *murder* and *rape* caught my full attention. The details hit me in my guts. "Hard to imagine a thing like that in such a quiet little town."

The red light flashed on the coffee machine and a buzzer sounded. "Coffee," the woman announced, tossing a hand towel across her shoulder. "Lemme grab ya a cup." She swung out from the back kitchen, her apron now showing wet handprints.

"Both of 'em," she said, "from right here in town. They was in here same night it all happened. Him sittin' 'bout where you are now. She was over yonder." She pointed to a corner table. "Got into a big fight—everybody heard him threaten her." She held a second mug under the spigot of the coffeemaker. "'Course, like I say, she was as bad with her language as any o' the men she chased around with." She flipped the spigot closed and dabbed at a spill before taking a sip from one of the cups. Sliding the other cup in front of me, she continued her tale. "Still, nobody deserves to die like she did…so young. Pretty girl, too."

The topic of young people dying before their time was a sore subject with me, but this woman couldn't know that. I let it pass. Clearly, we were coming at the death of young people from two different places.

"Daddy's a big shot here in town. Owns the mercantile," she said.

That last revelation made me go queasy and I cut her off mid-thought. "You talking about Sal DeCosta?"

"His oldest daughter Miranda that was killed," she affirmed, looking up at me. The woman must have seen into me because she stopped speaking and touched my hand gently before she asked, "You know the DeCosta family?"

"Yeah," I said, more to myself than in answer to her. "I know them—knew them—all of them…the DeCostas." But I had no interest in revealing any more to her about what was gripping me inside. "Jesus. Miranda dead. How can that be?" I whispered.

"Sounds like you knew 'em pretty well." She was niggling after details by that point.

I ignored her. Memories drifted like grey clouds across an ominous November sky. "I went to school with her," I heard myself droning. Maybe I was just thinking it, I'm not sure. It felt as if I'd slipped down a long constricted tunnel; a VC warren. I was back in the jungle. Steven lay dead beside me. What was left of Randy's life was oozing out of him thirty yards away. No way I could get to him. Ray's remains were unrecognizable the way the grenade blew his face and chest wide open. One moment we were there, giving each other a raft of shit. I could hear them, feel them, smell them. In the next instant, nothingness. And it could never be undone. Whatever was left unsaid between us, between everyone they ever knew, would remain unsaid forever. Life became appallingly finite in an instant.

The nightmare was happening again. I'd come here to speak to one person—Miranda DeCosta. Not for the first time, I found the cruelty of life overwhelming.

"You don't look familiar," the woman on the other side of the counter said.

"I gotta go." As I stepped away from the counter and opened the door, the big orange cat slipped by. I lunged for him, but just touched his tail as he broke free.

"It's okay," the woman assured me. "He usually goes out about now anyway."

"You said they were both from here. Was there more than one person killed?"

"Meant Miranda and the guy who killed her. Both from right here in town."

I stood in the doorway, holding it half open. "They caught who did it?"

"Had to know him too you went to school here." The woman had pulled the bottom edge of her apron up, wrung her hands nervously. She studied my six-foot frame thoroughly. I'd filled out a lot since high school; wore my hair longer now, down over my ears and to my collar in the back. I didn't want people to recognize me as a Vet. None of what she saw answered the question in her mind; who was it she was talking to?

The phone rang before she could dig further. I let the door swing closed in front of me while she went to answer the call. "No, Jorge," she said. "Everything's fine. Just didn't know what time I opened." She shook her head a few times and thanked the caller. She walked back toward me. "Local deputy checking up on me." She jabbed her thumb over her shoulder in the direction of the phone. "Not normally open this hour."

I grabbed the handle to the door once more and began to push.

"Fella name o' Caputo—Vinny Caputo—guy who murdered Miranda."

The revelation stunned me and I stood with my head buried down the front of my chest. "Knew him, too," I confessed.

"And you say you went to school right here in town." The woman went on probing the depths of her memory. The unanswered question of my identity was grinding on her. "Been around these parts thirty-five years. Oughtta know who you are."

Suddenly I just didn't give a shit about anonymity any longer. "Charlie Caldwell."

"Oh, my goodness," she bellowed, drawing both hands up to her mouth. "I woulda never recognized you." She stepped back to survey me closely. "Why, you seem—taller?" She hesitated. "You remember me, Charlie? You went to school with both o' my boys, too. Jeffery and Dennis Ponder. I'm Dorothy—Dorothy Ponder." She smiled up at me, reaching over to run her hands down the full length of my arm as though she were caressing something venerable or expensive.

The instant she told me her name, I knew who she was. "Sure, Mrs. Ponder. Now that you remind me, I do remember you."

"How long has it been?" Dorothy Ponder dithered, trying to recall things from the past. "You left town right after high school graduation back in…'62. People talked about that. You just up and left."

Too much information coming in, going out. "Another time, Mrs. Ponder," I said, pushing out the door.

"Dorothy," she called after me. "Call me Dorothy."

I turned to face her. "Okay…Dorothy. Another time." This time I gave her no opportunity to corral me and moved up the street, headed back to the Trail's End Motel.

Why I didn't immediately check out of my room and return to Mexico, I can't tell you. But I didn't.

I wasn't surprised to learn Dorothy Ponder had gone straight to her telephone and dialed her closest friend. By the end of the day, nearly all of Divina, California, population two-thousand-plus, knew Charlie Caldwell was back in town.

Chapter 2

ON THE EASTERN SLOPE of California's Diablo Mountains, perched well above the floor of the sprawling San Joaquin Valley along side Pacheco Pass, sits the tiny rural town of Divina. State Route 152 is the closest highway.

In 1769, a Spanish Monk by the name of Junipero Serra began establishing a string of missions stretching from Baja California all the way north to Monterey.

Serra built a mission at San Juan Bautista, close to a well-worn footpath over the mountains leading to the interior valley. Mission San Juan Bautista was situated at the trailhead, about half the distance between the path over the mountains that would later come to be called Pacheco Pass and the larger settlement at Monterey. The southern tip of San Francisco Bay lay close to the north of the pass where the Mission of San Jose was a burgeoning settlement.

As religious zealots since the time of Christ are given to do, Fr. Serra and his small army of brown-habited crusaders for the Lord went on to enslave the local heathens to do the work of God so they might know the salvation of heaven; a destination they were generally dispatched to in fairly short order. Those Ausaymus Indians had been the first to use the goat and deer path over the mountains into the great valley lying beyond to the east.

During the early 1800's, Don Francisco Perez Pacheco—whose land grant from Mexico stretched from Mission San Juan Bautista to Gilroy, California—established his Rancho Divina at the eastern trailhead exiting the pass into the San Joaquin Valley. One should not be surprised to learn the pass carries his name.

By about 1848, immigrants who arrived in San Francisco hoping to unearth their fortunes in the California gold fields poured over the coastal range mountains like ants out of a nest.

Among those heading east over Pacheco Pass in route to Angels Camp along the banks of the Columbia River were two Portuguese immigrants who'd survived the historically brutal trek across the Isthmus of Panama.

History teaches these men were skilled livestock handlers. Work would have been easy for them to find at Rancho Divina, which by then had spawned a small settlement nearby. Both men needed to earn enough money to fit-out for their mining expedition to the Sierra Nevada.

In late winter, California's coastal fog would roll in and creep up the western slope of the pass, finally spilling over onto Rancho Divina where it condensed and dripped in a fine mist over the rolling foothills, turning them into a verdant paradise. Each day as the misty shroud of fog receded, the two Portuguese immigrants stood in the open grassland of the foothills, gazed wistfully out across the vast valley stretching before them to see the towering, snow-covered peaks of the Sierra Nevada. Their will to leave the place receded permanently with the fog about early June that year as the rolling foothill grasses began to turn golden. California would take its name, "The Golden State," from those yellowed grasses and fields of golden poppies as much as it would from the gold rush itself.

By the end of the nineteenth century, Rancho Divina, having been divided into many smaller ranches and sold off, had become simply Divina, the small settlement now a township. The only remaining trace of Divina's Mexican origins lay in the pronunciation of its name. The Portuguese, speaking little English, pronounced both "i's" in Divina like two hard "ee's", and by that quirk of language, the beauty of the Mexican name of Don Francisco Perez Pacheco's *Devine Ranch* was saved.

What would attract and bring the extended families and friends of those early founding settlers to immigrate to Divina would come to be the same reason I had to get the hell out of the place the summer I graduated high school. Funny isn't it? One man's paradise—another's hell.

Don't miss the next exciting novel in the Charlie Caldwell series
SLAUGHTERED
Coming Soon